I0678281

SCARRED

Book 2
The Collectors Series

◇◇◇

S. M. Yair-Levy

DNYL PUBLICATIONS

SCARRED

The Collectors Series

S. M. YAIR-LEVY

Published by: DNYL PUBLICATIONS LLC

Copyright©2018 S.M. Yair-Levy

First Edition, published 2018

ISBN: 978-0-692-04459-9

Cover design by: Noa Yair-Levy

*This one is for my girls
with fiery hearts.*

SCARRED

Book 2
The Collectors Series

CHAPTER 1

"Hell is empty and all the devils are here."
William Shakespeare

PAIN.

All that Dylan could see, taste, or feel was the agony slowly shredding her apart from the inside. A crippling nightmare from which she couldn't seem to awaken.

She stared at the love of her life after he had been pronounced dead on the floor of her room in Silas' castle. Her heart crushed and contorted into something dark and forgotten.

This wasn't how her story was supposed to end. Silas wasn't supposed to get away through a Portal, and Tristian, her beautiful soul, wasn't supposed to die before they had a chance to escape. Before they even had a chance to *be*.

It was all her fault. If only she hadn't given up hope. If only she had waited another hour before taking Peppi's soul. Perhaps then Tristian would still be alive and she would be on her way back to Los Angeles; not waiting to die by the Shadow Horde's final blade.

She listened to the smiling King in golden robes, with a long jagged scar over his right eye and cheek, as he told the Shadow Horde to leave Tristian here to rot. *Here*. In the middle of nowhere and without a proper burial. How could they?!

Dylan wanted to scream but the wire wrapped tightly around her wrists was acting like some kind of sedative. She felt weak and limp, unable to so much as stand.

5

One of the Horde soldiers, the King called Soren, held Dylan upright until it was time to go. Then, he hefted her up in his arms as if she weighed nothing, surrounding her in heady scents of leather, spice, and musk. The aroma oddly comforted her when she knew she should be anything but. Soon she would be dead. She just hoped she would see Tristian on the other side, even if only to say she was sorry.

Dylan continued to sob into Soren's leather jacket as he carried her bound and bloodied body from Silas' abandoned castle in Zadar to the heart of the demon worlds: Elon.

Over the next week, Dylan recuperated in a small infirmary with a dozen empty beds divided by pale yellow curtains. The place reminded her of being in an emergency triage room, apart from the eerie silence.

Since the moment of her arrival she had not once seen another creature despite the fact her dressings and IV's were regularly changed. She assumed they knocked her out with an automatic dose of something in her IV before coming to check on her or, perhaps, to calm her down from screaming fits of hysteria.

It seemed like all she did was sleep dreamlessly; and that was almost worse than being on death row in this new world. When were they going to kill her? What was the point of healing her wounds before they did?

She had been staring at the machine to her left, beeping in time with her heartbeat. She had been unsuccessfully trying to speed it up or slow it down with her breaths—a ridiculous game that was helping pass the time—when a petite man in green robes with a stethoscope draped around his neck hurried in. His sneakers squeaked against the blindingly, white, linoleum tile floor.

The machine's rhythm finally picked up as fear and curiosity rushed through her veins.

"Hello there, sweet girl," the Medic's greeted, implying familiarity.

6

Dylan simply looked at him, unable to smile back.

He didn't seem to care that Dylan didn't respond. He just went about turning off all of the monitors before removing the IV from her arm and the wires stuck against her chest.

Then, he gripped her upper arm and hauled her up into a sitting position.

"What are you doing?" Dylan asked hoarsely, feeling stuck in a fog and wondering if this was all just a dream. Maybe, she had finally snapped.

The Medic hesitated. "You're healed," he answered as if that was a given. "You're allowed to get up and get clean before the trial."

Trial? Dylan took in a deep breath as renewed fear slipped inside her.

"Come on, now. Try to stand."

Dylan grimaced when it took her several tries to get to her feet. Once she succeeded, she swayed slightly; but, the Medic steadied her.

"Easy there," he sighed. "It might take a bit to get used to the new *Binding*," he said, motioning to her throat.

Dylan's fingers instinctively traced the thin wire around her neck. It was stuck to her skin like it had been superglued, or surgically applied just like the one she had been cuffed with in Zadar by the Shadow Horde. Could this be what was draining her energy and powers?

She frowned deeper and tried to walk with stiff, lurching movements, unable to command her body to move as she willed it. But the Medic stayed at her side, patiently urging her along.

He pushed open a solid, white door close to the front of the infirmary. Inside was a white and blue tiled room with six exposed shower stalls and a couple of wall-mounted, porcelain sinks with mirrors.

Dylan looked to the Medic, waiting for some privacy. The man just smiled tightly before turning his back to her. "You have five minutes to shower and change."

7

Dylan turned away and wrapped her arms around herself, not exactly keen on the idea of showering under supervision. Although her baths at Silas' weren't nearly as private as she would have preferred, at least there he had given her the illusion of privacy.

She ambled awkwardly toward one of the shower heads and stopped short when she noticed a strange girl in the reflection of one of the spotty mirrors over a sink.

No, it wasn't just any girl. It was *her*.

Shocked, Dylan stepped closer to the mirror as she took in the full image. Trying and failing, she barely recognized the haunted girl looking back at her. Her cheek bones stuck out grossly and her skin had lost its healthy glow. She had thick, dark circles under new eyes which intensified a deep shade of teal. It reminded her of where the sky and ocean meet. They were crystal blue with a wash of light green. *Just like Peppi's*, she thought.

Dylan lifted a strand of oily hair. It was what startled her the most. Her beautiful hair had been chopped off to just under her chin in careless, uneven cuts. Never in her life had she cut her hair so short or so badly.

Dylan blinked several times, not completely believing the sight before her, as if any moment the image might disappear and the real Dylan would appear in its place.

The Medic cleared his throat, tearing Dylan out of her personal assessment.

This girl wasn't going anywhere.

This was who she was now.

This was Temperance Elementa.

Dylan swallowed back her looming tears as she shakily reached for one of the taps below a shower head and switched it on.

She unsnapped the gauzy hospital gown as discretely as she could and tossed it in the corner.

The hot water felt amazing as it rained down, peppering her skin. She stepped further inside the all-encompassing

8

heat and sighed.

In this tiny, fragmented moment, it was like the world around her wasn't about to crumble. Maybe she was back home. Tristian was alive and would soon meet her in class. Aria was lounging on their overstuffed couch with a large cup of coffee and a book. Their plans for the day included school then lunch with Isabel. However, all it took to crush the daydream was the Medic reminding her she only had three minutes left to shower—the moment rotted and withered into something ugly and innately wrong.

She scrubbed and soaped quickly, glancing repeatedly over at the Medic who still faced the wall.

Dylan was rinsing her body when she noticed a small patch of sensitive, raised skin on her right shoulder. She craned her neck and lifted her right elbow to take a look at the black crest of flames and crowns painted on her upper arm. She scrubbed at it with soap before conceding to what she already knew—they had tattooed her.

No, she gritted her teeth, they had *branded* her. She felt her new necklace again. Her new slave collar. If the OP wanted to show Dylan that she was completely powerless here, they had succeeded. The message was clear. Contract or not, her free will was gone.

They owned her.

When she finished showering, she was handed a stiff, light-blue jumpsuit and a pair of white panties. She slipped on the clothes and zipped up the front of the jumpsuit, feeling truly like a prisoner. She moved to the mirror again and began to comb her fingers through her hair. She gave up when she realized it was pointless.

The Medic wasted no time escorting Dylan out of the infirmary and down a white hallway lined by parallel, polished steel chair rails and occasional industrial doors with black control panels embedded beside them. They stopped at one of the doors. The Medic placed his hand on the control panel's screen and the red light blinked green, granting access.

Inside was an empty white room save for a female soldier in a leather pantsuit. It took Dylan a moment to recognize the soldier as Astrid from the Shadow Horde. Her short height and exuberant voice were hard to forget. She had been part of the raid at Silas' and the one to find Peppi's family and then coordinate safe refuge for them. Dylan wanted to thank her for that.

Astrid jumped up from sitting on the floor, brushed off her leather uniform, and pushed back her shoulder-length, walnut hair—grinning like she was excited to finally see some action. The Medic spoke a few words about how Dylan had yet to be a problem and Astrid set her jaw indicating her obvious disappointment.

Once the Medic left, Astrid grabbed Dylan by the upper arm and led her to the wall directly across from the door where there were row after row of iron shackles and urged Dylan down.

Dylan didn't fight or cry as her arms were hoisted above her head and locked securely. Nor did she flinch when Astrid tightened the links a bit too tightly. Dylan simply sat cross-legged, too numb to react.

Astrid's rich hazel eyes inspected Dylan for a second longer than necessary before finally standing up and walking away to the corner where she took out a small leather-bound book and sighed.

Dylan flicked her gaze around the room. She could tell she wasn't the first prisoner to be held here. Long scratch marks streaked the white-painted, cinder-block walls and rusted blood caked the metal cuffs. Dylan knew she should feel fear from the pain that radiated off these walls, but a kind of detachment had overtaken her body. It wrapped around her like a fortified shield protecting her heart from remembering the realty of her situation and numbing the pain inside her chest.

It was about an hour later before the door opened again

revealing another Horde soldier: Soren in all his intimidating, leather-clad glory.

Out of all the demons she had met, his features were the most real. He had three thick scars, like claw marks, along the right side of his head and neck which was mostly covered by shoulder-length raven hair; and broken bones in his hands and nose that appeared not to have healed correctly. She wasn't sure why he looked like that when his comrade against the wall still looked like a model. Dylan knew from Tristian there were healers out there that could take away your scars if you cared. Perhaps, that was the reason right there. He just didn't care.

Dylan was about to go back to staring at the floor when she noticed Soren pulling someone behind him. It was none other than Silas' mother, Lucia Planto. She was shuffling in, dressed in similar fashion to Dylan but with chained wrists like an animal—a far cry from her typical pristine couture.

Dylan straightened. She hadn't realized her former kidnapper had been taken as well. She assumed the woman had escaped with her son... which was odd the more she thought about it. It didn't seem like Silas to abandon his lovely mother; no matter how much he wanted to remain free. But she surmised not even Silas was brave enough to go against the Shadow Horde.

As the soldiers secured Lucia to the adjacent wall, Dylan noticed a couple of bruises decorating her neck and jaw as if someone had knocked some sense into her, recently. Dylan found it hard to ignore the satisfaction at seeing Lucia disheveled and scared.

"Had any issues with her?" Astrid asked Soren, putting her book away.

Soren leaned against the wall opposite from Dylan, picking at his nails with a small blade. His head was tilted down in a way that made his jet-black hair cast a shadow resembling a Horde hood over his features.

He shook his head. "No. It only took two beatings to get

her in line," he said, causing Dylan's heartrate to kickstart at how casually he mentioned it. "You?"

"Nothing. Not even a dirty look."

Soren's face darkened at that.

Had he expected Dylan to struggle? What was the point when she was going to die no matter what she did? Why inflict more pain on herself when it wouldn't change a damn thing?

Dylan couldn't process why she had felt comfortable in his arms during one of the worst moments of her life. Perhaps she had only been suffering from blood loss and hallucinations.

Or it was all just another demon mind trick, Dylan thought, disgustedly.

Lucia let out an irritated huff, catching Dylan's attention.

"*What?*" Lucia hissed at Dylan's watching. "How about you stop staring like a dim wit and start using some of that Elementa strength to get us out of here."

Dylan lifted an eyebrow. Ha! Even if she could use her magic, like hell would she ever help *Lucia*.

Dylan shifted away, too exhausted to retaliate.

"*Coward*," Lucia sneered.

This made Dylan flinch.

Astrid whirled around. "Did I say you could talk?"

Lucia just grinned, choosing to remain silent instead of stoke a fire with the Horde. Dylan was disappointed. She wouldn't mind seeing another bruise on Lucia's bony face.

Dylan clenched her hands into fists that were tingling with pins and needles from gravitational blood-loss. She stared up at her pale fingers, pumping her hands and hoping for some of the feeling to return. They ached, but in a way she needed the pain. If anything, it reminded her that she was here not still in the hospital bed having a crazy dream.

She was really going to die soon.

Dylan looked away from her hands and noticed Soren's vivid-blue eyes focused on her. His expression was indifferent. He worried her the most. Maybe it was only because of everything she had gone through—some broken part of her forever afraid of male attention... or maybe, it was because he hadn't stopped fingering the knife in his grip, as if he couldn't wait another second to rip her heart out of her chest and mount it as a trophy.

He pushed himself off the wall towards Dylan causing her to stiffen.

"What are you doing?" Astrid questioned, suddenly in front of him as if she knew exactly what was on his mind.

"I was going to debrief her before we went to The Gates. Or would you rather do it?" He lifted a corner of his mouth in a frightening grin when Astrid didn't say anything. "What? Are you honestly not the tiniest bit curious about what she has to say?" He nodded his head toward Dylan.

"Yeah... but, I don't trust her." Astrid glanced at Dylan cautiously before looking back at her comrade. "I mean, she's too willing, you know? She just gives me a bad taste in my mouth. It's like she's waiting for something and I don't know if I want to know what that something is. Besides, we don't *have to* debrief them, and you know it."

Dylan thought about Astrid's words and immediately knew she *was* waiting for something. She was waiting for this day to end. For the moment when she would be set free from this terrible life. For the moment this ache, this emptiness, this fear of the unknown, would end.

She felt almost as thirsty for it as Soren seemed to be for her blood.

"Just let the OP deal with her," Astrid added, while meeting Dylan's stare as if she had just heard her thoughts. "It won't be long now."

"You fools," Lucia sneered. "You're afraid of her?" She let out a vicious laugh. "She was a youth until you showed up. She has absolutely no control over her powers. You could simply tie her up with an ordinary rope to have her *Bound!*"

13

"*Right*," Astrid deadpanned, folding her arms across her small chest with a terse shake of her head. "There's no way *Temperance Elementa* is that weak. Shut up, you witch."

"How do you think I'm still alive if she even remotely has the ability to kill me?" Lucia added despite Astrid's warning. "Before you all showed up, we practically had the youth *Signed*."

Astrid and Soren both stopped what they were doing, unable to contain their shock.

"You're with the Elementas too, then?" Soren asked Lucia.

Lucia smiled coyly and shrugged her shoulders—neither confirming nor denying.

"We need to tell the Kings," Astrid said, pulling out a small cellphone-looking device.

Goddammit! Dylan wanted to scream. What in the world was Lucia trying to do? Was she trying to expedite their sentencing? Dylan didn't want herself or her family to be grouped in with the dirty Plantos!

Dylan growled deep in her throat at Lucia. Her rage skyrocketed. She knew she hated the demon chained next to her but now others were seeing them as coconspirators, villains, *comrades* because of this woman and her damn mouth.

"You know that's not true," Dylan hissed under breath unable to keep it to herself.

Lucia's snarky attention shifted to Dylan and her smile turned cold. "My, my. Is that any way to act toward your future *mother-in-law?*"

Dylan's mouth dropped open and she felt her face heat from embarrassment.

"Oh, hell," Astrid laughed, "this just keeps getting better and better."

Dylan tried to collect her thoughts to respond, to deny Lucia's ridiculous claim. Except, it was true. Dylan had been mere hours away from marrying Silas before the Horde showed.

Astrid sniggered under her breath and Dylan felt herself pushing back against the wall. Her confidence had fled, retreating into old habits of acquiescence and submissiveness.

"Go ahead and ask her," Lucia said, looking down her nose at Dylan. "Ask her about the late-night rendezvous with my son. The pool, the library... *her bedroom*."

Dylan felt sick to her stomach as she remembered Lucia's voice over the intercom when she had first arrived in Zadar. '*I can see this entire plot of land. Not an inch hidden.*'

Dylan couldn't believe she thought Lucia wasn't a threat. Silas may be in charge of their rotten family but Lucia was no pawn, by any means.

The room was silent now, not that Dylan noticed. Her mind was far away. Her thoughts circled around those times she had allowed Silas to touch her. The times when she enjoyed it.

Dylan wasn't sure why, but she looked to Soren as if he could make sense of it all. Maybe because he had been there at the end. He had worn her tears and felt her heartbreak as she screamed over Tristian's death. The moment she had, she regretted it.

Dylan knew that while she wanted she to die, the look in Soren's intense eyes said *torture* and *pain*. Not mercy. Never mercy. Well, at least never to *her*.

Dylan suddenly pushed herself backward as much she could, forgetting about the debilitating embarrassment. It was like the anger in his eyes was reaching out to her, wrapping its fingers around her throat and squeezing until she felt its terror.

He grinned at her reaction as he stepped toward her and crouched down. He was so close she could smell the smoke and spice on his skin. He reached for her wrists to check the intact manacle before moving his hand to her throat.

Dylan squeezed her eyes shut as he dragged his thumb

across her neck where her *Binding* was.

"*Now*," he husked under his breath as if they were sharing a secret. "Tell me everything that happened. And start from the beginning."

Dylan clamped her mouth shut and shook her head slightly but firmly.

She heard him sigh before her will began to quickly break under his invasive stare. She clenched her teeth as she fought the returning memories. It felt like sifting through needles— each tip of a memory more painful than the last. The flashbacks were relentless, building and building like a pot of water on the verge of boiling over.

Why was he doing this?

How was he doing this?

It was like he had somehow gotten inside her mind and sliced open her box of pain with a single look. Everything, from the moment she woke in Silas' prison to the screams that tore from her throat as Tristian took his last breath.

No matter how hard she tried to stop it... the flashes of Silas' sultry grin... Tristian gasping as he stumbled into her room covered in blood... Peppi giggling with her as the little girl combed her hair... even Lucia sliding the small box across the dining table that held the Planto family ring. It all started replaying in her mind's eye like a virus—multiplying and dividing until it was taking up every nook and cranny of her body and swallowing her whole.

Sweat dappled her forehead and she wanted to jump out of her skin. She couldn't sit here any longer. She needed to run and get out of this room. She needed to take Soren's knife and plunge it deep into her stomach. *Anything* would be better than feeling this agony collapsing her insides. He was suffocating her, exposing her, and slowly cracking her open... couldn't he see she was shattering? What had she done to deserve this?

You killed Tristian, a voice inside her groaned under the pain. *You killed him. You.*

The ache in her heart suddenly exploded and Dylan threw her head back to scream.

And then it was gone.

She felt just as numb as before.

No anger.

No pain.

No memories.

Empty. Vacant. Soulless. Just like before she had met Tristian.

Alive but not quite living.

Dylan opened her exhausted, glassy eyes to find everyone staring at her in silence.

"Good morning!" exclaimed a round, bald man at the threshold of the open door. Astrid and Soren were instantly at attention and bowing. Even Lucia lowered her chin in an awkward prostration.

Dylan was still panting heavily, completely thrown off kilter by everything she had just experienced, unable to bow to this random demon. Who was he, anyway?

The demon shuffled in. His crimson, velvet robe swept across the floor as he moved with grace. He wore several gaudy golden rings and a thick chain necklace.

The demon stopped in front of Soren. "Lieutenant Soren Verbeck."

"Lord Struo," Soren greeted, curtly.

Struo nodded, not taking his eyes off of Dylan. "Is this she?"

Soren kept his eyes on the round man as he replied, "Yes, sir."

The demon in red robes stepped closer to Dylan, examining her trembling form. He grinned, exposing an array of needle point teeth as excitement gleamed in his eyes.

Dylan gulped.

Lord Struo spoke over his shoulder, "Has she been debriefed?"

"We were just getting to that," Soren stated, tossing a pointed look over to Astrid as if to say, '*see?*'

Struo stared back down at Dylan and giggled under his breath. "Well, that will just have to wait." He glanced over at Lucia who still had her head tipped down. His smile vanished.

"The Kings are waiting."

CHAPTER 2

"Help me...
Save me from the ghosts and shadows
Before they eat my soul"
Mercy-Muse

DYLAN had new clunky, metal cuffs wrapped around her wrists as she walked out of the white-walled prison room with Lucia next to her, Astrid leading the way, and Soren following.

It didn't take long to reach the end of the hall where an arched, frosted glass door loomed ominously over them.

Astrid quickly rapt against the pane. The door silently opened, revealing a few guards on the other side. They straightened and saluted before pivoting on their heels and leading the way into the room.

Dylan couldn't contain her gasp as the simple hallway transformed into an enormous cathedral. Everywhere she looked shouted prestige and wealth, from the crystal chandeliers with bright gold and jewel accents to the elaborate glass roof that bloomed open like a lotus flower to reveal a beautiful day.

Tall and narrow stained glass windows lined the wall to their right, separated by thick, marble pillars. Each depicted gruesome tales of war, death, and power. It felt like she had fallen inside of a book. The fantasy too amazing to grasp as reality.

Sharp words struck Dylan's ears like rocks before she

realized the sides of the room were full of demons, restrained by a twisted rope. She shifted her eyes to the hundreds of star-shaped eyes of all colors and sizes as the crowd snarled and laughed at the prisoners. Each attendee was dressed in finery, dripping in diamonds, precious stones, and gold.

It wasn't until she saw the magnitude of hate directed at her that she understood her place here. It was a horrible thing to be an Elementa in Elon. It made her wonder what Tristian had left out of her story. She couldn't imagine so many beings hating her simply because she had been hidden for protection. Had he lied? Was there more to the story?

Dylan's fear multiplied with each passing step. The more drawn out this became, the more cracks penetrated her resolve. A part of her wished she was that strong, scary demon everyone here apparently saw, not the girl that couldn't even stand up to her captors. She was nothing but a coward like Lucia had said.

Their group stopped in the middle of a large design of a shield etched into the granite floor. Dylan quickly recognized it as the same marking carved into her shoulder; the Collector's Crest.

Soren stepped in front of Dylan and grabbed her wrists, making speedy work of releasing the manacles.

Without thinking, Dylan whispered, "Thank you," rubbing the ache away. He didn't seem to appreciate her thanks. Soren snatched one of her wrists and squeezed so hard she heard a small bone snap. Dylan cried out and dropped to the floor from the pain.

Soren simply crouched down and got into her face, still holding her agonizing wrist captive. "You may have escaped Hell, but don't confuse this for a place of refuge. You left one only to enter another." He sneered at the torrent of tears falling down her face. "Oh and you're welcome, *Tempy*."

He dropped her wrist with disgust etched on his face, stood and proceeded to unlock Lucia's cuffs as if breaking a girl's wrist wasn't anything new. Dylan cradled her trembling, throbbing hand against her chest and stared at him in shock.

It really had been him. He was the one that evoked her pain earlier. He had ripped through her mind and forced her to face those memories simply to obtain information.

Dylan balked at the idea of someone flipping through her mind like a rolodex, yet, was it really out of the realm of possibilities here? If Silas could slip thoughts into her head and make her believe she was truly out of all options for escape, couldn't Soren scan her memories for truth?

Astrid and Soren were mostly busy talking to staff or other lower ranking soldiers when she heard Lucia clear her throat.

Dylan glanced sidelong at her kidnapper as she struggled to stand. The rage she had affixed to Lucia had long since expired. The issue of her own wellbeing was now very much taking precedence.

"What in the worlds did you expect?" Lucia hissed under her breath. Dylan turned to look at her and Lucia snapped, "*Keep* your eyes forward."

Dylan clenched her teeth once again feeling the anger. *Oh, well,* she thought. She was used to anger and pain. It was this helpless feeling that she couldn't seem to swallow. It sat in the back of her throat like glass.

"He wasn't doing you a favor," Lucia whispered, "None of them are. And if they ever do, be scared. Only curses follow gifts here."

"Save your advice for someone who cares," Dylan muttered.

Lucia scoffed. "You're worse than a hormonal teenager."

Dylan sighed loudly, hoping Astrid would come along and shut the bitch up like last time.

"I guess, it's a good thing that it's against etiquette to wear the cuffs in here." Lucia smiled. "...for us."

Dylan turned her head at that. "What on earth are you planning?"

"Hey," Astrid said, shoving the hilt of a weapon against Dylan's shoulder blades, causing her to jolt forward and wince.

"No speaking."

Lucia snickered.

In front of her, a couple of lower-ranking soldiers that had been conversing, turned and nodded at the Horde soldiers then moved to their positions at the sides of the room. Dylan's mouth suddenly went dry at the unmistakable, clear view of an enormous black, granite stage. Royal red curtains were draped across the back, displaying three golden seats with delicate etchings and a single panel of black velvet backing—tufted with small gold and crimson shields.

Thrones.

Her breath picked up as the ice of looming death crawled along her spine. It didn't matter what Lucia was planning. There wasn't time for anything. They were going die.

Tears filled Dylan's eyes. None of this was fair. She wanted to live. She wanted to go home. She wanted her grandmother and her bed. She wanted a tomorrow.

Closing her eyes, she released a shaky breath and tried to pull herself together. But, it was no use. She couldn't stop shaking.

A side door to the stage swung open, revealing the same round man from earlier: Lord Struo. The room silenced so quickly, Dylan felt momentarily deaf.

She watched Lord Struo march to the center of the platform. Once he was in front of the audience, he called out, "I, Edward Struo, Lord of Souls, announce the *Omnipotence!*"

He bowed and shuffled backward to the side of the stage next to a podium. Demons all around Dylan dropped to their knees in prostration.

A hand clamped down on the back of Dylan's neck, harshly shoving her face to the floor. She tried to catch herself only to cry out into the silence at the impact her injured wrist had against the unforgiving floor.

"*Bow, you cunne!*" Soren snapped in her ear.

Dylan shook from the all too familiar cocktail of rage, fear, and pain swirling inside her. A violent mixture in her body that begged to be released on the demon squeezing her neck. It was all pushed to the back of her mind when she noticed the golden-robed demons pouring into the room and sweeping across the stage.

Dylan shifted her head to get a better look, not caring one bit about Soren's tightened grip at her nape or the ache in her jaw from the icy floor. Something inside her faltered.

She knew that last golden-robed demon King. She had dreamed of him when Tristian had taken her to meet with the Oracle Sansvi. It was her father. What was he doing up there in a King's robe?

Each King stepped in front of a lavish throne. From the left, was a woman almost too beautiful to be real. A perfect DaVinci creation brought hauntingly to life. Her curls were placed precisely, like a giant coil collected on one shoulder, the rest pinned to the top of her head; and her smooth brow and classic features were calculating as she smiled to the bowing crowd.

The demon in the middle Dylan recognized as the "Master" that had accompanied the Shadow Horde to Silas' castle. He had a glossy sheet of black hair brushing his shoulders and a pointed nose. The way he always seemed to be smiling even in the most dire of situations made him hard to forget.

Then lastly, her father. His pale-blonde hair, crystal blue eyes familiar from the dream they shared. But that was where her only memory of him vanished. This man was regal and stern. His square jaw clenched in annoyance as he gazed upon her with eyes full of loathing and fire. He wasn't her father now, or maybe ever.

The disdain he harbored as he stared down at her hurt. It

hurt so much Dylan found herself looking away—trying and failing not to cry again. She felt rejected and humiliated. How could her own flesh and blood put her in such a position? And what about her mother? Had he turned on her, too?

The Kings sat followed by a loud hum that vibrated the ground as everyone in the room shifted back up to stand. Soren knotted a fist into Dylan's hair yanking her up to her knees. The Queen smiled at this.

"Welcome to The Gates, Elon," the Queen sang from her throne, gathering a chorus of *"Pleased"* by their audience.

"As you all know, a couple of decades ago our realm was greatly affected by the family that chooses to call themselves the Elementas. Since then, we have lived in fear of our... own... kind," her voice cracked on the last words. The King to her left laid a comforting hand on the arm of her chair as she fought tears. Dylan glanced around the room at the many faces mirroring her compassion and hanging on her every word. The Queen took a moment to compose herself, wiping away the tears that never fell with a handkerchief offered by Lord Struo.

With her voice steady, she continued, "We lived in terror for the day the Elementas would attack us again, led by their powerful daughter. Surely, to end us all." The Queen effortlessly fixed her invasive eyes on Dylan. "Not anymore."

A shuddering breath hitched out of Dylan's chest from the brutality of the Queen's stare. It was more than terror for what happened to her race. This hate was personal. But why?

"Today I am happy to announce that we will finally be able to put a piece of our terror behind us. Let the trial commence, Lord Struo."

The Queen nodded to Lord Struo. He lifted his shoulders and smiled, teeth and all. "Lucia Planto, you may stand and address the court."

Lucia returned Struo's smile brilliantly, and stepped up

with a type of grace Dylan wished she could possess in a moment like this. Or any moment for that matter. She looked relaxed and stately as if she had been invited, not beaten and forced here against her will.

Lucia curtsied. "*My Masters.*"

"I must say," Lord Struo crooned, staring at Lucia as if she was an interesting but dangerous new creature. "I am quite surprised to see you here so soon. I had imagined our differences had been settled with the execution of your late husband, Roman Planto."

Lucia shifted crisply—her knuckles turning white under the tension as she visibly fought scoffing.

Dylan lifted an eyebrow, surprised to see the crack in her armor. Perhaps, Lucia wasn't as tough as she made herself out to be.

"Hmm," Struo hummed, looking delighted to have driven the knife so deeply into Lucia's confidence. "So, do you agree the problem wasn't with Roman at all but with the entire Planto line?"

Lucia pursed her lips and met the Lord of Soul's defiant stare.

Struo looked down at a small card on his podium and giggled.

"You *have* been quite busy, haven't you? Taking in guests, creating portals, and holding humans…" he looked up and tsked, "but that wasn't all, was it, Ms. Planto?"

"*No,*" she finally huffed.

"No, it isn't. What else might you add to this ever growing list of delinquencies?"

"We took the girl."

"Oh?" Struo laughed once. "*Just* a girl?"

"We took Temperance Elementa," Lucia corrected. "And almost had her *Signed,*" she added with a hint of superiority, as if she wasn't the slightest bit apologetic.

The crowd murmured softy and Dylan grimaced at more creatures hearing about this; and the thought of how Silas

25

convinced her. Would she tell that part, again, too?

"For what, might I add, would you need the most powerful and dangerous demon in our realm?"

Silence ensued and Dylan found herself staring at the woman who in every sense of the word radiated demon. Her kinked, black hair was like a veil of shadows. Her insidious green eyes like lifeless holes.

"I think you know enough."

Lord Struo's eyes flashed at Lucia's statement and a hush of whispers spread like wildfire throughout the room. It was Dylan's guess that not many demons talked back to the court.

"We need to hear you say the words," the Queen interrupted, smoothing her robe in her lap. "The populous needs to hear it from your mouth."

"It doesn't matter, now does it? You will never find him," Lucia called out.

Dylan's head popped up.

"Excuse me?" the Queen laughed humorlessly, giving the demon a chance to recant her words. Lucia didn't falter.

"He will carry out our plan. Nothing you do will change that. Mark my words. *Gerion will come for you. All of you.*"

"End her, already," the Queen groaned with an exasperated sigh, looking anything but threatened. Dylan didn't share her ease.

The room erupted in rising levels of hushed chatter.

"He will come! He will kill each of you! And I will laugh from my throne as I watch you scatter in the void you're sent to!" Her eyes swung to Dylan and she flinched back, afraid the woman who once held her captive might suddenly strike her. "And *you* are coming with me."

What? Dylan frowned at the woman's growing grin until it was like a slash across her face.

Lucia swung out but Dylan was tugged out of the way, at the last second, by Soren. Astrid charged and Lucia spun around her so fast Dylan had a hard time keeping track.

Suddenly, a knife was in Lucia's grip as she held it up to Astrid's throat. Demons all around them began pushing and shoving their way to the exit. The moment Lucia noticed Dylan's horror, she laughed wickedly.

"End her, NOW!" shouted Dylan's father from behind a wall of several armed soldiers protecting the Three Kings.

Dylan looked at Soren and two other Shadow Horde soldiers that seemingly appeared out of nowhere, expecting them to be doing some sort of magic to save their comrade. Not... standing completely still!

"What do you want?" Soren asked, calmly, despite all of the screaming and chaos.

Lucia yelled, "Temperance Elementa!"

"And then what? You think you can just walk out of this room unscathed?"

"*Yes*," Lucia snapped. "Not only will you let us leave, but you will walk us out yourself. Otherwise *she* dies, forever." She motioned to Astrid.

Soren smirked under his breath at the challenge. "*Okay*."

Dylan gasped, ready with a slur of "no's" while she ran for her life—when she noticed Astrid watching her comrade tap his foot. Once, twice, three times—Astrid squeezed her eyes shut just as Soren flicked a small dagger in their direction. It sailed through Lucia's skull and into the stage's platform.

Dylan recoiled, expecting blood and a body slamming down to the floor. Instead she watched clothes flutter to the ground like fallen leaves.

Dylan stared at the heap of clothes, detached and frozen as her inner self stood just outside of her body, screaming.

Lucia was gone.

She had freaking *vanished*.

The lingering crowd erupted in wails and angry questions.

Soren hastily picked up the *Binding* laying on the heap of clothes and growled, "Fake!"

A blonde Shadow Horde soldier with wind-swept hair and sea glass green eyes joined Soren and took the small pointless necklace. "Looks like we have a traitor in our midst."

Astrid immediately began feeling her belt and then frantically rifting through the crumpled heap of clothes before gasping at their small group, "She got my *Daleon*!"

The soldiers were all silent.

"*No*," Astrid said to herself, trembling, "*nooo...*"

"It's okay," Soren finally said, lowly. "Go grab mine. I still have my father's blade."

"Soren, that's..." Astrid looked sick as if she was the one about to be on trial. "What she can do with that... No! What the Kings will do to me!"

"We'll tell them," Soren consoled, "just give me some time. I'll say it's mine."

Astrid nodded shakily before her scared eyes met Dylan's along with the rest of the Shadow Horde.

Dylan looked straight at the floor.

She wondered why they cared so much about Astrid's dagger. Didn't they have a plethora of weapons? Who cared if one was taken?

It took a while to regain control of the room. There were a lot of questions from the crowd and several groups left, too afraid to stay in the company of an Elementa who might suddenly lash out as Lucia had. The Kings made an effort to show that Dylan's *Binding* was working. But when that only appeased a few, they conceded by replacing her manacles for the remainder of the trial.

Her father suddenly shifted in his seat. "Lord Struo," he boomed, impatiently.

Struo jolted and scurried back over to the podium.

"Temperance Elementa," he announced to the room, "you may address the court."

Dylan took a deep breath and reluctantly shifted her face

28

up. She opened her mouth and stopped when she realized she had absolutely no idea how to address them. She racked her brain for the very proclamation Lucia had just used, but her sheer terror dried her mouth and drained her brain. Her breathing became erratic. All she could see was the glittering blade that would soon be shoving itself into a bed of her skin, sinew, and bone. This in no way felt like a trial but a shaming before death.

"Well?" Lord Struo pressed.

"I-I'm sorry. I don't remember how."

The Queen chuckled, silencing Dylan's pathetic confession.

"You d-don't remember?" she mocked, prompting the crowd to laugh with her. "You don't remember what, my dear?"

"I wasn't raised here—"

"*Oh*," the Queen smiled patronizingly. "You don't know how to address the court."

Dylan nodded as a startling current tickled her fingertips. The sensation frightened her and she felt her hands tighten into fists in an effort to stop it. Could her *Binding* be a fake as well? *No*. They had just checked it.

"Lesson one: you will always address this court with eye contact and *'My Masters'*. Is that clear?" the Queen snapped.

Dylan nodded again at the floor. Then, realizing her mistake, tossed her gaze up at the tribunal. "My Masters." It came out strained.

"Ah! She is a quick one, right, Damen?" the King in the middle japed, slapping her father on the shoulder in good nature.

"She would be wise to listen," the Queen said.

The King in the middle throne leaned forward, setting his unnerving attention on Dylan. "Temperance Elementa, why what a pleasure it is to finally meet you."

Dylan felt herself shrink at the announcement. *That only makes one of us.*

"I feel like we should introduce ourselves," he said, glancing at his counterparts before looking back at Dylan. "I can tell by your expression you have no idea who we are, other than Kings, of course." The way he spoke to her felt intimate as if it were just the four of them in the room and not thousands.

Dylan just stared back with terror-fueled stillness, unsure if she should even speak.

His eyes narrowed but his grin never abated. "I am King Zirk Abores," he motioned to the Queen on his right, "This lovely creature is Queen Vashti Monita." His eyes then slipped over to her father. "And this... why this is your blood, King Damen PyroVentus."

Damen... wasn't her father named Atticus?

"We apologize for restraining you in our holy court, but I am sure you can understand why."

When she still didn't say anything, King Zirk sat back.

"Very well. Go on now, Ms. Elementa. Tell us how you were found in such a," his eyes roamed her, "predicament."

All eyes swung to her.

"Uh..." She cleared her throat feeling her cheeks heat from all of the attention. She had never been one for public speaking. "I was..."

Dylan fisted her hands tightly, renewing the searing pain in her wrist, before finding the confidence to speak louder. "I was kidnapped by a vampire." She internally cringed at the memory of Erez and his *bite.*

"That must have been a powerful vampire!" King Zirk smirked.

Dylan tried to not let his comments get to her. Of course it was a powerful vampire. What vampire wasn't powerful?

"I woke up in a cell. Sil- I mean, the Plantos," her eyes flicked to Lucia's heap of clothes instinctively then back to her new rulers, "they held me hostage for almost two months."

Two months before Silas touched me. Two months before

he was able to reach my mind… it was still too late. She felt the familiar golf ball rise up into her throat as tears threatened.

Tristian. Don't think about Tristian. Not here.

"The Plantos made me feel…" She cleared her throat again when it became wobbly. "Like I had no other option but to–" Dylan paused as she found the words 'marry Silas' hard to say, because it had been so much more than that. Silas had cornered her with fear while marriage didn't sound so awful. It wasn't. Not when it's with the right person. "They tried to persuade me to sign a contract," she said instead. Her mind flashed to Lucia's satisfied smirk.

"And what was this contract for?"

"I don't know," Dylan shook her head. "That was why I took Peppi's soul, knowing full well it would call the Shadow Horde. I may not have known what the contract was but I knew my life depended upon not signing it."

Out of the corner of her eye, Dylan noticed Soren's posture straighten. It suddenly hit her that he already knew everything. Would he tell the Three Kings she was purposely omitting parts of the story? She stiffened, feeling even more threatened by him.

"You did not seem happy to see us," King Zirk countered, looking skeptical.

Dylan opened her mouth then closed it again. How could she voice everything she was going through when they arrived? How could she possibly put that moment into words?

"I was in shock," Dylan stated flatly.

"How well did you know Tristian Effingo," the Queen interjected, "and the Planto brothers, before your alleged kidnapping?"

Brothers? Dylan frowned. What brother?

"I, um, never knew the name Planto, or Effingo… Tristian only made himself known to me right before I was taken. I didn't even know what I was until he told me… I

31

mean, Effingo," she corrected belatedly.

"You expect us to believe this?"

"Yes," she breathed.

"Were there relations with any of these demons?" the Queen asked.

King Zirk sneered in disgust at the Queen's ridiculous question; but, she ignored him while keeping her eyes trained solely on her prey: Dylan.

Dylan suddenly felt her face heat with embarrassment. She glanced at the crowd, watching her intently, before clearing her throat and looking up at the Queen. Had Astrid already told them what Lucia confessed? What would they do to her if she lied?

"Yes," Dylan blushed and looked to the floor.

"Yes?" the Queen perked up. "Yes, with who?"

"Remember, her love life isn't on trial, my Lady," Zirk mentioned lightly.

The Queen simpered. "Of course, my Lord."

Dylan exhaled, thankful that King Zirk stopped her from further embarrassment.

Dylan was too deep inside her thoughts of Tristian and Silas to follow along with what King Zirk was saying until he inquired.

"Have I summed it up correctly, Ms. Elementa?"

A thousand eyes swung to her. She wanted to ask him to repeat what he had said but she had a feeling the request wouldn't go over too well.

"Yes?"

"So, it is settled." King Zirk stood. "She wanted to come here after discovering her true identity from Tristian Effingo, but couldn't because she had been kidnapped by the Plantos. She then waited until an opportunity struck. Alas! A soul from a slave girl!" He chuckled, gesturing wildly for the audience that was eating it all up before turning to her and looking satisfied.

What? She thought dumbfounded.

"You are turning yourself in...?" her father asked, less bitter and more confounded.

"You cannot be so foolish!" the Queen suddenly demanded, bashing her heavily ringed fist against the arm of her chair. "She just admitted to a plan!"

"A *plan* to turn herself in," Zirk said as if it was obvious.

"You cannot believe for one second that an Elementa would tell the truth. How foolish do you have to be to think she couldn't squash the Plantos like insects! She is working with them, with *all* of them!"

Dylan quickly stopped nodding.

"Just because she can doesn't mean she will."

"Maybe because she's waiting to crush us! Perhaps she came here with the intent to take over!"

"You never wanted her from the get go."

"That isn't a secret, Zirk! I didn't want her. Damen didn't want her. Hell, half the worlds didn't want her! It was all *you,* " the Queen growled.

Dylan felt herself filling up with anger as she watched the Kings bicker back and forth over her life.

Let me live, goddamnit! Let me live and send me away!

"You and your damn experiments," the Queen continued. "You're going to ruin us all!"

"*I am not working with them*!" Dylan suddenly screamed. Why was that so hard to comprehend?

The room silenced and the Kings all turned to look at her. The Queen's cheeks were pink with angered passion, as if she were about to explode.

Dylan's shoulders bunched up in horror.

"Four years," King Zirk finally said, corking the buildup of ire threatening to burst out at the Queen. "We shall have your retrial at your turning age. Until then you are sentenced to remain in this world. You will not step a foot outside this compound. You may think of it as probation, of sorts." He glanced at the Queen and raised his eyebrows, appeasingly. "A way for us to watch you until you gain our trust. *If* you ever do."

Her world seemed to tilt as her sentence sank in like concrete. It was hard at first. Like trying to break through solid ice. But, once it did, something clicked and light flooded the darkness.

They never intended to kill her or set her free.

They wanted to keep her, too.

She was distantly aware of the Queen's voice inquiring on the location of Tristian's body and the uproar of frantic voices opposing the verdict from the audience as the soldiers shoved and jerked her to the exit... to her new prison.

CHAPTER 3

"Beauty is terror.
Whatever we call beautiful,
we quiver before it."
Donna Tartt

ASHER tried to sit still, but his mind wouldn't stop working. It spun and twisted with dark thoughts and sickening scenarios of murder and pain. He stared at the amber liquid in his coffee cup before bringing it to his trembling lips and finishing the last of the whiskey. Even though he knew Aria wouldn't wake for several more hours, he still felt guilty for drowning himself in the burning liquor at an hour when coffee should be in this mug.

There was a light knock on the door. Asher jumped up from the couch and quickly cracked open the door.

Ulysses stood outside issuing his "hello" through a tightly held smile. He was wearing a long sleeve white T-shirt and ripped jeans. He looked mostly the same as the last time Asher had seen him back in Lamu, Kenya. He still had a ton of piercings and colorful tattoos covering his neck and the tops of his hands. The only difference was his hair. Before it had been a short Mohawk. Now his light orange hair was buzzed close to the scalp.

Asher peered around him into the outdoor hall of Aria's apartment looking for uninvited guests.

"I wasn't followed," Ulysses said, cautiously.

Asher nodded and let his friend in before shutting the door quietly so as to not wake Aria and let her in on what he was up to. Ever since learning about the underworld, about what happened to Tristian and Dylan… and then almost losing Asher in Zadar during the battle with the worms… Aria had developed difficulties functioning at what used to be normal tasks.

Sleeping was one of them.

Most nights, Asher would be startled awake by her screaming and ripping her nails across her chest. She told him once that the nightmares were always of a faceless man who barged into her apartment and killed everyone, leaving her for last to witness it all. Asher never told her his immediate thought was Gerion and not PTSD. He didn't see how that would help at all. If anything, it would probably make her depression worse.

Asher led Ulysses to the quaint living room with charmingly mismatched furniture. The angel sat, but Asher walked over to the large picture window and peered out through the metal blinds, taking his time with what he wanted to say. He wasn't even sure where to start. He didn't want to start. He just wanted to move on. Dylan was a lost cause. Tristian was gone. And Aria…

Last night after she had awakened him with her nightmare, Aria cried that she had failed Dylan by not keeping her safe. Asher knew Isabel had trusted Aria to watch out for the shy, suicidal girl; begged her to include her in everything when the girls first met. At first, Aria had played the role almost too well–memorizing Dylan's schedule, looking for her when she was late, and pulling her along to every school function. Then it became second nature as her protectiveness wedged itself deeply into their bond.

So, Asher understood the dark feelings of failure gripping Aria's mind. It wasn't until she pleaded with him to kill the faceless man before he killed her that he fully awoke. He hadn't even stopped to think about the can of worms he was about to open.

He just wanted her to be her again.

Asher had immediately called Ulysses and told him to come here first thing in the morning. It was urgent.

He finally looked over at Ulysses. The angel had a resigned look on his face as if he knew exactly what the demon was about to say.

"We're going after him?" Ulysses asked.

"I am," Asher corrected, before running his hands through his wildly curly hair. He suddenly wondered if he looked as crazy as he felt. "I need to kill him." He needed to do this. It was his fault. He had failed to bring back Aria's best friend, failed his friend, and failed to kill Gerion. Now Aria was tortured every night by nightmares that they were all dying. That they were all going to die.

He knew Gerion was singling out those that mattered to Dylan, hoping to dig the Elementa demon out of the OP's clutches.

"*We* need to kill him," Ulysses emphasized.

Asher looked at him for a moment before shaking his head. "No. I need someone with Aria. I need you to protect her."

"Aria has Isabel," Ulysses said. "She will survive being alone. What she won't be is fine if you don't come back."

Asher grabbed the neck of a new bottle of whiskey and took a swig. He swallowed and tilted the bottle towards Ulysses in silent offering.

"You need to understand that we might die doing this."

Ulysses grabbed the bottle and set it down on the coffee table before smiling and walking over to his friend. "Without the threat of death where would the adventure be, my friend?"

Asher let out an exasperated laugh. "You're one sick bastard, you know that right?"

Ulysses just shrugged again before turning away and

peering down the shadowy hallway to Aria and Dylan's rooms. "What about the demon girl?"

"Dylan?" Asher grimaced, looking back out the window. He didn't want to go there. He wanted to accept that the fight was out of his hands and focus on his mate.

"Tristian wouldn't want us to give up."

Asher scoffed. "Yeah, well, do you see Tristian here? Because I don't."

◇◇◇

"Grab her legs," voiced the Medic to Soren.

Dylan kicked violently and grabbed hold of the trim on her bathroom door before being yanked back and flipped over.

Soren laughed, but it sounded more like a growl as he straddled her. Dylan cried out and hit him, trying and failing to get him off of her. She spat in his face and watched in silent horror as his sick humor intensified.

"Here we go," sang the Medic.

She began to pant fiercely. "I can't," she sobbed, not wanting anything to do with human souls.

"Oh, dear," the Medic sighed as he held it delicately to her mouth. But, before she could hit it away, her reflexes shot into action. She wrapped her lips around it and kicked the vial back like a shot.

A delicious shot.

"There you go, sweet girl," the Medic hummed, caressing and petting her sticky, sweat sodden hair like she was a feral animal finally eating from his hand.

She moaned through the glorious high growing within her. "There you go..." he repeated, "You should be proud. I've never seen anyone go that long while completely abstinent from food. Your Kings will be pleased by this."

Her breathing soothed and her muscles loosed. Her head lolled to the side, lax and floating as she appreciated the sun spilling inside her small eight by eight room from the barred window like a waterfall of warmth.

A black crow appeared on the stone sill, interrupting her joy like a stain on her moment of peace. She stared into the tiny, green beads for eyes. Her smile warbled and reality snapped. She had done it again. She had consumed the souls of people.

Guilty sobs replaced her relaxed limbs and bile rose up in her throat. After Peppi, she never thought she would have to do it again; and now, she wasn't sure if she was going to cry or be sick.

Distantly, she was aware of the room settling into silence. Both demons had left her to grieve, curled in a fetal position and gasping tears.

Alone. Always alone...

"Damn," a woman's voice whispered, jolting Dylan out of her memory of a month prior.

Dylan looked up from the scratches she gouged into the door frame that first time she was forced *Essence* to the demon sitting in a metal folding chair directly across from her, cursing a broken nail. Her name was Anna Cacia and she visited Dylan several times a week. She had dark blonde hair pulled tightly into a sleek pony tail and down-turned, violet eyes.

The first few times Anna visited, she fumbled around, talking about herself and about her day. From those visits, Dylan learned that Anna was highly educated with several degrees in psychology. She was also well respected and the main benefactor of the schools, which to Dylan, meant she was wealthy but didn't have the status of a court official.

Anna spent two visits trying to get Dylan to open up about her past. When that didn't work, the demon started bringing textbooks on Demonology and reading to her from them. Dylan often wondered what Anna's true intentions were. Was she here to report back to the Kings? Or was she here looking to get close to her—hoping to score some Elementa connections in the future? Maybe it was to study her as part of some research project. Dylan couldn't fathom anyone braving a "dangerous prisoner" for two hours every other day simply because they just wanted to. But, Dylan wouldn't tell her to stop. As stupid and useless as it felt, Dylan liked the company. Besides, even if Anna's motives for visiting weren't as innocent as she claimed, Dylan liked learning the in-and-outs of those who imprisoned her.

Today, Dylan couldn't have cared less about Anna's motives or the content of what she read. As hard as she tried, Dylan just couldn't seem to get Silas out of her head. Last night had been like every other night— hours spent trying and failing to reclaim some normalcy within her mind. Unfortunately, the dark was when Silas *loved* to visit her. He always picked random nights to taunt her with memories of being imprisoned within his castle while then adding little sadistic twists.

In this particular dream, he had created a maze of the castle's duplicate hallways. She was dressed in the wedding gown he had picked out for her. She was running and trying to reach Tristian's voice that called out to her. When she thought she had made it to him, Silas was there, painted in Tristian's blood. He was laughing and holding her signed contract to marry him. It was then that she realized she was sinking onto the hard floor.

"Now, you'll never leave," he laughed. "Now, you'll always be mine."

"How are you feeling today?" Anna asked suddenly, looking sympathetic.

Dylan's lip curled, hating that her emotions were written all over her face. Out of all the reactions she evoked from the demons in Elon, sympathy had to be the worst. It was a look she knew all too well from her troubled past as a human.

Dylan looked away from Anna's prying eyes and around her plain room. A wooden twin bed, a matching dresser and desk with a plastic chair. Everything was simple, generic, and *white*. White cinderblock walls. White linoleum floors.

White starchy sheets. White oak furnishings. However, her clothes were all black. Two extremes that managed to make her eyes hurt whenever she focused too long on one or the other.

At least her window was open so she could gaze outside at the vibrant world of Elon, even if there were bars keeping her from imagining she was free.

"As I was saying," Anna said before continuing where she left off and giving up on the hope that Dylan might confide in her.

A sharp buzzing caught Dylan's attention and she shifted her glare from her monochromatic room to the Shadow Horde soldier she hated: Soren Verbeck. He stood off to the side by the door and was dressed in the Horde's typical leather uniform of head-to-toe leather sans hood and combat boots. He pulled out a thin, black rectangle from his back pocket, looked at the bright blue screen for a moment, then put it away.

By now, Dylan was used to seeing him even if she did loathe him; and she was pretty sure the feeling was mutual. Anna and Lord Struo never visited without having him or another soldier present. The other soldiers made it a point to stay out of the way while Soren seemed to like making himself known—always silent and watchful like a lion hunting and stalking its food.

He met Dylan's glare and the two continued their silent war until his phone vibrated again.

"Lady Cacia," Soren said gruffly, looking away from their staring contest.

Dylan smirked at the victory, then frowned as she realized how bored she must be to get any enjoyment out of *that*.

Anna looked back at Soren as if she had forgotten he was even there. "Yes?"

"King Zirk is on his way."

"Fine," she said, immediately going back to reading

41

about different powers and how they related to diverse bloodlines. The difference between the pure and the tainted; the wealthy and the poor...

Soren must have expected a different response because he looked a bit uncertain.

Despite Anna's aloofness at the announcement of a King about to visit, unease infiltrated Dylan's nerves. The Kings never visited her... so what did Zirk want?

Dylan felt along the thin tangle of threads of the *Binding* wrapped around her neck and thought about the many times she tried to manipulate various object since she arrived. It always seemed like the closer she got to wielding her powers, the more the wire would strangle her in the process. The last time she had tried, she had been so determined to overcome the *Binding's* barrier she didn't stop at the initial slice of pain but continued until blood was pouring down her chest and back. Thankfully she was in the shower and able to hide the evidence well. Or at least, she thought she had. Was this why King Zirk was coming? Did they know she was mentally trying to break free? Were they coming to punish her?

It didn't take long before the door opened revealing the two members of the Shadow Horde: Astrid and the blonde with wind-blown hair. They stepped inside followed by King Zirk.

Dylan looked to Anna as she quickly bowed while Zirk made his way to the front of the soldiers. Dylan followed suit—easing herself off the chair and onto her knees. It still felt uncomfortable to bow to anyone, especially now that the tiny room was crowded, but she wouldn't dare test the Kings when her life was constantly on the line.

"Lady Cacia," Zirk sang. "I apologize immensely for the interruption."

"My Master, there is no interruption. You are always welcome during our lessons."

"Wonderful," Zirk grinned fiercely, taking a seat on

Dylan's unmade bed and looking awfully out of place. "Please, continue as if I'm not here."

Dylan waited for Anna to move back into her seat before reclaiming hers as well.

For the remainder of the lesson, Dylan tried to keep her breathing level and her attention focused solely on Anna rather than the King as his speculative eyes roved around her sad little room and examined her sloppy attire.

Dylan sensed that Zirk was displeased by everything he was seeing even though a smile never left his face. She didn't know why, considering he had been the one to give her the room and baggy, hand-me-downs.

Anna's book closed, startling Dylan out of her thoughts.

"Amazing," Zirk commented, holding his head in one hand like an enraptured child. "And to think of all of those poor running amuck in our cities." He tsked. "I must come back for another lesson to hear the end!"

"You are always welcome, My Master."

"All right, Ms. Elementa, I'm going to need you to come with us."

Dylan visibly swallowed. She wanted to ask where they were going but found her tongue unable to work just as it had failed to do the last time she was in his presence. Oh God, they *were* here to punish her.

"My Master," Anna suddenly chimed in. "Do you mind if I accompany you for her comfort?"

"I believe that unnecessary," Zirk dismissed. "But I must say. It is such a delight to hear of your strong bond to the girl."

Anna nodded curtly before slipping on her crisp, khaki, suit jacket and allowing Astrid to escort her out of the room.

Dylan tentatively got to her feet and waited for the words: cuffs, trial, or death, but they never came. Zirk simply stepped out of the room as Soren and the blonde soldier ushered her out behind him.

Dylan kept her head tipped down as they turned down

several white hallways that matched her prison room. She wondered how they would do it. Would they use the special dagger Astrid had called a *Daleon*? From Anna's lessons, she'd learned the weapon was more than special. It was the only armament in the worlds laced with death's magic to completely sever a demon from ever returning back to life.

Good, she thought. *Make it final.* If she had to go, she definitely never wanted to come back.

It didn't take her long to realize they weren't walking to the trial room but passing through the threshold of some kind of gymnasium or multipurpose space. Wooden floors, mats, a far wall lined with equipment.

Dylan instinctively recoiled, feeling the déjà vu like hands around her throat. She stumbled backward into Soren and gasped through the dizzying fog as strong hands landed on her shoulders to steady her.

"Don't make me carry you," Soren warned from behind her. "*Move.*"

Dylan took a deep breath and forced herself to place one foot in front of the other.

It's just a gym, she chanted to herself, urging herself to relax. She couldn't continue to be afraid of everything that reminded her of Silas. To allow the fear was like willingly leaving the door wide open so that Silas could walk in whenever he damn well pleased. She needed to figure out how to close the door, once and for all, before he managed to tear her apart.

The group crossed over the four-lane indoor track and passed a wall of grey and white bleachers that could easily seat hundreds. There was a narrow, empty glass room with sliding doors and a control panel under the words, "*ENTER AT YOUR OWN RISK*" before coming to the back wall that held an area of weights, equipment, and bars cantilevered out from the wall. Above it all was a phrase painted in bold, black letters:

"VINCIT QUI SE VINCIT".

44

She briefly contemplated what language it was until her eyes settled on something a bit more enticing.

The enormous wall of weapons.

Axes, swords, clubs, bows, arrows, spears, and guns—anything dangerous that she could ever think of was right in front of her, mounted to the wall.

Dylan ran her eyes along the ominous wall, feeling elated and terrified at the same time. Escaping suddenly became a very real possibility. If she could grab a few weapons and somehow overcome to the *Binding*, she knew she might be able to fight her way out of Elon. Then she could hide or even search for the Elementas.

A side door next to the weapons wall suddenly opened, snapping Dylan out of her fantasy and unveiling King Damen, Astrid, and a soldier Dylan didn't recognize who was holding a large, black duffle bag.

Zirk walked up to King Damen as the men greeted each other with formal bows before turning and settling their scrutinizing eyes on Dylan.

"Ms. Elementa," Zirk said with a thoughtful smirk. "This is King Damen PyroVentus as I'm sure you remember from the trial."

And among other things, she wanted to say, but didn't.

She politely bowed to her father. He was dressed in the same golden robe he had been wearing at the trial. However, today he wore wire frames and looked a little more disheveled, as if he'd been in the middle of a deep sleep before coming here.

What the hell is going on?

"Ms. Elementa," King Damen greeted in a steely voice.

"We have been contemplating what to do with you for the past couple of months," Zirk continued. "And I think we would like to give you a chance here. After all, this was where you were meant to serve when we decided on your conception."

Wait. Dylan thought. *They are going to make me… a*

soldier?

"King Damen is in charge of the military sectors of Elon. So, he will be in charge of you from this point on as long as you stay in this sector. If it doesn't work out, we will discuss a different path. Good luck." Zirk stepped away and she thought she saw his smile falter as he passed.

The group bowed at his retreat, with Astrid following.

What just happened?

"James," King Damen prompted.

The soldier Dylan didn't know straightened and brought the duffle bag to her. She took it nervously, still trying to comprehend all that was happening. He then bowed to everyone and left the room.

"In there," King Damen said, "you will find appropriate training clothes and gear. Mr. Verbeck here will be overseeing your practices and he will also be the one conferring with me about your progress. Is that clear?" He seemed to be talking to not only Dylan but Soren as well.

"Yes, My Master," they both said.

"All right," King Damen said, before snapping to the blonde Shadow Horde soldier, "Ian. Follow me."

Soren and Dylan bowed as King Damen and Ian left the gym. Only when they were out of sight, and Dylan could no longer hear their foot falls, did she look at Soren with wide, panicked eyes.

"What just happened?"

Soren sighed and looked at her pointedly. "I've just received one hell of a headache, that's what happened."

"Wait. You didn't know about this either?" Dylan asked, hurrying after him as he stomped to the bleachers.

"No."

"I thought… maybe you had gotten me in trouble and I was having another trial."

Soren's brow furrowed as he regarded her intensely. "Trust me when I say I have better things to do."

"*Great*," Dylan replied sarcastically, when in fact she was relieved.

She hefted up the bag and placed it on the first row of the bleachers before unzipping it to see what was inside. Boots, leather gear, sneakers, socks, tanks, panties, sports bras, and yoga pants; all new and in the wonderful shade of black. Dylan found a plastic bag at the bottom with bottles of shampoo and conditioner, soap, a comb, hair ties, and deodorant.

"Looks like you don't have an excuse to look like a slob anymore," Soren said, leaning over to get a look in her bag.

Dylan curled her lip. "Asshole much?"

Soren shrugged. "Every day, pet."

She scowled from the atrocious nickname as she closed the zipper on her bag and placed it on her shoulder. She glanced down at her too short pants, giant tee-shirt, and bare feet before deciding to head to her room to change.

"Where do you think you're going?" Soren called out before she could manage two steps.

"To change...?"

"There's a locker room over there." He pointed to a door by the glass enclosure. "Hurry up. You have a lot to learn and I've got shit to do." Soren lifted his phone to his ear and began talking to someone in another language.

Dylan watched him for a moment, deliberating what language he was speaking and if it was the same as the one written on the wall. It flowed romantically off his tongue, like Spanish or Italian, but there was an accent leaning against each syllable that was otherworldly. She blinked a couple of times, reminding herself who she was listening to. She turned away from him before he could notice her staring and headed to the locker room.

She entered through the door Soren had motioned to previously and found a foyer with a worn wooden bench between two more doors. Dylan pushed through the door marked "Women" not at all surprised to see a traditional locker room. Porcelain sinks on the right. Brushed aluminum lockers on the left. Showers with washed out, blue curtains in the back and cream plastic stalls in the center facing the sinks.

Dylan strode to a bench near the lockers and opened the bag.

She put on a dri-fit tank that crisscrossed in the back, a padded sports bra, high-waisted yoga pants, and sneakers. Once dressed, Dylan looked at herself in the full length mirror next to the row of sinks and mirrors. She still looked haunted, gaunt, and pale. Her hair was a little longer; the edges still resembling the nice hack job the Medic had done. But, she couldn't deny that wearing clothes made for an actual woman made her feel less like property and more like a person, again. Not that she'd tell anyone. She still remembered the way Soren growled in her face at the trial when she thanked him for releasing her chains. No, she wouldn't thank anyone either.

What the hell am I doing? she thought as she fished a hair tie out of her bag. Did the Kings seriously think she'd make a good soldier? Or was this just another distraction until they decided her fate?

As she tied what she could of her hair back in a low pony tail, a plan began to slowly unfurl inside her head. Dylan decided she didn't care what their true intentions with her were; because she planned on memorizing every single detail of these training sessions. Then she would gain the necessary strength to escape with her choice of weapons from the smorgasbord out on display. That's when she would ultimately confront Silas and kill him. She needed to. Maybe not tomorrow or even four years from now, but she would. She knew she wouldn't be okay until Silas was finally dead. Until the entire Planto line was nothing but ash for what they had done to her life and the lives around them.

And then she would be free of Elon and Silas.

Free.

Dylan walked back into the gym with the bag slung over

her shoulder, feeling rejuvenated and strong from the oath she had just made to herself.

Soren glanced over at her as she set the bag on the bleachers and whistled sharply. "Get on the track. I want three miles every day before practice."

Dylan paused. *Three? Every day?* How the hell was she supposed to master one mile without passing out? He *did* realize she had been confined to a room for a while, right?

"All right," Dylan muttered before stepping into a lane and settling in to a slow pace. She could do this. She ran an easy three miles during college all the time. She just had to get back into the groove.

She had barely made it to the first curve when Soren jogged passed her in a loose black tank and cargo pants. Dylan took a second look, wondering when the hell he had time to completely change out of his uniform.

"Loser gets another mile," he called out.

Dylan threw up her arms. Was this honestly a competition? He had unfiltered demon speed and she was basically an out-of-shape human!

Dylan focused her thoughts and pressed on harder until they were sprinting side by side, determined not show her weakness.

Hot bile erupted from Dylan's mouth and into a trashcan Soren had snagged for her. She had barely sprinted half a mile before her empty stomach cramped up, making her sick.

She groaned. Her throat burned from the acid, seeing as that was all it was. Stomach acid. She hadn't eaten a thing since her "engagement lunch" with Silas and Lucia. For months, she had been living purely on *Essence* as if her new keepers couldn't be bothered to feed her a meal.

Once her stomach stopped seizing, she stumbled to the bleachers and collapsed onto her back. Beads of sweat dripped along her hairline as she tried to slow her breathing.

Ughhhh. I'm out of shape.

"Water?" Soren handed her a bottle and she took it a bit too eagerly. "You have five minutes then I want you in the octagon."

What?

Dylan could only stare at him in horror as she sat up just enough to sip the cool water that was almost too cold to swallow. She wasn't sure how she would be able to stand now, let alone train.

Soren walked over to the weapons wall, perusing the deadly arms. With his back to her, Dylan's eyes shifted down to his loose tank and cargo pants. It was so unlike his uniform. This attire felt more relaxed and showed off a hell of a lot more skin.

Her gaze locked onto the labyrinth of black, tribal tattoos wrapping his ripped shoulders and torso. She had gotten so used to seeing him in his uniform that she was almost surprised to see a different side to him. To see such a badass side. There were a few times that she tried and failed to imagine Soren drinking out with friends while wearing something casual. She always assumed the giant stick up his ass wouldn't allow him in jeans.

He reached out and grabbed a small black satchel and headed to the middle of the gym. He took out a thin blade and suddenly threw it across the room, the point sinking into the center of a target on the wall.

Bullseye.

Dylan's lips parted as she watched him throw dagger after dagger in effortless precision. Each dagger glittered dangerously with every swoop and flick of his wrist. It suddenly made sense how Astrid could trust him to make a killing shot when Lucia had taken her hostage during the trial. Soren was an expert when it came to knives.

When he was done, he simply removed the daggers from the target and put them away as if it were nothing. He then opened a large chest below the weapons wall and pulled something out before heading to a padded grey octagon in the center of the room.

She was still staring raptly when he looked over at her and lifted his eyebrows.

Dylan snapped out of her daze and urged herself to stand and hobble over to him.

"What are those?" she asked, her eyes running along the thick play swords in his hands.

"Wasters." When the confused look didn't leave her face, he added, "Training swords."

"Oh, right," she took the offered sword and examined the weapon, feeling his eyes upon her face. Comparing, judging, dissecting. Probably trying to figure out just how much she knew. She forced herself to lift her chin with confidence, despite feeling insufficient in every way.

"Stand with your legs at an angle and hold the sword out above your head."

"Um, like this?" she mumbled, lifting it up with the tip pointed straight out in front of her and angled her feet. God, she felt ridiculous.

He began walking around her, circling like a shark. Before she could say a word, his hand landed on her shoulder, shoving it back to straighten her posture. "Good," he mumbled, snatching her hips and shifting her a fraction more while kicking her feet open for a wider stance. "Better."

Dylan's expression turned sour. She didn't care one bit for the unforgiving way he touched her.

"This is the Och's guard," Soren said, moving to the space in front of her and ignoring her glare. "Every time I tell you to get into position, I want you to start here. Memorize it. I won't tolerate laziness."

She nodded, remembering the oath to herself.

Don't worry soldier boy, I plan on memorizing every single detail until I'm free.

"Got it. What's next?" she suddenly asked, not waiting for him to move on.

Soren's expression didn't change but she saw the challenge form in his sparkling cobalt eyes.

An hour later, Dylan was covered in sweat and groaning on the floor in the middle of the octagon while a composed Soren stood over her, holding both of their wasters, and his challenge conquered.

He had started out by teaching her a few drills and defensive stances; how to swing the sword for a strike; how to block. Then they parried, which was basically Soren kicking her ass, repeatedly.

"That wasn't fair," she cried, holding her legs to her chest and knowing he added yet another bruise. This time it was to her shins.

"You say that a lot," Soren crossed his thick arms. "It's not my fault you keep cringing every time I engage."

"Well, it's kind of hard not to when someone is swinging a huge stick at your face!" Dylan rolled into the fetal position and tried to breathe through the throbs of agony wrapping her body. Honestly, where had he *not* hit her?

"Come on, pet," Soren crooned. "Get up."

"Just give me a moment, Soren," she demanded, ignoring his degrading name for her.

Shit. She squeezed her eyes shut and counted to ten. *It's just physical pain. You can handle that kind of pain. Just breathe.*

Dylan forced herself to get up one last time, holding out a shaking hand once more to take the wooden sword from Soren.

He was glaring at her and she realized, belatedly, he didn't like how casually she had just said his name.

"We're done for the day," he snapped.

He turned away and went about putting the wasters away.

"That's it?" she called out with a sudden bravado when all she felt was relief the torture seemed to be over for now.

Soren looked back at her with the same coldness she

recalled from her trial.

"I'm tired of listening to you whine," he said, letting the chest slam close, "and I doubt I'm allowed to break the OP's new toy."

Break me? She scoffed. He thought he had that kind of power over her? Didn't he know it was impossible to break what was already broken? Although, he did seem like the type who would enjoy dancing on her shattered pieces just for the fun of it.

Fine, she mentally growled, already marching to her duffle bag resting on the bleachers. She had just placed the strap over shoulder when he appeared in front of her with demon speed, looming over her like a shadow of pure brooding male.

"Go on," he hissed, cocking his chin to the exit. "I expect you here tomorrow. Same time, *pet*."

Dylan narrowed her eyes and instead of telling him what was truly on her mind, limped out of the gym to the safety of her white-walled prison.

CHAPTER 4

*"You tell me that these blades are dangerous
but so are my thoughts."*
m.m

NADIA Burke pounced through the dark Topanga forest in her wolf form, flanked by her vigilant first and second in commands: Jax and Garret. She felt the crisp air of freedom rush through her coat as she dodged trees and boulders. It was truly the perfect night for a hunt. Unfortunately, hunting would have to wait as she had business to attend.

Leaping over a thorny bush, Nadia bumped into Garret and snapped at him with a nasty growl. He quickly moved to give her a wider berth, shaking his silvery coat in the moonlight as he trotted beside her. Garret was still technically on Nadia's bad side since failing to make sure the Collector, Tristian Effingo, killed her vampire lover, Datu at her villa in Lamu, Kenya.

Once she had found out Datu was still alive, it took several of her ladies in waiting to hold her back from ripping Garret to sheds. After her initial anger died down, she had been pleased with the way he had stood his ground, willing to take any punishment she dealt. So, she only demoted him to second in command and hoped his loyalty needn't ever be tested again.

Tonight though, her anger was back in full force after Garret came to her with a request to meet from another Collector. She found then that Garret Cottom indeed held a special place like a wound deep in your leg, unwilling to heal.

Goddamn annoying.

Nadia's first in command, Jax, dashed up ahead as they got close. He howled that everything was clear; she and Garret cut through the thick trees to a secluded opening in the Topanga wild. A large fire roared in the center, licking flames into the night and spitting embers like fireflies.

Nadia and Garret slowly met back up with Jax, who was busy assessing the four figures waiting silently next to the flames. Three men and one woman. When Nadia noticed who it was, she unabashedly turned. Her auburn coat shifted into silky russet waves of thick hair and dark human skin. She knew her guards would choose to stay in wolf form. Nakedness was viewed as a weakness for male werewolves. The females were different. They preyed on others with their sexuality. For it was the women who ruled and the men who protected.

Nadia caressed one of her bare shoulders. As much as she loved her wolf form, there was something irresistible about smooth skin.

She smiled furtively at the detested demon in the center. He stepped forward and shifted into something more appealing. She almost laughed outright but quickly held her tongue.

Men and their stupid egos.

His hair was a pale crown of blonde and his body nicely tanned and trimmed, but nothing compared to his eyes. They were a color that rivaled the flames behind him: blood-orange.

"Gerion Planto," Nadia greeted, before nodding to the others behind him: Gerion's mother, Lucia, and his brother, Viktor. She then snarled at the worthless existence being held captive, her old lover: Datu.

The vampire was cuffed with chains interlaced with crosses and wincing away from the threatening heat of the fire.

"Nadia," Gerion crooned informally before adding a seductive smile. "Please, call me Silas."

She merely raised an eyebrow. While her guards tensed and snarled, she lifted a delicate hand, silencing them.

"I see you have brought me a gift where my own guards have *failed*," she snarled in Garret's direction. "But, the question remains, why are we meeting..." she looked around the empty field, "here?"

"As you must have heard, our family is on the rise against the Omnipotence," Silas smiled brightly. "We have joined forces with many other families and species, and now we would like to proposition your pack. The more support we acquire, the greater the chance we have at dethroning the disgrace that is the Three Kings."

Nadia remained silent, soaking in the thought of a war with the root of the Collectors. Perhaps after she tore the throats out of enough demons her thirst for revenge would fade?

"And what makes you think I would be interested in such a..." Nadia inspected the ends of her locks, "inconvenience?"

Gerion held out his hand to his mother as she produced a small stiletto blade.

"Because we have this."

Nadia froze at the rare sight of a Collector *Daleon* dagger. She wondered how the hell they had acquired it. But, then she realized she didn't really care how. She only cared about the end; and a *Daleon* blade would kill not only the body but the soul attached to it as well. With this, winning was a strong possibility.

"Kill him," she snapped.

Datu's eyes flung wide in terror and he began to plead for his useless life. Gerion flicked the blade in his hand and sank it deep inside Datu's cold heart. Datu looked down at the blade as his dark veins cracked and bulged down his arms and up his neck. Gerion ripped the blade out as his brother pulled up Datu's arms and shoved his foot against the gasping vampire's abdomen, dismembering him in one swift movement before tossing the remains into the flames.

Nadia watched the last of her lover burn as Gerion removed a handkerchief from his front breast pocket to wipe off the clotted blood. Her lips curled above her teeth in a satisfied snarl. She would forever remember his screams like a lullaby to which she could enjoyably go off to sleep.

"You have our loyalty," Nadia said, turning her attention to the demon family. "Now, what is it that you need from us?"

"Two things," Gerion said, handing the blade back to his mother.

When the request issued from his beautiful lips, Nadia grinned.

◇◇◇

His eyes were like living monsters burning into Dylan's eyelids every time she shut her eyes. Silas seemed to pick up right where he left off after a two-month break. She could still feel the ghost of his fingers wrapped around her throat; the slick, warm coating of Tristian's blood running through her fingers.

It was just a nightmare, she reminded herself. A nightmare she had experienced countless times before. Other than her sweat-soaked skin and racing pulse, she knew it wasn't any more real than trying to remember a distant thought.

Dylan turned on the shower attached to her room and undressed. She needed to wash away the devastation slicked across her heart, renewed by her dream of Tristian's lifeless eyes, and the memories pooling and spilling over like the tears silently trickling down her cheeks.

Dylan stepped into the tiny stall of her shower and let the cold water envelope her. She gasped out a sob at the icy burn, finally succumbing to the tears she had protected since the moment she arrived in Elon.

She wrapped her arms around herself and pressed her back against the cold tile—needing to feel anchored while everything felt beyond her control. She tried to calm down and breathe through the pain that coursed through her veins like a violent storm. But, it was hard. She had this burning need for comfort. For something to stabilize her and bring her back to ground zero as the desire to give up attempted to fill the gaping hole left inside her chest. It felt like she was scrambling for the surface that was constantly out of reach.

Torturous minutes dragged by before she was finally able to locate that mask deep inside that kept this part of herself under lock and key. With it fixed in place, she let out a long, shuddering breath before vacantly switching the water to hot and washing her hair.

After getting dressed, she stepped out of the steamy bathroom and stopped at the sight of the sunrise drifting up in deep orange, almost red, waves. It felt like some kind of sick joke the way the sky's colors mimicked the orange of Silas' eyes.

It made her wonder what Silas had been up to for so long. She had been so busy focusing on her new training sessions with Soren that she hadn't given the nights she was nightmare-free a second thought.

Dylan was so engrossed in her thoughts that she didn't notice anyone else in her room until that someone shifted in the dark.

She jumped and looked over at the shadow leaning against her door with his hands in his pockets. Dylan quickly backed up until she stumbled against her dresser.

Silas! She screamed in her mind. *That's what he was working on: getting to me!*

The figure stepped forward, letting the growing sunlight illuminate his body just as his hand jutted out and flicked on the lights. When she realized it was only Soren, she felt her

58

knees weaken in relief.

"What the hell are you doing here?" she asked, through heavy breathing.

He was in his uniform and she was starting to distinguish his moods in correlation to how he dressed. The uniform told her he was here for something. He was here to work.

His eyes drifted down her body in assessment. She followed, making sure she was completely dressed and not forgetting anything embarrassing. She was wearing her usual attire of black on black: a pair of yoga pants and one of her old, oversized, long-sleeved tees. She suddenly wished she had worn a bra.

She looked up with a frown. "What?"

"You look clean."

"*Clean*?" She lifted her eyebrows.

"Usually, you're stinking with sweat," he said with a shrug.

"Usually, we're working out."

He smiled at her glare but it came off more like a sneer.

"I'll ask again... what are you doing here?" She knew it wasn't time for *Essence* and it was way too early for a visitor. Could he be here to tell her she wasn't cutting it at training?

"I'm just here to say hello."

"Okay," she responded warily. *And why are you sneaking around in my room?* "You know, knocking is a thing most people do when they want to say hi."

"Right," he clipped out.

Dylan ran her hands over her wet hair and sat in the chair next to her desk, watching him. He made a quick turn because there wasn't much to look at. Her walls were still blank and her desk vacant. Besides, it wasn't like she took pride in the space. Mostly, she just wanted to set fire to it all.

He picked up the notebook gifted to her by Anna and flipped through the blank pages. Dylan perked up both of her eyebrows at his obvious lack of understanding of the word *boundaries.*

By all means, she thought.

"Hmm," he hummed before throwing the notebook across her room with a loud snap against the door. "Where is it?"

Her eyes followed the notebook, landing haphazardly on the other side of her room. A sudden warning of danger pulsed in her ears.

"Maybe you should be more specific. Not everyone is a mind-reader." She tensed. "At least, I'm not."

"The dagger, *pet*." He was suddenly in her face. "Don't think I didn't notice it was missing."

Dylan tried to jerk back but he fisted Tristian's chain and twisted it until it was like a collar around her neck and pulled. "Where. Is. It?"

"Stop!" she gasped, clawing at his grip and not wanting him to break Tristian's chain nor the Elementa ring strung through. "I didn't take anything!"

He released her and was dumping out the contents of her duffle bag before she could even catch her breath.

Stuck in the chair and still holding Tristian's chain against her heart protectively, Dylan watched him rip her room apart. He upended her mattress to check underneath then threw it back in place and ran his hands in and around her pillows and sheets.

"All I have is what King Damen gave me," she panted. "I wouldn't dare steal anything." *Well, not so soon*, she added to herself.

Soren stopped and stared down at her. He suddenly seemed so dauntingly tall, towering over like the Devil himself.

"Where is it?"

"Does it even matter?" she snapped, feeling like she was on the verge of screaming. "You won't believe a word I say!"

He lunged for her, shoving her up against the wall and knocking her chair out from under her. "I'll take you to the

Kings. Do you have any idea what they'll do to get you to speak?" he hissed, as she shook her head no, repeatedly. "They'll rip you apart. They'll start with your skinny, little toes and finish with your arrogant head; all upon a stake in the Tower of Souls for everyone to see." He roared, "WHERE IS IT?!"

"I don't—"

She felt him invading her mind like fingers sliding into her brain as a knock sounded at the door, interrupting him from taking her thoughts.

"Who is it!"

Dylan threw her head to the side as a whimper left her lips.

"Commander Verbeck?" a muffled male voice said from the other side of the door.

Soren growled and rushed to the door, reining in his temper just before flinging it open. "Yes."

The soldier glanced inside at Dylan, shaking and still clutching her necklace, before returning his determined stare to Soren. "The contraband has been found."

Soren paused. "Where?"

"In the men's locker room. Seems as though a trainee forgot to put it away after practice. I put him on suspension. Would you like to speak with him before he leaves?"

Dylan's shoulders slumped in exhaustion and relief. She stumbled to the edge of her bed and sat; ignoring that the mattress was very much askew or that the sheets were rumpled and halfway to the floor. She didn't know why, of all the things he had done or said to her, she felt so betrayed and rattled by his accusation. Of course, he would immediately come to her for something stolen. She was the *Elementa,* after all.

As the soldiers spoke of more specifics, Dylan rubbed her temples and then her neck, trying to rid herself of his touch. But it was inside. The feeling of him combing through her brain made her want to retch.

When the soldier left, Dylan could feel Soren's eyes on her as she righted the mattress and fixed the sheets. She wondered if he felt an ounce of remorse; if he would apologize or attempt to justify what he had done.

She wasn't surprised to hear the door shut a moment later as he walked out.

◇◇◇

"*Uhn*," the pixie demon grunted from Asher's right hook into his gut.

"Where is he?" Asher asked, once again, holding the demon against the alley wall behind an underworld club.

Asher held on to him tightly as his hairless, pale blue body tried to claw and twist out of Asher's grip. But there was no way Asher was letting go of this lead. It had been days of dead ends before he came across a traveling siren one night at Spin. She had bought him a drink and admitted to watching him question creatures about information on Gerion Planto. For a small price, she told him the name of one of her clients who bragged about knowing the demon from being in business with him. The only problem was that the client lived in Germany.

The pixie sneered through blood stained teeth. "You think I am afraid of you and your fists?" he said, his words heavily accented.

Asher sighed. He was growing tired of this game. Didn't the pixie know he was going to cough up the information at some point? Why prolong the inevitable and waste both of their time?

"You are nothing compared to him," the pixie added.

Asher lifted his brows. Nothing in comparison to Gerion? Well that may be the case but he damn well wasn't nothing to this pixie.

"Nothing, huh?" Asher smirked. He really didn't want to resort to using his powers, but, you know, if the little guy insisted….

Asher stared deeply into the pixie's eyes that were like tiny, pitch-black marbles, and shot his Unda out through his fingertips. He imagined manipulating the Pixie's thoughts one by one, pulling every thread of his control apart while inserting his own desires.

The pixie's eyes bulged at the feeling of magic pouring into his body through Asher's tight grip around his short neck. He wanted to struggle but his body wasn't his anymore.

"You can use your manipulations all you want, but you still can't make me speak."

"Wrong answer," Asher crooned, this time using his thoughts to twist the pixie's thumb. He yanked it backwards in a sickening crack.

The demon roared.

"And now?"

"I lied!" he cried. "Stop! I lied!"

Asher paused. Was this seriously another dead end? *Damn that swindling siren!*

"I don't really know Gerion. I only know that he has been working with a wolf pack here in Munich," he sobbed.

"Where is this wolf pack?"

"Gone. They all got up and left about a month ago. The fey owns their territory now."

Asher thought about this for a moment and wondered what Gerion wanted with a German wolf pack. Could this be the only wolf pack cooperating with the Plantos? He seriously doubted it.

"Can I go?" the pixie begged.

Asher focused back on him. *Go?* No. This one was too much of a liability.

"You talked quite quickly," he said looking apologetic.

The pixie tensed and his head suddenly twisted to the side with another snap before his body crumpled to the ground.

Asher took a deep breath before lifting the hood of his sweatshirt and disappearing into the night.

◇◇◇

She saw the floor first. Crimson crushed velvet soft beneath her bare feet. Dylan was walking along Silas' hallway in Zadar and wearing a teal sundress just like the last time she was here. Her hair was long again, tickling her exposed skin and raising a wave of goosebumps along her arms.

She followed the red carpet and tried not to think of blood. Of her blood. Of Tristian's. Of every servant that lived and died here. Even of Silas' childhood beatings.

Everything was just as she remembered from having lived here. Uneventful and oddly comfortable. A part of her wondered if everything in Elon had been the dream and now she was actually awake.

But there was something different about this moment. She couldn't explain the strange freedom she felt from just being able to walk around without pondering who or what was going to come popping out around the corner. And then she knew. He *wasn't here. She just wasn't quite sure why she was.*

Dylan ran her fingers lightly along the frame of a floral oil painting, leaving a trail in the dust. She stopped and looked at the grey grime on her finger. The Plantos may have been creepy and dysfunctional, but one thing they were not was dirty.

A noise sounded from her left and she looked down a new hallway with a set of stairs leading down; stairs she hadn't ever seen before. It was dark, damp, and rock-like. It didn't appear to be a part of the castle. It was as if she had suddenly been transported into a dungeon.

She started down, ignoring the slickness of the stone under her toes or the coolness she felt from being deep underground. She was in the place Silas had warned her to stay away from: the North Wing. Yet, she couldn't stop herself from continuing on. Her breath picked up when she came to a set of stairs leading farther down into the darkness.

A torch flickered on a stand to her right and she grabbed it, descending the steps. One by one, she moved cautiously.

Something shifted in the air halfway down, prompting her feet to move a little quicker. It was a tangible darkness. Something that urged her to hurry.

Dylan reached the bottom, almost immediately coming to a set of opened, double doors.

Inside, an array of torches lit the opulent, stone room. Several glass tubes filled with greenish liquid lined the far wall behind a man standing next to a metal table that seemed to run on for miles. Bodies were placed carefully, head to toe, one after the other. All pale. All motionless. All dead. Well, except for one.

Dylan froze. On the very end of the table was Peppi Calibri. She was strapped down and crying softly. The dark haired man had been experimenting on the little girl. Her amazing strength was just as visible as it was the day she offered her soul so that Dylan may live.

The dark man wore a lab coat and a demented smile. He held up a syringe and flicked it twice with long, alabaster fingers before sinking the needle into the girl's upper arm. Dylan jumped as Peppi began to scream.

Peppi's body bucked, throwing her head back in piercing agony. Dylan raced to her friend, yanking the needle out of her arm and tossing it aside. Tears poured down Dylan's cheeks as she tried to console her friend but Peppi wouldn't stop screaming in horror.

Dylan suddenly looked up at the man standing near. He smiled. His eyes were like shadows on his face.

"Ah, Temperance. You're just in time." He picked up another syringe. Behind him, Aria and Isabel were floating lifelessly in large tubes. Grotesque claws contorted their hands and feet.

Dylan jerked awake in her room in Elon. It didn't take

her very long to piece together that she had slept the day away, that it was well past midnight.

She jumped up, unable to sit by herself in the dark a second longer and rushed through the halls—not caring if anyone saw her. She just needed to breathe. She needed fresh air and space to scream.

Somehow, she knew whatever she had seen in her dream had been real or was about to be. Her friends were in danger of being killed by a demon with black eyes she hadn't ever met before. She almost wished she had dreamed of Silas instead, because knowing her loved ones were being hurt when she couldn't do anything to help stop their pain was worse.

Dylan was near the gym when she saw the exterior door that she had been sneaking out of for several months. She shoved open the door and spilled out into the night.

Trees, cobblestone, the smell of earth and cut grass. A sensation tumbled through her body and lifted tiny strands of her short hair. *The wind.*

Dylan already felt lighter as she hurried to the precipice of the courtyard just before a steep rocky beach surrounded by black depthless water. Just staring at the same lake that rested outside her window made her remember the first time she had stumbled out here and the disappointment upon finding that it was a dead end. Now it was her secret retreat in the night when she couldn't bring herself to sleep.

Dylan crouched and clambered her way down the rock, trying not to fall and break an arm. She quickly found the secure, flat boulder she always sat on near the shore and sat with her toes just inches away from the water.

She stared out at the black, starless sky mirroring the lake. It was almost impossible to distinguish where the sky ended and the lake began. But, Dylan knew from the days gazing out her window, there was a clean, rolling ribbon of land across the horizon separating the two bodies. It brought back memories of dreaming about her parents being here.

Elon's glass city in the background. A time when she thought this place was beautiful and magical. If only she had known.

Dylan wrapped her arms tighter around herself. The long-sleeves of her shirt did nothing to ward off the chill. The air was absolutely frigid tonight and her breath plumed out in front of her like tasteless smoke.

She didn't think she could stay much longer and withstand the cold, but she needed this. She needed the fresh air. It was like a drug that calmed her soul. She breathed in deeply, letting her mind and body relax. She assured herself her dream had only been another nightmare conjured by Silas. Her friends weren't in danger. Silas didn't even know about Aria or Isabel. He only plucked the images out of Dylan's head to toy with her. But, why the demon man? Why not Silas himself?

Dylan's teeth chattered as she tried to force all of the nonsense out of her head before resting her chin against the peaks of her knees. A crow cawed above her before swooping down and perching itself on a nearby rock.

"Hello, you." She smiled, petting the black beauty as the bird briefly nudged its head into her palm before fluffing out its feathers and taking off again. She watched it go, wishing it would have stayed longer. She had never desired a pet, but she could see the appeal. The creature was a small comfort where life had fallen short.

With a sigh, Dylan hugged her knees. She needed to go back inside, but three suffocating days trapped inside her room were enough to push her to brave five more minutes in the cold following Soren's harsher than necessary interrogation.

It took her awhile to understand why she felt so betrayed by him. She realized it was because she had spent every day training with him. The small complements on her form. The easy banter. The way he worked out with her instead of just telling her to run. She thought he was coming around, perhaps, even starting to realize she wasn't the demon everyone in Elon thought she was. That was her mistake.

Now, she secretly hoped he'd walk into one of his swords.

"What are you doing?"

Dylan jumped as Soren's voice emerged from behind her. *Goddammit.* Had she thought of his name too many times and conjured him?

Dylan bristled from a sudden icy breeze and wrapped her arms tightly around her knees. Soren hopped off the ledge and swiftly sat down next to her.

"What are *you* doing?" she asked, once the initial shock of his presence wore off. She really *hated* being snuck up on. "Here to say '*hello*' again?"

"I'm sitting," Soren said, as if that were obvious.

Dylan pressed her frozen hands to her face and groaned. This wasn't happening. "I would like to be alone." She sighed forcefully. "Please leave."

"I'm good."

She looked at him as if he had two heads. Hadn't she dealt with him enough? Why couldn't he just let her be? Unfortunately, she knew that wasn't his style. If Soren wanted something he'd stop at nothing until he obtained it.

"Fine. Just get it over with," she said, holding out a hand. He looked at her in question; so, she clarified through gritted teeth.

"You're obviously missing something else. So just take what you need and leave me the hell alone."

Dylan turned her head away, bracing herself against the memories about to erupt within her. She thought about how he would see everything. Her passing thoughts, her nightmares of Silas, even her sexy dreams about Tristian. Private moments, now his.

If only he had the power to erase memories, too.

Dylan glanced over at him when she realized he wasn't doing it.

"I don't know how you sit here," he said, ignoring her offered hand.

She retracted her hand before he could change his mind and tucked both hands in the crook of her bent knees.

What the hell was that supposed to mean?

"Um, well I bend my knees. Then I kind of slowly fall on my butt." She looked at him and raised her eyebrows.

Why won't you tell me why you are really here? she wondered warily.

She thought she saw a ghost of a smile in his eyes when he glanced at her side long. "I guess, I have to give you credit. You have balls."

Balls, why? Because she didn't cower down and wait for his inner bully to show? Or because she had offered her thoughts?

"Well, I didn't want a repeat of your lovely interrogation. I like my dignity, *thanks*."

Now Soren looked confused. "I don't think we're talking about the same thing."

"What are you talking about?"

"The Void of Bones." He pointed out at the lake.

"The what-of-what?"

"The world of the dead," he answered casually.

Dylan looked at the water again, noticing for the first time how it kind of looked less like water and more like a black, murky cloud. She suddenly scoured the surface for the moon's reflection. Her eyes widened when she realized it wasn't reflecting anything, that she was sitting on a cliff. She ripped her feet away from the precipice, scooting further back onto the rock.

"You didn't…"

"I thought that was a lake!" Dylan barely gasped out.

Soren pressed his lips together as if that made more sense than her being brave.

"I guess the way it mimics the sky's color makes it look like water."

Dylan thought about all the times she had been outside. How the wind never caused a ripple. How there were never any boats or swimmers. Then she thought about the pull she felt around it. If it wasn't water... then what was calling out to her? She felt her neck.

Dylan suddenly got up and stumbled backward. She cried out but Soren already had her upright.

"Wouldn't want you to fall in there. That is… not unless you want to become one of *them*," he said, dramatically.

Dylan stared wide-eyed. "What?" she asked gripping his calloused hand for support as he pulled her up to the courtyard.

"As the story goes, anyone who jumps in becomes the living dead," Soren muttered as they walked side by side to the door. Dylan glanced behind herself several times. "Their craving for flesh is so great they wake from the dead when the moon is highest and prey on little girls who sit alone."

Dylan stopped and looked up at the moon, horrified, and she had been... wait. Soren smirked.

She glared and suddenly wrenched her arm out of his grasp. God, she was such an idiot for believing him, even if it was only for a minute.

"Enjoy that fake story?" she snapped.

He shrugged. "Not as much as you did."

"You're such a tool," Dylan scoffed, walking around him toward the door.

"I may have embellished a bit but it's still the Dead's world. I've never known of anyone actually coming out or going in. Only stories," Soren added as he followed her to the door and pushed it open before she could, "but that doesn't mean it's okay to sit next to it where accidents can happen."

Dylan stopped and looked at him. Was he seriously lecturing her on safety? *Him?* Her eyes skirted his uniform. "You're on duty," she said, more as a statement than a question.

Something flickered in his eyes. Dylan wasn't sure whether to be afraid of or not. "Yeah," he said, drawing the word out. "I'm on watch tonight."

"Watching what?" she laughed once. ...*me?* she thought.

"The grounds," he said, turning away from her and walking through the door. Dylan slowly followed. Despite knowledge of the zombie story being fake, she still didn't feel comfortable spending another moment at the shore. Besides, it was freaking cold.

Dylan nodded as they passed the gym even though he wasn't looking at her. Him patrolling the grounds made more sense than a soldier constantly watching her; but, it still didn't explain why he chose to annoy her with his presence.

"I do it about once a week. Usually Augusto does it."

"Who?"

"One of my comrades."

"Oh." How had she never seen this person at night?

Soren flattened his palm against a random door and shoved it open. He walked into a large room and strode over to the other side with Dylan trailing not far behind.

She could barely keep her chin off the floor when it dawned on her they were in a cafeteria. How hadn't she ventured in this direction and come across this place by herself? What else was in this direction? She had been so consumed with her little adventures outside by the lake and the gym, she had forgotten to finish exploring on her own.

The room was brightly lit and filled with about thirty or so empty tables with metal chairs. A long buffet was stationed across the far wall complete with trays, an espresso machine, and drink dispenser.

Dylan stopped in the middle of the room. Why was she even following him? She was still angry from the interrogation. Plus, he hadn't even apologized. Not that she would accept it, but it was the principle that mattered. She turned around to leave but stopped again at the sight of the large plaque near the door identifying several centuries

71

worth of "Commanders of the Shadow Horde"; and there it was at the very end: "*Soren Verbeck,*" etched in granite, as the current commander of the Shadow Horde under Dorian Verbeck.

Dylan remembered the soldier that stopped Soren's interrogation of her and how he had called Soren commander. Regardless of everything, she had been curious about it ever since.

She continued to read the names following the last two Verbecks. There were at least ten more. Perhaps, Soren *was* bred for this job.

"I guess congratulations are in order," Dylan said, whipping her head around just as Soren kicked a chair out from a nearby table and set down two paper cups. An amazing aroma filled the room and she moved forward instinctively before slowly pulling out the chair across from him.

Soren took a gulp of his coffee, "Whatever for?"

Dylan sat, feeling awkward and conspicuous for some reason.

"You're commander now," she answered.

"Right." Soren lifted his cup to her before taking a gulp. There was something in his face that looked uncomfortable. A part of her wanted to pick at his feelings until he exposed more, but the look was gone in a blink.

Dylan stared down into the cup of black liquid. Tendrils of steam invaded her senses, reminding her of a different life. She carefully wrapped her fingers around the toasty cup, trying to remember what coffee even tasted like.

"It's customary to return a toast."

Dylan glanced up at him. "Right," she echoed. "I'm not from here, remember?" she said, sarcastically.

She returned the toast with a forced, tight-lipped smile and brought the cup to her lips. She took a small sip—too afraid to consume too much too fast.

The bitter liquid slid down her throat and settled

deliciously in her stomach. It felt incredibly strange to drink something substantial after so many months living solely on Essence and water.

She took a larger gulp.

"This is *really* good."

Soren pulled his phone out when it vibrated. "It's pretty shitty coffee, actually."

Dylan tried to pace herself. "Why haven't I been offered food before now?"

Soren's jaw twitched and he set his phone down. "King Zirk was in charge of you before, as you know. He had this idea about making a perfect demon that only thrives on Essence. He used to check on your status daily. Other than handing you off to Damen, I haven't heard from him about it."

Dylan wondered if this King was the reason simple necessities like bras and shoes had been withheld from her for so long.

"And what does my father think of his new burden?" Dylan asked. She thought of his cold eyes every time he looked at her and completely lost her appetite. She set the cup down even though some of the coffee still remained.

Soren frowned deeply. "King Damen PyroVentus is not your father."

"What?" Dylan smiled, nervously. Of course, he was her father. She would never forget that warm face from her dreams. "Then who is?"

"His twin brother. Atticus, is your father."

"So, King Damen is... my Uncle?"

"That would be the definition of an Uncle, yes."

Dylan ignored his comment. Her mind widening with the thought of more family. For most of her life it had been only she and Isabel. Now she had parents and an Uncle. A *demon King* Uncle.

"Do I have any other relatives?"

"Anna Cacia."

"Anna!" Dylan almost shouted. "H-how?"

Soren shook his head at her outburst. "She's married to your mother's only brother."

Dylan was wide-eyed as she placed a hand over her mouth and spoke through her fingers. "I have another Uncle?"

"Yeah, come on," he sighed. Soren stood and Dylan watched him take their coffees and toss them in the trash next to the door. She jumped up and hurried after him, throwing a scowl at the trash can as she passed. How could he waste perfectly good coffee?

Down a few hallways, they were near the Kings' Chambers when a couple of lilting voices reached her ears. Soren suddenly grabbed her by the arm and rushed them into a dimly lit room.

Dylan jerked out of his hold, ready with snarl about him not touching her, when she found herself looking out the door's window at what had Soren so rapt.

There in the corridor was the Queen, in her traditional golden robes, coming out of a room. Her hair was styled artfully in a braided twist. She was conversing with a stunning woman in a cream pantsuit—the color complementing her dark complexion and long, russet locks.

The women smiled through the conversation Dylan couldn't hear. Both of them looked relaxed and relieved, as though an agreement had been reached before the woman in the cream suit bid the Queen farewell in a graceful curtsy. She then left through a side door, where two men obscured by the dark night waited for her. The Queen returned to the room and shut the door.

Dylan looked up at Soren, noticing how anxious he looked. His corded muscles tensed and readied for a fight. But... it was just the Queen coming out of a meeting...

"What is it?" Dylan whispered, not liking one bit the way Soren seemed on edge. "Who was that?"

He flicked his gaze to her and she watched as the look of

calculation dissolved from his eyes upon remembering that he wasn't alone.

"No one." He moved around her as if nothing had happened and strode deeper into what could only be deemed the saddest library she had ever seen. If you could even call it a library. Two bookshelves occupied the center each holding a little over a dozen novels and textbooks.

Soren scanned the only packed shelves labeled: *Community Records*. He skimmed his fingers along the row until he found what he was looking for and pulled out an enormous binder. He hefted it up in his arms and flung it onto a table in the corner then flicked on a small green lamp. He began flipping through the pages and stopped somewhere in the center and motioned to the page. "Your family trees."

Dylan stared at him in shock, the strange sighting of the Queen now forgotten.

Trees? As in plural? How much family did she have?

Dylan slowly moved closer and peered down at the elaborate series of brackets and handwritten script. Her name was at the very bottom without space beneath or any brackets other than her parents, attached. She knew it was because they didn't expect her to have children. Didn't want her to.

"What's up with King Zirk?" She turned her head to the side and looked up at him. It was a strange thing to ask, she realized, because she didn't expect a truthful answer from him. She was asking for information on a King which could be misconstrued as treason. "I mean, why was he in charge of me?"

"He was the reason your parents were granted the right to bear a child as long as they signed your life over to the OP's army. He was also the reason you were pardoned in Zadar to stand trial. Most demons in your situation would have been eliminated on site," Soren said without emotion. "So I think it was only natural that he volunteered to be your guardian after the trial."

75

"I still don't know why I wasn't killed," Dylan murmured, as she remembered that day in Zadar and the decision to call on the Shadow Horde.

Soren was silent for a moment as if he was remembering something from the memories he'd taken and then brushed the thought away.

"Do you think I might be sent home one day? I don't mind keeping the *Binding* on if my powers are the problem."

"Even weak, you're still a threat. You're connected to too many demons who want control over you. And believe me when I say, Gerion Planto wouldn't mind keeping the *Binding* on."

Dylan involuntarily shuddered. Maybe, staying *was* better even if she never saw another human for as long as she lived.

"Look, I need to get back to patrol. Stay," he motioned to *all* the books, "read."

"Okay," Dylan said, softly. "Have... fun."

Soren winked and left the room.

Dylan stared after him. Did he actually just *wink*? She chuckled to herself and looked back down at the binder on the table. She smoothed her fingers over the delicate parchment paper that felt like cloth—her mind spinning out of control from everything she had just learned.

Hours passed quickly as she gobbled up the information like an addicting novel.

Dylan was already on her fourth binder. The royal ranks laid out in front of her dated back several millennia. Each of the higher ranks, with separate family trees, had comments on their unique powers.

"Queen Vashti Monita
First female King.
Oracle.
Daughter of Mara Sors - Deceased and Dek Monita.

King Zirk Abores
Third generation King.
Manipulator of Nature.
Brother- Pike Abores- Deceased,
Sister- Svet Abores- Deceased.
Son of Eri Pron- Deceased and Dimetri Abores-
Deceased.

King Damen PyroVentus
First generation King.
CoCreator of fire and wind.
Brother- Atticus PyroVentus- Rogue.
Son of Aeliana Ventus- Deceased and Marcus Pyro-
Deceased."

So, Soren was right. King Damen wasn't her father. Dylan smiled, relieved that the cold demon wasn't her parent.

She scanned the following pages for the name Effingo. A couple of pages flipped and then her heart dropped.

"Tristian Effingo- Deceased
Highest rank- Lord of Souls.
Manipulator and healer of the body.
Son of Adelaide Sanaret– Deceased; Rogue, and, Gale
Effingo– Deceased; Rogue."

She flipped through several more pages, landing on a blank page. Dylan startled when it lit, revealing a glowing, white square like a tablet or computer screen. She lifted the typical parchment page, looking behind it with knit brows. It had to be magic.

She delicately released the page and warily placed her fingers on the corner of the glowing square. An array of colors began spinning across the page. She yanked her hand back and the blended colors slowed until she realized they were pictures. It finally stopped and Dylan bent over to get a better look at the image. She thought it was Soren, at first, but this man didn't have his unique, blue eyes or twisted scars; this man's black hair was thick, short and clean cut. He was dressed in a Shadow Horde uniform with three other Shadow Horde soldiers she didn't recognize flanking him. Could this be Dorian Verbeck with his Shadow Horde? She started to trace the side of the man's uniform and sent the pictures scrolling instead.

Dylan slowed the montage with a more careful touch. There were pictures of ceremonies and *Signing*, parties and the aftermath of wars. She scrolled, feeling Anna's words about history coming to life within the screen. Dylan gasped when two beautiful, emerald eyes stared back at her. It was a picture of Tristian scowling next to Queen Vashti, sending Dylan's stomach into knots. His hand was possessively gripping her shoulder and her delicate body turned into him at a party. It didn't take much to conclude they were lovers.

Dylan had hoped to see photos of Tristian's past. She just hadn't thought about them including another woman; and the Queen, for that matter.

She leaned closer. Something about him was off. The light she knew wasn't visible in his eyes. He seemed hardened and just as frightening as Queen Vashti. This wasn't the Tristian who tenderly cared for her in the old motel and held her hand tightly as they drove through Topanga. No, if she had met this Tristian she would have been more than happy to stay far, far away.

An awful thought suddenly popped into her mind. What if this was the real Tristian? What if his story about taking her to her parents had only been a ruse to gain her trust? What if he had been after her and the Elementas, like Asher had been, only to be screwed by a greedy vampire?

Tristian repeatedly told her it wasn't going to work out. That they couldn't be together. What if he was only trying to convey his true intentions, so she'd flee. Was that why he fought with her that night? Was he planning on bringing her to Elon, to Queen Vashti, as a prize all along?

What a stupid girl she was! Love sick over a boy who wanted nothing more than to manipulate her for a payout.

Someone cleared his throat and Dylan jerked, about to slam the book closed when Soren caught the edge. He leaned over her and she let out a long sigh as he invaded her space.

"He's not who you thought he was?" Soren asked. "Big fucking surprise."

She fisted her hands to stop them from trembling. She was still battling with the picture of Tristian and Queen Vashti, too overwhelmed to respond to Soren's vulgar comment. The image was hardening and blackening parts of her memory and replacing what she thought she knew with doubt.

Had he even loved her... at all?

Her heart ached. It hurt so much she had a hard time breathing. So, she just let it all hang there like an enormous black cloud.

Soren straightened his spine and cleared his throat again. "It's morning. Time for practice."

Dylan nodded, silently closed the book and returned it to the shelves.

CHAPTER 5

"Be fearless in the pursuit of what sets your soul on fire."
Jennifer Lee

A few days later, as Anna left the room, Soren instructed, "Get up!"

"What do you want?" Dylan whispered, staring out her window at the Void of Bones. She squinted, trying to see past the mirage of a glistening, emerald lake and into the damned world underneath, but she couldn't, no matter how hard she tried.

"Since when have I ever explained myself over the past eight months?"

Dylan frowned. Had it been that long? The sudden awareness of time caused her energy to drain.

She shrugged, not wanting to fight with him. What was the point?

...Eight months?

"I think I'm going to just stay here today."

"Like you've 'just stayed here' for the last few days?"

He had a point, she thought, considering she had been in the library a lot lately. Ever since seeing the picture of Tristian, she hadn't been able to stop herself from breaking apart his every memory, his every touch, his every word. She felt like she was going crazy. So, she had spent the last few days sneaking into the library and staring at all of his pictures—needing to distinguish what she knew from what she was seeing.

She looked over her shoulder at Soren. He leaned against the doorjamb in his uniform, his hands in his pockets. Would he be able to tell her some truths?

She shifted to the window and focused on a black bird fighting the wind. Was that her crow?

"What was Tristian like here?" she asked, before she could think better of it.

It was so hard for her to ask this. Soren was an unlimited fountain of knowledge that she typically refused to tap into out of fear of appearing vulnerable. But, she needed to know. It was killing her not to.

After a long moment, she turned and tentatively met his eyes. He looked like he hated her for even asking. But why?

"I wouldn't know. I never met him."

She stared at his ridged body, unnaturally tense beneath the rich leather of his uniform.

He was lying.

If Tristian was the Lord of Souls, then the Shadow Horde did his bidding. Why would he even feel the need to sugar coat or deny it? Didn't Soren enjoy tormenting her?

"Is it because he was deemed rogue?"

Soren pulled out his phone as if he was intentionally trying to get away from the question without anywhere to go. "What about it?"

"You're... never mind." It was useless to try and talk to him about this. She wasn't completely inept. Soren may tolerate her but she knew he wouldn't choose to hang out with her unless it benefitted him in some way.

Dylan started piling a few of her lesson books on the corner of her desk. There was an astrology book at the bottom that Anna had brought two days prior.

All the talk about demon eclipses, stars, and other worlds had Dylan thinking of a riddle she had mostly given up on. *The energy flows where the balance lies.* The words of her parents resonated in her head quickly followed by the flash of heat from Tristian's touch on the beach and the sting of

Erez' bite. She forced herself to banish the thoughts. Her parents were hiding, possibly dead. Tristian was dead. And Erez... well, she hoped he was dead, too.

Why was she still looking for answers within a past life that was no longer hers? It was probably best if Soren kept whatever he knew to himself. She didn't need any more pointless hope.

"No, go on." He crossed his arms.

She sighed and turned her body toward his. "It's nothing."

He made some kind of noise. "Get up."

"What?"

"Let's go."

"I'm not training today," she reminded, looking at him pointedly. "Unless you're ready to teach me how to throw those daggers of yours." She smiled sweetly.

He smirked at this. "You would think by now I wouldn't have to repeat myself."

Her smile dissolved and she narrowed her eyes, not liking one bit how his voice grew darker, more sinister. Most of the time she fooled herself into thinking their work-outs were a mutual agreement.

"I own you, pet," he confirmed aloud. "Follow me. *Now*."

Dylan felt an influx of hate pour into her.

"You *do not* own me," she snapped.

He stepped closer and let out a long breath through his nose as he tried to intimidate her with his darkness.

She didn't back down. "Besides... Haven't you ever heard of the word *please*?"

"Oh, right." Soren said. "Get off your ass and follow me, *please*."

Dylan slipped her sneakers on and grabbed a hoodie, tugging it over her head. She figured it might do her some good to punch something. She only wished that something included his face.

Dylan flipped her head over and tied her hair into a high

pony tail before straightening and motioning that they could go now.

"You know I might be more inclined to go with you next time if you bring coffee."

Soren tipped his head back and flexed his jaw like he was trying not to laugh or scream. He faced the door and muttered, "Noted," as he turned the knob.

They didn't train or even go to the gym. For an hour he led her around the building, making periodic stops and shoving boxes into her arms or making her wait outside doors. There weren't many demons milling about and those that were always did a double take while giving her a wide birth.

She was starting to wonder if the place was always this quiet when Soren told her it was a holiday weekend and most demons were celebrating or visiting friends. Apparently, the streets were filled with demons dancing and drinking. She couldn't help her eyes from lighting up at the thought of seeing it; but, it was clear the way he turned away that any requests about seeing it would be quickly shot down.

"What is the holiday?" Dylan huffed, as she set a box down on the floor in a small closet full of office equipment.

Soren set a box on top of hers and said, "The Day of Mourning."

"That doesn't sound like a day to party."

She followed him out of the closet and he locked it with his hand print on the control panel.

"It's... complicated," Soren murmured, as he checked a list on his phone.

Dylan sighed. "I'm sure I can understand it easily enough."

He suddenly stopped and glared down at her. "Today we commemorate the Elementa War." Dylan's eyebrows shot up. "Yeah. The war where your family slaughtered thousands trying to take over. We celebrate because despite everything going against us, we still won. Your parents fled like cowards, leaving their loyal followers here to die."

Dylan swallowed as she leaned against the wall for support.

"No wonder everyone hates me."

"*No wonder*," he echoed, returning to his typical angry gait.

Dylan pushed herself off the wall and rushed to follow him. Her mind still reeled with thoughts of her parents as a couple of mercenaries trying to conquer kingdoms and worlds. But, she couldn't seem to connect the parents she met in her dreams with those that would murder thousands only to rule. And Tristian had been working with them? That, coupled with his relationship with the Queen, began to cast doubt on every memory she had of him. She was almost certain she had never known him at all.

Soren stopped in another office and shoved a box of folders into her arms. Dylan winced at the weight, but it felt fitting considering the added weight of everything she'd just learned.

"I was fine in my room," she suggested as they left the office, "if you want to go have fun or visit family."

His teeth clenched together and she sighed at his monotonous glare for an answer. He was probably being forced to work and wanted to torture her in the process.

"Wish I could visit my family," Dylan mumbled, thinking of Isabel and Aria. She thought about their last gathering, the night before Isabel started going through her parents' boxes. Isabel and Aria's parents had met the girls at a hole-in-the-wall grille, a place where fish tacos were considered revolutionary. They were toasting to another successful year at college and the start of another over huge, frozen margaritas with blue salt rims. It tugged at her heart.

Would she ever see them again?

Soren was suddenly shoving her against the hallway wall, upending the box of folders from her arms and scattering them all over the floor. Dylan gasped, too caught up in her memory to notice that what she had said could have been misconstrued.

"Do you now," he seethed. "Care to share that with the Kings?"

"I meant *my* family," she groaned, sick and tired of Soren's damning accusations. "The human ones."

He quickly released her and shook out his hands as if forcing himself to regain control.

"Goddammit, you're pissed today," Dylan glowered, rubbing her arms where he grabbed her. "I'm going back to my room." She turned on her heel and started back in the direction they had just walked.

Soren sighed, loudly. "I thought they were dead."

She froze. How did he even know that? Was her life story public record or something? *Probably is*, she thought sullenly.

"My *parents* are dead," she paused. No matter how many years passed, those words never ceased to sucker punch her right in the gut. "But, not my grandmother or my friends."

His brows crinkled in response.

"What?" she crossed her arms. "Is it so hard to imagine me in a normal circumstance that doesn't involve trying to take over the worlds? I had a normal life! It might have been hard, but it was a hell of a lot more normal than before a bunch of demons and vampires came and *destroyed* it!"

"No one's life is normal," Soren said, rubbing the stubble along his jaw. He suddenly looked exhausted.

Dylan dropped her arms in defeat. "Why are you even dragging me around? You look like you would rather eat glass."

He looked at her for a long moment before deciding to answer. "I didn't think you should be alone on your birthday... even if it is the Day of Mourning."

"My..." Dylan trailed off, as her mouth seemed to fill up with cotton.

I'm twenty-two? she asked herself as reality sank its claws into her mind.

Her heart started to gallop inside her chest as thoughts of her infinite life stuck inside these walls began to multiply.

Forever.

Never to be trusted. Never allowed freedom. Never allowed to love. Never allowed to have a family. All because of her parents. All because of some stupid war she barely had anything to do with.

Her parents were the traitors, not her!

Dylan didn't even realize she had walked away from Soren until she was staring up at the words "**VINCIT QUI SE VINCIT**" across the far wall of the gym. The foreign words mocked her like the cruel voice in her head, reminding her she didn't belong here. She wasn't born here. Yet, she would die here... if the Kings even allowed that.

She wasn't sure why she had come to the gym but she needed to clear her head. And to do that she needed to do something mindless, something repetitive.

So, she ran.

Her shoes thrummed against the indoor track like a drum, getting faster and faster with each painful thought of her future. She circled the track so many times she lost count. Her mind spun. Her world tipped and tore off its axis.

She rounded another lap. Her vision blurred around the corners, only allowing her to focus straight ahead. Her lungs burned, but she kept running until her knees gave out and she collapsed.

She let out a yelp as she tripped over her feet and slammed against the hard floor. She laid there, face down until a pair of heavy combat boots slowly stomped over, stopping next to her side.

"Did you die?" Soren asked from above her.

"This is it," she groaned against the floor. "This is my life."

"You're just now figuring this out?"

Dylan ignored him and shifted her head in his direction. She stared at his black boots. As clean as they were, they were seriously worn. She vaguely pondered how many demons he killed while wearing them. Would she ever need to kill demons? If she kept training and was eventually placed in the army... was she expected to murder those that were against the Omnipotence?

"Would it be completely awful if I asked you to take me back to my childhood memories and just... leave me there? At least then you wouldn't have to worry about me leaving my room anymore."

Soren let out a short laugh at the joke but she was dead serious.

"I can't do this." She closed her eyes as the words resonated within, zapping all hope and leaving her nothing more than an empty shell. "I can't be who they want me to be," she added. "It's not who I am."

"Get up."

"I can't."

"You're so fucking dramatic."

"I'm serious." Dylan tried to lift a limp foot but it barely budged. "I think I broke something, or everything."

Soren leaned down and grabbed her by the arm pits, lifting her like a feather. He set her on her feet but her knees wobbled and gave out, refusing to hold her weight. Soren caught her against him before she could fall again. Their eyes met.

"I'm not being dramatic," she insisted, gripping his leather jacket for support. And for the first time, concern laced his eyes. She imagined she could see the wheels turning in his head as he carefully lifted one of her hands, plucking it off his jacket and turning it until her palm was facing up.

"How long have you had this?" he asked, his voice low and threatening.

Dylan stared at her palm. There was a prominent web of

splintering blue veins splashed across her hand. She blinked, trying to clear her vision. "What is this—*AH*," Dylan recoiled against the impact of a sudden migraine.

"*Shit*." Soren flung her up in his arms like a doll as another slicing pain blasted into her skull. "How did you not know you were starving?" Soren roared.

"I don't know!" Dylan flattened her hands against her head. "Oh my God. Make it stop!"

Dylan felt the ends of her hair lift as he used his demon speed to get them to the cafeteria.

Once they reached the entrance, Soren deposited her in an abandoned chair against the wall by the doors. She slumped backward and peeled open her eye lids, freezing at the sight of the Shadow Horde sitting around a long table. Soren didn't flinch at their presence. He tore through the large space and headed straight for the cabinet marked *Resident Essence*.

The group of three demons paused as Soren rushed past them, and then, one by one, they looked over at her.

She never wanted the power of invisibility more than at this moment.

Now that *would be useful*, she thought.

Astrid jumped up from the table and nodded at the other two to follow Soren before she walked quickly up to Dylan.

"Don't touch her!" Soren snapped across the cafeteria as he rounded the corner with two vials. Astrid complied but her eyes didn't stop their curious flight along Dylan's pale and shaking features, as if seeing an extinct animal for the first time. Which in a weird way, she was.

Dylan felt her entire body burn with embarrassment.

Soren pushed past Astrid and a vial was suddenly thrust up against her mouth. Her eyes slipped shut as her body blossomed with warmth and her skin sang and tingled. She struggled not to moan at how good it felt. Another vial was pushed against her lips and she inhaled through a blissful smile.

More, always more...

"Better?" Soren's husky voice filtered through her delicious haze but all she could do was nod and bite her lip. It was always so strange to her how inhaling Essence sated and quenched her entire being.

He chuckled, the sound like honey slipping down her throat as he inspected her hands.

Moments ticked by and her high began to slowly dissipate until reality snuck in like a cold bitch. Dylan was still leaning against a chilled wall surrounded by Soren's smoky heat as his arms caged her in—blocking her from the others. His blank eyes roamed around her flushed face and she wondered if she hallucinated his silky laugh. Probably.

He leaned in close, so close she could feel his breath against her lips. She instinctively closed her eyes.

Soren whispered, "If you want a purpose then get off your ass and make one. This won't be your life unless you allow it to be." He leaned back as she opened her eyes, greeted with nothing but distaste. "This won't *ever* happen again. If you're hungry you do something about it. Next time I won't be the one to save you. That's your job. *Are we clear?*"

She nodded again as embarrassing tears blurred her vision before she looked away, trying to shake the feeling of abasement. He knew she didn't do this on purpose; yet, he still chastised her in front of the other soldiers just to make his authority known. He grabbed her chin and yanked her gaze back to his. "Are. we. clear?"

"*Yes*," she hissed, but he still didn't look satisfied. "What do you want from me?" she added. "To bow? To call you Sir? How about My Master? *Oh, My Master*," she clasped her hands to her chest in mock prostration, "I don't know what I would have done without you!" He growled, and she yanked his hand off her chin. "*Step back.*"

"I will step back whenever I damn well feel like it!"

"You both are so adorable," Astrid's voice carried around

89

them. They craned their necks to scowl at her. "Oh, I'm sorry, was that not foreplay?"

Astrid's smile only seemed to grow at Soren's pointed glare. He turned back to Dylan's glower. "Training, first thing in the morning. We meet in the gym." He looked around. "All of us."

Dylan was about to speak but he chose that moment to brood his way out of the cafeteria like an irritable child.

"I guess we'll see what you're really made of tomorrow," Astrid smirked. "What does he call you? Oh, right. *Pet.*"

Dylan tensed.

Had he told everyone about her? Of course he had. Why wouldn't he?

It made sense that they all gossiped and mocked her behind her back. She wanted to slap herself for thinking, even if for only a moment, that he might be on her side. She needed to remember her place and who they both were.

Astrid laughed at her startled expression before flouncing back to where the others were whispering and staring.

Dylan hurried out of the gym, with only one thing blaring like a fog horn in her mind… she would be training tomorrow… with them.

◇◇◇

Nadia sighed sleepily as she awoke under silky, white sheets in a seaside cottage far away from all life. The room where she stayed was quaint, to say the least. White paneled walls adorned with photographs of sea life and boats; luxurious grey hardwood floors; an antique, iron chandelier and matching four poster bed in the center of the room. There were no televisions or electronics of any kind for distraction. A paradise for the overworked mind or for someone simply looking to get away.

The floor to ceiling, sliding glass doors framed by gauzy, aqua curtains were the true attraction. It granted her a breathtaking view of tropical warmth, crashing waves, white sand, and palm trees as the sun melted into a golden pool over the vast ocean. This sight was so much better than the freezing world of Elon.

Nadia slid her bare, voluptuous body out of bed, and stalked to the mirrored buffet. She lifted a bottle of Monet Chandon by its neck out of an ice bucket and poured herself a glass. She brought the lip of the flute to her nose, reveling in the fruity effervescence tickling her senses.

She smiled when light fingers slid around her waist followed by a flushed, hard body pressing itself against her.

She took a small sip and moaned. Champagne and sex always went well together like chocolate and wine.

Nadia raised the crystal flute again, but now those same fingers that had been around her waist wrapped around the stem of her glass, deftly pulling it out of her grasp.

She licked her lips and smiled, wolfishly, over her shoulder.

"*Salut*," she crooned, gazing deeply into Gerion's fiery orbs.

Naked, he politely raised his glass to her before striding over to the sliding doors. Nadia allowed her gaze to roam appreciatively over his lean, muscular body, feeling a pang of disgust for the handsome disguise he liked to call Silas— the mask he always insisted on wearing every time they met. She couldn't explain *why*, yet, a part of her was more attracted to the ghastly demon underneath. She preferred the true state of most creatures, appalled by the anonymity of spells.

Nadia watched him as he glared out at the sunset without truly seeing, knowing he was thinking of the Collector girl. How she had gotten away and how fast he could get his hands on her, again. What it would feel like to rule over the most powerful demon with a legally Binding contract. Perhaps, this Temperance would share his bed even if he would have to use force to make it happen.

Not that any of it mattered to Nadia. Gerion's heart could

lie in the hands of a blood-thirsty lion for all she cared. This was purely an arrangement to take down the root of the Collectors. That's how it would stay until she had her revenge.

Nadia shifted her gaze to the champagne bottle sweating in the humidity and rubbed her belly. It was probably best if she didn't drink afterall.

"When would you like for me to send in my Ladies?"

Gerion turned to her, returning from whatever distant thoughts that were plaguing his mind.

"Now," he threw back the rest of the champagne in his glass and grinned, "if you think you're pregnant."

◇◇◇

The morning came like a wave of fresh air. She couldn't handle another nightmare and she had a strange feeling she shouldn't leave her room. So, after an entire night of pacing, all Dylan wanted to do was cuddle with her pillow and feel Tristian beside her—even if it was only to hear his lies. She just wanted to be held as if she meant something to someone. Besides, she didn't want to face Soren with his Horde posse through what was bound to be a humiliating hazing for the rookie. No, she wasn't excited about this but she knew not showing up would be worse.

Dylan lay her head down. *Only for an hour*, she told herself. Then she would go submit to the torture.

When she woke, the suns were already setting, saturating her room in various hues from rose to violet. She sighed, still feeling Tristian's fingers threaded through hers and the gentle whisper of his lips against her flesh. She placed a hand over her heart, basking in its frenzy from being close to her soul and knowing the feeling would soon leave her.

It was well past dark when she decided to finally reopen her eyes. It didn't take long to know something wasn't right. She felt her heart race without the slightest clue as to why she suddenly didn't want to move or even look around.

She swallowed, then bit her lip so hard that only when she tasted blood did she accept that she was awake.

But he was here. He was here and she was *awake*.

She let out a shaky breath and muttered the one name that haunted her.

"*Silas*."

She flicked her gaze to the dark column of shadows in the corner of her room. Her lips quivered as she slowly rolled up to a sitting position. She was afraid to look away. Afraid he'd move so fast...

A glimmer of serrated silver slipped out of the dark and she knew he had come to finish what the Horde interrupted. She lunged for the door and fell face first on to the hard floor, still tangled in her sheets. Tears pooled in her eyes as his fingers tangled in her hair and yanked her head back, exposing her neck.

"Did you enjoy your nap?"

And like that, her consciousness slammed clear with the release of her hair.

Dylan flipped around and fell on her rear.

Soren pocketed his dagger and got in her face.

"It better have been a good one," he snapped, "because we're done."

Her excuse danced on the tip of her tongue. It had only been an accident. She was just tired. She *needed* this. But, she was in so much shock that it was only Soren, all she could do was blink back her tears. Her lips glued shut.

Soren curled his lip and stormed past her, slamming the door closed.

How could he do that? To use her worst nightmare against her like it was no big deal. As if it were *punishment* for ditching. The longer her mind replayed what had just happened the more it made her want to scream.

How dare he!

She pushed up to a wobbly stand, still unable to shake her nerves, and dressed quickly. She couldn't let him get away with this.

The walk to the gym was short. Once she got there he was nowhere to be seen. She laughed bitterly. So, he could hide in her room and threaten her life over *skipping* a stupid class, but couldn't show his damn face?

Dylan turned when a shift in lighting caught her attention. It was Soren walking into the empty, glass room as if she were seeing some sort of apparition instead of a person. The doors whooshed shut behind him.

Dylan gritted her teeth and power walked to the doors. She slammed her palm against the glass as she had just seen him do, and to her surprise, they slipped open at her command.

"I'm done coddling you," he said, but his voice seemed to come from behind her.

She flipped around and gasped, Soren stood behind her. His jaw clenched.

"How did you…" Her voice trailed when she looked back to where she had first seen him, but the apparition slowly dissolved like a drop of color in water.

"Wait, Soren?" She looked behind herself. Her senses prickling. He was gone again. She twirled around, finding herself alone in the creepy glass room.

Dylan pinched her arm. *Nope, I'm awake…*

"If you think you're too advanced for my classes, you might as well skip ahead to facing a real threat."

What? Face a real threat? Hadn't she already faced his darker side since the moment she entered Elon? What else was there to see? Goodness, wasn't his mind-reading enough?

The light blinked out and she tensed, trying with everything she had not to think of the prison in Silas' castle. But it was hard. The dark silence frightened her. Everything about it screamed panic. Her hands fisted, turning her fingers white against the pressure as she brought them close to her chest. What if Soren was a shifter too?

94

Oh God.

Why hadn't she ever asked about his powers?

"Please, don't do this!" She shook uncontrollably as she felt the ghost of *his* fingers slip around her neck. Deep down, she hated that she was begging Soren, but it was out of her control. Her heart couldn't withstand an actual visit from Silas. Even if it was all just for show.

Dylan slowly backed up, blindingly searching for the exit. She couldn't remember if it was behind her or in front of her. She felt completely disoriented.

Looking down, she could see everything on her body but nothing beyond. It felt like living within a shadow. Like living within the *void*.

"Soren?" her voice came out just as small as she felt.

"Tell me…" His voice echoed from the right before shifting from the left. "What you would do if you were expected to fight… blind?"

She backed into something tall and hard. Before she could react, he wrapped an arm around her neck in a tight hold.

She gasped.

He started to say something but she couldn't hear over her beat of her own heart. All that registered was she was going to die. She wanted to struggle, to fight for her life, but her mind had somehow detached from her limbs. She screamed at herself to move while her body remained immobile.

His arm squeezed tighter the longer she refused to struggle.

"Come on!" he growled in her ear. "Fight me!"

"I can't!" she gasped, barely above a whisper.

"You aren't even trying!" he hissed in disgust.

"I am," she mouthed. Everything was so fuzzy she wasn't sure if her words even made a sound.

When her lungs screamed for a breath, she instinctively grabbed hold of his forearm, trying to pry her fingers between him and her neck.

"Fight me harder!"

"I'm… not… strong… you…" She twisted and pulled at his arms with weak hands.

His grip barely faltered and she felt the beginning of a blackout. "You don't need it to be as strong as I am. There are demons out there that can zap your powers. That can be stronger than even *you* without a *Binding*."

"I can't!" she cried out. Her thoughts drifting to Silas stealing her life and how she had let him.

Her grip slipped.

"Fight it!"

She tried to shake her head.

"Stop going there. You need to learn to block those thoughts. I'm not even holding you that tight!"

What was he talking about? His arm felt like an anaconda squeezing her neck in a lifeless vise.

"Pathetic." He released her, pushing her out in front of him. Light inundated the glassed-in space. Awareness of her wet face and still surroundings brought a level of calm to her panic.

Her head felt like it was spinning. *What just happened?*

"You are to never miss practice again," he growled. "You made me look bad in front of my crew. Next time you do, I won't be so gentle."

"*Gentle*," she gasped, still reeling from the onslaught of debilitating terror like a slippery slope into Hell. "What… What was *that*?!"

He smirked icily. "I forgot to welcome you into my little Hell." Her eyes unwillingly swept back up to his and frowned. He leaned down. "I can make you loathe, lust, fear, or trust. I can make you feel *whatever* I desire. So, I wouldn't overlook my command unless you want your reality to be as much of a fucking nightmare as your dreams."

"You're sick." Dylan spat out.

Soren grinned. "Maybe."

Dylan curled her lip and marched toward the door. Screw him and his damn practices. Tomorrow she would tell King Damen that she quit. Whatever they decided to do with her then, so be it.

"Stop being so fragile," Soren called out. "No wonder you didn't attend today. It's embarrassing."

"Fine. You know what?" She looked back at him. "I quit!" She slammed her palm against the glass to leave.

Fragile? He thinks I'm weak? Then take off the damn Binding *and we'll see who's weak!*

She growled through clenched teeth when the doors wouldn't open and slapped the glass again.

"I'm not surprised," Soren spat. "Giving up is what you do best, isn't it?"

She flinched.

"I'm not giving up. Not even close," she said, pounding her palm against the glass. *What the hell!* She glared at the door that wouldn't budge. "I'm only refusing to waste anymore of my time with a psychotic freak who hides in my room and gets off on screwing with my emotions!"

She groaned, giving up on the door for a moment, but her eyes glistened with hate as she fought against resurfacing tears. Why was he doing this?

Dylan flung herself around and scowled at Soren. "Let me leave."

"No."

"*Why?*" she snapped. "What do you want from me?"

"I want the truth. All of it."

She wanted to ask what truth he was talking about; but, she decided she didn't really care because she was done being a part of his twisted games. He could apparently make her trust? Then do it because there was no way she was going to give him an inch, willingly.

"Well, welcome to *my* Hell where you never get what you want."

Dylan partly expected him to just take what he wanted out of her mind since it hadn't ever stopped him before. Instead, a drawn out silence ensued when neither one of them chose to bend within their endless battle of wills.

She was still staring icily and about to demand that he open the doors again when they suddenly slid open. She didn't stop to ponder how exactly Soren was controlling them before swiftly pivoting on her heel and seizing the opportunity to run back to her room.

CHAPTER 6

"Damaged people are dangerous.
They know how to make Hell feel like home."
via

ASHER searched for the extra key along the top sill of Aria's door. His clumsy fingers uprooting dirt and spider skeletons.

Just before he had decided to come home, Asher visited one more connection in his search for Gerion. A bartender at the local human club. Of course, the bartender wouldn't speak to Asher unless he was a paying customer. And of course, Asher couldn't let a perfectly good whiskey go to waste. Okay, maybe three.

Had she moved the key?

It was the middle of the night and he really didn't want to wake Aria by knocking. He'd much rather sneak into her bed like an incubus and rouse her in a more pleasing way.

Damn, he missed her.

Months had passed during his search. Months of trying to stay away from her. Months of seeing her from afar and not touching her. Months of listening to her cry on his voicemail.

Months of pure Hell.

But, he had to try and find Gerion for her... for them. He just hoped she understood his intentions.

Asher dragged his fingers along the opposite side of the door trim before finding the small key painted hot pink. He blew the coating of dust off and suddenly imagined a future where he didn't have to searched for a key because he owned one. A future of *their* apartment instead of just Aria's.

Asher had barely stuck the key into the lock when the door flew open and the sexiest woman alive stood in the doorway in an off-the-shoulder UCLA sweatshirt and cotton shorts. Aria jumped into his arms, kissing him as if her life depended on it.

Asher grinned against her urgent lips, quickly kissing her back as he stumbled against the door frame. He gripped her ass and sank his fingertips into her supple skin.

"Ah, damn. I've missed you too, baby."

Aria suddenly shoved herself out of his arms and slapped him.

"What—" Asher started, his cheek stinging.

"You thought you could just walk back into my life after disappearing?!" Aria roared, looking like a fireball ready to wreak destruction. She curled her upper lip and looked him up and down. "You're *drunk* again, aren't you?"

"Baby, let me explain."

"*Let* you explain?" she sneered. "Explain *what,* exactly? Why you left me without so much as a note? Or why you thought I'd be okay with you sneaking into my apartment after I spent half a year trying to get over you! *Six months*, Asher!"

Aria suddenly grabbed the closest heavy object and chucked it at him.

He expected this and caught the vase full of dried up apricot roses and moldy water. The flowers he'd sent her a month ago. No note. Just flowers like a true dick.

Her eyes bugged when he effortlessly caught what had been intended for his head.

"GET OUT!" She whipped a finger towards the door. "Take your awful flowers and get out! I *never* want to see your face again!"

Her words plunged deeply into his gut like a fist. *No,*

please.

"Please, I had to go." Asher sank to his knees not giving a shit that the entire complex was listening to him grovel. He shuffled towards her on his knees. "I couldn't bare seeing you out of your mind with those nightmares. I had to do something!" She stopped shaking her head at him and he knew he had his opening. "The nightmares... They stopped, didn't they?"

She didn't say anything but he knew they stopped. It had taken him several meetings until he found the right warlock to put a block on Aria's mind while he looked for Gerion.

"Why couldn't you call me?" she rasped, her throat gritty with tears and pain. "Why disappear like that?"

How could he explain that just hearing her cries had become the worst kind of pain he'd ever known? That he was falling into a pit of despair with each wail screamed into his chest.

"I was failing you," he said. "You needed someone to fix you, not stand by and watch you suffer."

"That doesn't explain anything," she sniffed and eyed the door. Asher quickly slammed it shut. The last thing he needed was a human picking up on his unique heritage.

"I knew that if I told you I was leaving, you'd want to come and then I'd have to explain what I was doing. You wouldn't have let me go."

"Thanks for the presumption, but I'm not a total crazy bitch. If you had said you needed to meet with someone to stop my dreams, I would have walked you to the damn door."

Asher flinched because that wasn't why he left at all. Yes, he had wanted to stop her dreams but he had wanted to kill the source, not temporarily hold them back.

"I'm not upset because you didn't give me a chance to tag along. I'm pissed you felt like you couldn't tell me at all. You just left." She crossed her arms, dejectedly. "I thought it was because you couldn't stand to be around me anymore."

Asher shuffled even closer to her on his knees until he was kneeling at her feet. "I am weak. If I hadn't gone when I did, I would have stayed and you would have suffered. Believe me when I say I had to go the way I did for your protection."

"They stopped." Aria brought a hand to his cheek and it felt like a weight had rolled off his back. She would forgive him… she had to. "A few days ago, I slept for the first time since we got back from Lamu. But it felt like a bad joke because my mind was finally better yet you were gone. You leaving was breaking me in a completely different way. Your absence broke my heart."

Asher grabbed her hand and pulled her to him. Aria fell into his lap with a soundless gasp. "My heart is bound to you," he said, "If yours is broken, mine is shattered."

"God, I love you," she hissed before reaching up and kissing him. She quickly pulled away before he could kiss her back. "I'm still mad," she said. "Promise never to leave me again."

She tried to kiss him again but this time Asher stopped her, causing Aria to look bewildered. "I have only come back to see you before I go again."

Aria was already sitting up in preparation for his words.

Asher sighed with a grimace. "I had planned to find and kill Gerion for what he was doing to you. That is the real reason why I didn't say anything. I knew if I did, I wouldn't have made it two steps out your door."

Aria's face paled and she jetted out of his arms. "You *were* leaving me," she gasped.

"No, baby,"

"You expected to die! Didn't you?"

Asher scrambled up on his feet and wrapped his arms easily around her. "It was a strong possibility." Aria tried to wiggle out of his hold but he grabbed her cheeks, staring her in the eyes because what he was about to say wouldn't be up for discussion. "But, I'm not stopping. Nothing you say or do will stop me." She gave up trying to fight him as a couple of tears slipped from her eyes. "I shouldn't even be here," he added. "He's going to catch wind that I'm looking for him; and the last thing I need is for some idiot to try and get to me through you."

"Then why are you?"

"Choosing to stay away from you has been the hardest decision of my life." Asher paused. "But it had to be done. I need to kill him for everything he has done to you, me, Dylan and Tristian. It's just going to take a bit longer than expected."

"I had wondered if he was dead." Aria swallowed back her emotion. "You know, when the dreams stopped."

"I couldn't even get a read on him." Asher dropped his hands, feeling like a failure. "Although, the word on the street is that he is partnered with some pretty powerful groups. I wouldn't be surprised if he takes over Elon soon. Then he'll really be hard to kill."

"But, Dylan." Aria's eyes widened, filling up with anxiety again. "You said she was safe there."

"She is," he immediately consoled, hating and loving how big her heart was when it came for her family and friends.

"I tried finding her in the Elon news again," Aria continued as if she hadn't heard him. "There's been nothing new since the trial. Just ridiculous gossip about her and Gerion being lovers. Can you believe that?"

"It's better to be gossiping about lies. That means none of the media has a clue where she is or how to speak with her. I imagine they are keeping her pretty secure and out of the spotlight, which is a good thing. Try not to worry." Asher kissed her cheeks and scooped her up in his arms.

"I want to continue Tristian's plan to get her," she murmured against his chest as he carried her to the bedroom.

Their bedroom, Asher thought, ignoring her idea. How would he be able to leave her again?

"I think about her all the time. I wonder what it is like there in Elon."

Asher set her down on the hand-sewn lavender quilt made by her great grandmother before climbing in next to her.

"Baby," he traced his fingers delicately along the vines of her cherry blossom tattoo that covered her exposed shoulder.

"Yeah?"

"Do you remember that werewolf, Garret? The one that Dylan was friends with."

"Of course… why?"

"His entire clan picked up and left their usual spot behind Cindy's and I need to talk to him."

"I think he's still working at the university gym."

"Really?" That didn't seem right but he'd check it out.

"Yeah… What would he know?"

"Something about Gerion that might help me find him."

She nodded, resolutely. "Okay. I'll go see him tomorrow."

"*Aria*," Asher warned but she silenced him with a kiss and rolled on top of him.

"I might not be able to kill Gerion," she hissed between soft bites along his neck as he fell victim to her seduction, "but I'm a damn good talker. I'll see what Garret knows."

Asher groaned and flipped Aria on her back, his expression serious.

"No. I won't have you put in harm's way."

"You couldn't even find him without me," she pointed out, "and besides it's just Garret."

"*Just* a werewolf, you mean."

Aria scowled for an answer. Asher knew for certain he wasn't going to win this one if he ever wanted to touch her goddess-like body again. And he didn't think the threat of death would deter her either.

"Fine," he sighed. "But, that's it. I'll need to leave again."

"As long as you come back."

I sure hope it will go that way, he thought as he peeled layers of clothes off his girlfriend.

"We should call some friends for help," she said, screwing him with her eyes.

Why in the worlds where they having this conversation, again?

"I already did," Asher said as he tore off his own shirt and stopped the discussion for good that night.

◇◇◇

Fragile.

Slamming the door to her room, Dylan began to pace in the tiny space, unable to calm down.

Five steps forward, five step back.

Soren was seriously messed up. And then he had to utter the one word that seemed to shatter her shell. A word that echoed in her mind, planting itself deep in her being. A word reminding her of every weak moment of her life that left a scar in her.

Fragile.

He took a sledge hammer at her, expecting scare tissue and steel, when in reality she was protecting something delicate. The rough facade she erected only protected brittle glass secreted away on the inside. An interior he penetrated with a game. *A scare tactic.*

Of course his power would be something so invasive. She could handle physical pain. But thoughts? Feelings? Soren had a greater power over her than anyone she had met and she wasn't so sure he realized it.

One thing she was not, though, was fragile; and tonight she planned to prove it to herself. Prove that she wasn't afraid of Silas.

Tonight she would sleep.

With the right mind set, she was sure she could overpower him. It was only a dream! …You couldn't die in your dreams... could you?

Her eyes flitted to the dark horizon. It was probably two or three in the morning. She couldn't wait any longer. She slipped into her bed fully clothed. Pulling her blanket up to her stomach with shaking fingers, she took a deep breath, repeating the mantra:

I am not weak. I am not fragile.

After several seconds, she closed her eyes and told herself to think of Silas over and over again.

"Silas Planto, Silas Planto... Silas *Planto... Silas...* "

Opening her eyes, she looked around unable to discern her surroundings. Everything was blurry as if looking through rippled glass. Suddenly, it came into focus with a snap.

She flinched, eyeing the black starless sky in front of her. The cold feeling of the stone courtyard entered her consciousness followed by the pain of her bare feet against tiny sharp stones. She was standing next to the Void of Bones.

Too close to the dead.

She quickly climbed up to the courtyard before taking in the familiar garden. A chilling wind tossed her hair. Had it all been a dream? What was she even doing here?

Dylan cursed to herself. Why couldn't she remember?

She wiped her hands on her pants, noticing the usually glowing candelabras now lifeless. She shivered.

Her crow was nearby perched on a boulder. It flapped its wings giving off a shimmer of green light, making her think of Tristian.

Green feathers. Green eyes. Was it possible for a demon to come back as an animal? She stepped closer to it, wanting to reach out to pet its silky feathers; to let him know she knew, but something about his panicked caws kept her feet planted. She didn't understand... until she felt it.

Her insides turned to ice and her entire body stretched taut as the heat of someone else could be felt from behind

*her. A sharp edge dragged slowly down her cheek. So
slowly, she could imagine the exact details of the chipped,
black oval nail curving itself down her cheek and over her
bottom lip. She squeezed her eyes shut as the hand attached
to that nail slipped softly around her throat, tilting her chin
up.*

*"Miss me, my love?" Silas whispered, his lips grazing the
shell of her ear. "Don't worry. Soon we'll be together
again."*

Dylan screamed and jumped out of bed. She cried for
Silas to stop while covering and scratching at her ears, trying
to rid herself of the breath that seemed stitched into her
flesh.

Fragile.
Fragile.
Fragile.

Her door snapped open revealing a wild-eyed Soren clad
in only a pair of leather pants, a blade gripped tightly in his
fist. His chest heaved as his eyes searched the room
expecting someone else to be in there torturing her. When he
didn't find anyone, he rushed over, seized her hands and
stopping the assault to her face.

Dylan pushed at him and tried to run, but he hooked his
arm around her waist, halting her from fleeing. She struggled
and cried, unable to remove Silas' touch. Soren's cheeks
reddened as he worked against her panicked strength, but he
only held her tighter. His hot chest melted the ice that had
splintered her raw. Her resistance became weaker and
weaker as tears and guttural moans spilled out of her.

She suddenly wrapped her arms around him, clutching
for dear life. She hated that he was seeing her this way, but
she wouldn't tell him to go. He resembled the protection she
desperately needed at the moment: A blanket of cold steel.

She had no idea how long she cried into his chest. But he
never said a word. He didn't caress her or question her. He
only held her tightly as if he sensed she might crumble if he

107

let go.

The next morning, Dylan became slowly aware of herself. Her dry mouth and tear crusted lids. Deep, slow breaths. An uncomfortable heat dampening her skin. The alien feeling of another body tangled next to her.

Wait, what? Her eyes flicked open.

She blinked several times wishing that she was only imagining Soren's body breathing deeply next to her. Soren's *half naked* body next to her. But, nope, this was actually happening.

She licked her lips grimacing at the acrid taste in her mouth. She wanted to get up and brush her teeth, possibly take a shower and rinse off the tattoo of Silas' touch… but she was afraid to move. It had been so long since she had wanted physical contact that she froze.

Was this wanted?

Sharp tingles of numbness pricked all along her left leg that was wedged between his while her other leg was cocked around his waist. She blushed realizing they were probably locked like this all night despite being mostly dressed.

Oh God. Her head lolled to the side and she tossed a heavy arm across her eyes, careful to keep her bottom half immobile.

He was probably stuck all night like this, unable to get free.

She still didn't know how he heard her and had come into her room like that, like he expected to save her from someone. It didn't stop her from appreciating him on some level. Because she did need saving… from herself.

What in the world had she been thinking conjuring Silas like that? Did she really think she could spook *him*? There was still so much more to learn. She knew it wouldn't be the last time she saw Silas, and she needed to prepare herself for their next encounter. Silas knew *exactly* what to do to her to creep her out. It had been foolish to think she was, or could ever be, a match to him. Even if someday she grew powerful enough to defeat him, she wasn't sure her fears would ever dissipate.

Soren stirred, causing Dylan to grow stiff as a board. A soft groan came from his lips and his arm flopped over her, pulling her closer—her arms bunching up between them. Her eyes must have resembled giant saucers, because his blissful wake turned into a reflection of her surprise.

He immediately freed her and pushed himself up, blinking his slumber away.

"Dammit," he rubbed his eyes with the heel of his palm. "Sorry."

"No, no. I should be..." She looked up at him, not feeling the urge to bolt. "Sorry."

His eyebrows crinkled as he regarded her intensely.

"I shouldn't have forced you to sleep here," she hastily added.

"Forced." He looked at her like she was speaking another language, then rubbed the area between his eyes as if to clear his head. When he looked at her again the usual icy stone had settled back into his eyes. He lifted an eyebrow. "We're going to be late for practice."

"Oh!" Dylan scrambled out of bed and rushed into her bathroom. She shut the door and immediately blushed when she remembered she had forgotten to grab fresh clothes. She opened the door and stopped short as Soren slowly stood. The thick packs of muscle decorated with black tribal tattoos tightened under her stare. He seemed to be brooding about something. Then again, he always seemed to be brooding about something.

"Sorry." She looked away squeezing her eyes shut.

The nightmare with Silas must have messed up her brain. She couldn't allow herself to appreciate Soren's body or even the way sleep came peacefully within his arms. She was only grasping at straws as she had at Silas'. None of this was real.

She heard the pads of his feet against the hard tile stop as she grabbed a pair of yoga pants from her dresser.

"I changed my mind…" he started, his voice raspy from sleep, but she didn't let herself look at him. "Nothing about you is weak."

She winced as the door shut. Her heart thundering inside her.

Collapsing on her bed, she pulled her knees up to her chest expecting guilt but, surprisingly, the feeling never came. What did come were his words about being late for practice. Perhaps he wasn't completely through with her, yet.

It wasn't much later when Dylan was peering into the gym showered and dressed in her usual active wear. The room held a throng of demons all dressed in black or dark grey and training in different forms. Two bleeding demons sparred bare fisted in the ring and a few practiced sword drills with which she was now familiar. Some more were in the glass room from last night, practicing their abilities against a kind of simulated target.

Mainly, she was surprised to see so many. For some reason, she had only prepared herself for the four soldiers of Shadow Horde. It made more sense if they had a larger army, but that didn't make her any less nervous about treading in on their territory.

"You're late!" Soren called across the room.

Great, she thought, hating that he'd spotted her before she had one hundred percent committed to walking in.

She shrugged at him and looked around once more before taking a large breath and entering the gym.

With each step the room grew quieter and quieter as demon after demon took notice of her. Dylan bunched her shoulders at the unwanted attention as her eyes drifted from Soren to the *others.* They posed behind him, appearing curious or impassive.

Dylan stepped in front of Soren and looked around again

at the completely silent room. A demon girl in the glass enclosure accidentally released a puff of black dust and cursed. Dylan couldn't help the tiny tilt of her lips as a couple demons snickered.

"Well, well," Astrid lifted a brow, stepping beside Soren and cutting off Dylan's smile. "Look what the worm dragged in."

"Astrid," Soren warned.

"What?" she asked innocently. "I'm just making sure she knows her place. Just because you're sleeping with her doesn't make her any less of an *insipid*."

Dylan felt simultaneously pale and flushed. Whispers commenced followed by low chuckles. "We're n-not," Dylan sputtered out.

"She knows that," Soren ground out to Dylan, while shooting daggers at Astrid which were ten times her glare.

She lifted her palms in surrender before cocking her head at Dylan.

"Soren, don't you have a meeting with King Damen today?"

"It can wait," he mumbled.

"If you say so... Ready to spar, Temperance?"

"What?" Dylan instinctively looked to Soren then winced.

Stop depending on him! she chided herself.

Schooling her features, she bounced her shoulders. "I mean, sure, why not. Wasters?"

"I don't think—" Soren started but Astrid cut him off, still battling Dylan's stare.

"I wouldn't keep a King waiting, Soren," Astrid said. "I'll go get the *Wasters*."

"I'll be back," Soren muttered, heading out of the gym.

Dylan proceeded to the outer ring of the sparring mat just as the two bloodied demons charged at each other.

Astrid returned holding two Samurai looking swords. She whistled loudly and told the two brawlers to scram.

111

"Wasters are overrated." Astrid handed her one of the swords as they stepped onto the mat and over splatters of blood. "Besides, you've been training with Soren for what, almost a year? I think you're way past the beginner's stage."

"I haven't held one of these, yet," Dylan mumbled, wrapping her fingers around the hilt and slowly peeling the sword from its casing. It slid out like butter and glinted like a diamond.

"A Katana sword," Astrid said, holding it flat with both of her palms up. "Deadly. And my favorite."

"Cool." Dylan cleared her throat, feeling the light weight and running her thumb along the edge. It nicked her and she flinched, expecting it to be blunt.

"Engage!" Astrid snapped, charging at her and bringing her weapon down in a single, swift motion. Dylan squealed and spun out of the way.

Astrid laughed haughtily. "Is this really the big, bad Temperance Elementa?" she announced as several soldiers gathered around the octagon, before Astrid began laughing even harder.

Dylan scowled and posed herself into a defensive stance.

"Hey, bitch!" Dylan barked, silencing Astrid's bout of hysterics. "I'm over here if you want to try that little move again."

Astrid grinned and rushed at her again but this time Dylan was ready. Their swords clashed in a T and Dylan grunted feeling her muscles scream and her *Binding* cut into her neck as she pushed Astrid off. Both girls stumbled away from each other.

"There she is!" Astrid growled, advancing yet again.

Dylan dodged and swung out unsuccessfully.

Astrid took the opportunity to swing again and met flesh, slicing a gash in Dylan's side.

Dylan stumbled as a cry ripped from her throat and a thin trickle of blood slipped down her hip.

"Oops," the other girl shrugged.

Panting, Dylan was furious. She righted herself and squeezed the hilt of the sword harder than necessary, as if she might be able to draw strength from the steel.

Astrid eyed her, and Dylan realized Astrid was waiting for her to concede. Not a chance.

Dylan pitched her body forward remembering Soren's lessons on using force behind her swings.

Astrid caught on to her form. She quickly blocked Dylan's predictable hit before driving a knee into Dylan's stomach and knocking the wind out of her. Dylan fell flat to the mat.

Astrid stepped beside her and pointed the sword at her chest with a smirk.

"I may be a bitch but I don't try to be anything other than what I am. *Traitor*."

Astrid was still smiling and bowing victoriously to the dissipating crowd when Dylan hooked her leg around the other girl, knocking her down with a yelp. Astrid immediately abandoned her weapon and scrambled on top of Dylan to throw a punch. Dylan threw up her arms and blocked the hit before getting her own in on Astrid's jaw.

Arms seemed to come out of nowhere, wrapping around the girls' chests and ripping them off of each other. Their legs and fists continued to swing violently until Soren's growl pierced the air, silencing the room.

"Let me go!" Astrid screamed, fighting against a huge Shadow Horde soldier that was about as big as a professional linebacker.

"I'm calm!" Astrid growled.

The large soldier released Astrid and she stomped her five foot four self over to Soren looking comical next to his height of six foot five.

"Why the hell is she even here?" she huffed, rolling her eyes when the large soldier appeared next to her again like he expected to intervene again. "We are four. Everything we know for the Shadow Horde is FOUR. She's like the slimy fifth wheel that can't be trusted! And who's going to lose their spot to her, huh?" Astrid looked at her comrades before returning her eyes to her commander. "She's a *traitor,* Soren. A damn manipulator. She manipulated Effingo, Gerion, even the Kings! Now she's manipulating YOU!"

"Are you done?" Soren's answer was like a verbal slap.

"No. I want her gone. Otherwise, I AM." She jabbed a thumb into her chest.

"You don't want to do that, Astrid. Don't make me choose because, unfortunately, you will lose."

Her mouth gaped. "You... you would choose *her* over your family?"

Dylan was just as shocked, not even trying to fight off the blonde Horde soldier, Ian, who hauled her upright after the fight. Why on earth would Soren say such a thing?

"Actually," a voice from the door thundered. "I am making him chose her over you," King Damen said icily. "So if I were you, my dear Astrid, I would accept the, oh what did you call her? *'Slimy fifth wheel'* before, you find yourself without a family."

Dylan didn't have to be a resident of Elon for long to recognize a death threat when she heard it.

Everyone in the room bowed and Dylan was quick to follow.

Cold fingers rested on Dylan's shoulder as King Zirk seemed to appear out of nowhere. His grip tightened and something deep recoiled inside her at his touch. She didn't think anyone noticed it until she glanced over at Soren staring darkly at King Zirk's hand. At least the rest of them seemed oblivious to her discomfort.

King Zirk bent down to her ear. "I suggest you make friends." Dylan's muscles tightened and she fought the urge to shove him. "I don't care if you manipulate them to love you. Just make it happen. Don't make me regret granting you this allowance." She suddenly felt as slimy as Astrid currently thought of her. She nodded slowly.

"Good girl." King Zirk smiled. "Now get up and make up." He tapped her on the back. "Go on now."

Dylan stood and walked toward Astrid, feeling the pain in her jaw throb.

"Good match." Dylan raised a hand. "I'm not sorry for punching you."

Astrid cocked a wicked smile and took her hand in a firm shake. "I'm glad you aren't sorry. Then I'd really know you were full of shit." Her eyes glanced over at the Soren and the Kings standing next to each other. "But... I guess I have no choice other than to welcome you." Astrid squeezed her hand so tightly Dylan felt her warning loud and clear, "*Trainee.*"

Dylan squeezed back, letting Astrid know she understood.

"Great," Soren added, dryly. "Now, can we get back to schedule?"

After practice, everyone headed to the cafeteria for *Essence* and food while Dylan got her side patched up by the Medic. She didn't want food or *Essence* but, one look in Soren's direction and she knew she needed to just go even if it meant sitting awkwardly at the table.

The Shadow Horde got to the cafeteria and immediately stepped in front of a long line of soldiers waiting for food and grabbed coffees, meals, or pastries. Apparently being a part of the Horde had its perks.

"Eat," Soren growled as he passed Dylan with a tray piled high with food.

Dylan sighed, scanning her eyes along the steaming muffins she used to love. "I'm not hungry," she mumbled to herself.

"I didn't ask if you were hungry."

She jumped, not expecting him to hear her.

"I told you to eat," he continued, "You need it. You can't keep practicing without sustenance."

He looked at her for a second before stepping even closer. He was so tall that her nose came up to the notch between his collar bone. A rich spice coated his skin and she wondered if it was cologne or his natural scent. He leaned down.

"Do you want a repeat of what happened the last time you were here?" His voice was so smooth and low it felt almost as if he were slipping his fingers into her hair. Was he warning her... or tempting her?

She blinked. He wasn't touching her. Not even his breath.

"Stop." The word came out in a rush of air.

He lifted his hands in surrender to her before selecting a muffin and handing it to her palms up. A silent peace offering.

She took it with a glare and started to turn around.

"Temperance," he cleared his throat and she looked back at him. "Coffee?"

"Sure," she said on impulse, holding her muffin close to her chest.

She looked all around the cafeteria for a place to sit, but she didn't know a single person. Everyone was in training clothes and almost every seat was filled. With a resigned sigh, Dylan headed to the exit. It felt like high school all over again. Eating in the library because she was too embarrassed and insecure to eat alone with everyone watching.

She was almost to the door when she heard someone call her demon name. She looked over at the side table closest to the door with the Shadow Horde sitting around it. They were all eating, the guys shoveling food down their throats as Astrid motioned her over with a curling finger before going back to buttering her bagel. Dylan set her muffin down on the table and their jests and movements slowed.

"Temperance," Astrid greeted. Dylan could tell the disdain was still present but she was at least trying. "This is Augusto," she pointed across from her to a muscular man big enough to take up two seats. She knew who he was but this was the first time she had ever gotten a good look at him. He had wide eyes and a square nose. His dark, sleek hair was pulled into a low pony—long enough to reach his lower back.

He nodded politely in hello.

"And this is Ian," she shifted her finger to a demon that didn't look any older than Dylan. If anything his baby face and platinum blonde hair put him at seventeen or eighteen. What was he doing in the Shadow Horde?

"Hey, Temps." He stuck out his hand and she shook it hesitantly. "You don't mind if I call you Temps, do you?"

"Actually—"

"Great!" He smiled before going back to his plate of eggs.

She sighed and finally plopped down in her seat just as a lidded coffee was set down in front of her. Soren sat opposite of her.

"You meet everyone?" Soren asked.

"Yeah—"

"Good." He took a huge bite out of something that resembled a panini with egg, cheese and veggies. "Eat," he mumbled, motioning to her muffin with his eyes.

"You just have to start doing it," Astrid butted in. "Otherwise, you won't ever grasp the urge for food."

Dylan swallowed against what felt like an extremely full stomach and picked up the cranberry muffin.

"Well, go on, Temps," Ian said, slapping her on the shoulder.

"Don't touch her," Soren snapped.

Ian yanked back his hand and looked at his palm for a split second before picking up his coffee and taking a gulp.

"Why the hell not?" Astrid dropped her half eaten bagel on the table. "*Don't touch her, Astrid. Don't touch her, Ian.*" She laughed humorlessly. "What is she, poisonous?"

"I just don't like to be touched is all," Dylan whispered,

opting to take a bite rather than take in the curious pity stirring in their eyes.

"Why?" Astrid leaned over the table in full attention, not getting the hint that Dylan didn't want to talk about it.

"Astrid—" but a monotonous buzzing cut Soren off. They all checked their pagers and the four of them quickly stood shoving the rest of their breakfasts into their mouths or shaking their trays into the adjacent trash.

Dylan's eyes bounced between each solider moving mechanically before following them to the side wall.

Soren pressed his hand to a patch of blank wall and it suddenly flipped. An array of different weapons appeared. They began pulling swords, whips, even guns off the wall, their fingerprints unlocking them.

Soren secured a fat dagger and something that resembled a flare gun to his belt. Even though Dylan was practically falling over him, not once did he acknowledge her.

Dylan's breathing sped up as Ian and Augusto started marching out of the cafeteria closely followed by Astrid. Before Soren could step around Dylan and exit with his crew, she fisted his sleeve, "*Wait.*"

He flipped his head around and hissed, "*What*?"

She took a sharp step backward but his hand came down on hers, stopping her retreat. He surprisingly looked apologetic at his outburst.

Dylan took a deep breath and met his harsh stare.

"What's going on?" She worked her hand free and pulled it to her chest.

"We've been called for a mission."

"Do I go, too?"

"No." He slammed his palm against the wall again, this time closing the hidden case of weapons. Dylan watched it close but when she looked back at him, he was gone—dashing after his crew.

CHAPTER 7

"It is the unknown we fear
when we look upon death and darkness,
nothing more."
J.K. Rowling

"HEATHER!" Aria called out to the willowy brunette sitting behind the welcome desk at the university gym. She wore the standard employee's blue collared shirt and khakis. It was the next morning and the place was packed with students powering away on equipment as Flume played in the background.

"Hey, girl," she said as Aria neared, stacking a few papers and stapling them. "Are you looking for a class or something in particular?"

"Hmm, maybe," Aria said, scanning the small gym. "Isn't there yoga or something with that hottie Garret?"

Heather smiled knowingly. *"Oh* yeah." She pointed to a room on the other side of the gym and then dramatically fanned herself. "Good luck trying to focus in there."

Aria laughed, "Thanks," and set off to the mirrored studio.

As she walked past the cyclists and runners, she found it hard not to think of Dylan here. It shouldn't have surprised her, considering the last time she had been here was when Dylan had coerced her into a pointless work out, but it did.

Garret was crouched over woman, correcting her form when Aria shoved open the door with a bang against the wall without thinking and interrupted the meditation class; which in her defense, looked more like sleeping than a work out. They could have probably used the wake up.

He looked up annoyingly along with the rest of room.

"Erm, hello," Aria said a bit contrite. "Sorry about the door."

"*Aria,*" Garret said, sounding irritated. She ignored it.

"Garret!" she smiled, just glad he remembered her name. It had been almost a year since he took her back home from Lamu, Kenya and stayed with her until Asher showed up with a whole new mountain of problems. She honestly didn't think he would remember her, especially since she had recently changed the color of her hair to a stunning, dark blue.

"Mind if I join?"

He tersely motioned to a stack of rolled mats in the back of the room and went back to instructing the class.

Aria tried not to roll her eyes at Garret's attitude as she dumped her purse on the floor and unrolled the mat next to a girl from her chemistry class. She got down on her hands and knees and lifted her rear in "downward dog" and immediately regretted it. To say she wasn't the most fit person would have been an understatement.

Thirty minutes passed and Aria was trying not to sleep in the Savasana pose when Garret ended the session with a mantra and "Namaste."

Everyone in the room quickly got up, chatting and rolling their mats, while Aria took her time, hoping to catch him after everyone left. There was a skinny blonde in red sports bra and matching capris that had been stationed in the front who wouldn't stop talking with Garret. When it became clear that the blonde wasn't going away, Aria stepped out of the room and stood near the door where she acted like she was texting someone.

"So, I'll see you tomorrow then," the blonde said as Garret exited and locked the room.

"Yeah," he said with a boyish smile that looked *really* good on him. When the girl was out of sight, he turned to Aria.

"What do you want?"

Aria grimaced. "Whoa, I can't just say hi or, I don't know, need an emergency work out?"

He just stared at her.

"Okay, jeez. I may have come to see you... for help," she said, realizing she had no idea what to say now. What the hell had she been doing for the past half hour? Meditating? *Hmm, maybe there is something to this yoga crap.*

"Yeah right." Garret turned to move past her.

She pushed off the wall and laid a hand on his chest to stop him. "Wait, please. This is important."

He looked back down at her and snapped, "How about you ask your boyfriend and his demon friends for help."

Aria quickly retracted her hand and crossed her arms. She had the sudden impression that he hated her. But, it was more than just her, it felt like he hated what she represented. Did she remind him of Dylan? Or was it just the demons he hated?

"Look, I can't go to Asher. I need," she dropped her voice, "werewolf help."

He glanced around her and spoke, "You have one minute."

"Okay. So, technically, what is one supposed to do after they get bitten?"

"I don't have time for this."

"Wait," she stepped in his way again, "I have this friend and she doesn't know what to do now... she's scared. I just figured, since you're, you know, then maybe you can help her?"

Garret suddenly appeared curious. "She was bitten recently?"

"Unfortunately."

He paused a moment before sighing, "Okay. Tell her to

121

meet me here tonight at eleven, alone. I don't want to see or hear from your soul sucking boyfriend or his friends, otherwise your friend is on her own."

She nodded and Garret took off towards the men's locker room.

Aria walked out of the gym and cursed when she spotted Asher and Ulysses conspicuously waiting on the hood of her black Volvo. Did they not understand how secret missions worked?

"What the hell are you guys doing?" Aria whisper hissed when she got close.

"Waiting for you," Asher said like that was obvious... which it was. Too damn obvious.

"You're going to ruin everything," Aria said, unlocking her car and jumping in. She looked at the gym's tinted windows, feeling as if she was being watched. Did this count as seeing her boyfriend?

Asher was on the other side of her car in a blink and getting into the passenger seat while Ulysses got in the back.

Aria gawked at Asher's use of his demon speed out in the open like that.

"Are you *trying* to draw attention to yourself?" she snapped.

"Babe, relax." Asher glanced at Ulysses, who just shrugged. "Since when do you care about my speed?"

Aria glared at the steering wheel and turned the ignition on. It almost seemed like he was being dense on purpose.

"What happened?" Asher asked. "Did he hurt you?" He reached for her and she felt her tight coil of anxiety ease from his touch as his fingers slipped between hers and gripped her hand. He was seriously impossible to be mad at.

"No... look, I talked to him and it was... weird."

"What do you mean?" Ulysses asked.

Aria turned in the leather seat and looked at both of them. "Does he hate us or something?"

Asher furrowed his brows.

"What?" she prodded.

"Well, we did kind of promise him that we'd kill Datu and we didn't." Asher shrugged. "Even though, word is the vampire is dead."

"Hmm," she hummed.

"It's okay if it didn't work out. You tried."

"That's not why I'm on edge."

"Babe…"

"It did work."

"What?" Ulysses said, leaning forward. "You got their location?"

"Well. Kind of," Aria looked apologetically at Asher, "I just need to pretend to be a recently bitten were-girl. Tonight. At eleven." she looked out the window again. "And alone."

"You *what*?" Asher said, sharply.

"Believe-me-when-I-say-this-is-the-only-way-he'd-give-me-the-time-of-day," she said hastily before Asher could get a word in otherwise. "And-now-he'll-take-me-to-their-nest-and-you-can-follow… definitely-try-for-more-stealth-though. He-really-doesn't-want-you-guys-around." Aria took a deep breath and grinned sheepishly. "It'll be fine. I promise," she assured as Asher rubbed his temples with a grimace.

Aria touched his elbow. "I've got this. I can do this."

Asher shook his head without looking at her. "I know you can. I just don't like it." Asher looked at Aria. "If something happens to you… I'm ruined."

She leaned in and kissed him once. "I'll be fine. I'll get their location and you'll kill Gerion and then maybe… maybe we can figure out a way to get Dylan back."

◇◇◇

The dark brown punching bag swayed back toward Dylan before she swung at it again. Her taped fist met the leather for what felt like the five-hundredth time. She shook out her

123

shoulder. Her arms ached and trembled, and a light sheen of sweat flushed color to her cheeks. But she was nowhere near done because she couldn't sit still. Not since the Shadow Horde left four days ago.

Was that normal?

She glanced up at the dark windows—guessing it was around three in the morning. Then wiped the sweat off her forehead with the back of her wrist and lifted her hand to continue when the gym doors opened revealing Soren.

Their eyes locked for a moment.

"You can't be here outside training hours without one of us," Soren called across the space.

Well, hello to you, too, she thought.

"Not even soldiers or trainees," he added as if sensing she might come back with the fact she was training to be one of their exclusive group.

She continued to look at him. He stood stoically, still dressed in his gear from the mission.

Her eyes did a quick scan of his body. He looked healthy and clean, not like he'd been injured or stranded on some remote world without a single way home while forced to fight off rabid animals and dig for water. No, he actually looked...

"Well?" he sneered, "Did you forget how to speak?"

Like an ass. He looked like a big, fat jerk.

Dylan rolled her eyes and began packing up the equipment. Had she honestly missed him? The thought almost made her laugh.

After putting the waster back in the trunk, she turned and walked toward him. But he just watched her.

He watched as she wiped her face with a towel and tossed it into the hamper. He watched as she unraveled the tape from her knuckles and chucked it into the waste bin. Then he watched her head for the doors.

Dylan thought she was going to make it past him unscathed. Perhaps, he wouldn't mind taking a break from his alpha brooding role for a moment.

His fingers gripped her elbow before she could hit the threshold, jerking her to a stop.

So much for hoping…

"Are we back to this?" he whispered under his breath.

She yanked her arm away and cocked her head. What '*this*' was he even talking about? He was gone for four days and came back ordering her around… just like before. Nothing had changed. So, what did he expect?

God, Soren was so contradictory. His words sometimes sounded honest and caring while his actions always appeared otherwise. He only cared about himself.

"I'm just tired," she said with an exasperated sigh. "I don't feel like chatting."

"Then why aren't you sleeping?" He narrowed his eyes, not believing her one bit. Except she *was* tired, just not in the way that evoked sleep. Her fatigue was mental and she didn't feel like explaining this with a man who seemed to hate her most days.

"I couldn't sleep, but now I can."

"The nightmares?"

Nightmare felt like such an innocent word for what she experienced. Night terror seemed more befitting.

She bristled. "Don't act like you know me."

As soon at the words left her mouth, she regretted it. It was as if something dark and deadly folded in over his eyes.

He chuckled. A delicious sound that grated her nerves and shot a dose of fear into her blood.

"That's funny, because I could've sworn we had gotten to know each other quite well last week."

Her entire face contorted and her upper lip curled. No way on earth would she dignify that with a response. Damn her for letting him console her. *Damn her!*

She pushed past him to storm off and stopped short at the unsettling sight of the rest of the Horde. The guys had the decency to look uncomfortable but Astrid looked a breath away from a full blown laugh before crossing her arms and raising two condescending eye brows.

"Well, you heard him. *Get*."

Dylan's cheeks reddened as a flurry of heat tingled her fingertips. The sensation startled her so much she jolted forward, dashing to her dorm room with the echo of Astrid's laughter chasing her the entire way.

Inside her room, Dylan stared at her fingertips as anger coursed through her veins like wildfire. They were flushed as if she had submerged her prints in hot water. She curled her fingers into a fist and continued pacing.

Was it possible to overcome the *Binding*? Or was she simply still growing in strength?

Goddammit! She hated being so alone. Hated figuring it all out by herself. Hated being *here*. But she couldn't say she regretted all of her decisions. She regretted not waiting long enough for Tristian. She regretted not fighting harder against Silas. She regretted not listening to Tristian in the first place; but she couldn't regret taking Peppi's soul—because it saved her. Silas would have murdered her. If not physically, he would have emotionally. He would have enslaved her. He would have broken her beyond repair.

Tristian's death may have doused the fire in her heart, but it didn't extinguish it. The ember still burned. It just needed a reason to ignite again. This... this fire in her blood was her purpose. She thought with him she had found herself but she hadn't. She had only just begun to crack the surface of Temperance Elementa. And a large part of her was hell bent on unleashing her.

She abruptly stopped and slammed her fist into the wall in frustration over the idiotic *Binding*. Except instead of only hurting herself as she had intended, she'd punched a gaping hole... in concrete!

Dylan pulled her hand free. Her fingers trembled sending stone shards and dust floating to the floor.

A sharp knock rattled her door.

126

A quick breath released from her lungs before she acted.

"Just a second!" Dylan scrambled to her dresser. Finding it moved with ease, she slid it in front of the hole. Dylan looked at her dirty hands once more then dove to wipe the evidence of her strength off her bed.

"What are you doing?"

Dylan whipped herself around. Her heart was stampeding a mile a second. "Nothing," she said breathlessly.

Soren closed the door and locked it.

"What," she swallowed, "are you doing here."

"I needed to see if you were at least trying to sleep." He frowned. His eyes swept over her body. Her pulse leapt at the thought of Soren finding out and turning up the *Binding*. His gaze made her feel as if her thoughts were ingrained across her skin like a neon tattoo. She forced herself to take in steady gulps of air.

A blush of goose bumps prickled her heaving chest.

"Still doing drills, I see."

Dylan blinked incredulously before letting out a bout of jam-packed air from her lungs.

"Maybe."

She cleared her throat and looked away to the new location of the dresser. Realizing that unless he frequented her room often, a couple feet to the right really wasn't that noticeable.

"Maybe," he echoed with distaste.

"It shouldn't matter to you what I do at night. I'll still be at practice tomorrow. I'll just sleep after that."

"What about your lessons then?"

He stepped in closer and the sharp look in his eye foretold of the upcoming reprimand.

"Then after that," she shrugged noncommittally.

"I don't think you're understanding me. If you can't keep up with the schedule, do you know who gets the reprimand? Me. I vouched for you to the Kings. So, like it or not, your safety is a top concern of mine along with my crew. I'm

127

responsible for you. For all of you."

Dylan's eyes widened in disbelief. *Safety? Concern... of mine?* No, no, no, she didn't need a babysitter. Besides, Soren a babysitter? Maybe in Hell. *...Did he say he vouched for me?*

"Well, you don't need to bother. I'm fine." Her lie slipped out of her lips and she pinched them shut and looked away to stop any more dishonesty from pouring through.

He saw right through her, like he always did. "'Fine' isn't avoiding sleep. 'Fine' isn't working yourself until exhaustion or to pass the time. 'Fine' isn't waiting until you collapse on the gym floor!" He stepped closer to her. "You. Are. Not. Fine."

"Okay!" She backed away from him and rubbed her arms. "I'm not. But I'm stuck this way. So, will you just..." she looked at him, searching for any sign of compassion. She shook her head. Still, nothing had changed. He was still the same psychotic demon only now he was covered in more lies. "Just *leave*," she sighed in frustration.

His lips turned down for a moment before bringing his hands up to his leather jacket and ripping the zipper down. He shrugged out of it and tossed it on her dresser. While he kicked off his boots, Dylan froze, in too much shock to ask what the hell he thought he was doing. Tatted, muscled, and shirtless, he walked over to the door and flicked off the light.

Dylan tensed in the dark. With her arms crossed over her chest, she felt the sharp pain of her nails digging into the softness of her upper arms. Her knees felt weak even though they were locked up tight, and her heart seemed to reach an entirely new level of haste.

But instead of closing the distance between them as she had partly expected, he rolled onto her bed.

"I'm not going to touch you," his husky voice snapped her out of her haze and she twitched.

"Then what are you—"

"Look, I figured, you slept with me fine the other night.

So I must have had some positive effect. And if I have to do this every night to keep your head right for the army, then fuck it, fine. But I won't touch you. I have no desire to. So you can stop worrying your bottom lip before it bleeds again."

Dylan released her lip and laughed humorlessly. He couldn't be serious. "It was probably only coincidence."

"Only one way to find out."

"You can't do this every night."

"For fuck's sake," he groaned under his breath. "Just get in the damn bed, *pet*."

She looked at his large silhouette taking up most of her bed before taking the first step. She laid awkwardly and board straight, feeling as if she had left the last piece of her old self standing in the middle of her room.

Then she closed her eyes.

CHAPTER 8

*"There she was, all dressed in adventure,
straddling the edge of a star."*
Jonny Ox

ARIA stood alone outside the gym in a pair of dark jeans, a black long-sleeve shirt, and Dylan's heeled leather boots. With her lips painted a deep shade of red coupled by a dramatic sweep of eyeliner, Aria was channeling her favorite super spy: Natasha Romanoff. She only needed some Widow's Bite bracelets to complete the outfit.

She was more than ready to break into the secret werewolf den. All afternoon, she had been sitting with Asher and going over every possible detail of her story and reading up on werewolves from books he had scored for her. She was the perfect imposter... as long as Garret didn't decide to test her first.

The gym doors opened and shut as she watched the last gym patron head to her car through the perfect, spring night air. The brightly lit street lamps swathed over her like amber spot lights on a stage.

"So it was you, this friend you were talking about."
Show time.

Aria spun around, coming face to face with Garret. His eyes seemed to glow as the car lights from the leaving patron slipped across them. Just like a wild animal's whose eyes light up when caught in headlights.

"I didn't think you would want to help *me*." She

swallowed thickly.

He cocked his head and circled around her. He even went as far as to smell her. Oh no, could he tell she was lying just by her scent? She hadn't read anything about that!

"I sense your demon lover. What does he think about the change?"

"Um, well, he doesn't exactly know."

Garret leaned back and crossed his arms as he waited for her to elaborate.

"See, he was gone for a few weeks when it happened." She looked away, remembering she was supposed to be a scared cub to him. "And now that he's back... I'm afraid to tell him but it has become harder and harder to keep it a secret..." Aria forced her mouth shut before she could ramble on.

He nodded like he could relate. "Where did it happen?"

"At a club. I had been trying to get over Asher because of something stupid. I guess, I picked the wrong guy."

"Do you remember his name?"

Aria narrowed her eyes, visibly trying to remember the name. When in reality, Asher had paid off another siren for info on a wolf known for biting women. "Drake... I think? He could have been lying. I don't know."

"I know a Drake. He's a damn hot head, too." Their eyes connected and surprisingly, she found empathy. "I'm sorry that happened. I wouldn't wish this on anyone."

She waited a few beats before asking the one question she never thought she'd ever ask a man, "What should I do now?"

"Aria," he said while shaking his head, "Maybe I can help you while you stay at your place. That's better. Safer."

"But, what about Asher? I can't tell him. I need somewhere to go."

"Listen," he lowered his voice, "You don't want to become one of my pack. The women are being manipulated."

"What do you mean?"

"They're being used as nothing more than sex objects for my Alpha's revenge. You can't come with me. Not unless you want that to be your life, because once you arrive, that's it. You're a part of us."

Aria felt the very first tingles of fear at the thought of being trapped in a place using women. What was to stop them from figuring out that she was a fake? And then what? What if they really turned her? ...or worse, killed her?

She suddenly thought of Dylan, scared, helpless, and trapped in Elon, and then of Gerion, knowing there was no other way. This was their only lead. Besides, it would be weird if she didn't go. New werewolves always desired a pack.

"I need to go."

Garret did a quick scan of her body before looking away with an odd look on his face and nodded. "I thought that might be the case. Come on."

He started for a green Ford pickup that was parked in the back of the parking lot. Aria hesitantly followed. She glanced briefly at the shadows beside the gym, knowing Asher and Ulysses were there, somewhere.

She hoped.

"There are a few rules you'll need to abide by once you're there," he said, as he pulled out of the parking lot.

She tore her eyes off the road and looked at him. "Oh?"

"For one, I am a delta, your superior. You cannot call me Garret there, but Lieutenant Cottom, or Delta Cottom."

Aria cocked an eyebrow. Lieutenant? *Oh damn, if only Dylan knew*, Aria thought trying to keep herself from smiling.

"Second, whatever my Alpha says, goes. And I'm not kidding, *what-ever* she says. She's in charge."

"She?"

Garret nodded like that was a given. Aria knew females were worshiped within packs but whenever she thought of an

Alpha, she imagined some thick, roaring male that had to fight his way to the top with his bare fists.

"Third, you'll be expected to cut all ties with the demons that are not a part of our alliance. Your boyfriend and his friends are not welcome in our home. Ever. In fact, it's probably best if you just don't talk to them anymore."

Yeah, right, she thought eyeing the simple black arrow that wrapped around her left hand ring finger. The day after Asher came back, they vowed over ring tattoos and champagne to never leave each other for as long as they lived. It was as close to a wedding ceremony as she would ever have.

"What alliance?"

"The Plantos."

"Who?"

"Fourth, you'll stay with the shewolves," he said, ignoring her question. "I can't help you after we arrive."

"What?" Aria's heart beat a bit faster when she thought about being alone in the werewolf den. For some reason she had assumed Garret would be with her. "But, I won't know anyone. You can't, like, show me the ropes before leaving me?" She sounded whiny, God, she hated sounding whiny.

"We are not mates, Aria, so no. I'm not even allowed to socialize with the shewolves unless my Alpha grants it." Garret's brows furrowed. "They're all mostly incapacitated right now, anyway."

Her eyes widened at that. "Wait. What do you mean?"

"You will see soon enough. Your... type... will be pretty popular."

"My type?" *Shit*, this wasn't good. She suddenly wanted to forget this suicidal mission, and the Black Widow never quit. "Garret. I really need you to be blunt with me right now."

What the hell did he mean incapacitated?!

Garret pulled over in front of a dark office building in a strange part of town she hadn't ever seen before, and turned off the engine.

"We're here," he muttered and got out.

Aria widened her eyes when it became obvious that he wasn't going to tell her more. *Oh no.* What had she gotten herself into? Aria looked around at the empty street. There were no cars or people in sight. What if they had lost her backup? What if Asher couldn't find her?

She startled when the passenger door opened.

"Ready to get the show on the road?"

"Not really," she said, gripping the side of the seat protectively. "Tell me more before I go in there. Please." Information was why she was here. If she could just get enough out of him maybe she could hit him over the head and run before she got stuck inside the building.

"There's really not much else to know. We have our ranks. The men work and protect. The women make sure we have food and cater directly to the Alpha."

"No, I mean," she lowered her voice, "you said they were incapacitated because of the Alpha's revenge. What is that about?"

"And I said, you'll see soon enough." Garret grabbed her by the arm and tugged her out of his truck. "This is why I asked if you were sure about being in the pack," he grunted.

"Hey!" Aria yelled as he guided her to the front doors with way too much strength for one person to have. It occurred to her then that even Asher hadn't ever used his strength on her.

She was seriously out of her league here.

Garret shoved open a glass door and waited for her to enter on her own.

"You know, you could learn to be a bit more accommodating since we'll be living together," she said. "And—"

"And what?" he cut her off. "Less... dog?" Garret growled apparently remembering a few remarks she made during their mission to find Dylan.

"Hey, you said it, not me," she muttered as she stepped inside. "I was going to say caveman, but whatever."

When she heard the door behind her close, cutting off the sounds of the night, her pulse rose even higher. Was she trapped?

She glanced around the foyer at the dirty glass and striped wood that would have made for a stunning entrance in another life. A crystal chandelier hung from the ceiling that appeared just as sad and debilitated as the small, brown couch seating area on her left.

There was a man with buzzed, mocha hair in a blue shirt and jeans leaning over a newspaper at the graffitied front desk. He looked up and immediately stood.

"Delta Cottom."

"Ryan," Garret greeted in return, "I've got a cub ready for initiation. Call one of the ladies to help get her settled."

Ryan nodded curtly and picked up his cell phone.

"Listen," Garret said to Aria while Ryan spoke to someone over the phone. Surprisingly, his voice sounded gentle, soothing her a bit. "Just do what they say and you'll be fine. I promise."

She took a deep breath. She could do this. She would see her boyfriend again. She would get the necessary information. She would get Dylan back.

She couldn't break down now, not when she needed to stay the strongest.

"Hi," said a feminine, silky voice from behind her. "You must be the cub."

Aria turned toward the voice and choked when she realized it belonged to a completely naked, very-much pregnant brunette with silver highlights.

"Hey," Aria replied, trying to act normal, because it *was* very normal... for werewolves. "Oh." She suddenly stuck out her hand. "I'm Aria."

The shewolf smiled at Aria's reaction before taking her hand and shaking it delicately. "Lady Kiera." Her eyes

135

traveled down Aria's body appreciatively. "She's cute, Cottom. Where did you find her?"

Garret had stayed perfectly composed since the shewolf arrived, as if her nakedness had no impact on him. "Believe it or not, she found me."

"Ah, it's his scent." Kiera grinned to Aria as if the girls might agree on something. "Deliciously strong, is it not?"

"Oh, yeah," Aria said a bit too sarcastically, amused at the thought of being lured by Garret's... scent. Well, they *were* dogs like he said. "Sexy."

Garret's lips twitched upward briefly. "Well, I'll leave you to it. Aria. Lady Keira." He tipped his head before turning away and disappearing behind one of the stairway doors.

"You don't like him?" Keira suddenly asked when Garret was out of earshot.

Aria widened her eyes, not expecting that comment. "He's... fine."

Keira narrowed her eyes. "Yeah, he *is* only a Delta," she mused. "I mean, he used to be a Beta, the Alpha's first in command, but he made a bad deal with some demons and got demoted."

She wondered if that was why Garret seemed to loathe all demons outside of his 'alliance'. Aria suddenly realized she liked this Keira with a big mouth. *Keep speaking, wolf-girl.*

"Anyway," she continued, "I hope you weren't put off by my flirting with him. I do it simply to screw with the males. Let us go."

Keira leapt, *turning* mid-way in the air, and headed for a different stairway behind the reception, dashing up the stairs.

Aria hurried to keep up.

"Is that good for the baby?" Aria huffed out of breath at the top of the stairs after Keira shifted back into human form.

"What? *Turning*?" she shrugged, heading down the hallway on the second floor. "Technically, it is better to stay

136

in wolf form, but no, changing does not affect my little wolf." They turned down another hallway and Aria noticed more pregnant women milling about or resting inside rooms with their doors open. None of them were naked like Keira and it suddenly made sense what she meant about screwing with the males.

"This is where the shewolves stay."

Aria looked inside a room. There were two infants sleeping in a crib. "Huh?" She looked at Keira. "Why is everyone pregnant?"

"It is a part of our new alliance with the demons. It's really too bad you missed it. Silas is *so* hot."

Aria nodded, wondering who the hell Silas was and what he had to do with the demon alliance, and everyone being pregnant.

"He's the demon you've allied with?"

"*We* allied with," she corrected. "And yes. Here's your room."

Aria abruptly stopped in front of an empty room with a single bed and private bathroom. It appeared clean, just older, as if the high days of the hotel were in the eighties. Dark green carpet. A mud brown comforter and cream sheets. A vintage photo of Venice Beach adjacent to the large window covered by sheer curtains.

"Feel free to look around some and get settled. Our Alpha wants to meet you in twenty minutes."

Aria shut the door carefully, and took a deep breath before rushing into the bathroom, closing and locking the door, then turning on the shower.

She pulled her cellphone out of her bra and called Asher.

"Babe," he breathed in relief, "You're okay?"

"Yes," she whispered. "I don't have long, I'm about to meet the Alpha."

"That's Nadia Burke," Asher said, reminding her of the shewolf Tristian had made the deal with.

"*That's* their Alpha? I remember her. Oh God, what if she

remembers me?"

"I think you have enough information. Get out of there."

"I barely have anything!" she whisper-hissed. "All I know is that they really hate demons not a part of their alliance with some guy named Silas Planto. *And* the women are all pregnant and being used for some revenge." The line was silent for a moment. "…Babe?"

"Get out of there. *Now.*"

"What?"

"Place the device and get out."

"I did, in Garret's car," she said, remembering the tiny microphone and GPS chip that cost a small fortune placed under the seat. "Why?"

"Silas is Gerion!"

Aria was up and shoving her phone in her bra in seconds. She closed the bathroom door with the water on, hoping whoever came in looking for her would think she was showering.

She hurried to the window. A couple floors couldn't be that hard to climb down. She had snuck out her second story window countless times in high school.

She yanked the curtains aside and balked at the wooden boards nailed across the length of the pane from the inside.

Aria grabbed the edge of one and tried to pry it off the wall without success. After a few more attempts she turned on her heel and faced the door. She was going to have to walk out of here.

She cracked open the door to her room and peeked out for any signs of Keira. When she didn't see the shewolf or really anyone, Aria decided to play it casually.

Channeling the Black Widow. You're a badass. You own this place.

Aria made it to the stairs fairly easily and started down. She was wondering how she'd make it past the guard in the lobby when she passed the first floor door. She stopped and looked over at the door before peering through the crisscrossed glass panel to see Garret talking to some guy with chocolate skin and blonde dreads.

He was her ticket out.

She closed her eyes for a moment, shoving away any doubt, and opened the door.

A light reflected off the door as it opened and Garret conveniently looked over. Aria quickly signaled for him to come with a single, spastic finger before closing the door again. She took another angst filled breath. So much for cool and calm.

She watched as Garret dismissed his friend and headed to the stairwell. He pushed the door open and found her leaning against the wall.

"I feel like we're having deja vu, or is it just me?" he smiled coyly.

Oh dear, he thinks I want to sneak around with him. Time to break his heart.

"You can drop the smile, Cottom. I need your help getting out of here."

His smile did disappear then. "I told you, once you arrived, that was it. You're in the pack, otherwise you fight your way out."

"I'm not a damn werewolf!" she hissed.

Garret froze. "…what?"

"*Yeah.* I only needed you to think I was to get in here but I'm just here for information."

His mouth curled and his teeth snapped like a wolf. "*What?*"

"Oh," Aria gasped. She backed up when he took a step toward her.

"I'm going to tear my teeth into that pretty little neck of yours while I take you to my Alpha. She'll reward me while she deals with you. Perhaps, she'll turn you, although, I believe that to be too merciful."

He advanced more as her back hit the wall. Aria threw up her hands in surrender. "Bringing me to your alpha has to be the worst idea!"

"For you," he barked.

"For you!"

Black Widow. Black Widow. Black Widow.

Aria ripped her hands down and met him, eye to eye. "Don't you dare forget, you were demoted for screwing up during the deal with Tristian. Now, what is your Alpha going to think when she hears that you brought in a demon spy. That you didn't even test me first! You're in just as much shit as I am, if not worse."

Garret bared his teeth before backing away.

"You are going to get me out of here," she said, shakily but strong. "And then you're going to forget me."

"And then what?" Garret growled. "I'm just supposed to forget that you know where we are and about the alliance?"

"Yes."

Garret suddenly laughed.

Aria continued, "You're going to forget everything, because of Dylan. Because I'm doing this for our friend."

"And what if I don't care about her anymore?"

"You have to," Aria said, evidently. "Once Gerion gets ahold of her, she'll be destroyed. And that's all he wants. To ruin her... to own her."

"We're not helping him get Dylan, we're helping him get Elon."

Aria stared at him, feeling tears well up in her eyes. How could he not see this?

"Elon is Dylan, you big idiot! Of course, you're helping him get her. You need to put a stop to this. Goddammit, Garret, remember what she was to you!"

"She's nothing to me," he husked.

Aria couldn't contain her gasp. This was coming from a guy who was fighting Tristian over her less than a year ago?

"How can you say that?"

A door slammed above them and they both momentarily froze when Kiera's voice echoed with another shewolf.

Garret suddenly grabbed Aria's arm and growled, "Fine. I'll get you out. But for your sake, disappear… because she'll find you and I won't be around to intervene then."

CHAPTER 9

*"And into the forest I go,
to lose my mind and find my soul."*
Anonymous

DYLAN stared at herself in the mirror in her efficient en-suit bathroom. Pale hair, straight, evenly grazing her shoulders. Faded teal eyes, captivating, yet still painful and hard to look at. Her tiny frame now layered with smooth muscle. An expression harder and more distant than she ever thought possible etched across her face. All and all she was still the same. She didn't feel older, or like a demon. She wondered if anyone actually felt like an adult, or if it was all a big hoax. Everyone just faking it to get by.

It was Temperance's twenty-fourth birthday and one year before her turning age. For some reason, she thought she would somehow be… different. Ever since she was a young girl, she imaged twenty-four as an age of independence. A time of careers, relationships, and adulthood.

She cocked her head to the side and assessed her features once more.

"Happy birthday," she muttered with a sigh.

Picking up her toothbrush, she squirted a glob of toothpaste and began brushing her teeth. A dark shape moved behind her in a slump before positioning himself next to her and proceeded to take a leak. Her head lolled over and she glared.

"Reawy?" she mumbled around her tooth brush.

142

"Yes, really," Soren grunted, discreetly pulling himself back together.

His face was still puffy with sleep and his hair was a perfect mess of tangles. He stepped next to her and snatched her toothbrush right out of her mouth and stuck it in his. She grimaced, just staring as he brushed his teeth.

Was this really her new normal?

He popped it out of his mouth a few seconds later, spat, and pushed it back through her lips, leaving it there to dangle.

He bared his clean teeth with its crooked incisor at the mirror. "Don't forget, you need to be at the gym in thirty," he said nonchalantly as he walked out of the bathroom in all his tattooed grandeur.

She quickly pulled the toothbrush out and shook her head, washing it off in the sink with her thumb. He didn't even wash his hands. Gross.

"You know, most people have boundaries because of a little thing called germs!" she called out to him, dashing out of her room and running smack dab into Ian and Augusto.

"Oh! Sorry!" she laughed.

"Not a problem," Ian smirked. "But I do have a question."

"Shoot."

"Are you planning on training in that today? And if so, can I watch?" He leered down at her as her eyes saucered. She had been so preoccupied with thoughts of her birthday that she had completely forgotten that all she was wearing was a towel.

Augusto sighed with annoyance, crossing his boulder trim arms. Dylan immediately scrambled back inside her room and shut the door.

"I have another question," she heard Ian say through the door.

"Go. Away."

"Would you care if I switched places with Soren tonight?

You know, if it helps, I could always shave the side of my head—"

Dylan flung open the door with a scowl which prompted him to jump then flee down the hall laughing.

Yes, apparently this was her new normal, but it wasn't so bad. It had taken a while, but the others finally accepted her as a trainee into their exclusive crew. She wasn't a hard ass by a long shot. She still craved Tristian's small touches in her dreams, but sleep wasn't as fearful next to Soren... as much as she still hated to admit it.

Life was almost... good.

After the second night of sleeping together completely nightmare free, Soren just started showing up every night around midnight. He would always stop her from pacing, pull her to bed and lay completely still next to her until a blissful and uninterrupted sleep overcame her.

They never talked about it or acknowledged it. The others knew and mostly thought they were screwing no matter how many times she denied it. What she had with Soren was an unspoken understanding.

A deal.

Dylan wasn't sure when it exactly happened but, at some point he had become the only demon she trusted with her life. He didn't seem to want anything in return besides her devotion to the crew, and for that, he gladly posed as her living dream catcher and withstood her tiny bed.

Only one more year and she would be at her re-trial, swearing in, free to leave but bound by blood to an army. She would finally be a part of the Shadow Horde. Or, at least, those were the promises from Kings Zirk and Damen.

"Hey," Dylan greeted Astrid who was practicing upper cuts and kicks on a punching bag. Astrid waved back with a tight smile, quickly getting back to work. Dylan passed a smirking Ian, and as she did, she shoved him; then nodded to Augusto, who stoically nodded back.

She continued across the nearly empty gym, because of

the festivities taking place amongst the streets in celebration of the Day of Mourning, and hesitantly stepped into the glass room to join Soren. Usually the room was devoid of equipment, but today there was a large porcelain crucible in the center and three targets set up to her far left.

Ever since the night Soren had scared her with his powers, she avoided the room whenever possible. It was the only room where demons were allowed to practice their powers, at will, outside of battle. Well, all demons but her. She was still bound by the electrum wire at her throat.

The sliding doors whooshed shut behind her and the glass instantly fogged over to keep anyone from seeing inside. The air thickened as a memory surfaced of the last time she stood in this very spot. She took a steady breath and shoved the feeling back down and locked it away.

Soren looked up from the control panel he was messing with and acknowledged her with a nod.

"You're two minutes late."

He set the control panel back on the wall and walked toward her. His stride was commanding and intimidating. The old Dylan probably would have blushed and backed up, but today she only planted her feet. He stopped just in front of her, causing her to crane her head back to look him in the eye.

"How can I be late when my watch says two minutes early?" She showed him her Hello Kitty watch that Ian had brought her from a mission in Russia. She usually wasn't into the brand but the fact that it wasn't black had her wearing it.

"Simple. It's wrong."

She narrowed her gaze at him. Sometimes it was like his eyes smiled at her in total contradiction to his set jaw. It was the closest expression she would ever get to a smile when he wasn't tormenting her. The problem was she liked this side of him that made her heart beat a bit faster.

"Maybe." Dylan knit her brows as she walked around

145

him to the large porcelain bowl before peering into it. There was a bed of black rocks at the bottom.

"What are you demonstrating today?" she asked. The bowl between them felt like a fence keeping her safe from the blood thirsty predator. "I'm not going to lie, it looks pretty interesting."

His expression turned skeptical.

"What?" Dylan wondered aloud.

He kept his eyes on hers and stepped around the bowl. Dylan found herself gripping the lip of the crucible until her fingers turned white.

Soren cocked his head as he rounded it. It should have come off as playful, but his expression didn't change. Her stomach knotted on the verge of panicking. What was he going to do? She forced herself to let go of the bowl only to lift her fingers to her mouth. He snatched them as he eyed the dried blood staining her chewed fingernails.

"I've been eating every day... I swear." She blushed instinctively. What was *wrong* with her?

It's only the damn room, she chided herself.

In the days leading up to her birthday, she had felt anxiety needling into her mind and planting itself deeply into her veins. It was hard not to listen to the gossip surrounding the Day of Mourning. The stories. The details. The conspiracies. It only reminded her of how the worlds still hated her. She had been here for nearly three years and still no one trusted her.

"I know," he said, rubbing his thumb across her torn nails, distractedly. He focused back on her eyes. "I have a gift for you."

"Oh?" She swallowed and slowly pulled her hand out of his grasp only to grip the bowl again.

He pulled out a small leather sheath from the back pocket of his uniform. She recognized it immediately as one of Soren's beloved daggers. One he carried around everywhere he went that wasn't a *Daleon*. She felt her lips shift a fraction upward. Only in the demon world would knives make appropriate gifts.

"We need to start working on your powers. And that's what we'll be doing today." He unsheathed the blade and used it to motion for her to step closer. "Come."

She took a step closer, reluctantly releasing the bowl.

He raised his hands to her neck. She flinched as his short nails wedged beneath her *Binding*, releasing a tiny shock.

"You won't be needing this anymore."

Dylan took a deep breath, trying to process that this was even happening. Despite King Zirk's never-ending promises, Dylan had resigned herself with the idea of living with it forever.

"This is okay…?"

Soren looked into her eyes as he quirked an eyebrow that said, *do you really think I'd be doing this if it wasn't?*

She shook her head, not sure why she was even arguing about her own freedom. "Never mind, continue."

She wrapped her hands around her hair and tilted her head to one side, exposing her throat.

He cupped her nape and focused back on the wire.

The moment felt frozen in time as she watched the strain in his jaw and the vicious throb of his jugular vein under a fine layer of stubble as he carefully pried the *Binding* off her skin. She pursed her lips at every flash of pain, imagining he had to dig the thread out of her flesh.

"Hmm," Soren groaned, his expression growing darker with each careful yank. "Maybe we should have a Medic do this."

Dylan took another deep breath and shook her head. She wanted it off. She wanted the damn thing in the trash!

"Suit yourself." Soren continued to peel it back. It was like removing several deep stitches.

He swallowed every time she winced, bobbing his Adam's apple. He finally placed the dagger underneath the thread and pulled. Soren stopped. His stare focused hauntingly on her aching neck.

She glanced up at him afraid to ask what was wrong in case he had changed his mind about freeing her. Perhaps, he was second guessing himself. The act of unleashing Temperance Elementa had to be the equivalent to untying a lion. He'd raised her from the feral cub, trained the wild out of her blood (or at least hoped he had) and now this was the test. But, no matter how much he trusted her, he had never known her true capabilities. Hell, she didn't even know her true capabilities.

Soren's eyes hardened as he dragged a finger over a bare spot; and by the sudden sting, she knew it was an open wound.

"Have you—"

The door suddenly slid open and the shock at seeing a King momentarily paralyzed her. Forgetting about her *Binding*, Dylan bowed along with Soren.

King Damen, clothed in his golden robe, entered the room.

"Leave us," her Uncle said.

Dylan immediately started to move up until she realized he meant for Soren to leave.

"Give it to me, Verbeck," the King said, holding out his hand as Soren passed. Soren stopped, tipped his head down and held up the thin, bloody rope of her *Binding*. Dylan was surprised to see roots connected to it, like the rope had been alive and growing inside of her.

Her eyes widened and her fingers flung to her neck. She gasped when she touched raw flesh but the wire wasn't there! A small laugh bubbled up from her throat and tears pooled in her eyes.

She was *free*. Holy crap!

She looked for Soren, wanting to share this moment with him, but he was already gone. The doors sliding shut.

King Damen examined the *Binding* with an unreadable expression before pocketing it.

"You may stand," King Damen's sharp voice brought her back to the moment, remembering there was a true family member—no, a King, standing near her.

He unwrapped his golden robe and hung the delicate fabric on a translucent coat hook by the doors. He was wearing dark blue dress pants and a simple white crew neck underneath. He looked at her and tilted his head as if to study her. "Well?"

"Oh," Dylan fumbled around her words unable to stop looking at him. "My Master," she mumbled and stood. He was wearing such simple—*normal* clothes that she felt oddly perplexed. She wasn't exactly sure what she expected... a fine suit?

She closed her mouth unsure of what to say... or do. It wasn't such a secret that he loathed her as much at the worlds did. What in the world was he even doing here alone? Was he not afraid of her?

He crossed the room and pulled out another ball of wire from his pants pocket. Dylan stilled as he untwisted it, revealing reading glasses.

She released her caught breath. For a moment, she thought he was going to *Bind* her all over again.

He perched the glasses on the tip of his nose and punched in a series of codes on the console next to the giant bowl.

"Age is funny thing. Is it not, Ms. Elementa?" It took a while for Dylan to register that he was talking to her. "Usually it is in reference to humans who grow old and die rather quickly. Beings who are subjected to death in contrast to divinity. But are we divine beings?" he glanced at her over the rim of his glasses. "Mortal or Immortal? Do we not age and die? You might say no, looking at our faces." He frowned, focusing back on the panel, "But, we do. Perhaps, not in the same way you are used to seeing in the human world. Though, I have found my eyes less focused and know others, too, have lost the luster of their powers after hundreds, or even thousands, of years."

He finally closed the panel and the lights in the room shifted to focus on the targets. He looked at her. "I noticed you eyeing my glasses."

"Oh," Dylan stammered. "I apologize, My Master."

"There's no need for apologies. But, it *is* important to understand the importance of age. The moment we are born, the peak of prowess, even the particular age your parents are when you were conceived may make an impact on offspring. Temperance, I'm telling you this because soon you too will be at a major milestone in your life. And, depending on how well you control your abilities over the next year, it will determine how bright your future may be."

"My future?"

"I do hope," King Damen continued as if she hadn't spoken, "you'll prove that my hesitations are purely spiteful and not of good reason."

King Damen uncrossed his arms and held up a hand. A spark flared with the snap of his fingers. A drop of fire now hovering close to his thumb and index finger.

Dylan froze. The fire… it had just come out of him. He had created it instead of only manipulating it.

She began racking her mind for the information she read about his powers. *PyroVentus*… Fire and air. *CoCreator*… Did that mean he could make fire? …could she?

"From now on you will have different teachers all specializing in a single subject, each grading one of your particular skills." The small flame slid and wove through his fingers before he flicked it into the giant porcelain bowl. It erupted into thick flames.

Startled, Dylan took a sharp step back. "Today's lesson is fire …If you hadn't already guessed."

She realized she didn't want to get any closer, not sure what she was more afraid of… the fire or her steely Uncle.

"You have permission to speak freely, Ms. Elementa."

She nodded, not exactly trusting him.

"I mean it. I am not your King in here. I am your

teacher." He frowned. "Your Uncle."

"It," she said, trying to ignore the way he seemed put off by the fact he was related to her. "It doesn't hurt?"

King Damen's eyes roamed over her, as if sizing her up. "Tell me, what do you know about your powers?"

"Um," she shook her head, "not much. I have controlled water... a few times. I have been told I have a keenness toward the four elements."

He let out a forceful sigh through his nose. "Sometimes I wonder what your mother was thinking housing you with that weak human family." He turned away just in time to miss her heated glare.

King Damen mumbled into the crucible, "*So much power nearly wasted,*" like he was mocking someone.

"You know, there are not many of us left," he said, surprising her.

"Us?" *Elementas*? she thought, but didn't dare say aloud.

"Pyros. Fire users."

"Oh..." she felt sudden pain and yanked her fingers away from kneading her neck. She idly wondered how deep the wound from her *Binding* was and how bad it looked. She probably did need to see a Medic. "Why?"

"They're usually not strong enough to live. The fire in our veins can be consuming, incinerating the weak before they even get a valid start. A Pyro that lasts out of infancy... well, I don't need to tell you how valuable you are." His eyes scanned her nervous form once more. "All right, come on now. I have a meeting in half an hour." King Damen turned back to the crucible and reached in, scooping out a fire ball the size of his fist.

Dylan forced herself to take a step toward him, then another, until she was close enough to feel the heat of the inferno against her bare arms.

"It shouldn't hurt you," he explained, "You are a Pyro like me. Atticus has the Ventus stronger in his blood."

"If you're so sure..." she said, staring at the licking

flames. She reached out with shaking fingers, unsure of how to grab it, and flipped her palm. She could already see the fire reaching for her as if it had a fingers of its own. *A mind* of its own.

King Damen twitched his wrist and the fire ball leapt from his hand to hers.

Dylan sucked in a breath as her entire body locked up, expecting pain.

But it didn't hurt.

No, if anything it felt... nice. Each lick of the flame like a toasty breath, lapping and caressing her skin. She loosened her breathing.

The sight of her fingers cradling something that had been so deeply ingrained as dangerous sent a series of memories spiraling throughout her brain. Holding a hot pan for too long. Burning herself with a curling iron without leaving a mark. Knocking over a candle and putting out the small fire with her palm.

How had she missed this? How had she missed never burning herself... ever?

King Damen made an odd, choking sound as he observed her take in the new sensation. "As I thought," he said, only looking even more distressed. "Get into position."

"Oh... we're... now?" He looked at her above his glasses and she shook her head at herself, groaning inwardly. Of course, he meant right now. What did she expect?

Moving awkwardly to the center of the room, she shifted her body towards the targets, trying not to drop the fire yet unsure of what to do next. His arm came around from behind and surprised her, causing her to fumble the fire. Thankfully, it seemed to cling to her.

King Damen waited for her to relax before continuing to lift and contort her hand until her fingers formed a fist in the air. The fire seemed to shrink and disappear. The throbbing beat of life against her palm was the only indication it still existed.

"On the count of three, aim and flick your wrist like this."
He rotated his hand next to hers and pantomimed the action.

She took a deep breath as he began counting just above
her head.

"One."

She aimed at the middle and closest target.

"Two."

He drew his arm away.

"Three."

She snapped her wrist just as he'd shown her and
simultaneously opened her palm... sending the ball of fire
flying, rocketing and blasting against the far wall.

Wow. Dylan gawked at the singed mark on the otherwise
pristine wall before turning to King Damen with a barely
suppressed smile. "*Wow*," she said aloud.

"Try it again."

Dylan blinked at his dismissive tone.

"What did you mean, '*as you thought,*' when you gave
me the fire?"

King Damen seemed to ignore the question as he scooped
another fire ball out. She stepped closer to him.

"Did you not know I was more of a Pyro than a Ventus
like my father?"

He scowled at the fire before glancing at something on
her shoulder. She gazed down at her bare shoulder; at the
small scars from the worm, her tattoo of the Collector's
crest, and a flat red mole... there wasn't much to be
fascinated about. Maybe the scars were too much of a
reminder that she'd been through Hell already?

King Damen thrusted another fire ball at her and she took
it. Imagining it as some kind of tangible ball helped her
better control it. She pivoted toward the targets, resigning
that her question would probably go unanswered.

"Lucky guess," he finally said.

Her aim faltered.

"*Guess*?" She craned her neck to look at him.

153

"Well, you'd either catch the fire ball or it would burn you. A fifty-fifty shot at best. Relax." He waved a dismissive hand in the air. "I was right."

She shook her head with a grimace and repositioned her aim.

A damn fifty-fifty shot.

She fired, and the ball exploded against the edge of the closest target.

Forgetting all about his blatant lack of regard for her well-being, she jumped with a controlled excitement.

He handed her another. "Put more swing into it." She shifted her body and looked at him. King Damen nodded that her position was good. She threw herself into it, hitting the first ring. *Yes!*

"Please don't take this the wrong way, but… why are you teaching me and not another Pyro?" She glanced back at him, schooling her features. "Or is it normal for a King to train a soldier?" She didn't think it was. Maybe powers were best learned from family?

"We draft the few Pyros alive into the army. Quite stubborn and arrogant bunch you are, and still no one willing to get close to you."

Dylan looked away, feeling the heavy uneasiness of doubt pour back into her heart. It was easy to think she fit in when the only demons speaking to her were being forced to be nice to her. She pulled her hand away from her mouth when she realized she had torn another nail to the quick.

"You need to work on your reputation if you want to win the vote for acceptance."

Wait, a vote? Dylan had thought the Kings decided those who entered the army, not the populous.

King Damen tsked as he ambled closer, handing her another fire ball. He looked down at her intensely. "For what will the worlds think of a delinquent girl who after three years hasn't even grasped the approval of her fellow peers?" He stepped closer and hissed, "Prove me wrong,

Temperance. Prove to me you are more. Because if I am not convinced of your loyalty, no one will be."

She aimed at the targets feeling anger shoot through her veins and spurn the fire hotter. She released the fireball, letting it slam into the far left target center. She took a deep breath.

"*Good.* Finding a way to control your anger and translate it into your powers is the only way to survive and thrive," he praised, patting her on the shoulder.

After a few more critiques on her form, King Damen slipped on his robe and left her to practice alone.

She couldn't stop thinking about all that he had told her. Despite being viewed as an Elementa who still evoked hatred, her Uncle saw refined strength underneath it all and not just because of her powers. *She* was strong. And this, Dylan took to heart.

An hour passed by and she found herself not wanting to leave even though King Damen urged her not to stay beyond an hour.

She grasped the edges of the crucible for one last fire ball, staring inside and wondering what it would feel like to immerse herself in the deadly heat. What it would feel like to test her powers on the fire. Could she manipulate it like she had with water? What would happen if she did? Then again, it had been so long since she last used her *Unda.* What if she couldn't even remember how to use it? A lick of orange reached up as she brought her hands out above the heat, palms face-down. She felt prickles of energy course all over her skin like a tiny shocks of electricity. She wasn't sure if it was from her desire to break the rules or her senses picking up because of her powers' hunger to break free after so many years of being restrained.

With a deep breath, Dylan tapped into that dark place in her mind. The place where her emotions rooted and pain sprouted. The place she held the miserable, bitter, and

155

dejected parts of her past. The place she suppressed the years she was abused and broken. This place was where she would unlock her *Unda*.

She hated this place.

It was an easy place to ignore when she had Tristian or Silas encouraging her forward while promising happiness. By herself, it was agony. She had to kick and shove through memories of slut-shaming and unwanted touching. Memories of hate and difficulties. Memories of loneliness and hurt. Memories she wished to forget. But the longer she fought and searched for that part of herself the more she wanted to give up and fall into the crucible—never to surface again.

Dylan gritted her teeth as tears rushed down her face. She didn't want to feel anymore. Her parents' screams during their car crash. Tristian's gasp and gurgle as Silas stabbed him. The nauseating pain as she tried to end her life with a kitchen knife. The sharp release from the razor blade against her flesh.

She searched harder inside the terrible pit of emotion until it grew slowly tolerable, until she felt… weightless.

Dylan opened her eyes and stared deeply into the roaring fire. It had somehow crawled out of the crucible and tangled around her arms and chest while she had conjured her *Unda*. She lifted it in her arms and slowly held it out in front of her. Fingers of fire screaming for her warmth.

Dylan then tried to contain the heat by balling her fists like she had with the fire balls from earlier, but it didn't seem to want to cooperate. There was too much.

Crap, she thought, peering into the empty bowl and contemplating setting it back down and leaving as expected. She wasn't so sure what she could do with it anyway.

She flicked her eyes left to the targets and suddenly had a better idea.

"Here goes nothing," she whispered before heaving the ball of flames with everything she had to offer.

The middle target exploded.

Shattered bits crumbled into a fiery heap on the floor and black smoke billowed up, filling the room with a thick fog.

"Wow," she whispered, still staring at the destruction.

I want to do that again!

The doors whooshed open as the Horde tumbled into the room, each holding a weapon.

"Everything okay?" Augusto's authoritative voice boomed.

"What happened?" Astrid said at the same time.

"*Whoa*," Ian choked, waving the smoke away from his face. He wasn't staring at the remains but at Dylan.

Soren was already voicing commands to the control panel. Canisters dropped from the ceiling and released a blanket of white sludge, smothering the flames and smoke.

Dylan looked down at herself. She sucked in a breath, quickly throwing her arms up and over her chest barely covered by minuscule scraps of cloth. She may have been fire proof but her clothes apparently were not!

"Practice is over," Soren snapped, shoving past her to leave the room again.

"Wait!" Dylan yelped. He halted but didn't turn. She wasn't sure what she wanted from him. To acknowledge her power? To give her a hearty pat on the back?

"Perhaps, next time you'll refrain from destroying the targets *and* your clothes."

Her teeth clashed together as she restrained herself from making an inhuman growl. Why did she crave his approval so much?

The others were quick to move out of Soren's way as he exited. Dylan looked back to the crucible. At the dying heat feasting on lumpy coals. She sighed.

Happy birthday to me.

"So... I'm not sure about you two," Ian said, pointing to Astrid and Augusto. "But I would like to see a giant fire ball demolish some shit. But you know, that could just be me."

He shrugged.

Astrid snorted and shook her head before walking up to Dylan. "I mean, I know it's been a while since someone damaged the targets. And just so you know, no know has ever *demolished* them." She quirked an eyebrow and smiled. "But don't listen to Soren. He's just pissed he can't do that."

Dylan wished that was the case. But she knew Soren couldn't have cared less about her fire power. He was pissed about something else. She just wasn't sure what.

Astrid unzipped her jacket and handed it to Dylan, before moving to the control panel and showed Dylan where to press for new targets. As she did, a door opened and the debris disappeared somewhere beneath leaving a brand new target.

"You don't have to stop practicing, but please don't forget to stop for food or *Essence*." She patted Dylan on the shoulder and walked out with Augusto. "Oh, almost forgot," she turned around, not stopping. "Happy birthday. Glad to see you're not murdering us all without your *Binding* on."

Dylan smiled just as the door whooshed shut. She noticed Ian hanging back, his tongue thumbing the inside of his cheek.

"What?" He crossed his arms. "I wasn't kidding. I want to watch some fire balls."

"Fine." She pointed at him. "But only if you teach me how to manipulate wind like you do." She wasn't sure when that lesson would come up and she'd rather study up before hand, minimizing the chance of looking like an idiot in front of whoever the teacher might be.

"Deal... Uh," he looked around, "should I move somewhere...?"

"Somewhere... safe? I can defog the walls and you can watch from outside if you're scared," she said wryly.

"Nah, just try not to kill me. I'd like to live until at least eighty."

The statement almost made her laugh. "You and most of

humanity," she mumbled to herself.

For the rest of the morning, she practiced with Ian who surprisingly helped her control the fire balls with more precision and speed. She could now shoot handfuls of fire quickly and efficiently, almost always hitting the targets.

She wanted to keep training with him but he persuaded her to go grab lunch in the cafeteria. Before they walked out, he handed her the last target she practiced on. It was incredibly heavy and took both hands and a bit of *Unda* to hold. Ian went on to tell her how it was crafted out of a local tree—magical and mostly resistant to the elements. Black singes marked her hits on and around the bullseye.

After placing the target in her room and meeting with the Medic to tend to her neck, she met the Horde in the cafeteria. She grabbed a muffin, coffee, and under Ian's advice, a vial of Essence.

She was thankful the vial wasn't marked with some sort of label like: "Evil Souls" or "*The Innocent*." Not that she thought they were above naming it something awful like "Consume thy unborn!" because she was still on the fence about it all and it helped to just not think about it among other things.

Dylan walked up to the rectangular table that held the Horde sans Soren. She couldn't deny she was a little happy that he wasn't here. She was starting to enjoy her day and he only seemed dead set on ruining it.

Sitting down, Ian relayed her "humungo fire balls" to the rest of them, earning a few impressed responses.

Astrid turned to Dylan. "So, how does it feel?" she asked before shoving a bite of eggs into her mouth.

"How does what feel?"

"No *Binding*, fire balls… come on… the list is endless."

"Good… weird. I'm just trying not to break everything."

"I think we all can relate. After Augusto turned, Ian kept coming up behind him yelling "HULK SMASH!" I really thought the idiot was going to die that day." She stuck her

159

tongue out at Ian and he flicked a spoonful of pasta at her. "Then again you were only, like what, nine?"

"And even then I whipped your ass," Ian said mischievously. "Go figure."

"I'm kidding. I don't really feel any different. Well," Dylan scrunched her nose, "I guess, I feel stronger?"

"I could see that," Ian said, nodding his head thoughtfully. "That *Binding* wasn't exactly allowing growth, you know?" He shoved another bite of egg into his mouth.

Everyone moved on to a different subject while Dylan tuned them out to inhale her Essence. Doing it in public was difficult and required concentration.

She closed her eyes for a brief moment as the life slipped down her throat and entered her veins. It still felt amazing but she figured moaning in public might be frowned upon. So as often as she could she worked on her control.

Everything was still saturated in vivid color and her extremities still shook with sparkling tingles as she picked up her coffee cup. She stared at it trying to work herself up to drink it. Ingesting anything other than Essence was the last thing her body wanted. She forced the first few sips down her throat before a ravishing thirst overcame her, as if her stomach had been suppressing hunger for *Essence*. It was always easy after that first sip, almost like she was human again.

"Where's Soren," Ian asked, grabbing Dylan's attention. She may not have wanted to see him at the moment but it didn't mean she wasn't curious as to why he wasn't here.

"He left for home early," Augusto answered.

"Home?" Dylan asked. She thought for sure he lived here like her.

"His parent's house. He usually goes home for the evenings but is back by nightfall."

"Oh." She nodded, bringing her coffee back up to her lips, trying to mask her frown. She forgot, from time to time, how little she knew him. Even if it had been years since they met, Soren was still a mystery to her and probably everyone else.

"When he gets back," Astrid jumped in, "You guys wanna go out tonight? For Temperance's birthday."

Dylan was already shaking her head no.

"*Aw,* why?" Astrid whined

"Yeah, come on. It'll be fun," Ian added. "You haven't been out in years… literally."

"Am I even allowed to leave?" Dylan asked.

"You've been cleared as of this morning," Augusto said sharply. "As long as you're with one of us."

"There's a bar down the street. Barely any Tainted. It'll be fun. Promise."

Tainted or not, at least it wasn't a club.

"I guess." She polished off her coffee before setting her eyes on the muffin. "What time?"

"Nine. I'll come find you a bit before. Do you have anything to wear?"

Dylan looked down at her black tank and yoga pants. She had acquired more clothes in the past couple years but nothing more than gym attire. "I have… leggings."

"You can borrow something of mine," Astrid said. "We're pretty much the same size."

CHAPTER 10

"Oh my darling, it's true.
Beautiful things have dents and scratches too."
writtenbyhim

LATER that night, Dylan sat cross-legged on her bed reading a non-fiction novel about a retired Shadow Horde soldier and his life in the Horde. Soren had been quite adamant that she read it but it was hard to imagine it as anything other than fantasy.

She rolled her eyes as the solider bragged about, yet, another kill. Honestly, what was she supposed to learn from this? How to inflate your ego?

A loud knock banged on her door. Dylan dog-eared the page and got up to open the door, half expecting Soren to be on the other side.

"Oh, hey."

"Uck, don't sound so excited." Astrid barged in wearing a navy bandage dress with cut outs on the side and a black leather jacket. Her eyes were lined in several layers of coal and her chocolaty hair was donning pastel pink highlights. "Who were you expecting? A Seiren?"

"You mean Siren?"

"No! Seiren: A male Siren... A stripper! I thought all you did was study all day. Why don't you know this?"

Dylan just shrugged, seriously doubting the history of male strippers would be listed among battle histories and fighting tactics.

162

"Although, I wouldn't be against getting one if you're in," Astrid added while perusing Dylan's things, lifting notebooks and peeking out the window with a frown... almost as if she were looking for something and coming up empty. She then did a quick scan of the blank white walls, probably thinking Dylan was some kind of psychopath.

Dylan stood next to the open door with her arms crossed, watching as Astrid poked around. She felt like she should stop her but couldn't find the strength to care. It wasn't like anything in the room was really hers. She had Tristian's necklace and her Elementa ring secured around her neck. Nothing else mattered.

Astrid flopped on her bed and started reading the back of Dylan's novel. Her lack of boundaries wasn't what had Dylan's sudden undivided attention; no, it was the small, plumb-purple *thing* she had tossed on the bed next to her.

"*No*," Dylan stated while vigorously shaking her head.

Astrid stopped mid-flip of the novel and lifted an eyebrow. "It was a joke. I didn't expect you to want a stripper."

"What? No. I'll just wear this." Dylan motioned to her tank and leggings.

Astrid glanced down at the purple mini she had brought. "Oh, shut up, Temperance!" Astrid tossed the book aside and jumped up, pushing the tiny fabric into Dylan's unwilling arms.

Dylan screwed up her face, not really wanting to go anymore.

Astrid laughed. "Fine! Wear your damn leggings, but the dress too, okay? I don't want to be the only one dressed up. I don't get many occasions to, as you can imagine."

"I'm wearing my jacket, too," she added crossing her arms.

"It's your birthday, nun."

Dylan got dressed in the little tube dress over her leggings with a pair of combat boots, while Astrid went back to flipping the rest of the way through the book and probably snooping some more. She stepped out of the bathroom as Astrid was touching up her makeup and looking like she enjoyed it too much to have the job she did.

"Why did you join?"

Astrid glanced at her, "The Horde?"

"Yeah."

"Well, it wasn't like I joined out of the blue. My specialty caught the Kings' interest after several trials."

"Trials?"

"Yeah, for growing and selling illegal herbs." She smirked. "I used to own my own nursery."

Dylan lifted her bows. *Like pot?*

"What? Can I not like plants?" Astrid closed the lid on the tube of her rose lipstick and chucked it back into her leather clutch. "It is known the Terra's have dealings with black magic but I changed the business and our reputation. My herbs were mainly for sustenance and that angered the OP. If you can't control it, can't kill it… you might as well work with it, right?"

"Wait… you were growing something equivalent to souls?"

Astrid smiled. "Yup!"

"Why would you need to find an alternative if everyone could just go out and collect?"

"Too many demons can't afford to buy government Essence. You don't know but only the extremely wealthy can afford not to collect. And most of the poor cannot afford to leave their families or their businesses. The people had a problem. I fixed it. Well, only for half a century or so, before the OP finally proved what I was doing."

"The Horde is your punishment?"

She smirked. "No. I was sentenced to the army. I was noticed by your Uncle during a fight. They asked, I assented." She shrugged. "King Zirk gave me a plot of green space on campus as a reward. Have you seen the Thorn

164

Gardens?"

Dylan shook her head. "Was it enough?"

The question seemed to catch her off guard. "I— It didn't matter what I wanted. I couldn't refuse the gift of a King… Not with the alternative."

It suddenly made sense to her why Astrid felt so strongly in the beginning about her becoming a part of the Horde. Astrid didn't want to lose her spot, her life. Dylan wondered if the girl still felt that way under all her forced charm.

"You must have gotten in a lot of fights to catch King Damen's attention." Dylan laced up her boots and looked at her. "Somehow I'm not shocked."

Astrid laughed and pointed to the empty spot on Dylan's bed. "Sit. It's your turn."

After some more arguing, Dylan allowed Astrid to draw an edgy, long sweep of eyeliner on her upper lids, mostly because she didn't want to be the one to deprive Astrid of these small girlish moments she seemed to crave.

Dylan hated every second of it. It reminded her too much of Aria. Her heart feeling like it was about to cave in on itself from the pressure of her best friend's memory. So, she steered clear of the mirror and took Astrid's word for it when the other girl told her she looked "*Smokin'*".

Dylan stepped out the side door by the gym. There were about four or five stone steps that lead down to the short rock-lined driveway with four ropy motorcycles parked off of a main road. Several lush maple trees and bushes stood along the left side of the drive and just around them she could see houses… businesses… a woman in a kaftan walking with a baby on her hip.

Dylan's heart kicked up a storm at the sudden air of freedom as she descended the steps. It had been so long that each step felt dangerous, as if she were doing something wrong or against the rules. She really hoped she had the clearance to leave and they weren't screwing with her.

Once they reached the gravel layered drive, they found

165

the rest of the crew standing around the motorcycles. Augusto was the first to see them. His eyes quickly passed over Dylan and landed on Astrid.

Dylan always wondered about their relationship. Sometimes it seemed like they were an item while other times they acted like either best friends or enemies.

Ian jumped off his motorcycle and flattened both palms against his eyes for a long moment just groaning.

"Dammit, Astrid. You had to go and make her hot?"

"She was already hot. I just turned up the flame a bit."

Dylan pushed her fists into her jacket pockets, a bit embarrassed. Her eyes hesitantly found Soren. He stood half on, half off his bike smoking something that smelled like black pepper and cloves. It was the smell she had come to recognize as his specific scent. It hung in the air like a warm blanket.

He wasn't looking at her but at the ground and he seemed even more pissed than before.

Soren glared at Ian. "Shut the hell up. You're making her uncomfortable."

Dylan wanted to snap at him for just assuming she needed saving, even if his assumption was right.

Ian pressed a palm to his chest in mock shock. "I?" He laughed. "I'm making *her* uncomfortable? No, pretty sure she's making *me* uncomfortable." He pulled at his crotch making everyone groan.

"Can we just get out of here already?" Astrid said, straddling an angry looking bike. She somehow got on it without flashing everyone.

"I thought it was just down the road?" Dylan asked, already taking a step backward.

Soren finally looked at her, but only briefly and impassively before getting on his own bike and flicking his cigarette to the ground.

"It is, but I don't want to walk in heels," Astrid said, revving her bike in several short blasts. "Ever ridden on the back of a bike?"

Dylan nodded. "Once." She thought about the ride on Asher's bike: her last weekend of freedom. She bit her lip.

"Well, let's go!" Astrid yelled.

Dylan nodded and walked up to Soren, trying as gracefully as she could to straddle behind him. She was thankful for the leggings, because she wasn't as practiced as Astrid.

Soren didn't acknowledge her or so much as flinch. She guessed it was kind of a given that she'd get on his bike, but not so much as a "*Hey*"?

He revved the engine and waited for her to grab on before taking off.

Soren took the lead as Augusto, Astrid, and Ian followed in synchronized motion. Her fingers gripped Soren's jacket with some restraint as she looked all around at the English style homes. A memory flickered in her mind from the passing houses that she almost forgot she was outside on the back of a bike.

She never realized it was here that she was dreaming of all those years ago when this new life first started. Except, unlike her odd dream of the deserted town and a cracking glass tower, the windows were lit and full of life. Dinners, parties, a couple relaxing, kids playing and then screaming with glee at the sight of the Horde. It was hard to imagine this place as a demon world. It seemed so... normal.

They rounded a corner and picked up speed, her hair blowing wildly in the wind for only a moment before they slowed down to a stop in front of a small building covered in green vines. Two torches illuminated the small arched entrance.

"Traverna!" Astrid squealed, jumping off her bike before everyone else.

The rest of them got off of their bikes but Dylan's hand gripped Soren's thick bicep, stopping him from following his crew.

"I need to talk to you," she said, waiting for everyone to disappear through the small wooden door. A burst of music and loud voices struck the air and dissolved with the shutting door.

Soren stopped and turned unwilling to meet her eyes. He searched his back pockets and brought out another cigarette. He lit it and took a long drag. His narrowed eyes finally meeting hers.

"Then talk."

She felt herself glare a bit at his aloofness. They hadn't been this cold to each other outside of training in a long time.

"Feel like telling me what happened?"

"Don't know what you're talking about," he said, releasing the white smoke from his lungs.

"You scream at me during practice, go MIA for the rest of the day, and now you're acting…"

He glared at her. "I'm no longer your mentor. I don't have to coddle you any longer."

"As if you coddled me," she sneered. "We're friends!"

A chilling laugh busted out of him causing her ears to turn red. "This is who I am. And I am not your friend."

"I don't believe you," she murmured, ripping the cigarette out of his hand. He only watched her as she placed it between her lips and took a puff. The taste wasn't entirely unpleasant but it felt too heavy inside her chest and she quickly let it out, trying not to cough.

"You don't need to prove anything," he sighed, taking the cigarette out of her hand.

"Tell me what happened." She cleared her throat. "You were fine until King Damen showed."

"You're so full of shit." He laughed as something sour twisted his features and looked away, blowing a trail of smoke to her right.

Dylan cut off his laughter by taking the cigarette back. She didn't smoke it this time, only wanting his full attention.

168

"*What*?"

"You can stop pretending like you don't know anything." Soren peeled the cigarette from her fingers before she could crush it with her surmounting anger. "I saw the *Binding*… the roots," he mumbled. He took a long drag and angled his head back to the darkening sky, releasing another trail of smoke.

The roots? What… she suddenly remembered the way the *Binding* had looked alive, like it had grown into her skin. Then she remembered how Soren seemed to shut down just before King Damen arrived. The roots must have grown every time she tried to harness her power.

"Tell me," Soren said, shifting his head down to look her harshly in the eye. "Was it all a manipulation? The helplessness, the vulnerability, the nightmares…"

"No!" she balked. Why did he think she had been lying?

"Whatever, Temperance." She recoiled at the use of her demon name. He hadn't called her Temperance in years. Even though she detested the endearment 'Pet' it was better than calling her an Elementa.

Soren took another drag of his cigarette before flicking it off to the side. "You got what you wanted. You're in line for the Shadow Horde. There's nothing I can do about it now other than accept it. But, it still doesn't mean we need to be friendly outside of the gym." The metal buttons on his leather uniform clicked against the teeth of his zipper as he moved around her towards the bar door.

Dylan's hand was on his arm again, halting him before he could get very far. She heard him sigh.

Before he could rip his arm out of her grasp she whispered, "My name is Dylan." An offering of a dark piece of her soul. "Not Temperance." She looked at where she still held him, the leather supple and soft beneath her fingers. She wanted to let go and let him be. After all, he said it himself; he wasn't her mentor any more. It didn't matter what he thought of her. But, she just… couldn't. Dylan had grown attached to him. They had a special bond without dredging up the past. She understood him and she thought he understood her. Well, maybe it was time he finally did get to know her.

With a heavy breath, she slid her hand down his arm until she was touching the course flesh of his palm. For the first time, she *wanted* him to take what he needed in order to trust her. She needed him to understand everything about her.

Dylan closed her eyes as she continued to slide her fingers between his until she was holding his hand. After a couple of moments, her stomach flipped when she felt his strong hand close around hers.

"Dylan," he said slowly and softly like he was testing the new word on his tongue.

She nodded and finally craned her head to look into his intense eyes. "I hate it when I'm called Temperance because I'm not her. I've never been her."

She could feel a tingling at the base of her neck and her heart picked up speed as she anticipated the pain and heartache, even the little bits of joy in her life. She wondered if he would notice how she looked up to him. Or how many times she wanted to hug him and tell him thank you for saving her when she thought all was lost. Or how she ached for his brief smiles which were like watching a storm clear, revealing blue skies.

Maybe then he would finally see that despite everything, it was because of him that she was even standing here, at a bar, without a *Binding*. It was because of his brash encouragement that she was even given a chance. She knew he didn't hate her anymore. He hadn't hated her in a long time because they were friends. He just didn't want to admit it to himself for reasons unknown to her. Now he was standing here thinking she lied to him and that everything he'd done to help her had only aided her advancement in some sick plan to take over the OP.

He needed to see the truth.

170

Dylan squeezed his hand. "Do it," she challenged him. "I want you to have it all."

A cloud slipped over his eyes when he realized what she was asking of him.

"I may not have been completely forthcoming in the beginning but I've never outright lied to you," Dylan continued. "I don't know why the *Binding* looked like it did. There were only a few times when I intentionally tested it because I had to see what my limits were; but even that was before I started training." She shook her head as she stared at their clasped hands, struggling with the possibility he'd already made up his mind about her.

The door to the bar burst open and they were quick to let go of each other.

Dylan shoved her fists into her jacket pockets, watching a drunk demon stumble out and down the adjacent alleyway until he was out of sight.

"You shouldn't tempt me into your mind," Soren rasped.

"Believe me, I know." She laughed humorlessly. "It isn't exactly a party for me."

Their eyes met. "I might have jumped to conclusions." He moved back a step to sit on the side of his bike. "It's been a shit day."

Dylan perked an eyebrow at his lame apology but shrugged it off, just thankful he didn't take up her offer to leap inside her mind. The way he said "tempted" made it seem more like a desire than a tactic. Then again, weren't they all drawn to their powers like a drug?

"I didn't know you had a family here," Dylan said as casually as she could. Ever since lunch, she had been dying to ask him about it.

His eyes flicked to her. "I never told you, so how would you know?"

"Wouldn't it feel odd if your friend knew everything about you but you knew nothing of them?"

"And I know everything about you?"

"Well, no—"

"Look, I'm not important. Learning the life as a soldier is important."

"Can *you* please cut the shit?" she breathed, tired of all the self-righteous-soldier crap. "Friends, remember?"

He rubbed his mouth, trying to obscure some kind of emotion until she realized it was a smile. "Yeah," he straightened up and chuckled. "*Friends*. I'm fucking friends with an Elementa. How fucked up is that?"

"What did they do to you?" she suddenly asked. Yes, she understood her parents were some horrible evil villains to the OP but what did *they* do to *him*?

"That's not how this works." He started to get up but she was quick to press a palm to his shoulder, stopping him.

"Then tell me how it works, because I'm *trying*. We've known each other for three years and I just found out today you have a family to go home to every day, and… you smoke."

"I didn't think any of that was relevant to training."

"It's relevant when you're sleeping in my bed every night!"

His expression darkened and she felt her pulse gain speed.

"You want to know me?" he asked, but it came out almost as a threat.

She nodded, tentatively.

"Fine. Yeah, I smoke cloves. Have for decades. My family… Well, I had a little brother and a father. They're dead." Dylan winced but continued to listen, knowing he was going for shock value just to end her prying. "A member of your valiant fucking family gutted my little brother, and ripped my dad in two if you need more of a visual. That was a *real* shit day," he taunted. "The anniversary is today, actually. The Day of Mourning."

She felt the hate radiating off him. It finally made since why he hated her name so much.

"So, you know, please forgive me for not divulging that I visit home every day for peace of mind."

"I'm sorry," she said, grabbing his hand and staring down at his fingers dwarfing hers. "I know what it's like to lose family. I wouldn't wish it on anyone. It's like having your heart ripped out. But, mostly, I'm sorry that it was someone I'm related to, that you're forced to shadow and mentor someone that only reminds you of that." She suddenly felt absolute hatred for her mother and father. "*God, I'm so sorry.*"

Silence seeped in between them as he thought about what she had said. After a few moments, Dylan looked up to find him staring at her. Her heart constricted. For the first time since knowing him, she saw sadness settle across his face. She brushed her thumb over his knuckles and he tensed, prompting her to pull away. She shoved her hands back into her pockets.

"Sorry," she mumbled again. Touching him had been an innate reaction to their conversation and she wondered if she had crossed a line.

She suddenly didn't want to be here anymore. "Go on." She tilted her head at the bar. "Take a shot for my birthday."

"You don't want to be here?" he asked.

I don't want to be anywhere here, the nagging thought surfaced in her mind.

"Don't you know me at all?" she said with a nervous laugh. "This," she motioned to her clothes. "None of this is me. It may have been once but not anymore. It's taking everything inside of me not to claw this crap off my face."

"Give it a chance." The corner of his mouth curved slightly. She knew on anyone else the expression would be light with an air of fun but on him it spoke of a certain dark come hither—as if the devil himself was trying to persuade her inside. "I'm done being a dick."

Her eyes widened in mock shock. "*For-eve-r?*"

"Tonight," he corrected. "I can't promise beyond than

173

that."

"I thought as much," she smiled tightly and looked back at the bar Astrid had called Traverna. As much as she wanted to move on with her life, the thought of drinking, dancing, and letting loose made her stomach queasy. Would someone try to take advantage of her once again? She glanced at Soren before finally letting out a long, worried breath.

"Just one drink," she said, "okay?"

They walked side by side to the bar's front door. Dylan reached for the knob but Soren grabbed it first, keeping her from opening it.

"What are you doing?" Dylan asked.

"This," he brought his hand up and fingered the lapel of her jacket, "You look good, Dylan," Soren said, effectively sending a pack of frantic butterflies to attack her stomach.

Soren let go of the doorknob and she quickly opened the door. Cheers welcomed them into the bar and Dylan stopped short.

Soren bent down and said, "Don't worry. The *commons* love us."

"*Commons*?" Dylan questioned over her shoulder.

"The town's people. Come on," he said, walking around her to lead the way.

Dylan followed, her eyes shifting around the room. The place was filled with dancing and mingling demons. The thick vine that covered the outside of the building flowed inside the bar, looping and twisting through the wooden beams and covering the roof. A band boomed indie rock and a sweet smell of liquor and cigarettes saturated the air. But, what made it even better was not a single demon batted an eye at her. It was like she was no one again and it gave her the confidence to stay.

They sat down at the round, wooden table in the back of the club that Ian had scored off of a couple of *commons* who had high respect for the Horde. Soren was quick to tell her the Shadow Horde never had trouble finding a place to sit, a ride, or food. That in a way, they were more respected than the Kings because they actually fought and carried the *Daleon* daggers. It was the first time she heard anything borderline traitorous come out of his mouth.

Soren nodded at a busty waitress with bright pink eyes. She smiled coyly and moved to the bar where she began pouring his drink.

"I already ordered," Astrid said, scoffing in the waitress' direction.

"*You* ordering drinks is exactly why I won't be drinking it," Soren said with a shrug.

The same waitress came over to them, balancing a tray, and set down a round of fizzy drinks and one short glass of ice water. Dylan reached for one of the drinks and wondered how often Soren came here to have a "usual" even if it was only water.

The waitress made small talk with the table for a few minutes. She giggled a lot and couldn't seem to stop touching Soren. Whether it was an accidental brush of her arm or a subtle squeeze of his bicep.

Dylan tried not to notice as she stared down at her bubbling drink in a tall tumbler. Thankfully, the waitress didn't stick around too much longer. But as she left, she made eyes at Soren; and Dylan felt an odd sensation in her gut that she could only describe as jealousy. He had definitely slept with the waitress.

"So, what took you so long?" Astrid yelled across the table, over the music.

"Smoke break," Dylan yelled back.

"You smoke?" Ian appeared doubtful.

"No," Dylan said without elaborating.

Astrid knit her brows before launching into a topic of carcinogens that affected plant growth, immediately causing everyone to lose interest.

Soren reached over and took Dylan's drink, sniffing it

with a frown. "Good luck," he winced, sliding it back over to her.

Dylan lifted the glass and sniffed it. Sugary, pineapple-infused bubbles tickled her nose and she quickly took a forced gulp before blurting out, "That waitress was flirting with you." She immediately bit her cheek, feeling a tight squeeze of regret for bringing it up.

"I'm sure," Soren murmured eyeing the woman as she flirted with another table.

"Do you not think she's pretty?"

He looked at her with the usual Soren frown, and mumbled, "sure."

"Go talk to her."

Dylan wasn't exactly sure why she was pushing him to pursue the waitress. But, she figured she just needed to push him away a bit. Ever since he told her she looked good, her belly hadn't stopped doing somersaults. Dylan instinctively smoothed a hand over her stomach, trying to stop the feeling.

"He doesn't date," Ian interrupted.

That got Dylan's attention and apparently Soren's. His eyebrows quirked at Ian.

Ian simply shrugged before leaning back in his chair, checking out the ass of another passing waitress

The band switched songs and Astrid's eyes widened.

"Ohhhh!" she squealed, startling Dylan out of her thoughts of Soren not dating. "I *looove* this song!" She turned to Augusto and whispered in his ear. He just continued to glare at his drink in brooding silence. Astrid furrowed her brow, looking somewhat sick for a brief moment, then looked at Dylan. "I want to dance. Let's go find someone to grind on."

Dylan locked up and quickly shook her head no.

"Oh, come on!" she whined.

"I don't dance," Dylan shrugged and went back to her drink, mostly just staring at it.

"What do you mean you don't dance?" Astrid asked.

"People who don't dance," Ian stated, keeping his eyes on the same waitress across the room, "are people who can't dance."

"Fine," Dylan raised her hands. "You got me. Can't dance."

"Fantastic," Ian husked, slamming his empty glass down. "Now if you'll excuse me, I have a present that needs unwrapping." He stood and followed his line of sight. To Dylan he looked as if he had been pulled into a trance.

"Sirens," Astrid grumbled into her cocktail.

Soren leaned into Dylan's ear, his breath stirring unwanted goosebumps in an exhilarating attack down her spine. "Can't? …Or won't?"

Dylan suddenly stood, bumping the table and almost knocking over a drink. "I'm going to get… something," she mumbled, probably a bit incoherently, as she shuffled away before anyone could protest or even remind her they had a waitress.

At the bar, she wedged in between several demons, not caring about the fact two large men were practically stepping on her. She just had to get away from Soren. She was sure he was using his powers on her because with the way her body responded to the mere sound of his voice… she just couldn't imagine feeling anything for someone again unless it was magic.

The woman bartender leaned over the counter at the far end, fiddling with a customer's tie. Her hair was dyed a light blue and her dark skin was decorated by several gold piercings. Her curved smile and movement of her hips to the beat of the music was seductive and practiced. Dylan rolled her eyes when the customer shoved a bill down her cleavage.

I wonder how much… wait.

Dylan was about to back away, figuring she couldn't order anything anyway without cash, when that very bartender appeared in front of her.

"I was wondering when I would see you," she smiled

knowingly at Dylan's frown.

"Hey, I was here first," the man next to Dylan growled in the bartender's face.

"Oh, you were, were you?" the bartender lilted, her doe eyes innocent but cunning. "My apologies. What can I get you?"

She leaned over the bar again, her breasts almost spilling out of her low V-neck top. Once the man tilted his head in her direction, she blew in his face.

Dylan flinched, mostly expecting the man to be roaring with rage. But... no. He stayed stock-still. Dylan poked his arm, he didn't move.

"You *froze* him?" Dylan hissed under breath. "Oh my God, is he... will he *die*?"

"It's only temporary. Don't be so dramatic, *Temperance*."

Dylan narrowed her eyes. "And you are?" The fact that everyone seemed to know who she was wasn't lost on her and, frankly, pissed her off.

A smile spread across the bartender's face like melted butter. "Cassandra. Or perhaps a friend of a friend?" She flicked her eyes to the man standing abnormally close to Dylan. "May I get you something as well?"

The man grunted something and left.

Dylan perked an eyebrow. "I don't have any friends you would know." She thought of the others, of Soren. Okay, so maybe she did have friends here.

"Hmm, really? Because this particular friend, *group* of friends has been waiting an extremely long time for you to return to them."

Dylan's eyes slowly grew as the realization dawned on her.

"Where are they?" she gasped under her breath. It hadn't been until that very moment that she realized just how much she still wanted to meet her parents. After everything they had done, and didn't do, she still wanted to know them. Perhaps, they had another side to the story that wasn't so awful. What if they weren't so bad?

Cassandra shook her head with a click of her tongue. "You of all demons should know what that kind of information can do if leaked. Not only what it could do to the demon holding it, but to those who had entrusted the information."

"Then how the hell am I supposed to know?" Dylan hissed. "Don't you think it's a bit ridiculous all of this secrecy with *me*? *Their daughter.*"

Cassandra narrowed her eyes. "Seeing as you wear the enemy's color; I don't blame them for being cautious."

"I wouldn't be if they had just trusted me from the get go."

"You really don't know where they are?" Cassandra asked, eyeing her guardedly.

"No!" Dylan all but screamed, but then quickly reined in her temper. "No," she said just loud enough for Cassandra to hear.

"Perhaps you should revisit your studies. I hear the library where you *live* is delightful."

Dylan rolled her eyes so hard it hurt. "If they wanted me so bad, they wouldn't be afraid to come out of hiding to get me. I have a sneaking suspicion I'm related to cowards," she sneered.

"Cowards?" her voice was eerily calm. "That's an interesting word for the thousands of demons who either lost or risked their lives *just* for you. I'm thrilled to see you hold us in such high esteem."

"That's not what I meant," Dylan said through a wince. *I just wish they showed me how much they supposedly loved me.*

"Whatever it is that you meant, I know they are waiting for you. We are all waiting for you. Entitlement and all!"

"All waiting...?" She didn't understand that comment. Why would so many demons risk their lives for her only to re-unite with her parents and possibly live in isolation? Had she had the culture all wrong? Were they really that romanticized? "What do you—" But before she could finish, Cassandra flashed her easy smile and interrupted her.

"And that is how the punch is made."

Dylan felt him before she saw him in her peripheral vision, like a stroke of heat down her back. Soren's presence was always difficult to ignore no matter how hard she tried.

He bumped arms with her and Dylan couldn't stop the small smile at his playfulness. It was something so rare.

"The punch, huh?" he asked. "Care to share the ingredients? Then we could start our own bar and we won't ever have to come here again."

"Oh... uh..." Dylan suddenly raised four fingers when she couldn't come up with a believable lie. "Sworn to secrecy. Sorry."

He closed his hand around her Girl Scout salute. "What is this? A human thing?"

"A promise in the human world?" she frowned then mumbled, "I don't know why that came out as a question."

He drew his lower lip between his teeth and nodded, releasing her. "So, you were only avoiding the dancing?"

"Yeah... Well, until I realized I didn't even have money for drinks, so I settled for annoying questions." She looked to Cassandra. "Sorry."

"No problem, sweetheart. Here," she pushed two cloudy, purple shots in front of Dylan. "*Happy birthday, Temperance.*"

Dylan murmured a thanks to Cassandra and clinked her shot glass with Soren's shot still on the bar in front of him.

Tipping back her drink, the liquid slid down her throat thick like honey. For something way too sweet it was really good.

Dylan eyed the glass. "Wow." It took her aback. She wanted to ask what was in it and possibly for another one, but when she looked back up Cassandra was gone, replaced by another bartender.

"What?" Soren asked. He still hadn't touched his. Actually, he hadn't touched anything all night.

"Nothing. Just a good shot." She cleared her throat. "Are you not drinking?"

"Someone has to stay on duty," he said

Dylan crinkled her nose. "You're always on duty."

Soren just shrugged before sliding his shot over to her. "Enjoy."

Dylan grinned and took the other shot a bit too willingly. She set the glass down and coughed hard. This one didn't go down as easily. Instead of smooth and sweet, it was chalky and burned her throat.

"You okay?" Soren asked, patting her back.

"Yeah," she rasped. "Oh wow. That one was a lot stronger."

The tension in his shoulders released as he nodded.

Whatever it was, it was working fast, because Dylan felt her vision waver a bit.

Was that the punch?

"A really strong shot," she found herself saying with a heavy mouth.

He frowned, as usual, but for some reason it made her giggle. She brought both hands up to his face and forced his mouth into a smile. "You frown too much. It's my birthday. You're not allowed to pout. Only I am."

Both of his hands came around her wrists and pried her away from holding his face. She pressed her lips together to stifle another laugh. She liked feeling his stubble. A large part of her wanted to rub her face across it and lick it. She burst out into a boisterous laugh at the thought.

"Maybe we should call it a night?" Soren looked a bit unsure before eyeing their shot glasses again.

"No way," she said, bumping into the frozen guy to her left. She quickly apologized then laughed harder when she remembered he was still frozen.

Dylan suddenly proceeded to pull off her jacket and

181

throw it across the room.

"It's too damn hot in here!" she yelled, as she skipped to the dance floor. She found Astrid and Ian and began to dance and jump with them to the heavy beat of the music.

Dylan's hands were in the air as she shook her head from side to side. The feel of her hair sliding across her face with each twist felt amazing. So amazing, she was surprised this was the first time she had ever noticed. Hot hands slid down her hips and she began dancing with the hard body now pressed up against her, still feeling her hair. It was so silky and soft. She just wanted to live in it. Make a tiny house out of it and never leave.

The demon she was dancing with was suddenly ripped away from her. She flipped around and giggled at the feeling of her hair again. Soren stood there, his eyes dark with disapproval and concern. He cupped her face.

"Are you okay?" She heard his words, but they sounded far away as if her ears were clogged.

"Feel my hair!" she yelled, putting his palm on her head and forcing it down to pet her. Soren didn't protest but he didn't exactly humor her either. His arm was tense and his face seemed strained. Not that she cared because she was feeling the other side of her hair and was on the verge of moaning.

"Temperance!" Dylan flipped around again but kept a grip on Soren. Astrid was laughing at Ian who was doubled over in hysterics, both of their lips purple. Dylan couldn't help but laugh with them. The entire world was suddenly light. A sunburst of life. And with it she felt like she was someone else.

Someone happy.

Someone with a normal life.

No dark shadows of death and pain woven into her. No inescapable burdens or planned destinies. Here, now, she was just a girl having fun, dancing with her friends and celebrating her birthday as she should be.

They motioned for her to come dance with them but Soren's arm stopped her, gripping the fabric of her dress near her stomach.

"Come on," he sighed near her ear. "Time to go."

She shook her head, trying to detach from him once more and dance at the same time. He finally let go and she skipped away to dance with her friends. Astrid and Ian howled in excitement. Both of them had dance partners Dylan didn't recognize.

Dylan moved her body with the upbeat music, her fingers trailing long paths across her bare arms.

Screw her hair! *This* felt good.

Dylan was starting to wonder if this was what Dickens meant about looking through rose colored glasses… when everything flipped. One moment she was dancing, the next she was looking at the room upside-down. Her legs were dangling as her feet kicked and she stared at an exceptionally nice leather butt.

She couldn't stop the laughing even as the blood rushed to her head making her dizzy and congested.

Darkness clouded her vision and her hearing was muffled. It took a full moment to realize she had left the bar.

"Dylan…" a voice connected to the body carrying her said.

Soren bent down and set her feet on the pavement. She wobbled and held onto his arms for stability.

"Why are we outside?" She snorted, something about his twisted face making it hard to be serious.

He shook his head, exasperated and backed her up until her thighs hit his bike. "We're going home." She sat suddenly, and her fingers latched onto his belt. Once the world stopped tilting, she sighed thinking of home. Her real home back in Los Angeles.

"Home?" she asked, looking up at him with an innocence that visibly hurt him.

His jaw tightened as he covered her hands, stopping her

from exploring underneath his shirt. "Not that home. We're going to our home, *here*."

She blinked rapidly and looked away. "I'm not ready to go back. I'm having fun."

He lifted her chin and brought her face to his. She closed her eyes as a warm feeling rippled through her belly. She could feel his breath across her lips but not his warmth. He was close but not close enough.

"You'll never be ready to go back, but that's what we do. We go back. We fight. We serve. It's no longer about ourselves. Not anymore."

"What are you doing to me?" she asked, still thinking about the assaulting butterflies thrashing around inside her belly.

"What do you mean?"

"You're using your powers again. How else am I supposed to reason this feeling?"

"Dylan," his voice came out in a warning. "I'll say it only once; I'm not doing anything."

She refused to open her eyes, her mind focusing on the exhilarating fingers of wind gliding across the nape of her neck and arms. A large part of her wanted to be kissed hard and long, to be taken against this motorcycle. She sighed and pulled him closer.

"Fuck, you're wasted," he said in disgust.

She smiled. "No, I'm not," and leaned in. He snatched her chin again, stopping her ascent.

Her eyes flicked open and he looked at her directly. "I'm not going to kiss you."

"Why—"

"Why? Because you're going to regret every single thing that happens tonight, tomorrow. And I refuse to be one of your regrets."

Her shock melted back into an easy smile. "What if I told you I wouldn't regret it?"

"Then I'd say I don't believe you, you're on drugs."

"I don't do drugs." She frowned.

"Not intentionally, maybe." His expression was hard and unrelenting.

"Fine, whatever." She motioned for him to back away from her straddled legs and yawned. "Your loss."

He seemed to find that funny. "I'm sure."

"What about the others?"

"They'll be fine," he grunted, pushing one of her legs over the seat until she was in the front like she was about to drive.

"Uh, you sure *I'm* the one on drugs?" She giggled and began to scoot backward. He stopped her.

"You can barely master sitting," he stated, throwing a leg over the seat and steadying her from falling off. "There is no way I'm trusting you to hold on behind me."

Her eyebrows shot up. He sat, scooting forward until the front dug into her stomach. "This won't work," she mumbled, suddenly feeling stifling hot.

"Well, if it doesn't, we'll walk. But I'd rather not leave my bike here all night." She nodded as he reached around her to ignite the engine. "Hold on."

She did, clutching the center of the handle bars. When he took off, her entire body clenched and she pressed her back into his chest. No matter how wary of his manipulations, Soren was still her safety net of protection from a sea of lurking terror. Her pounding heart began to slow at the thought and she released her hold slightly. Craning her neck a bit, she peered at him sidelong.

"What?" he asked after a moment.

"Where's my jacket?" Her eyes began to droop from the rumbling of the motorcycle, but it didn't stop her from cocking an eyebrow.

"Well, you stripped in the middle of a bar. Just be happy I got you out, all right?"

"That was Astrid's. She's not going to like that..."

Soren sped up and Dylan gasped as the frozen air rushed

against them.

"Do you ever miss the stars?" she asked out of nowhere.

"No," he said without hesitation. "Stars make the sky feel crowded."

"I miss the stars," she sighed as he slowed down, the gravel crunching as he stopped. The tall glass tower of her home seemed to lean over her, mockingly.

"Home sweet home," Soren sang.

A pain stabbed Dylan deep in the heart. This wasn't her home.

"I think, I'm sober," she mumbled not wanting to go inside.

"Great," he deadpanned.

She sat up and before she could even yelp, the world spun and she fell off the bike. Soren caught her just before she hit the sharp pebbles, his arms cradling her like a child.

"*Whoa*," she giggled, her legs still in the air. She shook her head slowly from side to side with an easy smile. "Nope. Not sober."

He began to help her up but stopped, his eyes locked on his hands gripping her thigh. The tips of his fingers brushed the jagged edge of raised skin through her thin leggings.

Dylan gasped and quickly tried to jump out of his arms. No one had ever touched her there and noticed. She felt suddenly ill as she failed to push him away. He must have gotten stronger because she felt like a weak little girl all over again.

"Tell me," he stated.

"*No*." She tried to shove his hand away but his grip tightened—his nails digging into her flesh. "Some things are just better left alone."

"Did Gerion do this?"

Her eyes flicked up to his before looking away to the starless sky like a void into which she could disappear.

"Tell me, Dylan. So, I can repay the favor before I hack off his head."

"You can't always assume I'm the victim," she mumbled. "Sometimes we are our own worst enemy."

His brows knotted and his grip loosened. She took the opportunity to shove his hand away. *I shouldn't be here… this exposed, this…* "It's *nothing.*"

"I thought we were divulging our secrets now. Or is it only I?" he sneered, appearing slighted.

Dylan stared at him pleadingly. "Not this," she breathed. "Anything, but this." She didn't want him to look at her the way everyone did when they found out about her troubled past. Soren had been deliberately skirting her memories for years now, which supported her false front that her human life was better than this one. When in reality, there had only been scattered moments of light within a wide sea of darkness.

Soren set his mouth into a firm line and helped her up. She leaned heavily on him for support as they walked back to her room in silence, thankful he had dropped it. But, it didn't matter that Soren had let it go. Her mind was already filtering through blackened memories all by itself. Lunches eaten alone, name calling, and tricks; how not even the nerds or mutually bullied kids wanted to talk to her; how she cleared tables simply by her presence. Of course, it wasn't enough to attempt suicide, but to a depressed teen, those years felt infinite.

It had only taken one day to reach her snapping point. A time forever burned into Dylan's memory. Just thinking about it dug out renewed agony as if it hadn't left but burrowed deeply under her skin just as alive as it had ever been… waiting for release.

She could still feel the hot pattering of water against her back as she rinsed off after P.E. as if it were just moments ago. The sharpness of fear striking her with the sounds of their giggles.

Their mocking unmistakable.

Dylan began shivering. Her teeth clicking uncontrollably

when she peeked around the cheap plastic curtain to the empty locker room.

She sucked in a breath, jamming air tightly into her lungs as she darted to a locker full of towels. Yanking it open, she felt her stomach drop at its bareness. Part of her had already known after her clothes disappeared near the shower, but still she had checked her locker for her backpack and phone.

Nothing. They had left her with only one way out.

No one would be here to help her. Not even Isabel was expecting her until much, much later. How would she call for help?

Her bottom lip quivered and she bit it, refusing to cry. She would figure it out like she always did. This wasn't the first time they had tried to pull a stunt like this and she knew it wouldn't be the last. It was her own fault for thinking it was okay to let down her guard.

After trying and failing to detach the shower curtain, Dylan cautiously looked out into the empty gym and spotted the stack of towels, her clothes, and book bag perched tidily on the bleachers across the gym from her.

She was half way across the court, when someone behind her yelled, "She came out!"

Her instincts burned hot, jolting her limbs into quick action. She made it to the bleachers just in time to grab a towel and wrap it quickly around herself, sending everything else to the floor. Except, when she turned to run, she was already surrounded by not only the girls but several guys, including Jacob Mancuso.

They had their phones raised when two of the girls snatched the hem of the towel and yanked it away. All of their faces became one giant blur of dares, shoves, laughs, and phone capture sounds.

It was all she could do to hold her arms around herself and not cry.

When she heard the voice of a teacher, tears released,

streaming down her face.

Dylan then thought of the cotton-like texture of the envelope. It was the weekend when she ran her thumb across the indentation Isabel's name made carved into the paper. The pictures and rumors had already begun circling the school. It was only a matter of time before Isabel found out. By then she hoped to be with her parents. Gone.

She set the envelope beside her on the glossy wooden bench in the same locker room. Her ears rang so loudly like an alarm only she could hear. Warning bells of her imminent death.

She dug into her backpack and pulled out the sharpened butcher knife. Its feather weight somehow weighing her down while her body fought to rise with the air. The searing pain that numbed her. The hot gush of blood that healed her. So much blood...

Soren's thumb pressed just under her eye and caught a lone tear. She was startled out of her memory and looked at him as he inspected the tear like a foreign object before placing it on his tongue. She felt the ache in her heart lessen; and it was only then that she realized they were laying on her bed. His arm was propped, holding his head up.

Her eyes looked to his. The blue truer in her room. But he wasn't looking at her. Not really. His eyes were on her face but he seemed a million miles away. Perhaps just as far away as she had been.

"Do I need to worry about you trying it again?" His pupils dilated with focus.

Dark, unspoken secrets tumbled and burned to the surface of her mind. Had it been that obvious from what she said? Perhaps, he had simply deduced what she had done from the scar and the few memories he had taken?

"Answer my question." He licked his lips still tasting her tear like a trophy.

There was something unsettling about the worry in his eyes. Soren was strong, sharp, and deadly. Worry wasn't a good look on him. It humanized him too much.

"Not unless you plan on doing the honors." Dylan still couldn't garner the strength to stab herself again. It had taken so much not to puke or pass out before she could finish.

"I would slit my own throat before I slit yours."

It sounded so romantic like a page from Romeo and Juliet but she knew better. Killing her would only result in the Kings ordering his death.

Her fingers lifted as if on their own accord, slipping beneath his hair and drifting along his scalp—the alcohol making her bold. The skin around his gashes crinkled and goosebumps broke ground. He swallowed and closed his eyes thinking of the day he got them, no doubt. She had never seen him so unnerved. He opened his eyes and she felt a gasp gather inside her throat from his intense stare.

God, he was beautiful.

Her eyes grew heavy and she blinked several times as his face distorted and blurred.

"Dylan?"

His hands cupped her cheeks, but it was strange. His touch was numb as if searching for feeling through an encasing of glass.

"Dylan, *answer me*."

She frowned at his words, wanting to answer him but she couldn't make her mouth work. She was so, so tired…

He cursed under his breath and got up.

She lazily reached for him to come back and stopped when she noticed the walls were dripping like melting wax.

What the hell?

Time seemed to cut out and fast forward, as Soren talked to someone in her room. That someone pulled on her outstretched hand and pushed in a needle connected to a syringe filled with clear fluid. She pinched her face.

"It's only to help, sweet girl," that someone crooned, gliding his fingers through her hair. *The Medic.*

She recoiled from his touching.

Soren was quick to remove him and take his spot next to her. Surprisingly, he took her hand and squeezed it as if to tell her he wasn't going anywhere and not to worry.

Thank you, she wanted to say, the words dancing on the tip of her tongue. She hadn't said thank you to him since the day of her trial. He hadn't given her a reason to until this night.

The feeling in her limbs began to return as whatever the Medic injected her with worked quickly.

She sighed when everything around her calmed and her body responded to her mental commands again. "I don't mind them," she croaked, squinting her eyes.

"What?" Soren asked still sitting next to her and watching the Medic like a hawk as he took her vitals.

"The scars. Actually, I think it makes you even better looking. Perfect is boring."

He let out a long breath. "Wonderful," he said sarcastically, yet his eyes told her another story. He was relieved. "And here I thought you were resistant to my charms."

She smiled. "I knew it. See? Nothing you do can get past me." She tried open her eyes wider but the light shot pangs into her temples.

"Noted."

"Why don't you date?" she asked, remembering their earlier conversation.

He ignored her and unclasped their hands to lay hers across her chest as he answered the Medic's questions.

Dylan focused back on the walls that were still melting. She slowly snaked her eyes along the creases then between the ceiling tiles that rippled like soft waves. She hadn't expected him to answer her and she wasn't entirely sure why she even asked.

She blinked.

It was like noticing a spot on a lens after looking through

it all day—easy to miss but hard to forget. It was her, as if someone had altered her room and added a mirror above her bed. Except her reflection was pale like marble statue, aged and chipping away, dissolving into meaningless ash—her mind breaking to forever be forgotten.

She was breaking, and she was allowing them to break her.

◇◇◇

Once her breaths became deep and even, Soren stood and motioned for the Medic to finish the sedative cocktails.

"What did she take?"

"She didn't *take* anything," he snapped. Reynold had the decency to look empathetic while Soren corrected his outburst. "Someone drugged her—and the Horde."

"Do you have a clue what it might be?"

"The way she was acting... maybe White Ash?"

Reynold stiffened but then quickly nodded, rummaging through his leather tote, pulling out vials and translucent liquids.

From the far wall in her room, Soren stared at her sleeping and thought about every memory he'd yanked out of her mind tonight. He knew she would be flipping her shit in the morning once she realized what he had done to retrieve the information. It was just so startling to see her mind opening up like a flower to him. He hadn't ever been able to reach the darkest depth of her memories before; and the monster inside him leapt up to feast on it like a starved lion—a pretty low move even for his standards, but he hadn't been able to get a memory he had taken years ago out of his mind. She had been unconscious in some sort of hospital with an older woman at her bedside; and for the most part, he'd convinced himself it was nothing... that was, until he felt the jagged skin on her thigh. Then he had to know if she was unstable enough to try hurting herself again with her new freedom.

Soren rested his head against the wall. It was a stupid thing to get so close to her. Yes, he told her they were friends, and maybe someday he would be without any pretenses, but for now he still *wanted* to hate her as much as he liked her. He wanted to torture her and make her life miserable. He wanted to kill her in hopes of settling the score between him and the Elementas. But that part was becoming undeniably smaller with each passing day.

She was just a girl with a big role. She didn't know those that wronged him and thousands of other demons in this world. He couldn't justify shedding her blood in the name of revenge, not when he knew her fears, hopes and shattered pieces. Not when he was *this* close. Her death would only tear the wound deeper.

He fisted his hands, feeling frustrated at how fucked he was. He knew his mistake. It was his weakness to protect. He should have let her scream her nightmares of Gerion away. But that wasn't him. He didn't enjoy that kind of pain. Her suffering from lack of Essence, while parading like a know-it-all bitch, brought on a certain satisfaction. Those nightmares on the other hand, were pure terror from a mutual enemy, and his innate reaction was to fight her battle, to slaughter the adversary.

And now a part of him ached for her. If she hadn't been drunk, he wouldn't have stopped her from pulling him to the dance floor or trying to kiss him. Her joy was contagious and he could suddenly see why Tristian and Gerion had been so infatuated by her. She was nothing but sunlight when she allowed it. But, she was intoxicated; and not only drunk, someone had spiked her drink with a hallucinogen that could knock the most fearing on their asses. He just couldn't pinpoint who had done it or even which drink. It could have been anyone, really. He would go back the next day to hopefully find out.

Soren cleared his throat loudly when Reynold pulled her top down to listen to her heart through his stethoscope—not enough to expose her but too damn close for Soren's liking. The Medic quickly replaced her top before packing up his supplies and leaving.

A small noise escaped her lips drawing him away from his thoughts. As messed up as it was, he itched to lay back down beside her. There was something unnervingly peaceful about sleeping next to a viper.

CHAPTER 11

"I miss you in waves and tonight I'm drowning."
Denice Envall

DYLAN jerked awake. She sat up on her elbows. Her body was still sluggish from sleep and the drug, but her mind was sharp.

She screwed up her face as the night flooded back into her mind. Her actions at the bar and *after*. Every single thing was painfully vivid. The hallucinations, the conversations, the *desire*.

But now wasn't the time to dwell on her mistakes. Something woke her up and it wasn't a nightmare. She looked around her room then down at her empty bed.

Where is Soren?

She took a deep breath, trying to recall why she had awakened. Was she one hundred percent sure that it hadn't been a dream that woke her? She dug harder into her thoughts and came up blank, which was weird. Her heart pounded audibly and her quick and shallow breaths felt congruent with one of her nightmares.

She sat straight up, the bottoms of her feet gently touching the cold tile floor. She brought a hand up to her aching head and a pinch tugged at the middle of her arm where the IV sat. She quickly pulled the long needle out before throwing it on the floor. The room tilted a bit and she squeezed her eyes shut automatically, trying not to throw up.

Then she heard it.

The sound that woke her was an alarm. A short, high-pitched wail that made her ears ring in the silence. It was also then that she noticed a slow blinking red light coming from the crack under her door. Dylan got up as fast as she could, not caring one bit that she was still wearing the stupid tube dress and leggings. All she could focus on was that something was terribly wrong; and with that thought came the fear of Silas and Lucia coming for her. She grabbed the first pair of shoes she saw and pulled on the leather boots.

On her way out the door, her vision fogged and she slammed into the frame, stumbling into the opposite wall.

Cursing the impact, she opened her eyes and stared down at a large heap of dark leather sprawled about on the floor. A dark circle of blood surrounding the head.

She shuddered. The solider was dead.

Dylan fought the images of lifeless eyes and tried to ignore the blood staining her fingers as she inched along the wall in an attempt to give the corpse a wide berth. At least it wasn't someone she recognized. She could almost convince herself it wasn't real.

Her feet were pounding with each beat of her heart when another violent wail ripped through the air.

She pushed off the balls of her feet in anticipation of speeding down the hall with demon speed; but, every time she tried, it felt like trying to turn the key on a dying engine. She didn't understand why her powers weren't working.

She could feel herself starting to panic when she passed the cafeteria. She skidded to a stop with the intention to grab some weapons from the wall just inside as she had seen the Horde do countless times.

The room was dark and empty like the halls. The only light was a flashing red bulb above the doors. The slow, strobe-like split-second cameos: a deserted cup, a chair askew.

She felt her way inside the dining room. The light flashed and she got a glimpse of her regular dining table. A sick feeling settled inside her gut at the thought of never sitting there again.

Dylan inched along, visualizing that movie: *Silence of the Lambs,* when Buffalo Bill had Clarice trapped in his house in the dark with only flashes of his camera to taunt her.

She slammed her hip into the end of a table and jumped.

Oh God. Stop it. Stop thinking right now, she told herself.

She darted forward on a whim, quickly slapping her hand to the control panel and bouncing impatiently as it loaded her prints.

A green light pinged and the wall flipped, unveiling the fully stocked arsenal. Dylan scanned the wall and snatched a belt loaded with six charcoal daggers primed for throwing.

She wrapped the belt around her waist, threading the strap with shaking fingers and yanked it tight. She was about to dart out of the Cafeteria when she doubled back to grab a vial of *Essence,* figuring it couldn't hurt to top herself off.

She inhaled the energy and stumbled back against the wall, coughing as she dropped the small tube. The glass shattered and she gagged. Her stomach burst with pain as she crouched, holding her belly.

"What. The hell," Dylan gasped through gritted teeth. It must be the drug Cassandra had slipped her. She couldn't think of any other reason for the agony. *Essence* felt good, not like your insides were ripping apart.

Dylan crawled a bit until the pain lessened and she could manage standing. She clambered up and planted her feet, suddenly wanting to *kill* Cassandra.

Happy birthday my ass, passive aggressive bitch.

Dylan took off out of the cafeteria just as another long wail pierced through the night air. Her body was lethargic, but thanks to the *Essence* she was getting stronger—*just* like the first year she had the *Binding* on.

Great, she thought sarcastically.

Grinding her teeth, she pushed her muscles further. Until that moment, she hadn't believed Soren when he told her about demons sucking your power. Thank God she was skilled in hand-to-hand combat and knew how to throw daggers with precision.

A faint scream followed another long wailing siren. Dylan ran faster, passing an exit. It was then that she realized she wasn't running away from the possible horror but running to it. She wasn't sure why, but it felt as if she needed to help her crew with whatever they were fighting, and she needed to help them *now*.

Dylan came to a hallway she recognized as the same place she had been during her first week in Elon. The infirmary was to her right and the room with the chains was five doors down, with the beautiful trial room at the very end.

She paused before forcing herself to run through the hallway, refusing to acknowledge the chill spreading through her body like frost. She opened the glass door at the end of the hall and burst inside the trial room, also called The Gates. In here, she could hear the unmistakable sounds of battle echoing from the foyer.

Before she knew it, she was standing in the opening of the main foyer. Her feet felt glued due to the gruesome scene in front of her. Several demons she recognized as Elon's interim army were fighting and dying at the hands of so many other demons adorned with war paint. They were clad in black leather suits like Elon's army but their faces were painted in vibrant designs. Each design was different but the colors were the same: blue, orange, and red.

There were so many of them it was hard to keep track. Her eyes bounced all over the enormous marble and gold encrusted atrium, stopping on a wall of painted soldiers blocking any access to the large glass tube called the Vat of Souls. Dylan felt her senses call to attention at the abundance of *Essence* while her heart burned with guilt for wanting every single bit of life in that tube.

She blinked several times to regain control of her urges

and focused on the wall of foreign soldiers when it looked like there was some sort of wolf creature behind them. She blinked again and then it was gone. Maybe she was still hallucinating?

A demon suddenly ran across her vision. He stopped short in front of her, looking down at a smooth dagger protruding out of his chest. His hands found the hilt, and he pulled it free just as his eyes connected with hers. Spurts of blood shot out with each dying heartbeat.

"Tristian!" she screamed, running to the dying demon. Silent tears rolled down her cheeks as she held the fallen soldier in her arms. His body trembled as she scrambled to apply pressure to his wound. "No-no-NO!" she slurred, her heart raw with renewed pain. The soldier took his last breath.

Dylan's heart beat a mile a minute as green eyes faded to dilated brown.

Tristan wasn't here.

He was dead.

This soldier was dead.

Everyone was *dying*.

She had to get a grip on herself!

Hands suddenly grasped her shoulders, yanking her upward.

"What are you doing here?!" Soren screamed over the cacophony that filled the room. Her eyes moved past him and locked on a painted demon across the room just as he threw a serrated dagger.

She didn't think, just acted. Dylan windmilled her arm under Soren's arm, knocking him to the side in one swift swoop. The knife missed its target of his heart and grazed her side instead. She gasped through the sharp pain and fell into Soren's body causing both of them to tumble to the floor.

Her hands clutched her waist as Soren loomed over her, his eyes wide.

"What do you think you're doing?!"

He straddled her and moved her hands to inspect the wound.

"I wasn't going to let you die!" Dylan said through a wince.

"Do you know what they would do to *me* if *you* died?" he panted furiously. Realizing it was only a graze, he got in her face. "You never fucking think! You aren't even supposed to be here!"

She gnashed her teeth and pushed him off of her. "You know, the next time I save your ass, a simple 'thank you' would suffice."

"*Right*," he glowered.

Soren continued to lecture her; but, his words were lost when she realized the demon that threw the dagger still stood, frozen and pale, as if he hadn't moved since the throw. The demon finally lowered his arm and nodded resolutely to another painted demon walking up to him with a red band tied around his upper arm. The red banded demon quickly slit the pale demon's throat and he collapsed to the ground. The demon with the red band turned around and locked eyes with Dylan. He seemed to smirk before disappearing into thin air.

Dylan narrowed her eyes, wondering if she had just hallucinated… again.

"They're just… disappearing," Soren said, his eyes running around the room. He rose abruptly and pulled her up, too.

"THEY'RE GONE!" Soren yelled to the room with his fist raised in the air. The remaining soldiers, wounded and standing, all mimicked his stance, chanting their victory.

But Dylan wasn't smiling like the rest of them because she couldn't get that painted demon out of her head. He executed the other demon for what? For trying to kill Soren? …Or for hurting her? Once the other demon had thrown the knife, he looked ashen as if he'd made a deadly mistake.

Who were those demons?

She suddenly thought of Soren's earlier words. *"Do you know what they would do to* me *if* you *died?"*

"Soren," Dylan gasped, clutching his arm. "Who were those demons?"

He turned back to her, his blinding smile faltering at her panicked eyes. She had never seen him so happy. It was death. Death and blood was Soren's bliss.

"Hey." Soren looked around before pulling her into The Gates. A shiver pricked her skin, and she rubbed her arms trying to rid the creepy feeling generated by the trial room.

"Are you okay?"

"Who were those demons?" she reiterated, pushing his hands off of her when he tried to look at her hurt side again. She looked up at him. He had specks and streaks of blood on his face. She imagined he had killed many painted soldiers without a second thought.

He frowned. "We don't know. We've been calling them The Scarred."

"Scarred? …Why?"

"Come on. I'll show you."

Back inside, soldiers all around her picked up dead Elon soldiers and Scarred demons, piling them in separate heaps by the enormous entrance between veiny, marble columns tipped by spires like spears against the very Gods above.

Soren stopped one of the soldiers carrying a dead demon. The soldier froze with his eyes locked on Dylan.

"Hello," she said, trying to smile reassuringly, but it came out lopsided and strained.

She looked down at the "Scarred" demon and couldn't help herself from taking in the strange designs painted on his face. This demon apparently couldn't get enough of the red paint. He had bared teeth and was dripping blood like a vampire. She glanced away before she was able to study his lifeless eyes.

Soren ripped open the leather jacket on the Scarred demon and pointed to his chest.

"See? Every single one of these fucks has this brand over their heart."

"Oh," she mumbled, eyeing the raised flesh. It was a stamp of a dragon with two heads. Their necks twisted together with their heads growling at each other. "What does it mean?"

Soren curtly nodded at the solider and he rushed away to set the dead Scarred down on the heap to be burned.

"My guess?" Soren said and Dylan nodded. "I think it's the Planto family seal. I used to think it was the Elementas until Lucia pulled that stunt at your trial."

"Wait, this isn't the first time?"

"This group has been slowly attacking us like this for decades. Draining our *Essence*. They always grab only a small piece of the Vat. But even small pieces add up." His eyes moved to the Vat of Souls and Dylan's followed. The blue mist that filled the tube was half way down from the top.

"What happens if they take it all?"

"We lose our power, our food. We lose the energy for our worlds. We lose... everything."

She looked back at him, yanking herself away from an array of conclusions she didn't want to reach. "Honestly, thinking it was your parents was just a theory... And mostly one concocted out of spite."

"It does make sense if it's Sil— I mean, Gerion because of the orange and red paint." When he didn't make the connection she told him how Silas liked to paint her nightmares in orange and filled them with blood.

"That's probably a bit of a stretch."

Dylan shrugged. "Like you said, it's all theory."

"Well, if you can think of anything else in relation to Gerion and Lucia that might be helpful..."

Dylan nodded, stepping around a large pool of blood.

"Thank you... by the way."

Her head jerked towards his. "For what?"

Soren gave her a look like *you're really going to make me say it?* He rolled his eyes. "For saving my ass back there. I wouldn't have been of much use with a knife in my heart."

No, you would only join the growing list of those close to me who died, she thought.

"Ms. Elementa?" a young voice asked from behind her. Dylan turned around to find the young demon that always seemed to accompany the Kings.

"Yes?"

"The Court would like to speak with you," he said before walking away and leaving Dylan in a state of sudden panic.

She flipped back around. "Di-did I do something wrong?" It wasn't until he pried her hand off her neck that she realized she had been rubbing the spot where she had been *Bound*.

"Try not worry. I won't let them *Bind* you again."

She wanted to believe him, but she wasn't an idiot. If the Kings wanted her *Bound*, his word wouldn't stop them. "I'll go with you."

Dylan nodded and they walked to what Soren told her were the Kings' chambers. Before they could enter, a rather large guard laid a hand on Soren's shoulder, halting him.

"Only her." The guard's eyes flitted briefly to Dylan.

"I'm sure they won't mind if I go in," Soren stated, but the guard kept his hand on his shoulder. She saw the man's muscles tense with his tightening grip.

"They told me not even to let *you* in."

"It's okay," Dylan said, trying to steady her wavering voice. "I've got this. Really."

Soren nodded to her before glaring at the guard.

She took a deep breath then pushed the heavy, wooden door open. The room beyond was warm and inviting, unlike the chill of death which filled the foyer. Apple and hot spice permeated the air.

A servant boy stood to the side holding a tray of *Essence*. He somehow found a way to look bored and rapt all at the same time. Dylan pulled her focus away from him and found five sets of eyes transfixed on her.

"Ms. Elementa, please step forward," said King Zirk.

She moved to the middle of the wood paneled space. Lord Struo grinned behind three wing-back chairs where only two of the Kings sat.

Queen Vashti stood off to the side next to a crystal bar with a petulant scowl gripping her pretty features. A man stood with her, tracing his fingers along her neck and collar bone. His black beady eyes were hollow and menacing.

Dylan found herself once again trying to imagine Tristian next to her, feeling her as she perceived this demon doing, but she just couldn't do it.

She bowed. "My Masters."

"Rise," her Uncle stated, his eyes hard like blue diamonds, so unlike earlier in the day when he was teaching her.

She rose.

"It has come to our attention," King Zirk announced, "we may need to re-examine your ranking here in Elon a bit earlier than expected—"

"Are we not going to cuff her first?" Queen Vashti interjected, sipping from a gold plated cup. "You can't even keep her contained in her room. How are we to trust she won't release her new power on *us*?"

"She has already proven her loyalty. She saved her commander just moments ago by putting herself in the way," her Uncle defended.

She was surprised they already knew of that and wondered if they had been watching through cameras...

Queen Vashti took a long sip of her drink and rolled her eyes, positioning her body towards, Dylan guessed, her boyfriend. "She didn't save her *commander*. She saved the demon she's fucking." Dylan bristled at her crass words. "Of course, she would save the man who gives her orgasms."

Dylan's entire body seemed to heat in embarrassment

when a flashback of trying to kiss Soren surfaced. The way he shot her down. He was right. She regretted everything she did after that shot. Now rumors were going to eat her alive just like high school. She had to put a stop to them. Now.

"I am *not*—" she gasped, throwing a trembling hand over her mouth when she remembered who she was standing in front of. She couldn't believe she had just talked back to the Kings.

She fell to her knees. "*Please* forgive me. I didn't mean... I shouldn't have... I am *so* sorry."

Stupid, stupid, STUPID!

"No, no. *Please* continue." Queen Vashti glared, appearing taut with ire. Dylan stilled as if one sudden movement would cause the Queen to snap. "Whatever were you going to say?" the Queen edged out.

"Be still my lady," King Damen warned. "I believe my niece is still under the effects of a drug slipped to her earlier in the night. It is truly remarkable she was even able to fight considering her condition."

King Zirk smiled at King Damen. No doubt, he was just as pleasantly surprised as Dylan to see King Damen's continued bold defense of her.

"Go on, Ms. Elementa," her Uncle nodded, "answer your Queen before she pops a vein."

King Zirk guffawed and Queen Vashti sat in her chair, ignoring her companion's hysterics. Her boyfriend leaned down to whisper in her ear. His eyes met Dylan's and he winked. Dylan looked away and tried not to show her disgust.

"I'm waiting," Queen Vashti announced, less threatening.

Dylan swallowed. "My... relationship with Commander Verbeck is strictly platonic—"

"So he doesn't visit your bed every night?" She laughed. "I do hope you understand the definition of platonic, my dear."

Dylan bit her tongue when the urge to snap back

surfaced.

"He does... visit me. But, for something completely unrelated to," she cleared her throat, "sex."

Queen Vashti's eyebrows shot up amusingly and Dylan felt her cheeks heat even hotter, if it were possible.

"*Enough.*" King Damen snapped. "We are not here to discuss Ms. Elementa's love life."

Queen Vashti rolled her eyes and grabbed her cup off the side table and brought it to her lips.

"Like I said earlier, we have decided to pull your trial up... to now. Please stand."

Dylan's eyes rounded. What if she had screwed up going to the bar or jumping into battle. What if they decided to *Bind* her again or worse... finally do away with her for good?

Dylan stood, fighting the urge to rub her neck. The skin was healed thanks to the Medic but just thinking about being *Bound* again made her neck burn and ache as if the wound was still open.

"Do you know what a *Daleon* is?"

Dylan stilled when it seemed like all three Kings were pinning her to the spot. *Oh no.* "Yes, My Master," she whispered.

"Then you know every member of The Horde has one?"

Dylan nodded.

"We need you to understand the importance of being a part of the Shadow Horde. It means you will be playing God—severing the diseased from our people and preventing them from making the same mistakes. It is *critical* for the survival of our species. You must understand this if you wish to be one of the guardians whom enforces the Law. A way of life that brings and sustains order to our reckless race."

Dylan's tension eased when it dawned on her what they meant about moving her trial up. Why they asked about the *Daleon*. It wasn't to punish her for withholding information on Astrid's weapon or for fighting in the battle just now. It was to offer a spot. But, who's spot would she be taking? Ian was a prodigy with wind, Soren was the commander, and Augusto the Lieutenant. So, what about Astrid? She was the newest to the Horde and the most hostile when it came to accepting Temperance. Was it possible that Astrid assumed Temperance would replace her?

"Can we count on you to help keep the Law alive? Can we trust you to give us everything—including your life—for the peace of our worlds? To become selfless under the Omnipotence?"

Dylan swallowed, remembering Astrid's words. *Nobody says no to a King.* "I accept."

"Very well," King Damen replied. Despite himself, he looked pleased.

She felt fear and excitement begin to take hold within her, but she was determined not to show it.

"When?" she asked tentatively.

"One month."

CHAPTER 12

*"She wasn't looking for a knight,
she was looking for a sword."*
Atticus

DYLAN sat on her bed just as the suns crested the horizon, staining her white room in soft pinks and purples. Soren sat next to her as she rehashed her impromptu trial.

"A month, huh," he grunted, frowning at the sun as if it scorned him.

"Yes," she whispered. "Soren... I need you to stop sleeping here."

"Why?" He flicked his gaze in her direction. His eyebrows scrunched together adorably. She forced herself to look away.

"They think we're being... intimate." Red pinched her cheeks. "I had to correct them."

"You did what?" his voice was accusatory, demanding.

"It was Queen Vashti. She pushed me and I couldn't help it." Dylan cringed, biting at the raw stumps of her finger nails. He gripped her hand, pulling it away from her mouth.

"It is for the best." He cleared his throat. "After last night..."

"I was on drugs, Soren. Please, don't take anything I said or did seriously."

"What?" he had the decency to look wounded before trying to suppress a smile. "Am I less kissable in the daylight?"

She smacked him in the chest playfully.

"I agree, though. I think it is smart we stop," he added. "There's something else."

Soren sighed, knowing what she was about to tell him.

"If you ever go inside my mind without my permission again, I won't hesitate to tell the Kings about Astrid's missing *Daleon.*" She hadn't forgotten about his little stroll into her thoughts after he noticed her scar. She had wanted to strangle him when she remembered, but exhaustion won, so she compromised with a gentle lecture and threat.

Soren nodded as if he didn't expect any less of her.

"Your secrets will remain under lock and key, I swear." He held his hand up in the Girl Scout salute and she tried not to laugh.

"No apologies?"

"I can't apologize for wanting to know everything about you," he said, using the same hand that motioned his promise to gently push her hair behind her ear.

Her eyebrows crinkled. She could finally remember why she had wanted to kiss him.

"You should go to the Medic," Soren said, dropping his hand. "I know he wants to see you after what happened last night."

She took a deep breath and stood. "Right. I'll see you at practice."

Soren left and she waited a bit before laying down on her bed. Working to slow her pounding heart, she couldn't tell if it was from Soren's simple touch or the thought of Silas invading her dreams again without her dreamcatcher keeping vigil.

Why couldn't she discern between fear and attraction? But then a thought crossed her mind that she may still be afraid of Soren. She had naively assumed that they were now somewhat friends, that maybe he'd keep his powers to himself. Except all it took was a weakened moment to take advantage of her. How could she ever feel safe around him again?

Dylan closed her eyes, feeling her mind spin with residual hurt, anger, and regret. It was stupid of her to trust him. Sometimes when she looked at him it was like he still hated her deeply, which contradicted how much he took care of her. Maybe she really was his pet. She had been beaten and abused then dumped on the lap of an owner who hated animals, but fed her nevertheless, just so she wouldn't die.

She had no clue why she had chosen to get so close to the darkness that was Soren.

Two hours and a cat nap later, Dylan was finally making her way down the hall to the infirmary where the touchy-feely Medic could take a look at her side and test for whatever drug had been slipped into her drink. Her mind still focused on how she was potentially killing Astrid by taking her spot on the Horde.

Even though a victory had just been won, everyone was still on high alert. All of the soldiers that were on leave, plus the ones that fought raced the halls in packs of three and four patrolling or rushing to and from their posts.

A soldier bumped her side and her molars ground together through sudden slice of pain. She growled at him but the soldier was long gone by then. She continued to hobble past Ian's room just in time to witness Astrid slipping out. They both froze, eyeing each other warily. Oh no, she needed to tell her.

"What?" Astrid asked with a quick shrug of her shoulders.

"Nothing, I didn't know. I thought you…" Dylan's entire face scrunched, unsure of what she was trying to say.

Were Astrid and Ian a thing?

"Stop thinking, *Temperance*," she snapped.

Okay, maybe not.

Dylan lifted her palms hoping to convey: I come in peace!

Astrid nodded once as a blush crept up her neck in angry red blotches. "Just don't—"

"I didn't see anything," Dylan cut her off, "Got it," before continuing to walk past the temperamental demon. Perhaps, now wasn't the best time to tell her she had a month to live.

"Wait," Astrid called. Dylan stopped and turned, causing a pain to shoot up her side from the small movement. "...What happened last night?"

Dylan flicked up her eyebrows. "I don't think I'm the one you should be asking."

"*No*. Temperance, seriously? I know exactly what happened *in there*." She hooked her thumb towards Ian's door. "Too many details are *forever* seared into my mind." They both cringed at that. "You're limping. We were drugged. Everyone seems to be on duty. What the hell happened?"

A couple soldiers rushed past them bumping into Astrid but giving Dylan a wide berth. She guessed some were still afraid of her.

"A group of Scarred demons ambushed us." *And I got your place on the Horde. Just say it,* she urged herself, *now is the time!*

"*Essence?*"

Dylan nodded. "The Vat is down to half."

Astrid gasped and the air around her body seemed to drop several degrees as she worked to contain her shock. Dylan took a cautious step back still unsure of the scope of Astrid's powers. She had mentioned being a Terra but temperature always seemed to fluctuate around her. "What about Augusto?" Astrid asked but then quickly added, "and Soren."

"They weren't drugged."

"You were... yet, you still fought?"

Dylan moved out of the way of a few more demons marching down the hall. "I probably shouldn't have.

Something… I don't know, I just woke up and ran towards the screaming, ready to help. I was probably more of a liability than anything else." She gave a small smile that didn't reach her eyes. "Um, look, I…" she trailed off losing her nerve again. "I need to get to the Medic."

"Oh, right. Well, thanks… for not seeing anything."

"Don't mention it."

With her wound patched up, Dylan headed to the cafeteria for a quick snack before hitting the gym. Apparently the drug in her system was something called White Ash. It was a hallucinogen meant to knock her out for the duration of the battle. The Medic told her if Soren hadn't called him when he did, who knew when she'd have awakened; considering the dosage was apparently meant for a male three times her size.

She just wanted to continue her day like any other, and definitely not think about how she was potentially killing Astrid or her failed attempt to tell her. Taking someone's spot on the Horde was something Dylan struggled with silently for years since the day Kings Damen and Zirk had forced the group to welcome her with open arms. Until last night she had honestly thought this day would never come. Now, she had Kings to impress, powers to learn, and nights alone to face Silas.

One month.

She had a month to become a badass. *Ha!*

Deciding on some waffles, Dylan sat down at an empty table in the cafeteria and took a bite, swallowing the dry, crunchy cake with large gulps of her latté.

A short beep sounded on the cafeteria speakers. Dylan paused half expecting a worm to come fetch her or for the lights to blink out.

God, I'm messed up.

"Elementa!" She jerked her head to the door where Ian was urgently waving her over. She frowned and got up.

212

"What's up?"

"Come *on*." He grabbed her hand and yanked her down the hall. She was too stunned to question what was going on when he came to halt in front of an iron door opposite of the gym. Ian shoved it open, revealing a wide room filled with strange contraptions, hanging chains, racks of numerous types of weapons and onyx gear.

At the very end was an archway. Except instead seeing a room beyond, there was a luminescent, beryl-blue mist door with ethereal wisps and breaks of light as if the outdoors were just on the other side of the strange cloud.

Dylan gasped when she remembered Silas creating something similar to leave Zadar.

It was a Portal. *Here.* Right under her nose for the last three years. Why the hell hadn't she ever wanted to try this door? Not that she knew how to jump through a Portal without getting lost… if this even was a Portal.

"*Hello*," Ian waved in front of her face. "Temps?"

Dylan suddenly looked at him before noticing the rest of the crew.

Astrid looked up from pulling on a pair of leather pants and a hooded jacket. "Welcome to the Iron Portal, *comrade.*"

"What?" Dylan asked as they shoved a hooded leather jacket and pants in her arms. *Comrade*? Shit. She knows.

"This is your first mission," Soren said, appearing next to her already dressed in his uniform and securing a dagger and gun to his waist.

"My first… *oh*." Dylan quickly pulled on the pants and boots, fumbling the laces and buttons, all the while the weight of Astrid's execution pressing upon her.

"Don't worry you're only observing this time."

Dylan nodded nervously, while zipping her jacket.

"Hey," Soren said as he pulled her hood up. It was like she was suddenly wearing a helmet outfitted with night vision and several different gauges. "You got this."

She nodded again, not really knowing what to do or say

but mostly kind of wishing she had finished her coffee first.

"All right, let's go," Astrid said, opening a printed paper. She read the words and handed it to Ian before leaping into the blue cloud. Ian and Augusto copied her and when it was only she and Soren, he explained that he always went last.

She looked at the paper crinkled in her fist. Written down were several numbers in a line separated by dots.

"What do I do with this?"

"It's the coordinates of our destination. Remember it and think about it as you go."

She looked down again.

"You got it?"

"Yeah, but—" Soren shoved her into the blue oblivion.

Dylan screamed, tumbling ferociously through what seemed like a never ending cloud. Her arms flailed as she tried to orient herself when everything felt backwards and upside-down.

Her hair flung and whipped her face painfully and pieces of her body felt frail and on the verge of giving out.

A scream tore through her throat, clawing its way up and out of her mouth, when long fingers hooked her waist and yanked her until her world jolted and she collided with a hard chest. She quickly grabbed hold of Soren's neck and jacket.

"Breathe," Soren whispered onto her hair. She fought through the violent wind for her stolen breath and when she found it, her eyes snapped open. They had stopped spinning frantically and were only falling with no end in sight.

She shifted her head, resting against the side of Soren's spiky cheek. They weren't falling through the clouds as she first thought, but were being sucked into another dimension. It was like traveling through a black hole or tornado.

Swirling air vacuumed all around them as glimpses of different colors of light, chartreuse, aqua, magenta, and emerald, filtered through the varying cracks—glimpses into other worlds.

Dylan pushed back against the pressure of the wind to look down into the swirling depths of the vacuum, and focused on the bright star of light they were quickly reaching. She could see the others falling, and one by one, disappearing into the light.

How on earth would they survive this fall?

"This might hurt."

Her head whipped back just as Soren spoke, her body flung and ricocheted through the trees as if a real tornado had actually spat her out. This time, though, her scream lasted and echoed until her back slammed against the ground with a sharp snap.

A pinprick of feeling started in her big toe and slowly spanned her body. Her muscles protested movement as she curled in on herself, trying to ease the stiffness clutching her like a fist.

Why had Soren just let go of her like that? Couldn't he have helped her land more softly? If softly was even a possibility…

Dylan groaned and took a deep breath as several sharp pangs sliced through her back.

Of course, he pushed her away. He was like that parent that shoved their kid into a lake to teach them how to swim.

After cursing Soren under her breath, she began to focus on the sharp smell of mulch and fungi. Dylan concentrated on an odd, twisting shape piercing the soil she laid on. A black and purple beetle scurried up with tiny squeaks over the thick root.

"*Elementa!*" someone called, the voice muffled by the overgrowth of nature.

"Here," she croaked in return, barely loud enough for anyone to hear.

She rolled over onto her back, yelling, "Here!" just a bit louder. Her tense muscles refused to heed her inner demand to simply stand.

A sticky, hot wind shifted over her in a soft caress, kicking up some dirt and ruffling the explosion of green leaves above her that blotted out the afternoon sun. The surrouding nature was so beautiful and new, she almost forgot she was a soldier on a very specific and time-sensitive mission.

After another shout of her name that honestly didn't sound any closer, Dylan sat up and batted away chunks of black dirt from her cheeks and tangled hair, realizing that maybe she didn't hurt so bad after all.

Looking around the shaded dense crop of trees, she was contemplating which way to start looking for her crew when she heard a stick break not too far to her right. She froze.

A bird chirped and the wind played music in the trees before she heard what sounded like a boot crunch on the ground.

Dylan deftly pulled her hood back up while a series of texts scrolled across the screen in a flash.

LOCATION: BRAZILIAN AMAZON, EARTH
LOCAL TIME: 15:43
TEMPERATURE: 85 F
HUMIDITY: 70%
VITALS: NORMAL, ELEVATED HEART BEAT

Dylan uncurled herself silently and extracted a simple, serrated blade from her belt with shaking fingers. She knew she was only supposed to be observing but she was terrified and thankful Soren had pressed the weapon into her palm. She just wasn't sure what to do if she found the rogue demon. It wasn't like she wanted to kill him.

Her pulse pounded violently as she inched closer and closer to the enhanced sounds made clearer by her hood. She felt herself begin to tune out the chatter of Nature, her fellow soldiers' calls, even the loud rush of her breath, and focus her ears to her victim's movements, like a panther on the hunt.

She could do this. She wasn't Dylan Prescott here. She

was Temperance Elementa.

She sensed someone around the thick Kapok tree with tall, twisting roots. After a deep breath, she released a battle cry, jumping from around the tree with her blade raised—her voice stilled at the sight of a jaguar mauling the stomach of a dead child.

The jaguar took one look at her, growled, and immediately dashed away. Dylan slowly lowered her weapon, watching with wide, confused eyes as it disappeared into the brush.

She reminded herself that she was a demon, of course animals would be afraid of her... even deadly ones.

Dylan moved her gaze down to the naked boy with a crown of matted dark hair and dirt smudges around his cheekbones and neck; and then to the discarded blowgun filled with poisonous darts. She thought about the fact that she was in the Amazon Rain Forest and wondered if this was a member of one of the last uncontacted tribes—the Kawahiva or the Awá. If he was, they were already teetering on the brink of extinction, and it pissed her off to see a demon carelessly leave him unconscious to the fate of the wilderness. Where the hell was his tribe?

She swallowed painfully as she forced herself to examine the extent of his injuries. She had always fantasized about interacting with an uncontacted tribe, but not like this. A whimper slipped through her lips as she fell to her knees. One touch told her he was cold, dead, and had no soul.

"Dylan." She started at Soren's presence. "Dead?"

"Yes," she said, loosening a breath. It shouldn't have been that easy to sneak up on her here. What if he had been the rogue demon? She needed to pay more attention.

"Good," Soren said.

She gaped up into his unrelenting eyes. "*Good?*"

"Yes, good," he growled. "It's less work for us. Now, follow me."

Dylan ran her fingers over the small boy's eyes, closing

217

them. She wanted to take him to his home but knew that would be impossible. Even if she did know where to go, they would most likely refuse his body from an outsider, from a *demon*.

She stood up, unsteadily, and followed Soren as he began tracking his eyes along the foot prints that lead away from the Brazilian Indian victim.

They jumped over a large tree root and ducked under a thick bush. The temperature reading on her hood still showed that it was hot and muggy even though her suit seemed to be keeping her cool.

Minutes dragged by in silence as Dylan tried to cool her anger from the rogue demon's carelessness and Soren's comment. How much work could justify the death of an innocent? Sometimes Soren seemed like nothing but a robot for the OP. As if someone back in Elon controlled him from within a room with many screens and a joystick.

He was just cold.

"What's wrong?"

"Nothing. I'm just not as immune as you are to everything around me," Dylan said, glancing at him before stumbling over some roots.

"No. Before we jumped. You kept staring at Astrid like she was about to disappear."

Dylan wrapped her arms around herself. Astrid *was* about to disappear.

"I'm worried about her. That's all. I know she didn't want me to join the Horde."

"Yeah," he said, stopping briefly to click something on his military looking watch then veering left. "The worlds know she doesn't want you to join, but what can she do?" He shrugged it off like her death meant nothing.

She felt the innate urge to growl at him. Soren just shrugged at the thought of his friend and comrade dying. He freaking shrugged!

"You are unbelievable," she hissed.

Soren stopped when he realized she had flipped back her hood and started walking away from him. She almost gagged at the sudden slap of humidity against her face but she powered through, not really sure where she was going. She just wanted away from him. She needed to calm down and get her head on straight before she did something stupid like punch her commander.

"Where are you going?" He caught up with her and grabbed her elbow.

"Away from you," she said, wrenching herself free and continuing deeper into the thick forest.

He laughed icily, throwing back his hood as well. "And where might that be? Are you finally going to try running away?"

She looked back at him and mimicked his shrug angrily. She faced forward and wasn't all that surprised he already stood in front of her.

"Go ahead and run, Elementa. I will make it my life's mission to catch you."

Her heart stumbled from the way he said he'd catch her. Dylan immediately tore the unwanted thought from her mind. "Oh, it's Elementa now? Not *pet*?"

"Not unless you would rather be my pet," he smirked.

She sucked in a breath, trying with everything inside not to scream at the top of her lungs. "She's going to die because of me! Does that not mean anything to you *at all*?"

He cocked his head just slightly, as if considering her words for the first time. "What do you mean Astrid is going to die?"

"I'm taking her place in the Shadow Horde! And you... you're just making jokes! And *shrugging*!"

He still stared at her lamely and Dylan shook her head, forgetting Soren just didn't give a damn.

She spotted a log off to the side and sat with a huff, wishing she had gotten more sleep. Soren checked his watch before deciding to sit next to her.

His mouth twitched. "Astrid isn't going to die."

"*What*?"

"If the Kings want you on duty, then they'll make room. There's no need to worry, *my pet,*" he said the endearment jokingly. "They wouldn't dare lose an investment on purpose."

"Oh." Well, that had been a bunch of stress for nothing!

"Don't sound so disappointed," he chuckled.

"I'm not!" she scoffed. "Just... relieved. She kind of grew on me a little."

"Sure. She grows on us all after a while." Soren stood and instead of grabbing her like he usually did, he held out his hand.

Dylan took it and let him help her up.

"You better listen to that thing on your wrist," she said, prompting him to look down at his watch. "All that beeping can't be a good sign. What is that thing anyway?"

Soren muttered, "A TAC."

"A what?"

"Tracker-Auxiliary-Communication. TAC. You'll get one soon, I imagine."

They started moving deeper into the jungle again, soon coming to a shallow stream surrounded by towering palms and overgrown trees bearing white flowers and fruit; creating a dome effect to blot out the sun. Dylan paused at the water's edge, gazing at the brilliant, hot-pink shrubs and verdant bushes with hanging, rose gold, trumpet flowers all growing naturally. Dylan had never been very good at keeping plants alive, so the fact that this all grew in the wild kind of amazed her.

Aria had once bought a cactus after the girls had slowly murdered several house plants, thinking they just needed something that could basically take care of itself.

It took about two months for it to die.

After the cactus, they had an unspoken agreement never to bring up the possibility of pets.

Soren glanced at her before stomping through the delicate stream. Dylan followed cautiously, hopping on the exposed pepper-colored stones—wary of the fragile ecosystem being destroyed by Soren's boots.

"So, who does the kill? Whoever gets there first? Or… is it always you?" she said, jumping to the other side of the stream.

"It's usually whoever gets there first. We tend to make it into a game. But we don't kill until we've all met up and confirm the suspect."

"Okay," she said, dodging a vine that closely resembled a snake, and then darted forward when she realized it was a snake.

Soren grunted in response and stopped his watch from beeping again. He peered over at her instep with him.

"What?"

Soren appeared hesitant when he said, "We're giving you dibs if you want it."

Dylan's step faltered. "Soren, I'm just observing. I can't—"

He suddenly turned to look at her, revealing an expression as hard as steel. "What do you mean you *can't*? What exactly did you think you were going to do in the Horde?"

Dylan held his stare defiantly, trying not to flinch. "I've never killed anyone."

A voice inside her mind screamed that she was a liar. She'd killed Tristian. She'd killed her parents. And it was only a matter of time before she killed her friends here, too.

He grabbed her by the arm and yanked her close until she could see the individual black lashes framing his intimidating cerulean eyes. Her heart had a mind of its own this close to him. It flipped and swooped inside her chest, and she couldn't stop the rapid beat no matter how hard she tried to remain stoic. He frightened her with the way he pushed her; but it scared her even more to know how much she liked the fear.

Only his fear.

It was one of the few things in her life she knew she could count on never to change. Because his fear was safe. No matter how many times he tested her boundaries, he never did it out of spite. He was not Silas. He was not the enemy. He was conditioning her into being a warrior and building her up while guarding her from the threats that tore her down. He was her shield and her blade. He was her protector made of thorns.

His grip tightened and it only seemed to remind her how small and impressionable she was in comparison to him despite her potential power. It felt like he could crush her with a simple clench of his fist.

"You see that dead boy back there?"

She opened her mouth with a retort of how it was kind of hard *not* to see the boy when Soren leaned in a bit closer. "Think of how the demon who did that didn't give a shit. Think about how it took his soul while he screamed, and then after the little boy passed out from the pain, he only woke to a jaguar making a meal of his stomach."

"Soren," she slowly gritted out as he released her without backing up. She looked up into his impassive eyes, wondering how anyone could be that numb to violence.

He seemed to pick up on her internal question. "The only way for your first kill to go smoothly is for you to be angry. Even if it's directed at me, or at a false story." The hilt of his *Daleon* was suddenly pressed into her palm. "Now kill the fucker like a good little soldier, and don't embarrass yourself in front of our crew."

Our crew.

He backed away and she rubbed her arm absentmindedly. She was pissed off but not *that* pissed off. "Wait, *now*?"

"Astrid has detained her up ahead." He yanked up his hood, turning his sharp features into a shadow of leather and smoke. He pulled out the gun with an extra wide barrel, the

222

one she always saw him grab before missions. He checked the ammunition and nodded for them to keep going.

Her. The rogue demon was a her. She had a harder time digesting this for some reason. It wasn't until then that she realized she had just assumed the rogue demon would be a man.

They rounded another thick tree and walked up to the others talking about the band at Traverna from the night before, as if they were just hanging out and not watching over a demon bound and forced up against a tree.

Dylan had a flashback of being bound in the chambers just before her trial. The paralyzing terror and acceptance of knowing her life was over. Yet, here she was on the other side and about to give the final blow. How the hell was she going to pull this off?

"Finally!" Astrid sighed, a good welt swelling on her cheek. "I almost took this one for myself." She glared at the woman.

Ian laughed. "Careful there, killer. She looks about ready to give you another roundhouse kick."

The demon growled through clenched teeth stained red with blood then fixed her bloodshot eyes on Dylan.

Soren leaned down next to her ear. "Don't forget, she enjoyed it. She enjoyed slowly ripping that soul out of his tiny screaming body."

Dylan shuddered and Soren stepped in front of her to place a black device to the rogue demon's hand. The woman tried to fight this, but her body was mostly unresponsive.

"Shit, she's been busy!" Ian exclaimed glancing at the rectangular device.

"Why, what is it?" Dylan asked.

"It's how we collect the souls she took," Astrid explained. "She's about three times over the legal limit. I'm surprised she went down so easily."

Dylan nodded, still not really understanding the whole 'limit' thing. About a year earlier, Lord Struo had taken her to a place called the Rose Hall to release her consumed souls through a similar black box. She remembered expecting to feel exhausted and strained without the *Essence* running through her blood, but apparently demons only needed the immediate energy. The rest could be reused in different ways.

Dylan's fingers shook as she readjusted her grip on the *Daleon*. Just holding the blade made her nervous. It felt like an unstable bomb in her hands.

"All right," Soren said crossing his arms. "You're up."

Dylan gripped the blade harder and stood in front of the woman. She had thick dark hair pulled back into a ponytail that was mussed with dirt and dead leaves as a result of the fight. She had a slight figure and her jeans and tank looked relatively clean despite recent blood stains. It made Dylan wonder where she came from and why.

Stop, Dylan told herself. *Do not go there.* She couldn't think of this demon as a person. Not when she was expected to put her down like a feral animal.

The woman began working her mouth into a frightening smile. "Why, look who it is." Her voice was low and rough from the strain of the *Binding*. "You know, there was a rumor back home that you were fighting with the enemy. I didn't believe it. Not until now, of course." She spat to the side, turning a couple of crushed leaves crimson.

Entranced, Dylan moved closer. The woman smiled knowingly. "You still want to know, don't you?"

Dylan glared, not daring to utter a word.

"You do!" she laughed. "Oh, but, sweet Temperance, I can't do that..." She flicked her eyes to the others and back to Dylan. "I know they still look forward to your arrival... despite how much of a fraud you are," she snarled.

Dylan blanched. This demon didn't know what she had to go through to survive. "*Be quiet.*"

"Have you no self-respect?" The woman laughed. "Pretending. Always pretending to be someone you're not.

Pretending and using anyone who gets in your way. Do you pretend to love him, too?" Dylan cocked her head at this. Was she asking about Tristian? "I'm surprised you were able to convince the Kings and your little Horde friends of any worth. But I know, don't I? It's why they don't come after you. It's why no one wants you. I can see the mark of death on you, and it's laughing. *Always laughing at the spineless girl*."

Dylan told her again to be quiet but the demon's voice kept getting louder and louder. Dylan began to worry the others would hear the thoughts that clouded her mind daily.

Pretending.

Fraud.

Spineless.

It's why no one wants you…

She squeezed her eyes shut, needing the demon to stop talking, needing her poisonous words to stop filling the cracks of Dylan's fragile foundation.

"But don't worry, my sweet Temperance. I'm sure they'll figure out soon how much of a *waste* you are. If they haven't already." The woman started laughing manically.

"SHUT UP!"

"The *all-powerful*—" The life shot out of the demon's eyes and Dylan looked up unable to believe what she had done. Her hand was still gripping Soren's knife now lodged deeply in the demon's head. A puff of purple mist dissolved around her like smoke.

It was her demon life, an *Elementa* life, and Dylan ended it.

Almost instantly, Dylan tried pulling the knife out as she stood but it didn't budge. She wedged her foot against the woman's neck and yanked the knife free. The demon fell over with a thud onto the forest floor.

Dylan's heart was screaming inside at what she had done, but outwardly she felt nothing.

"Damn Temperance!" Ian laughed. "Remind me never to

get on your bad side."

Dylan didn't dignify him with a response. She just wanted out of here. The woman's words were eating away at her mind like acid. Placing the bloodied dagger in Soren's hand, she pulled her hood up and walked away.

"Where is she—where are you going?" Astrid yelled.

Everyone seemed confused except for Soren.

He looked like he heard everything even though Dylan knew that to be impossible. The rogue demon had been inside her head—neither one of them uttering a word until Dylan killed her with a scream.

"Forget it," Soren grunted, looking away from Dylan. "Let's just get out of here."

CHAPTER 13

*"She wears strength and darkness equally well,
the girl has always been half goddess, half hell."*
Nikita Gill

"So, I was thinking about going for a ride."

Dylan turned to Soren as he sat next her in the cafeteria. She wasn't really sure why he was telling her. Usually he just did whatever he wanted and expected her to accept it.

She nodded. "Have fun. I'll probably just work on drills," she sighed as she took another bite of her sad, rubbery omelet. Oh, what she would give for a breakfast taco.

"I'm not giving you an update on my schedule." He tossed her a jacket, light leather and heavy zipper hitting her in the face. "I'm telling you to come with me."

"Huh," she grunted, yanking the jacket off her head. "I must've missed the part where you asked, *would you like* and *to go* and," she boosted an eyebrow, *"with me?"*

"Don't be a smart ass," he added, jumping up and heading to the hallway as if he expected her to follow.

She groaned. Of course she would follow. She threw away her snack and quickly got in step beside him.

Ever since they had gotten back from the mission, Dylan hadn't talked to anyone. Not even Soren, and he appeared to want to give her space as well. She went to her lessons with various instructors, still mainly working on controlling and summoning the elements. So far air seemed to be the only nonexistent element despite the strong pull she felt for it.

Dylan skipped down the front steps behind him as she pulled the jacket's zipper all the way up to her chin to fight off the hard chill in the air.

Elon was a lot different during the day. Instead of charming and quaint, there was an air of seriousness. Demons rode bicycles and horses or pulled carts filled with baked goods, liquor, or metal work. Everyone seemed to be diligently working, bartering, or heading somewhere specific. No one mingled or even laughed. She wasn't sure how a world so beautiful could hold people who looked so miserable.

"Get on."

"What? Oh." She marched over to his bike and hesitated when he didn't get on first.

"Well?"

She frowned. Did he want her to get on first again? "Soren, I'm not drunk. We don't have to ride in that ridiculous—"

"Get *on,*" he insisted. "You have to learn how to ride at some point."

"Oh… Oh!" Her eyes lit up and she beamed skipping up to the roping hunk of metal and slid on slowly already feeling the enormous weight under her.

He smirked and showed her how to turn it on and which lever was the gas verses the clutch and break.

He moved behind her and she sat up straighter.

"Now try not to kill us."

Her mind sputtered and she turned her head to look at him. "Th-that's it? Just *go*?"

"Yes," he sighed. "Just go."

She sucked in a deep breath and switched on the bike, forgetting the clutch. It stalled. Her breath released in a disappointed rush.

"Try again," he pushed.

She nodded and turned the ignition again. This time the bike started successfully.

"Ha-*ha*!"

"Yeah, yeah," Soren said, his suppressed smile practically heard. "Now ease the throttle—"

Dylan clutched the little lever and jerked forward violently. Her grip instinctively tightened and the front wheel lifted a bit, catapulting Soren off. She gasped as the wheel slammed back onto the pavement and swerved, startling a demon pulling a vegetable cart. The cart tilted, spilling a dozen tomatoes before it corrected itself.

Dylan panicked as she headed straight for a shop window. The woman inside screamed just as Soren rushed behind her and jumped back on. His arms flew around her and took control of the throttle in seconds, yanking the bike back on to the road.

Dylan whipped her head around yelling, "Sorry!" to the victims of her driving only to be rewarded by curses and raised fists.

Soren chuckled in her ear and pulled the gas, steering them out of town and into the surrounding subdivisions. The homes here were the same English Tudor style as the city center only with wider lots and lush landscapes.

It occurred to Dylan, Soren might be taking her to his house when several children who had been playing in the street started running alongside them yelling both of their names in barely controlled excitement.

Dylan couldn't help but smile and wave.

Soren didn't stop in the neighborhood. He wove through the streets before turning onto a long and hilly road that curved around the sparkling blue-green mirage of the Void of Bones.

The city of Asau moved farther and farther behind them as the Collector's world became more vibrant. Beautiful trees and thick greenery blanketed the sides of the road, granting glimpses of sprawling farm houses on many acres. Corn stalks, wheat, cotton. Fields of lavender and lilac. All beneath the denim blue sky.

It felt like she was flying, soaring through the rolling pastures and it was absolutely breathtaking.

She settled against her friend and smiled at the welcoming sight.

"I could do this forever," she muttered.

His chin shifted against the top of her head and he began to release his grip off her hands. Dylan straightened and held the throttle at the same pressure.

"Good," he said into her ear. "Now, just keep going. We'll take a turn in a couple miles."

Dylan nodded and pulled more on the gas. She imagined Soren smiling as they raced down the road, hitting unsettling speeds that pulsed adrenaline into her veins.

She felt alive, dangerous, and somehow safe all at the same time, wondering if this was what Soren felt during battle. If he did then she understood the appeal.

They soon slowed and he directed her through a couple turns. While jerky, she made the turns successfully. She was just glad she didn't stall out or crash.

They quickly began climbing altitude and her heart pounded as they traversed the edge of a mountain. She didn't realize she was hugging the wall until she felt Soren steer them away from the jagged rocks.

"Just around the corner," Soren urged. "Then we stop."

Dylan exhaled in relief when she caught sight of a white food truck with steam sighing through the windows. As "freeing" as the ride had been she was eager to hand the controls back over to Soren.

Dylan listened to Soren's careful instructions as she tried to stop next to an old picnic table but the bike stalled leaving it half on, half off the road.

"Good enough!" Dylan announced, wasting no time in jumping off.

Soren shook his head to himself while grabbing the handle bars and pushing the bike to the side, next to a cedar tree with peeling bark and spiny, emerald leaves.

Dylan had her arms wrapped tightly around herself and was bouncing on her toes as Soren jogged over to her cupping his hands around his mouth to warm them.

"Holy shit," Soren shuddered. "It's cold. Here." He produced two beanies out of his pocket, giving her one.

"I feel very unprepared for this weather," Dylan grumbled as she pulled the black knit hat over her hair and ears.

"It'll get better soon," Soren said as they hurried over to the little window on the side of the food truck.

Dylan highly doubted that. It may have been too early for the sun to properly warm anything but she couldn't foresee the temperature rising to a comfortable level up here where it could possibly snow.

Soren rapped his fist against the side of the truck twice. Someone inside moved around, rocking the truck with vigor. That someone swung open the concession window and stuck his head out. It was an old man with graying hair, deep lines around his thin mouth and sharp demon eyes.

Dylan gawked. He was a Collector... but aged!

"Ah, Verbeck!" the old man hollered, "I'd wondered when you might be back."

"It's commander now," Soren corrected, prompting Dylan to roll her eyes.

The old man whistled in delight. "Just like your papa. Good for you, son."

It struck Dylan then that Soren wasn't bragging but simply sharing news with some kind of... friend?

"Now, I know you didn't come all the way up here to see little old me, so what'll ya have?"

"Two of Elon's finest cocoas," Soren said with true enthusiasm.

The old man's eyes seemed to zero in on Dylan as if he'd just noticed her presence.

Dylan politely said, "Hello."

The man didn't respond. His gaze flicked back to Soren

231

with a frown before he ducked back inside and slammed the window closed.

"I have a sneaking suspicion he doesn't like me," Dylan murmured.

"He doesn't like many people," but even as Soren said it, she could tell it was lie. Something had shifted inside him; and it was almost as if he suddenly regretted bringing her. "He's just old. You have nothing to worry about."

"Speaking of, how *did* he age? I thought all Collectors stayed miraculously young looking."

"He refuses to consume Essence. Without Essence, we age almost like humans."

Dylan listed her head. "Would we die like humans?"

"Considering Mr. Bryant is about three hundred years old, I would say no," Soren said, pulling a pack of cigarettes and a lighter out of his jacket pocket.

Dylan widened her eyes at the man's age. "Oh, wow." She thought about Tristian's age of over two hundred years and then Soren's of fifty years. "So, you're like young then."

"No," he lit his cigarette, inhaling the calming smoke and filling the air with spices. "You're young."

Dylan nodded thoughtfully.

He flicked the bottom of the pack against his palm and a thin brown cigarette pushed out. He held out the pack to her and she shook her head—not really enjoying the taste as much as she liked the smell.

The window snapped open, giving Dylan a start.

"Two world famous cocoas!" the old man beamed, holding out two steaming, red paper cups.

Soren dug out a couple of silver coins and Mr. Bryant acted insulted.

"I cannot accept money from the commander of the Horde." He shook his head, shaking the loose skin on his cheeks. "Take your drinks and pay your respects. Your money is no good here!"

"Oh, come on!" Soren scowled, apparently not liking the

232

special treatment.

"Then perhaps you might accept it from a trainee?" Dylan took the coins from Soren's hand and slipped them onto the shelf connected to the window next to the two cups.

The old man grunted and slowly took the silver suspiciously while Soren grabbed the cups with his cigarette between his teeth.

Soren handed Dylan a cup and she brought it close to her nose, letting the steam warm her face.

"This cocoa better be good to have come all the way up here for it."

"It is," Soren confirmed, walking to a small pathway between the trees.

Dylan followed closely behind, marching up the rock staircase deeper and deeper into the woods.

"Where are you taking me?" Dylan asked, as she eyed the dense forest around them.

"You'll see," was all he said as he crested the top where the forest ended.

Dylan broke through the trees and almost dropped her cocoa at the sight. Her feet carried her forward mindlessly until she was a few feet from the lip of the canyon.

"The Valley of Ashes," she whispered.

A cold gust of wind picked up from behind her, shuffling the trees and swooping down into the pit of white ash. It kicked up remains, revealing spikes of black granite. Dylan took a couple steps back; afraid the wind might shove her off the cliff's spine.

"Yes," Soren confirmed, sitting on a nearby bolder.

She looked at him. His usual frown set securely in place.

"Was this what that man meant by paying your respects?"

Soren nodded. "It is the highest honor to be lain here."

She waited for him to tell her who he visited but he took long drag of his cigarette and silently stared into the canyon. She wondered if his father and brother were here. But, of course they were. Where else would a soldier and the

233

commander of the Shadow Horde be placed?

Dylan suddenly felt like she was intruding on some sort of private moment for Soren. She stared out at the canyon and tried to imagine what it felt like to dump your loved one's ashes here. She couldn't. She was so used to speaking to the ocean when she needed her parents' guidance, not a giant chasm filled with burned remains.

She took a large gulp of her cocoa, realizing it was pretty darn good. It was the perfect balance of creamy chocolate and milk with only a touch of sugar.

"I know he's not here," Soren said, "but if you need a place to go…" he clenched his jaw. "I thought it would make you feel better. After the mission, after what was said," he trailed off and took another drag.

She knew he saw her scream Tristian's name when they were fighting the Scarred. He *knew*. And he also somehow knew about the rogue demon's thoughts just before Dylan killed her. But looking at Soren now, Dylan almost wanted to laugh at how uncomfortable he looked saying these words to her; she held it in. He was trying to be thoughtful, even if it looked like it pained him to be.

She walked over and sat next to him.

"Thanks." She offered a small smile and looked back toward the valley. It was really quite wonderful in a weird and messed up way. She could almost imagine the ash was snow.

"Where did you guys take Tristian?"

"We didn't."

She jerked her head in his direction. "What?"

"King Zirk ordered us to leave him. We did."

She shivered at the indifference in his words, and then shivered at the thought of dying in Silas' castle only to forever be confined within his twisted walls.

They sat for a while, both thinking about the past in silence. Dylan noticed that other than the random bursts of wind the area was devoid of life. Not even the sound of a bird chirping could be heard.

"We shouldn't stay here too long. It looks like it might rain."

Dylan looked up at the darkening clouds like stained, pulled cotton closing in over them and stood with Soren.

"What about your cocoa?" she asked as Soren started back down the steps inside the forest.

"It wasn't for me."

Riding back into town, Dylan drove with more confidence. Her grip was relaxed. Even Soren held the back of his seat instead of the handlebars.

They were still several miles out from the town square when the clouds closed over them, blackening the sky and stealing any warmth from the air. A fork of lightning struck a tree in front of them, splitting it like a knife down the middle. Half of the tree landed in the road, startling Dylan and causing her to swerve the bike off to the side.

They tumbled into the grass just as another burst of lightning struck the Void of Bones. Her head and shoulder snapped against the hard ground.

Soren rolled out from under the bike and pulled her free. Dylan sat up and looked around hazily. Fat drops of rain rushed down like a waterfall, soaking them instantly.

"Crap!" she groaned over the downpour of rain.

"Are you okay?" Soren yelled.

"I think so." She tested her arms and legs then confirmed, "Yeah. Are you?"

"Yeah."

They both stood unsteady, when something hard struck her head. "Ow!" But just as she spoke several more hail stones began to shower overhead. Soren yelled something that she couldn't hear and snatched her hand, yanking her towards a farm house in the clearing.

They stumbled into an old, screened-in porch wrapped around a white paneled home.

For several moments they just stood, soaked, watching the hail falling in waves over the field accompanied by violent wind. Their breaths came in quick, smoky pants as lightening crackled against the gun-metal-grey horizon.

Dylan couldn't believe she had just wrecked a motorcycle without breaking something or dying. She had heard so many horror stories about motorcyclists that she always assumed you were immensely lucky to walk away. Perhaps, they were... or maybe it was because they were demons. She suddenly felt idiotic for not wearing a helmet. Wouldn't that cause a change in events. How in the worlds would Silas pass his time if she died?

Soren turned to Dylan in a sudden moment of determination. He threaded his fingers through her soaked locks, pushing back the hair from her eyes and tilted her face up. Her breath caught at the unexpected touch. At the way he didn't hesitate with each movement.

His beanie and hair were just as soaked as hers and it dripped down on her relentlessly as his blue eyes looked her over, inspecting her wounds. She couldn't help but do the same. He had a gash on his cheek with smeared blood from the rain and he looked about ready to... his touch trailed across her jaw to the apex of her neck. She tensed, not exactly at his touch but at how gentle it was; how open he seemed. It felt like he wasn't about to just kiss her, but love her.

She pulled away and winced when the sudden movement caused her head to hurt.

"I probably should have worn a helmet," she said mildly, answering the bemusement in his features. She looked away from him, feeling the tear of flesh on her jaw. It felt like a broken goose egg. Her hand drifted to her pounding head when she noticed that she must have lost Soren's beanie by the bike.

The sound of a screen door squeaking and snapping shut brought her attention to the entrance to the old home, into

236

which Soren had disappeared. She shivered again, wrapping her arms around herself and trying to rub warmth through the slick, leather of her jacket.

Her eyes scanned the porch. It was dark and dusty; a stuffy, earthy smell spoke of the home's extended vacancy. She wondered who lived here and why they left; why no one had chosen to take the home and make it their own afterward. Her eyes flicked back to the front door of the home as her breath plumed out.

She wanted to go inside, but an odd feeling gripped her and she wished she had the option to leave, so she didn't have to face Soren right now. Not after wrecking his bike and turning away from him during... whatever that was.

With one more glance at the vicious hail that obviously had no intention of stopping any time soon, Dylan opened the screen door and stepped into the dark room filled with white sheets covering lumps of what she guessed were sculptures, furniture, and lamps. A burst of lightning flashed, giving her a moment of clear vision and an even longer moment of blindness.

"Soren?" she called out. There was a shuffle behind her and she spun around. Her heart thudded when she bumped into a marble sculpture.

Dylan took a deep breath. She never liked old, deserted places. Haunted houses not exactly her go to Halloween stop. A crack of thunder shook the house and she jumped. Was Soren messing with her again?

"Soren!"

Another sound muffled behind her and she flipped around again, still only surrounded by white mountains. But when she blinked, two flecks of dark orange seemed burned into her retinas.

Something heavy fell on her shoulder and she screamed.

"Shit!" Soren grunted, blocking Dylan's right hook and knee.

When she registered it was him, she fell into his arms and

hugged him tightly. She didn't want him to know how scared she was, or how hard she was fighting tears. His arms hesitantly encircled her.

"Dylan?"

She took a deep breath before looking up at him. His hair was tangled and unruly as if he had just ripped off his beanie and didn't bother to fix it. He frowned down at her with a blanket in one of his fists.

Dylan quickly stepped away. "Sorry." Her hand came up and she pinched the bridge of her nose. "God, I'm so sorry."

"Fuck it," he muttered, giving her a puzzled look before turning away and leading her back into the living room and to a clearing next to a small, white hearth.

There were a couple worn, crocheted blankets laid out in front of a sheet covered couch.

Soren sat on a blanket and Dylan copied him. He handed her the other faded blanket and she wrapped it around her shoulders. The thing stank but her need for warmth won.

"It's not the first bike I've wrecked," he said, running his eyes all over the dark room, suspiciously. "It's really not a big deal, so stop beating yourself up over it."

"I'm still sorry."

"It's okay, Dylan," he sighed, finally resting his head against the couch. His head hurt just as much, if not more, as hers. She idly wondered why they weren't sitting on the couch instead of the floor but she figured Soren had his reasons.

She looked around the small living room,

"Does the fireplace still work?"

"I don't know, Pyro, does it?"

"What? I don't know how to *start* fire."

"After seeing the roots on your Binding, one might assume you were an expert."

"And where would I practice this?" she snapped. "My strength was the only thing I noticed, never something I practiced." She ground her teeth, angered that he was still bringing it up.

"Well, you might as well try. We'll probably be here all night."

"You don't want to try hiking back in an hour?"

"We probably could if we were in gear."

She sighed. "Okay then... Pyro it is," she mumbled, crawling towards the hearth. She looked back at him. "Uh, any advice?"

He lifted an eyebrow. "How about *touching* the wood?"

She cleared her throat, "right."

She shook the cold out of her fingers before setting her fingers on the dusty, crumbling wood that rested inside.

She closed her eyes and thought of fire, of life, of the will to live, the hot fire festering within her heart—the fire she never thought she'd have again, and surged her *Unda*. Her hands tingled and her fingertips burned almost too hot to tolerate. It didn't feel like what she remembered the flames felt like. This almost pained her. After a moment of burning her fingers, her lids flipped open to disappointment, followed by astonishment.

Her fingers ran across the live, rich wood, stopping at the green flower curling up and out of a small hole.

"Dylan...?"

"*Soren*." She smiled, fingering the glossy petals. He moved next to her. "I created... life," she whispered. Why did life have to hurt so bad?

"Huh," he grunted over her shoulder. "Well, maybe the wood will light now."

Her mouth dropped open.

"I can't just destroy it!"

"Dylan," he chuckled a bit exasperated. "I'll get you fifty sticks to decorate with little flowers when we return home, but right now it's damn cold."

When she didn't move, Soren lifted his boot and brought it down on the emerald flower. "There. I destroyed it for you."

She gaped at the crushed flower then back at him. "*Ass.*"

"I've been called worse," he smirked, laying back and closing his eyes with his hands pillowing his head.

She scowled and reached for the wood. This time instead of thoughts of beauty, her mind sizzled with irritation and resentment.

It didn't take long for a flame to ignite.

They spent the next few hours warm, talking about her lessons with the new teachers, and King Damen whom turned out to not be so bad. Soren even admitted that her powers were coming along fine; and from Soren, Dylan knew that was as good as praise got.

They also talked about the games they played during missions and how she would be expected to catch the demon next time as a kind of initiation they had all been through. Then, their conversation drifted to when he learned to ride a motorcycle and his many crashes. Some drunk, some distracted. One that was completely not his fault, or so he said. And every now and then he would smile or laugh in rare carefree moments. It felt like she was sharing something sacred with him that no other person had the privilege to experience; because if there was anything she knew about Soren, it was that he never shared.

Dylan's eyes fluttered open sometime in the middle of the night. The room was silent except for the occasional crackle or pop from residual fire. A low flicker danced shadows along the bare plaster walls. Her side ached from sleeping on the floor, but her head felt better and was, surprisingly, being pillowed by Soren's leather arm. She hadn't even remembered falling asleep like that.

She sat up and rubbed her eyes. She hadn't dreamed of anything so she attributed her midnight awakening to just sleeping on the hardwood.

She glanced down at her commander. He slept on his back, one arm for her, the other securely gripping his *Daleon* as if he expected to be lurched awake for battle.

There was something beautiful about watching him sleep. His icy exterior melted and smoothed in the midst of dreams. She could almost imagine that he was kind, selfless, *sane;* but she guessed, in his own way he was all of those things.

Who do you mourn? she wanted to ask. He had only left one cup for whoever he visited today and she had a feeling it wasn't for his dad or his brother. And the way Mr. Bryant had spoken to him and looked at her like she was an unfortunate addition, made her think perhaps Soren had lost the girl he loved. But, that could merely be her jumping to romantic conclusions.

Her fingers came up to the gash on his cheek. It was swollen and red, and even just hovering, she could feel its warmth of a nearing infection. She moved her hand up to his hairline just about to push his hair away from his eyes when a weird sensation tickled the back of her neck.

Dylan paused.

Her gut screaming, '*Move!*'

With the rain still pounding against the tin roof it was difficult to listen for anything out of the ordinary. Her head turned slowly to look around the flickering room. It felt like someone was there, watching her.

Her eyes locked onto a dark space between the small foyer and dining room where she had initially entered. The white sheet-covered furnishings glowed like human shaped ghosts.

A hand closed around her wrist and she gasped.

"What is it?" Soren asked, eyes alert and blade drawn.

"Nothing." She looked back to the storage room briefly before turning back to him. "I just don't like old houses. Everything feels alive, even though I know it's all in my head."

"Everything in our world is old... but, you are right, none of it is alive." He sighed, holstering his blade. "I assure you."

"The rain should've stopped by now."

241

"If it doesn't by morning, I'll figure something out." He sat up and ran a hand through his locks. "In the meantime, I need to find more wood."

"Oh, yeah," Dylan said, starting to stand.

"No, stay here. I'll be right back. I think I saw some wood on the porch. If not, that rocker's meeting its maker."

"Fine," she yawned, as Soren got up and left through the front door.

Dylan looked around briefly before getting up. She peeked outside the dusty window, but it was like a black tunnel without moonlight. The violent slap of wind and icy rain was still going strong.

She yawned again and peeked under a few sheets at the floral furniture before ambling into a breakfast room with wide bay windows and a matching floral bench. The thought of this home vacant for the rest of its existence was almost sad. She could easily imagine it bright and cheery during the daylight without the sheets and dust. She turned another corner and stopped.

It was pitch black. The light of the fireplace unable to reach what she guessed was the kitchen. She wondered what it looked like, if there was water or food. Who knew how long this rain would last—a faint sound, like the shuffle of a boot or whisper of a step stung her ears.

"Soren?" she called out, unaware of which way she heard the movement, behind her or... Her eyes widened at the gnawing feeling, yet again.

Something was wrong.

She backed up, retreating into the living room. She was about head to the front door when the front exterior wall exploded, sending Soren through the debris like a sack of bloody potatoes.

Dylan slammed down into a crouch behind the sofa, her arms flying up over her head in protection. After a few moments, she inched around the armrest until she spotted Soren groaning on the floor, surrounded by splintered siding and shattered glass.

He rolled onto his stomach, trying to get up. Dylan started to get up as well, to dart toward him but stopped when a brawler type with green, orange, and red paint on his face sauntered inside. His foot came down hard between Soren's shoulder blades, shoving him back onto his stomach.

"Where do you think you're going, rodent?" the Scarred demon laughed.

Dylan's stomach turned over in terror, and she began scooting backward towards the hearth—to her only weapon, to her flames. She told herself it was only one demon and they were two. They could still take him. They were all supernatural. None of them were exceptionally special except for her. Even if she was just learning her powers.

She could feel the heat kissing her clammy skin as she reached around behind her. Her hand knocked against a leather boot and she gasped, turning to look into the eyes of another Scarred demon painted in red and green stripes with slicked back, pale blonde hair. But, it wasn't just any Scarred demon. He was the one who had the red band tied tightly around his upper arm.

Dylan flipped around and scrambled backward. He chuckled when she hit another boot and yelped.

A new Scarred demon looked down through thick green paint and dark brown eyes.

She screamed this time and scrambled into another direction.

"Dylan," Soren's pained voice stole her attention, "*run!*"

The demon standing over him slammed his foot into Soren's ribs with a scowl. "No one asked for your advice."

"Fuck... off," Soren spat.

The Scarred demon laughed humorlessly while pulling out a small cell phone like device and aimed it at Soren. Soren's body jumped and convulsed as if electrocuted.

"Oh God! Stop!" Dylan cried in horror at the blood trickling out of Soren's ears and eyes like tears. The demon stopped, but he seemed to smile at her concern as if putting together a vital piece of the puzzle.

"Or what, *Dylan*?"

Her lip curled instinctively, but she didn't have an 'Or what.' she just wanted him to stop and go away. She stood when it seemed like no one was making any moves toward her and she took a chance.

"Don't you know who *I am*?" she asked defiantly.

The demon with the red band next to her grinned. His eyes were alight with amusement. "The Elementa *child* with little to no control over her abilities? Why else would we be here?"

The blood in her veins ran cold. In the back of her mind she had known, only she didn't want to accept it. She had left her cage and now Silas' minions were here, ready to take her back to their master.

"I'm not going back," she all but gasped. "I won't."

The demon with the red band smirked at her words. "I don't believe you have a choice."

"I would rather *die*."

He nodded, as if what she suggested could be arranged before looking at the demon standing over Soren. "Red, do it."

Dylan's eyebrows furrowed but the sound of Soren's rippling scream and his body seizing against the electronic pulse yanked her out of her confusion. She leapt toward him as two of the Scarred demons grasped an arm on either side and tugged her to her knees. She struggled against them as Soren convulsed until the icy prick of a sharp blade met her throat.

The commander leaned down close to her ear. "I'm not sure how many more times your boyfriend here can withstand the *scrambler* before he kicks it." The leather of his gloves creaked against the hilt of his weapon. "Care to keep testing me?"

Silent tears raked down her face as she watched Soren

gag and struggle through pink, foamy spittle. The Scarred demon wrenched him up to his knees and pressed the device squarely against his neck. Soren's eyes were glazed like he'd just woken up.

Dylan opened her mouth to tell them she'd cooperate if they leave him alone, but she couldn't speak the words. To go with them would be walking, willingly, into a life of slavery and torture.

She knew then she had barely changed, if at all. She was still a coward. The only difference now was that she was a coward with lame magic tricks.

"Red, do it," the commander sighed, annoyed.

"Okay!" Dylan screamed. Shocked that she was doing this. "Okay," she said with less fight, "I will go," she forced out, "but, only if you let him go."

Soren became coherent enough to glare at her. Her cheeks heated in shame. His hate didn't matter. She just couldn't justify killing Soren to only, possibly, save herself. It went against the grain of her very being.

"*Good*," the Scarred commander said, so close to her face that his breath touched her cheek. Her face crinkled and she lifted her shoulder abruptly, wanting his disgusting breath off her skin. "Now that wasn't so hard was it?" He straightened and directed the Scarred demon nearest to him to create a Portal.

The demon marched to the wall between the living room and the kitchen and placed his hands on the plaster. A brilliant swirl of blue light emanated from his fingertips, expanding until it was the size of a door.

The Scarred commander yanked Dylan up until she was standing and shoved her to the Portal. Her eyes instinctively sought out Soren. When she caught his gaze, Soren's eyes narrowed, retreating into a dark path of incredulous hate. Dylan couldn't take his dissatisfaction any longer and stared at the floor.

You're doing this for him. She told herself, *Yes, he's*

pissed... but pissed is better than dead.

Dylan's expression hardened just before she was shoved inside the blue cloud.

If felt like hours before they tumbled onto a dusty, wooden floor. The Scarred commander landed on his feet while Dylan landed hard on her knees. She lifted her chin and blinked through her hair that was a mess of tangles, sticking to her tear stained cheeks. They seemed to be in some sort of barn with a high-pitched, gabled roof supported by bulky, oak rafters. A couple bales of rotting hay sat in the corner by an aged, narrow ladder that led to a sparse hayloft and a dark, circular window, giving nothing away of what was on the other side. The smell of wet wood and manure was sharp against her nostrils.

Dylan gritted her teeth as the commander dragged her across the room by her arm where two figures stood. Looking at them, Dylan felt even more perplexed.

"Oh, good," a woman said, staring down at Dylan in delight. "I don't think we've had the privilege, yet."

Dylan glared. No, they hadn't met, but she had seen this woman before. Once. In the middle of the night with Soren.

She was the Queen's friend.

"My name is Nadia Burke."

Dylan looked her over, trying to discern what her roll here was. Her russet locks were pulled tightly into a high bun and she wore an impeccably cut pant suit as before; only instead of cream it was a pastel blue. She looked almost the same. The only major difference from then to now was her quite rounded, pregnant belly.

Had Dylan completely misread this kidnapping? Who was this lady and what did she want with Temperance?

Dylan moved her eyes to the wolf sitting calmly next to her. It had a shimmery silver, almost blue, coat and sky blue eyes. It shifted uncomfortably when their eyes met and she had the strangest feeling that she knew this animal. Dylan blinked several times, determined to correct her mind from playing a joke. That was impossible. It was only another wild beast uncomfortable around a demon.

More boots stomped behind them followed by Soren's groan. Dylan craned her neck back in shock at seeing him… here.

Nadia's cold eyes flicked to the demons that had just fallen through the Portal and she snapped, "Who is *this*?"

"This," the Scarred demon, Red, yanked Soren up and sneered, "Why, this is our leverage for Temperance's cooperation. Hurt him and we can get her to do anything."

Dylan gaped.

"Well, we have her now, so get rid of him," Nadia snapped, drifting her fingers lazily in the air.

"NO!" Dylan screamed, before pleading frantically to the demon that gripped her arm. "The deal was that I go with you and you let him go." Dylan seethed. "So, send him back!"

The Scarred commander smirked. "Oh, we'll let him go all right. But, we never said alive."

Dylan gasped as she jerked her head around and watched Red pick out a blade from his hip. He lifted it to Soren's throat. "Don't worry," he crooned to Dylan. "I will make it quick."

Dylan's fists clenched as the urge to scream and launch herself at Red flared. It suddenly felt like everything around her was moving in slow motion as she watched a sadistic smile spread across his face. And then she was looking at Soren. His face flushed and his nostrils fared as he waited for the inevitable.

"I'm sorry," she suddenly said, knowing if she went with them now her sacrifice would have meant nothing. She needed to fight. They might be surrounded but like hell would she go down willingly. When Red glanced at her after she spoke, Dylan used the distraction to rear back her elbow and strike the commander in the crotch.

Soren seemed to follow suit, snapping his head against

Red's temple. Red stumbled, giving Soren enough time to reach for his dagger, flipping it straight into the demon's throat. Soren yanked it to the side and blood gushed through the opening as Red collapsed to the floor.

Dylan shot out of the commander's grasp when she felt his hold weaken from her hit. He scrambled after her, his blade sliding across her shoulder in a sharp burst of pain as she rolled away.

A terrible stinging seized her, but she forced it to the back of her mind and pushed herself to get as far away as she could until she hit the wall.

In her peripheral vision, Soren fought the other Scarred demon with jerky and sluggish movements probably the effects from the *Scrambler*. In front of her, the Scarred commander was eyeing her like a snake tracking its target—just waiting for the perfect moment to strike.

Her thoughts were tumultuous. Wondering where were they? The odds of getting to the Portal; and if not, were they somewhere they could easily find help? She needed a weapon. Who was Nadia? Soren's face when she turned away from him on the porch.

Dylan fisted her hands and forced herself to stay on track. Weapon first.

Her eyes landed on Soren's fallen cigarette pack.

Of course! Dylan almost squealed. *The lighter!*

She took two steps toward it and stopped when a dark brown wolf darted in front of her and dove into the Portal. Dylan looked over where Nadia and the wolf had been only to see the wolf with a silver coat standing on all fours with its ears back.

Dylan felt momentarily dazed while she watched it dart to the Portal as the other had. It stopped just before diving in and looked back at Dylan. The wolf's teeth bared and it barked a warning. In a strange way it kind of sounded like... Dylan looked to her side and gasped, ducking just in time to miss the commander's lunge for her. He had snuck underneath the hayloft while she was focused on the Nadia's wolf form. Dylan knew without a doubt that if the wolf hadn't warned her, she would be in the commander's clutches yet again.

Dylan grabbed the commander's blade-ridden hand and shoved him back with her demon strength. He growled and lunged again, this time slicing his blade through the air between them. Dylan jumped back and stumbled over Red's body, falling hard on her rear. She kicked over Red's body, trying to put distance between them. But, the commander only grinned as if she amused him with her struggling.

Dylan turned and rushed halfway up but before she could stand the Scarred commander grabbed her ankle and yanked her down. She reached for the pack, her finger tips just barely grazing the worn paper siding.

He pulled her back but she held onto the Red's body, anchoring herself to the floor and kicked, hitting the commander in the chest and shoulders. When he finally snatched hold of her other foot, he ran his blade in one swift swoop across the back of her ankles. Dylan bowed through a screeching cry and black spots of sheer, nauseating pain clouded her vision. It wasn't until she tried to move her legs that she realized they were useless and paralyzed. The pain rattled deeply into the core of her bones. But... she... had... to...

Slapping her palms on the ground, she knew she had to try. She pulled herself forward—a good twelve inches, before feeling the Scarred demon's weight pin her to the floor. He yanked one of her arms around to her back and pulled it taut.

"You know my orders are only not to kill you." He flipped her over until they were two sets of blue eyes staring at each other. He settled the blade just under her jaw, again. "No one cares what I have to do to get you restrained. Perhaps, you'll listen after a few scars to your face?"

"The only way..." she panted, "you'll get me back

there…" She cringed through the stinging shots firing up her legs and into her spine. "…is if I'm dead."

"Well, it seems you are at a disadvantage." He laughed, his tight skin pulling at his features unkindly. "Death is not on the table tonight."

"No, it isn't," she agreed and he looked pleased for small moment. "Well, at least, not for me."

Her free hand snapped to his jaw where she flicked the lighter open and fired her *Unda*.

She closed her eyes as she focused on feeding the fire and holding him down—feeling the heat surge out of her fingertips. The commander released a blood curdling scream, but she didn't stop. She couldn't. She wanted to fill his veins with the blaze, with a torturous demise. She wanted to make him combust and die a slow death inside *her* hungry flames for thinking he could just take her. For ever thinking he could kill someone she cared for.

Not anymore.

She wasn't weak or unable to control her powers. Nadia had been greatly mistaken.

Dylan shot an even more violent stream of hate into the commander's heart.

Her entire body vibrated with heat. She let her *Unda* escalate until it flooded every single nerve inside of her. Life around her became a numb and distant, a background for her own refuge without pain or fear.

She felt the fire crawling along her bones when the high pitched screams of the commander reached her ears, his thrashing, fiery form fleeing until he smacked his head against a log column and collapsed.

Dylan's eyes jumped open wide in shock. She wanted to stare at the disfigured man lying unconscious under the hayloft; at the fire slowly dying across her bare skin, but the Portal was closing.

With one last look at the Scarred commander covered in flames, she flipped onto her belly, needing to get to the

Portal before it left them there to die.

Panting, she hauled herself forward, yet she knew she was too far as the ethereal blue window began to shut from the top like a sliding piece of glass.

Her fingers brushed Red's jeans and with only seconds closing in on them, Dylan shoved him half inside the sliver of blue mist. The Portal slowly reopened and she collapsed on the floor in relief.

She pushed herself up on her arms as Red's lifeless body vibrated and jerked wildly like sticking a flimsy doll inside a wind tunnel. She could tell the Portal didn't like being held open and she worried it would suck him inside before she had a chance to escape.

"Soren!" she screamed over her shoulder.

There was no response and only then did she realize how different the air was from earlier. The stillness of vacancy. It almost felt like she was alone. She turned her head to look for him. He wasn't far, standing a few feet away and completely covered in blood.

A fiery clump of wood fell from the ceiling and she inhaled sharply. Staring at the small lick of fire sent a wave of awareness through her. The barn was on fire. Everything to her left was ablaze and quickly spreading along the beams and roof.

She snapped her head to where she saw Soren. The Scarred demon bled out near his boots in a mess of puncture wounds. His arms were hunched as he clenched and unclenched his fists, just staring at the Scarred demon, as if he was mentally daring the demon to move so he could stab him one more time.

She never thought she would ever see him brought to a point of absolute mania. He always appeared like this impenetrable pillar of balance. The man who thrived on killing. Loved wearing his enemies blood. Now... he only looked sick. Like he had lost control.

What had they done to him?

"Soren!" she screamed again over the roar of the escalating fire. But he just continued to stare at the demon.

They weren't far apart, but with her injuries, she wouldn't be able to make it to him. It was only then that she realized her beautiful moment of fire had completely incinerated her clothes as well.

"Wake up!" she yelled again, her voice cracking. "Goddammit," she panted. "We have to get out of here!" She tried to move but the strain on her injuries pushed her into a fit of gasps. "*SOREN*!" she choked.

He blinked several times as his dilated eyes refocused. He looked around at the fire as her words sank in, then down at her. The curtain of bloodlust was gone from his eyes, replaced with something akin to fear. Fear of the fire? Fear of their injuries? No. It was fear of *her*.

A small cry escaped her lips. "I need your help." She motioned to her legs and at the pooling blood escaping her body.

Soren blinked away the emotion and immediately bent down to scoop her up in his arms. Even though she was sticky from her own bleeding wounds, the slick feeling of other people's blood from his uniform made her stomach turn.

"Listen to me," she gasped through the pain. "The Portal won't hold. You need to *move*!" Just as she said the words, she heard a single shot.

She felt Soren tense and then he stumbled, falling to one knee. He struggled to hold her, but with the pain and all the blood, she slipped out of his fingers and hit the floor.

"*S-shot*," Soren edged out, holding his side in obvious pain before falling against the wall.

Dylan's eyes saucered and looked under the hayloft at the chard commander, laying sprawled out on the floor with the gun trained on her. She scurried for Soren's dagger and grasped the hilt just as the commander gripped the trigger. It clicked. Empty. He discharged the magazine without missing a beat and reached for another just as her thrown dagger slammed into his skull. His head thumped to the floor.

Dylan released her caught breath and collapsed backward as she tried to catch her breath.

"Oh God," she gasped, gripping her chest and feeling her heart pounding like a fist against her rib cage.

The circular window atop the hayloft exploded just as the Portal pushed at Red. She heard a snap and she could only imagine a piece of him broke away.

Soren's free arm came up and grabbed her leg. Their eyes met and she shook her head determinedly.

No.

No one but the Scarred were dying tonight. She wouldn't allow it.

Dylan reached over and pulled Soren as close as she could with a long, groaning cry. He let go of his gushing belly to wrap his arms around her waist until they were locked securely together. She felt his hot blood spurt out against her skin just before she shoved Red inside and fell backward against the Portal, letting it swallow them in a single gulp.

The ride felt infinite and instant all at the same time. Most of her senses felt null and void to anything but the strong metallic tinge of blood and the pain mirrored in his beautiful eyes.

It wasn't until the gasps hit her ears did she let herself look away from Soren and whisper a single word before passing out with Soren's deadweight still gripped in her arms.

"Help."

Aria stood outside a cabin in the middle of woods with a steaming cup of coffee cradled in her hands. It was early morning and she had yet to change out of her velvety, red pajamas. She lifted the mug up to her lips as a whack echoed through the trees. She looked up through her lashes at Asher, bare chested and wielding an axe as he chopped fire wood like a damn God.

A gust of chilly wind sliced through the air and she pulled the heather-grey wool shawl on her shoulders tighter around her body before curling into the padded porch swing at her left.

Right after Garret helped her escape the werewolf den in Los Angeles, Asher had picked her up and the two of them escaped to one of Tristian's houses in the Elon mountains. For the past two years, she had been able to continue her studies online and secure all her and Dylan's things into a storage unit.

Oh, and dyed her hair a blah shade of brown. Now was not the time to be extraordinary. Hopefully, it wouldn't be forever.

Aria placed the tablet they were tracking Garret's car with on her lap and opened it to see if there had been any change in his daily schedule.

Nope. Gym, home, gym, home, she thought.

A ping sounded from her pocket and she dug out her cell. "Check the news."

She glanced at the familiar unknown number and switched tabs to the Elon news. She came across a couple stories about Elon being attacked the week before and then the impending ceremony to welcome Temperance Elementa into the Shadow Horde.

"BABE!" Aria yelled, just as Asher swung the axe… nearly causing him to lose his grip.

He sighed before wedging the axe into the stump of the tree used as his chopping block, and sauntered over to her. "Yeah?"

Aria rushed down the porch steps with the tablet and shoved it into his hands.

"Look!" she gasped, wide-eyed and pointing to the screen. Asher licked at the sweat dotting his upper lip as he read the story about Dylan.

"She's going to be sworn in and I want to be there," Aria burst out. "I want us all to be there."

Asher looked at her without a trace of excitement in his face. "I can't promise anything but I'll call Ulysses."

"This is good," Aria said, hugging the tablet. "She's okay."

Asher smiled then and bent down to kiss her. "Of course she is."

She released a forced breath and suddenly declared they were going to celebrate. "I hope you're hungry because I'm making pancakes!" she squealed, hurrying inside.

CHAPTER 14

"She wasn't scared to walk away.
She was scared he wouldn't follow."
Atticus

"**ASK** her again," Queen Vashti's acidic voice cut through Dylan's ears like needles.

Dylan wasn't sure how she got to the white-walled prison room she was in now. She vaguely remembered someone barking orders in Traverna, where the Portal had set them down, and a *commons* healer curing her major wounds as they whisked Soren away. She knew it had been a risk picking the bar but she needed somewhere crowded and no Portals would have been granted entrance inside the Glass Tower without a key.

Now she was being questioned by the Kings with three guards, weapons drawn, standing near. If she wasn't so drained and preoccupied with her thoughts of Soren's wellbeing, she knew she'd feel like a criminal; even if she hadn't done anything wrong. But the fact she wasn't anymore trusted than the day she arrived felt like a slap in the face.

"We've been here for four hours," King Zirk sighed. "Either you feel her dishonesty, or you don't."

The Queen's fingers pressed harder against Dylan's sweat and blood dappled forehead like probes fishing around in her brain.

"Ask her, AGAIN!" she screamed. Dylan recoiled,

256

wanting to slap some sanity into Elon's beloved mistress, but she was cuffed to the chair.

King Damen growled and quickly stormed out of the room as if he had had enough entertainment for one day. Dylan scowled at the shutting door.

King Zirk shook his head then slowly began to reiterate the question Queen Vashti so desperately wanted them to ask, "Please, tell us again why you were in a damned domain."

Dylan repeated her statement, telling them everything from the Valley of Ashes to the wreck and the weather and then the Scarred's failed kidnapping attempt. She mentioned the werewolves and Nadia Burke, waiting for the Queen to give away anything at all that she might have known about this all along, but the Queen was unflinching.

When she wasn't speaking, Dylan could only think of Soren. Was he okay? Was it possible that he had died?

It wasn't too much later that they decided to release her. Dylan practically raced out of that suffocating room, but not without seeing the terrifying look on Queen Vashti's face. It told her the Queen wasn't done; no, not by a mile.

Dylan rounded a corner on her way to the infirmary and ran into the rest of the Horde.

"Watch it!" Astrid snapped. "Wait, Temperance? Are they done?"

"Where is he?" she panted. "He's okay?"

It seemed like the guys suddenly couldn't look at her and her heart felt like it was quickly filling with cold lead, on the verge of falling out of her chest at any second.

"*Astrid.*" Dylan couldn't stop the tiny flood in her eyes. "Tell me he's okay, *please.*"

"He's—" Astrid's skin blotched and for the first time since she met the demon, she watched as tears threatened to fall.

"No!" Dylan shouldered through them and began to run again.

"Temperance, *wait*!" Astrid yelled after her. But she didn't stop. She couldn't let another friend die. Not someone else she cared for. It was her fault! It was always her fault. She got too damn close, again.

Down the hall, she pushed open the wide, metal doors of the infirmary. The sterile scent of antiseptic and death hung in the air. There were dozens of beds lined along the walls with light yellow curtain dividers, but she didn't have to look too far. He was set up on the second cot. Tubes and wires covered his naked body and blood stained the usually white sheets in blooms around his injuries. A machine beeped steadily at his side telling her he was alive.

Tears finally fell as she slowly stepped to the side of his bed. Her trembling fingers reached for his pale hand. She let out a sob as she cupped his warm hand.

"Ms. Elementa?"

Dylan yanked her hand back when she heard the Medic's voice.

"I'm sorry," she mumbled, failing to stop her embarrassing hiccups.

"I didn't mean to interrupt."

Dylan looked away and to the floor—worried she'd break down completely if she looked at Soren again.

"You are free to stay. He's in a medically induced coma while he heals."

"Will he be okay?" Her voice sounded small and insignificant, again, and she hated herself for it.

"Only time will tell," the Medic admitted. "There were significant injuries to his brain and the bullet obliterated his spleen and crushed his left lung."

Dylan felt breathless and dizzy as she grabbed the bed for support.

The Medic took a step toward her. "I need to finish taking a look at you."

She shook her head with a frown. Her injuries seemed so trivial. "I'm fine."

258

"You are still bleeding. I was only able to heal your internal injuries. You need Essence—"

"I'm FINE!" she screamed in his face. Her heart pounded at an incredible speed of rage. If Soren wasn't able to make it, like hell she'd let them erase her scars.

The Medic stumbled back in shock, quickly making himself scarce. Her anger crumpled into a painful heap of guilt and sobs. Without letting herself look at him, Dylan pulled up a chair and sat where she would wait until... well, until something happened.

Her eyes opened, but Dylan didn't move her cheek from the pile of drool she had created on Soren's cot as she slept. It had been about two weeks and she had only left his side three times to shower and change. She couldn't force herself to eat any more than she could force a smile.

Soon she would be expected to swear in. How could she do such a thing when her friend was deteriorating every day on the verge of death? While she questioned her very existence?

The others visited now and then, urging her to eat or clean up. They all looked resigned at Soren's state and a little ticked off at how hard Dylan was taking it.

Astrid reminded her several times, *Death is the way of our life.*

Well, it's not the way of mine, she'd snap back.

But wasn't it?

Dylan finally sat up and popped her neck. Her entire body ached and as she pulled her hands away from rubbing her eyes, she noticed the dark streaks marking her skin. Still Essence was last on her list.

"You're awake."

Dylan gasped when her eyes connected with Soren's pissed off stare.

"Oh my God," she whispered. "*You're* awake!"

"What," Soren's impatient, raspy voice cut through her

smile. "What are you doing here?"

"Wha-what do you mean?" she stuttered. "You're hurt. Someone needed to be here."

"I don't need anyone, least of all, an *Elementa*."

Dylan jerked as if he'd stabbed her in the chest.

"Medic!" Dylan jumped again at Soren's sudden boisterous call.

The Medic scurried around the corner, all smiles at Soren and nervous glances at Dylan.

"Yes, sir? I must say, it is a real pleasure to see you up and speaking."

Soren gave the Medic a tight nod in greeting before speaking, "I don't want any visitors. And I believe Ms. Elementa has over stayed her welcome."

Dylan stared at him.

"It's time for you to leave now," the Medic said, just an edge away from smirking.

Dylan glowered at his smug expression and enjoyed the way he shrunk back, stepping down from his brief moment of superiority. She stood up, but stopped just before turning to leave to glance back at Soren. His cold eyes lifted a brow in challenge.

"I'll let the others know you're *just* fine," she sneered and left the room.

A few days later, Dylan was dressed in her usual gym clothes. She marched to the cafeteria; her mood still sour and petulant. Before she could enter, she noticed Soren walking toward the gym. Dylan followed him from a distance and watched as he exited through the side doors by the weapons wall. Apparently he was out of the infirmary and aiming to skip practice.

Dylan ran after him on a whim. He was already taking off down the road on his fixed bike as Ian was parking his.

"Let me borrow your bike?" she pleaded Ian.

"You and lover boy having a fight?" he smirked.

"*Please*," she wined impatiently.

He laughed. "Didn't you just wreck one?" he asked, eyeing her in suspicion.

"Yes!" She bounced on the balls of her feet worried she was going to lose him. "But, I need it. Now!"

"Whatever. You break it, you buy it."

"Thank you!" she squealed jumping on the rumbling leather seat.

"At the first row of houses, take a left."

She frowned at him, but he only pushed his hands into his pockets and headed inside.

She jumped on the bike, not even waiting a beat to calm her nerves before taking off after Soren in a wobbly skid.

Near the end of the street, she took a left like Ian had suggested. Homes lined the gravel street like neatly packed boxes with whimsical wooden, gable roofs, only varying in height by one or two stories.

It was barely a minute before she caught sight of him and had to slow down. It was an understatement to say she was curious as to where the he was going. Was this home? If so, then *who* was home? Did he have a lover, a mate, a gigantic family or just a grandma like her Isabel?

Who was Soren, really?

Since he had dismissed her so easily from his bedside, Dylan couldn't stop wondering *why*. They had been through so much together. It seemed like he was finally letting her in, so why kick her out now?

Soren stopped in front of a quaint two-story with overflowing flower boxes, aged stucco, and dark wood shutters. It was so cheerfully normal that she almost laughed. For some reason, Dylan expected his home to be darker and colder. Something more in tune with his *spectacular* personality. But perhaps his mother was the bubbly affectionate type who spent her days tending to the flowers with rich soil coating her baby pink gloves.

Dylan pulled off the road and jumped off Ian's bike

before Soren could hear her. She waited for him to disappear inside the home and ran over as covertly as possible.

She wasn't exactly sure what she was doing. Not that it mattered, because she was already venturing up to a small side window and peering in.

A large inset porcelain sink was the first thing she saw before scanning around the dated kitchen through a crack in the curtains. It was the kind of kitchen you expected to retrieve well water and use fire to light the stove. It was as if she had stepped back into time into a farmhouse set in the 1800s.

A young woman with vibrant red curls laughed and twirled into the kitchen. Dylan's eyes widened and she ducked, flattening herself against the facade. After a moment, she slowly inched upward; her fingers curling around the stone sill. At the view of an empty room, she let out a large breath of air.

That was close.

The whole situation was becoming a tad ridiculous. She needed to retreat before she made a fool of herself in front of his family. What would she even say if she got caught?

Ohhh, hey. Ha-ha. I've only been stalking you since you kicked me out of your hospital room. Oh, and who is the red-head?

Pushing away from the small home, Dylan turned around and yelped.

"I can explain."

Soren crossed his arms. His stance was wide and domineering... his face set into his usual take-no-shit frown.

"Go on," he rasped.

Dylan swallowed and lifted her chin, hoping to convey her own version of the Soren frown.

"You were skipping practice. You can be an ass to me all you want, but when did you get special privileges?" She gulped.

He lifted his eyebrows. "I'm to check in with you now?"

Her lips parted but she didn't have an answer.

"What right do you have to be following me? Or to be *here*?"

Dylan cringed. "I should go…"

"Yes. You are not welcome here. *Ever*."

She stopped dead in her tracks and looked at him. "*Excuse* me?"

"Leave, Dylan," he said sharply, "There are some aspects of my life I cannot share with you."

"Can't? …Or won't?" she asked using his own words against him.

He apparently didn't feel obligated to give her a response. This bristled her the wrong way, considering all of the unsolicited strolls he had taken through her mind over the years.

"No, sorry." She tossed her palms up briefly. "I forgot." She started to brush past him. "I'm the *Elementa*. I basically killed your father. Of course, you don't want me anywhere near you. I should have just let him take me, right?"

His hand snatched her elbow, stopping her. Her glacial exterior melted a bit as she waited for his comeback; the one that told her she wasn't just an *Elementa* to him. The one that told her she was his friend as much as he was hers. The one that soothed her thorns of insecurity that perhaps she wasn't all alone.

Soren leaned down until his hot breath marked the shell of her ear. "Don't ever forget your place."

Dylan ripped her arm away. The sudden slap of reality stung as it crawled back inside crushing her heart. She was only what was convenient for him, a burden, a chronic thorn under his wing.

She nodded and walked back to Ian's bike, her shaking clenched fists wrapped tightly around her ribs.

Dylan rode slower this time, wishing she didn't have to go back; that she could return to home simply by ride. As she neared the Glass Tower, she found herself continuing until she was in front of Traverna. She parked her bike and walked in.

Unlike last time, the bar was quiet, only serving a few patrons who looked at her with confusion laced with terror. Despite wearing mostly street clothes, everyone knew who she was and wondered if she was there on a mission. As much as she hated to admit it, their fear of her presence soothed the burning words Soren had said and gave her the confidence she needed.

"May I help you, soldier?" the bartender asked. His hair was cut close to the scalp and he wore a long sleeve, green shirt over his olive skin that matched his demon eyes.

"Is Cassandra here?" Dylan felt like a kid asking if someone could come out and play. A couple of the patrons looked away, sensing this to be a leisurely visit.

"She'll be here soon, at five, for the next shift."

"Thanks." She pulled out a chair and sat.

"Can I get you something while you wait?"

She crinkled her face, afraid to drink anything from here. "I don't know…"

He laughed and it pinched his eyes warmly. "Yeah, I heard about last time." He shook his head. "I promise, no funny business on my watch."

"Do you have regular liquors here?" she asked, remembering all the odd drinks that were ordered that night.

"Anything you could want."

That was good to know, she thought. Not that it mattered. It wasn't like the Kings gave her an allowance, or paycheck, or… anything.

"The Horde has a special privilege here. So, it's free," he said as if hearing her thoughts.

"Oh," she chewed her lip a moment before conceding that she could use a real drink. "In that case, I'll take a vodka, water with lime."

"Girl after my own heart," he smiled again, pouring two, one for him and one for her. "I can't stand all of those sugary drinks."

"Me either." She took the drink and brought it to her lips just as the door opened and Cassandra walked in. She spotted Dylan and her step faltered.

Her pastel hair flounced as she sauntered behind the bar and tossed her purse on the counter before pulling the bartender into a quick kiss. Dylan looked away and took a sip of her drink. Seeing such easy love made her heart hurt. With Tristian, everything had been so rushed and short, she felt as if she had missed out on that comfortable part.

Noticing that the sip did nothing to alleviate the pain, she took an even bigger gulp.

"Temperance," Cassandra said. "Care to follow me?"

"Um," Dylan set down her empty drink, "Sure."

She moved off the stool and followed Cassandra. There was an opening off to the side with hanging beads for a door. Dylan slipped through after the demon. Cassandra turned on a set of lights, and the room illuminated with a soft glow. A round, wooden table with several chairs sat in the middle surrounded by shelves of books, little knickknacks, and treasures.

Cassandra sat in one of the chairs and eyed Dylan as she walked around looking at everything.

"I don't really know why I'm here," Dylan said, examining a small tea cup that had looked broken and repaired with gold. She suddenly remembered hating Astrid looking through her stuff and stopped perusing.

Dylan looked at Cassandra straight on. "I should have told the OP about what you did the other night."

"Yet, here you are." She motioned with her hands wide.

"What is this room?"

"Depends who I'm talking to."

"To an Elementa," Dylan said, feeling the alcohol like an added boost of confidence. "...To an ally."

"You should watch your words, Ms. Elementa," Cassandra tsked. "To some it may be taken as treason."

"But not to you…"

"No," she gave a rueful smile, "I tend to deal with many… questionable things."

"Dark… things?" Dylan tiptoed.

Cassandra tilted her head. "Who is it?"

A part of Dylan wanted to tell Cassandra to go screw herself for implying, but mostly she was too curious to do so. "Tristian Effingo."

"Ah, the Effingos," she mused. "I did not know their son, but I can only imagine he followed in their footsteps."

"I guess," Dylan said, shrugging one shoulder.

"I heard he died by the Horde's blade, though. I cannot bring back that which is destroyed."

"He isn't." She took a deep breath, thinking about how Tristian pulled out his own blade, the one that Gerion ultimately killed him with. "He died by someone else's hand."

"That!" Cassandra exclaimed, "Is something I can work with. Please sit."

Dylan pulled out one of the chairs across from Cassandra and cautiously sat.

"Do you have something of his?"

Dylan nodded, partly shocked this was happening, that it was this easy, and pulled off his chain, handing it to her.

Cassandra eyed the Elementa ring attached to it and smiled knowingly. "There is only the matter of payment."

Dylan's hope vanished. Of course. "I don't have…" She forced a smile. "I didn't mean to waste your time." She started to get up to leave when the demon stopped her.

"I take favors as well as finery and gold."

"Favors?" she slowly sat back down. She didn't think the kinds of favors Cassandra would ask for would be innocent. "Something in mind?"

"Not at the moment, but I would like to be able to collect whenever I see fit." She slipped off the Elementa ring and slid it back across the table to Dylan. "And I will collect.

Maybe not tomorrow or in a year, but you will be in my debt."

Dylan chewed her lip, mulling this over in her mind. Could she possibly go against the Law, against the Kings to bring him back? Her heart fluttered just thinking of actually being near him again and knew she would do *anything* to have him back.

"Deal."

A sly smile edged the corner of Cassandra's mouth as she held the chain and looked off to the side. Her eyes were glazed over as she focused on something inwardly. After a moment or two, she frowned and placed the necklace back on table.

"There are too many souls attached to this." She shook her head. "Do you know if this was entirely his?" she hesitated, before asking the next question. "Or if he killed often while wearing it?"

Dylan felt her resolve crack. "No," she whispered. "I wouldn't know."

"Hm... Mind if I hold onto this? I just need time to sift through the lives attached to it."

Dylan nodded and stood, as did Cassandra. "If I have any luck, I will get started and let you know by letter. Otherwise... I will have a carrier return it to you."

"That is the only thing I have left of him."

"I will give it back, don't worry, *my friend*."

Dylan was almost to the exterior door when Cassandra came rushing after her. "Something wrong?" she asked.

"No, here." The woman thrust a small book into Dylan's hands.

Dylan looked down at the small, leather bound hardback.

"If I cannot bring him back... this might help you ease the pain in your heart."

Dylan brought the book up to her chest, hoping that her heart could be calmed by just the pressure. It felt like Cassandra was already telling her it wasn't going to happen, crushing, once again, the hope that had bloomed inside of her. It was stupid to come here, anyway. To have tried to bring him back was only a desperate plea for companionship after Soren's second, painful rejection.

"After all the lives we lost in the Elementa War, I was given this book to help with mourning. Perhaps, it will lead you on the path you are hoping to travel."

Dylan nodded. "Thanks."

◇◇◇

A door slammed shut, rattling Nadia's golden mirror as she dabbed a bit of pink gloss on her lips. She mashed her lips together, smearing the color, and listened to the heavy foot falls barging through her jewel-tone villa on the secluded beaches of Lamu, Kenya. She stood as elegantly as she could, her back aching from the pup growing rapidly in her belly. She turned to the side and appreciated the curve her belly made in the new, gauzy, white dress.

Today was the day her pup would come into the world. She would love it for six weeks before it was old enough to join its many siblings, when it would be able to start training. It was already her and Gerion's tenth creation of demon and wolf and his two hundredth. He would soon have his army and she would soon get her revenge.

"*Nadia,*" Gerion fumed, stomping into her bathroom. He was wearing the face of Silas again and appearing quite handsome in his tailored khaki suit with a white button down. His collar was unbuttoned, giving a hint of tanned skin across his collar bone.

Nadia forced a coy smile and tossed it over her shoulder.

"Why, what a surprise, my dearest. Felt like witnessing one of my births?"

Silas' teeth crushed together in response and it only made her that much more delighted.

"You do remember how I like my privacy after my pups are born," Nadia reminded as she stalked to her bathroom's

268

exit, stopping just passed him. "I'm afraid I won't be of much use to you right now." She touched his shoulder delicately and he snatched her hand, twisting and caging her against the door frame... careful not to touch her stomach.

She bared her teeth and her eyes flashed, appearing canine for a blink. "Perhaps, I do have some time now." She grinned, curling one of her fingers around his belt loop.

"Tell me," he hissed close to her face, ignoring her lure. "Tell me you didn't try to take Temperance behind my back."

Nadia narrowed her eyes and dropped her hand. "I saw an opportunity and I wanted to surprise you."

He suddenly shoved himself away from her to stop himself from taking her by the throat and crushing her wind pipe.

"You're just so tense, lately." She crossed her arms. "I only wanted to give you a gift."

"A *gift*." His chest rose and fell rapidly as he listened to her.

"Yes, of the woman you are truly craving."

She had barely stopped speaking when he lunged for her vanity and shoved everything off in a crash.

"You set us back!" he growled; and against her better judgement, she flinched. "She knows who you are. She knows you're a werewolf! What the *fuck* were you thinking?!"

Nadia glared at the ground filled with broken oils and smashed cosmetics. The air was already inundated by a mixture of overpowering perfumes. Yes, she had wanted to grab Temperance, but not for Gerion. After one of the soldiers bragged about seeing the girl during an *Essence* mission, she made it her business to watch the girl and wait for an opportunity to intercept. It didn't take long. She would have eventually given the girl to Gerion, she just wanted the little bitch to suffer at her hand first.

Nadia smoothed her expression before lifting her eyes

innocently to the father of her pups. "I only wanted to please you, my sweet."

Silas grabbed both sides of his head, exasperated. He pointed a finger at his chest and spoke loudly like she was deaf or dumb. "*I* will be the one to get her. *Not* you," he seethed, before storming out of her bathroom and passing several of her ladies awaiting the birth.

Nadia waited for her front door to slam before letting herself smile with her ladies. Oh yes, soon Gerion would have his army, but so would she.

CHAPTER 15

"He lies so well
It is almost as if he knows
I am not going anywhere."
Sx

DYLAN stood as Astrid fixed the lapel on Dylan's new uniform of head to toe black leather. It was light weight and customized to fit her form, even her powers, or so the designer that just left had said.

Someone had even appeared to fix her hair and makeup. She felt polished, pristine, and dangerous on the outside, while inside she was a mess of nerves. She knew it was normal to feel anxious, even excited, for the upcoming ceremony but she was too busy worrying if this was all just a giant mistake; and her dream the night before hadn't helped ease her concern in the slightest.

She had been back in her old room in Los Angeles, stuffing her bag to go to her grandmother's, as Aria asked once again what the matter was—why Tristian had acted the way he had in class after he and Dylan had kissed. Instead of evading the conversation and heading out the door, Dylan had stopped moving about her room and told her everything. She just let it all spill out of her in giant rush. When she was done, Aria believed everything much to her surprise. Dylan had then stayed home and missed Asher's interception at the cafe and the Hick's SUV. Tristian never took her to Sansvi's or the beach, so they never got in a fight. Most importantly, she never went to the party where she met the vampire who had bargained with her life.

Every decision she made felt weighted by a thousand pounds. A part of her was afraid to move the wrong way or utter the wrong words for the chain of events that could be set in motion leaving her in a situation far worse.

"I know it's not really my business or anything, but…" Astrid blurted out, pulling Dylan out of her haunting thoughts. "What's going on with you and Soren?"

Dylan stared into Astrid's round chestnut eyes as the last words Soren spoke to her bounced about her brain. *Don't forget your place.*

Oh, she knew her place and it wasn't anywhere near him.

"You're right. It isn't your business," Dylan said, calmly.

She was so sick and tired of everyone assuming Dylan and Soren were anything other than friends, if even that.

"Look, I get it," Astrid said. "You thought he was going to *die*. But you can't blame him for getting upset over the way you acted. We are selfless to the OP, not to each other."

"So you're saying, I was supposed to let them kill him? And then to just leave him there?"

"No…" Astrid shook her head vigorously like Dylan was missing the point. "This is just the way of the Shadow Horde. The way of our *lives*. Friends, comrades, lovers die and we move on. You just can't let that break you, is all."

"Are you done?" Dylan spat.

"Stop being such a bitch, Temperance. You need to talk to him. He's been a giant dick since he woke."

Dylan huffed out a short laugh. "I don't think you want me to say what's on my mind."

She did feel better knowing she wasn't the only one he was being an asshole to. She just didn't know what Astrid wanted from her. She was going to deal with tragedies however she wanted, whether it was the "Horde" way or not. Putting that all aside, it still didn't excuse his attitude toward her. Even if she did creepily follow him to his home and peeked in his kitchen window. Dylan scrunched face and pinched the bridge of her nose as she remembered the embarrassment vividly. But, she had just wanted to know something, *anything* about him. It wasn't fair how closed off he could be.

"Don't worry about him or me. He'll get over it." Dylan sighed, looking away to the window.

Dylan didn't feel like placating her or anyone for that matter. The only thing she wanted to do was get through the day, crawl back into bed, and forget her new role that included murdering and possibly watching her friends die, all the while feeling no pain.

"Well, that's it," Astrid mumbled, stepping to the side and eyeing Dylan once more.

Dylan nodded and sat on her bed to lace up her black combat boots.

There was a knock on the door and Astrid answered, murmuring soft words that Dylan couldn't hear. Finally, the girl turned around and handed Dylan a heavy, cream envelope. She could feel Trisitan's chain through the thin paper and set it aside to finish lacing up her boots.

Once she was done, she stepped into her bathroom and closed the door. She finally looked at herself and grimaced. Her makeup looked perfect. It was mostly thick eyeliner with a pale lip, but it was unnerving her to see herself made up. It reminded her of times when she thought her life could be changed by working on her appearance: getting a boy to like her or simply boosting her confidence. Now it did the opposite. They might as well have painted her face neon orange with the words "ELEMENTA" or "TRAITOR" across her forehead in black.

Dylan gazed away from her reflection, unable to look at that familiar vacancy settled deep within her eyes. She opened the envelope and pulled out Tristian's chain. She unhooked the clasp, looped her Elementa ring through and slid it over her head. She knew without talking to Cassandra

273

that she had been unsuccessful. Without the possession, she wouldn't be able to bring him back.

She braced herself against the sink with both arms.

What was she doing? She didn't want this. No one saw her any differently than the day she had arrived. She could continue going on, acting as if she fit in, as if everyone liked her and trusted her… go on as a *fool*. She was simply an unstable weapon to them. She would forever be questioned, interrogated, watched, and tested. She didn't doubt that one misgiving would lead her to be *Bound* again, even if it was fifty years from now without a single hiccup.

She lifted her fingers and snapped. A tiny ember jumped out from her fingertips and dissolved into ash when it hit her suit. At least she didn't have to worry about incinerating her uniform.

"Come on, Elementa!" Astrid's voice called through the door.

Dylan pushed her necklace inside her jacket and, with one last look at the white smear of ash, stepped back into her room and following Astrid to The Gates.

Astrid brought her to a small room off to the side of the trial room where she was due to have her ceremony. Servants and soldiers milled about, either on duty or grabbing food at a long buffet table filled with refreshments. Even King Zirk was there sipping on a cocktail as they arrived.

Astrid spoke with the King and left to stand her post in another room.

Dylan continued to stand in the middle of the room. No one approached her, not even King Zirk. He just studied her from afar, and she wondered if he was weighing whether having her in the Horde was a mistake or not. Or perhaps he saw her just as cornered as she felt and didn't want to cut himself on her broken pieces.

"You look… well put."

Dylan frowned at Soren's sudden and lame complement.

She glanced at him out of the corner of her eye. The only people unafraid of her seemed to be the already broken, and she knew Soren was beyond fixing, like her.

"What I look like is scaring people." Her brows puckered, and she corrected herself, "Demons. Scaring *demons*." She glowered at a staring solider. He immediately looked away and visibly swallowed. "Even King Zirk won't approach me."

"I assume he doesn't want to frighten you off before the ceremony."

"Or set me off. Heaven forbid I forget *my place*," Dylan sneered, crossing her arms.

Soren released a rush of air from his nostrils. "Can we not do this now?"

"If you don't want to 'do this' then leave. I didn't ask you here."

"Well, I'm escorting you, so get over it."

"Oh, *lucky* me." Dylan rolled her eyes.

"I don't even know why you are mad," Soren pointed out. "You are the one that snuck up on me and peered into my house."

Dylan brought a hand up to her face feeling a headache coming on. He was right. He was always right. He had every reason to be pissed at her; yet, here she was trying to make him feel bad.

"Did you honestly think I wouldn't catch you?"

Dylan stared daggers at the ground. It felt like Soren was yelling at her despite his voice never rising above a whisper.

"No... yes." Dylan shook her head. "I don't know. I wasn't really thinking."

He grabbed her chin, trying to steal her gaze for a moment. She batted him away.

"No, you *were* thinking." That caught her attention. "You wanted me to catch you. You wanted me to just let you in." She knew he wasn't just talking about letting her in his home, but being let into his past.

"And that's so bad?!" she suddenly cried out, not caring that they were now the center of attention.

Soren grabbed her arm and yanked her into the hall. He waited until the door shut before pining her to the wall with his stare.

"It wasn't so bad until you tried to kill yourself for me."

"*That's* what you're mad about?"

"That and you didn't leave. You had your chance and *you didn't leave.*"

Her thoughts quickly turned inward as she scanned the last few weeks for a time when she could have escaped. To be honest, the thought hadn't even surfaced until this moment. Until this morning, after her dream, she hadn't minded Elon so much. In fact, she had liked learning here and getting to know her Uncle. In a way, she had found her place; whether Soren liked it or not.

"I told you to go," he said, piecing it together for her. "Back at the Damned Domain. You had a chance to disappear!"

Dylan glanced up at the security camera angled away from them. Soren followed her line of sight and forced himself to lower his voice.

"Yet, you still stayed. You were actually willing to give yourself up to them. For fucking what?" he snarled, his face red. "For me?" He suddenly looked so disappointed.

"Why is it so hard for everyone to understand that I care about you?" Her shoulders dropped. Saying the words felt like an admission of guilt and she suddenly wanted to stuff it back in her mouth and forget this entire conversation.

"Because when you start caring, you might as well sign your own death warrant." Silence settled between them before he gently touched her cheek. "You start fighting with your heart instead of her mind and that is when you make mistakes. That's when you lose control."

She looked up into his bottomless blue eyes, wondering if that was why he looked afraid of her just before he picked her up; just before he got shot. He must have realized then that she was too invested, that he needed to sever whatever budding relationship they had. But, she knew she would have done the same for Astrid or Ian, or even Augusto. This wasn't about him and her. It was about doing what was right.

He dropped his hand from her face. "Come on. It's time," he said, eyeing the soldiers getting in line near the steps that led to the stage.

Dylan smoothed her sweaty palms on the slick leather of her pants and stepped back into the small, side room. She stopped when she felt rough warmth slip into her fingers. She looked down at Soren's hand gripping hers before looking up at him in question. Except he wasn't looking at her. He stood next to her like a pillar of strength.

She sighed, accepting how scared she was and squeezed his hand, silently thanking him for the much needed support—even if deep down he thought caring, helping, and comforting were pointless, damaging traits.

They walked up the metal stairs and out on to the stage as a deafening roar greeted them. Dylan tried to drop Soren's hand but he held on even tighter. They stood in their designated spots towards the back of the podium next to a line of chairs. Dylan spotted the Kings on the other side sitting on their elaborate thrones.

"What are you doing?" she hissed under her breath. "*Let go.*"

"No." He whispered it so relaxed and indifferent that she couldn't stop herself from turning and gaping at him.

"You're going to make them think—"

"Think what? That we're together?"

"*Yes.*" Her cheeks heated, trying once again to pry away his hand from hers.

The same tainted demon from her trial, Lord Struo, walked out to the front and began a long dramatic speech about protection, loyalty, and commitment.

"Look around, Dylan," Soren whispered. "It's what is

expected of us."

She frowned at him before reluctantly letting her eyes wander across the crowd. A chill spread across her body. Instead of seeing the hatred she was welcomed with the last time she was here, it was now all smiles and *acceptance*.

"Why?"

Soren gripped her almost painfully and leaned into her ear. "Smile as if I'm telling you something encouraging."

"There is nothing encouraging about this." But when her gaze locked on a pair of gushing girls up front, she faked a smile. No matter how much she hated the act, being on this end of things was a lot better than shoveling through the residual pain of what her parents caused.

"You're awful at this." He chuckled deep within his throat.

"A little warning would have been nice."

"You are even worse with warnings."

She let out a single huff of humorless laughter. "*Thanks*."

After the speech, Soren was called forward as the new official commander of the army and presented a badge. It was rectangular and red with three golden stars. Lord Struo pinned it to his breast and announced that he was the tenth Verbeck to ascend as commander of the Shadow Horde. Dylan hadn't known this ceremony was to honor him as well; and seeing him light up as he took his late father's position made her smile, too. He had never seemed more proud.

After a few more words to the crowd, Soren accepted a short dagger from Lord Struo. He then stepped up to her and kneeled, holding up the blade with both palms up.

Dylan looked down at the weapon with the Omnipotence's crest wrapped around the hilt. It was carved from the hardest metal in all the worlds and infused with death's magic. She was kind of afraid of it.

"By accepting this sword, you swear to forever protect our worlds and uphold the laws set forth by the Three

Kings."

She looked into his eyes and her right hand came down on his, covering the blade.

"I swear," her voice cracked a bit as she grasped the hilt. Once she had, Soren nodded and stood, resuming his position beside her.

Dylan knew this was it. She stepped up to the Book of Swears. It was a giant leather bound book with crisp, antique pages laid out across a wooden podium. There she saw a blank space under the long list of Horde soldiers before her. She swallowed and using the sharp tip to her palm, pressed deeply until blood pooled around the polished metal and the blade turned purple. She removed the edge and closed her hand, lifting it over a small bowl. Once there was enough blood to cover the bottom, she picked up the small quill and began to write her name in blood.

She was nearly done when her eyes glanced up to the crowd that seemed to be holding a collective breath with her, and paused when two amber eyes gazed back at her.

Asher lifted his hand and waved with a sad smile. Two tall hooded figures flanked him, each donning traveling robes. But before she could completely take in that she was seeing someone from her past, applause and shouts rang out in a unified roar.

Dylan looked down, realizing her bloody signature was finished, forever sealing her into the Shadow Horde. When she looked back up at her old friend. He was already turning away, closely followed by his companions—a lock of brown hair slipping out the side of one of the hoods.

She wanted to scream *wait!* but she held her tongue when King Damen lifted her left arm high over her head with a congratulatory remark as the Medic attended to her other hand. She smiled numbly to the crowd except her attention was still on her past slipping away as if it had never occurred. Part of her began to wonder if it actually ever *had*.

She mentally tried to clear the image just as Soren began

ushering her off stage.

As they descended the steps, Soren turned to her. "Who did you see?"

"What?" she looked at him as if seeing him for the first time. She still felt sucked into her old life and wondered just how much of a mistake this ceremony really was. What terrible chain of events would this cause?

He stopped at the bottom and pushed her to the side, locking his arms on the wall to cage her in.

"Who did you see?"

"No one."

"*Don't lie to me.*"

She looked him straight in the eye. "I'm not lying. He was no one. Well, at least no one important to me. Just someone I knew before I— before."

"Who?"

"Asher... I don't know his last name."

"How long did you know him?"

"Not long. I found out he was only using me to get to my parents."

"Using you..."

"He acted like he wanted to be my friend... or whatever." She didn't feel like getting into details of kisses and heated dances. She scowled, shoving him away. Soren didn't budge very much. He merely dropped his arms. "But I'm sure you could have figured that one out for yourself. Manipulation seems to be an art here."

"What's his patronymic name?"

"I told you I have no idea. And I don't really care." She sighed in annoyance.

Soren finally took a step back, giving her space. She adjusted her jacket noticing no one was around anymore.

"Was he contracted by Gerion?"

"What? No. His vampire friend was. ...I think. I don't even know if he knows what happened. Besides, do you really think he would show up here if he had been a part of it?"

Soren thought about it for a moment before agreeing and turning away from her. "We need to get to the party in the foyer."

"*Wait.*" She grabbed his arm and he stopped. "What if he was his contact? What were you planning on doing?"

His head tilted a bit in consideration.

"Gerion is still a fugitive and the likely suspected father of the Scarred army after what happened to us. If this Asher even has an inkling of an idea where he might be, then it's worth exploring." His eyes danced between hers. "Just because we have you doesn't end our search. We'll never stop searching until he's dead. Until his whole family is nothing but ash."

"Okay," she whispered. A feeling of relief settled into her bones. He would make sure Silas paid. "But, I want to be the one to kill Gerion if you're ever given the chance."

Soren nodded curtly.

"Promise me," she urged.

"Okay," he affirmed. "I promise."

For the next hour, Dylan smiled for interviews with the local news and replied when spoken to like a good little soldier; but all she could think about was how close Soren always was to her. The way his body seemed constantly turned towards hers, or how his hand occasionally slid across her lower back, possessively. It was confusing and frustrating. She wasn't totally sure if it was an act only for the party or if he planned to be this way from then on.

When she noticed Anna across the room, she felt relief at the opportunity to dislodge herself from Soren's side.

She marched across the crowd and glanced back, seeing Soren hurrying after her with Astrid close behind. Eyeing the distraction, she didn't even realize she was bumping into Asher until it had already happened.

"Oh!" Dylan squeaked when his hands came up to her

arms, stopping her from an even larger collision.

He chuckled and dropped his hands. "Long time no see," his pupils winked as he whispered her name, "*Dylan*."

"Asher," she breathed. "What are you doing here?"

He pushed his hands into his suit pants pockets and looked behind her for a split second. "Just had to see how you were fairing for myself. But you look..." he glanced at her uniform and something in his eyes flickered disappointment in his smile, "Like you are adjusting."

She opened her mouth to speak but Soren's voice stopped her.

"Verso," he greeted.

"Verbeck," Asher greeted in return with a dip of his head before turning to Astrid with a similar indifference, "Crystallos."

"Verso." Astrid suddenly turned into Dylan's ear and hissed, "*Tainted*."

"Great. Now that's over with," Dylan turned to Soren and Astrid, "can you give me a second alone with... *Verso?*"

Astrid gaped. "You're choosing to hang with a—" she stopped herself. "How do you even know him?"

Dylan only lifted an eyebrow in her direction. She was taken off guard by Astrid's act of superiority. She would have thought the demon who had once gone against the Law for the people would have a little more compassion.

"Come on," Soren interjected, pulling Astrid away.

Dylan tried to not think about how suspicious he had appeared as she watched them retreat and become swarmed by reporters and supporters.

"Your boyfriend doesn't like me," Asher stated.

Dylan looked back at Asher blankly. "What are you doing here?"

"It's great to see you, too."

"You can't blame me for being a little upset at your presence. The last time I saw you was just before I got taken by the guy you introduced me to."

He ran his fingers through his golden mane. "I hold penance for that every single day of my life."

"You don't even know me." Dylan sighed. "Why would you care?"

"Let's just say I got to know you a bit more than you realize."

"Still after my parents, I see. Well," she lifted her arms and spread them wide, palms up, "they aren't here, obviously. And even if I knew where they were, I still wouldn't tell you."

"Does Soren know that?"

"Leave me alone." Dylan turned away knowing her comeback sounded childish and lame, and headed back to her crew.

"Aria misses you," Asher called out causing Dylan to stop dead in her tracks. "Isabel, too."

She flipped around and rushed at him. She ripped her new blade out of its holster, flipped it deftly between her fingers before laying it against his throat. The edge grew a dark purplish hue when it connected to his skin. "*Stay away from them,*" she spat. "You have no right to be near them."

Asher swallowed against the sharp imposition. He held his hands up in surrender and a sad smile fixed in place. "I have more right than you do."

Her eyes widened and she felt herself pressing down on his neck before she could help it.

Soren's fingers suddenly slipped around hers and yanked her hand back.

Once he had her submitted and pressed against his chest, he told Asher to get lost.

"Walk," he demanded Dylan, urging her away from the silent and watchful party.

She was aware of everyone staring at her, but she didn't care. She ached to feel along her neck where it was hard to swallow. The iron braid of Tristian's chain keeping her together when all she wanted to do was fall apart.

She kept her head down until they made it to a vacant hallway where she pushed away from him and collapsed against a wall, letting her forehead rest against a cool, decorative, metal panel.

Seeing Asher had ripped open one of her mental boxes. All she could see was Isabel, Aria, and Tristian. She missed them so damn much. She was trying to let go like she should, and mostly had. But it still hurt to think of them, and she wondered how long it would take for that pain to leave her or if it ever would. And how the hell did Asher know about them? Where they in danger?

"I could have handled myself," she finally said.

"I know." She felt the warmth of his body before his touch caressed her shoulders. She stiffened.

"Stop," she whispered. "Stop touching me as if I mean something to you."

"I didn't know it was making you uncomfortable."

She yanked herself off the wall and flipped around. "*Really*?" she shrieked in mock shock. "Because, I haven't changed. Whoever you were touching in there," she pointed down the hall with a severe tilt to her head. "Must be someone else then."

"I was only trying to make the guests comfortable around you," he lurched closer and hissed, "which, if you haven't noticed, their comfort relies on your ease. Not that you're very good at ease either."

"I'd rather everyone hate me than for you to touch me," she blurted on impulse.

He lifted a single brow. "Don't mistake my comfort for something more than what it is."

Footsteps echoed down the hall and she was suddenly thrust up against the wall. His lips were a breath away from hers, causing her heart to palpitate.

A camera flash stung the air just before the reporters shuffled back into the party.

They still didn't move, and she couldn't help but look at

him—really see his expression. He wasn't about to kiss her. She had been too keyed up to notice the lack of emotion in his eyes. The dead facade that he mostly wore was fixed in place. It made her wonder if he even forgave her for following him to his house or trying to save him by sacrificing herself. This, everything during the ceremony, was only leverage. She just wasn't sure for what.

Her lips parted before she spoke, and her voice was soft with a hint of agony shedding the pitch, "I don't want your comfort anymore, Soren. I only want to be stronger. Not made to feel as weak as I am. And if *you* haven't noticed, you're amazingly great at making me feel small."

He released her and she turned away from him, walking back to her room in conflicted silence. It was just too hard sometimes to accept her life as it was, and she was done wondering why it had to be her.

CHAPTER 16

*"She has been through hell.
So believe me when I say,
fear her when she looks
into the fire and smiles."*
e.corona

THE *sky overhead was cloudless, blue, and beautiful as Dylan and Tristian drove along terrifying cliffs overlooking a golden ocean. She didn't know where they were headed but it was clear they were on the run.*

Free.

Their hands were interlocked over the center console and he gripped her so tightly she could feel the desperation in it. She couldn't stop looking at him. The way the sun shined brightly behind him, filtering through the trees and outlining his features, making his hair appear more golden and rich.

He suddenly pulled over and parked his car under the cover of a forest. When he got out, Dylan followed and stopped in front of the car, staring at a small home that seemed to appear out of nowhere. It looked like a traditional log cabin but had been merged with a modern home. The thick, flat roof matched its foundation like two parallel tree trunks with a wall of illuminated, frosted glass between and surrounded by a large, planked patio complete with a porch swing.

It was small, simple, perfect.

Subconsciously, she knew this place even though she hadn't ever been here before. It was going to be their place whenever she was free again. Inside, Aria was cooking with Isabel as the scent of banana muffins permeated the air.

She felt Tristian move behind her and wrap her in his strong arms. He tilted her head and began kissing her down the side of her neck. She knew if she could just make it to this cabin, everything would be okay. They wouldn't have to worry about Silas or the Kings, or tortured destinies.

She turned around in his arms and looked up into his intense eyes that smoldered like liquid emeralds, and kissed him long and hard until she woke.

Dylan opened her eyes and blinked several times as she tried to reorient herself when all she wanted to do was go back to that cabin in the woods and lose herself in the fantasy. If only it were real and not just a dream, but that was all it was… a dream. A *really* good dream that made her homesick for a place she'd never been to.

Dylan shifted her stiff body when she remembered that she must have dozed off on the floor while reading the Elon Newspaper. It had conveniently appeared on her dresser earlier while she showered. Had Soren stopped by? Astrid? Anna? It kind of ticked her off that she didn't have a lock on her door like a normal person. What was honestly stopping anyone from waltzing in here at any given time?

She made a mental note to ask King Damen for a lock while she examined the new tattoo on her shoulder.

After the ceremony, she had returned to her room to find a tattoo artist waiting for her against the door, ready to mark her with two black stars indicating her rank. He had given her the choice on where to place them. So she chose her arm underneath the Omnipotence crest.

The artist had nodded and cleaned her skin before drawing it perfectly freehand. The painted needle dragged over her skin in sharp movements that felt oddly good in the way pain sometimes did. The way that bleeding could feel like a release.

When he was done, the demon slathered some ointment over the tattoo and packed up.

It had been days since then. She didn't feel the need to show herself or even train. She was officially their weapon. If they needed her, they'd page her on her new TAC watch.

Dylan lifted her *Daleon* knife by the point and let the fading sunset refract against it, painting her bare walls with spots of rich color. It felt so strange to be left alone with such a powerful weapon. If she didn't know any better she would have thought they were beginning to trust her.

It was really too bad that she did know better.

She shifted her head in the direction of the Elon News article laying on the floor by her head, featuring her and Soren in a *"lover's embrace after a spat during the Signing Ceremony's Reception."* In the photo, it was easy to believe the two demons in the picture were indeed lovers. It was all a ruse though. She just wasn't sure for what. Why did he feel the need to exploit their relationship and call it something it was absolutely not? She had the worlds' acceptance, what was the point in furthering a lie?

Dylan flipped onto her belly and traced the small space between herself and Soren with the knife. A part of her wondered what would it be like to be his lover, to see obsession and warmth in his eyes. It made her think about that day and night she was trapped in the damned domain with him. It had been strangely perfect until the Scarred showed.

The sound of paper tearing caused her to look down where she had stabbed the couple in the photograph. It was ridiculous to think about such things. They were just pretending and she wouldn't let another guy into her heart, not until she felt ready enough to move on from the one that was already there. Dylan was pretty sure Soren was not that guy.

A muffled, sporadic buzzing came from her nightstand

and she shifted, craning her neck back to try and see her TAC watch without getting up. From her vantage she could see the three star symbols on the screen which meant one thing: *Mission*.

A sudden thrill prickled her veins. She jumped up and shook out her uniform from where she had chucked it on the floor after the tattoo artist left. The watch stopped buzzing. She halted mid-pull of her pants wondering what it meant. She ignored the sudden feeling of doubt and finished pulling on her uniform.

Grabbing her jacket, she dashed down the hallway and shoved open the door to the Iron Portal. She skidded to a stop as she watched her crew disappear through the ethereal cloud. Soren's cruel eyes flashed to hers at the very last second.

All of the air inside her lungs rushed out of her as she felt herself deflate. She wasn't anymore a part of the crew now than she had been before her ceremony. Everything was a lie just like their "relationship."

The training. The mission. Even the ceremony.

It was only an illusion for the worlds to see that she wasn't some psychotic murderer ready to end them all with a swift flick of her wrist. Or maybe it was all only to secure her, enslave her, and forever use her as their weapon. Perhaps the Omnipotence wasn't any better than Silas. Only they succeeded.

Turning around, Dylan gasped, caught off guard by King Damen standing silently behind her. She instantly bowed.

"My Master."

"I was told you were not feeling well enough for the mission. I believe you look fit for duty."

"I am ready," she panted, still reeling from his sudden appearance. "They should not have assumed."

There was a long silence and she bit her tongue and held her form so as not to accidentally question him.

"Soren's a great soldier; one of the best," King Damen

finally stated, causing her to look up. She internally winced at her thoughtlessness. He motioned for her to stand anyway. "I approve of your relationship."

Oh God.

"We don't have a…" she trailed off, glancing over her shoulder at the Portal which still glowed like an arched cloud. It was hard not to imagine diving into it, going back home, especially after everything that had happened. To go on the run, as Soren had to asked of her in the heat of the moment. To tell everyone to take their expectations and shove it— "I need to talk to him about that," she finished and looked into her Uncle's clear blue eyes that rivaled the Elon's skies. It didn't feel right to tell him that what everyone saw at the ceremony was staged. She wasn't even sure how to explain it.

King Damen looked at her as if doing so pained him. "I apologize for not congratulating you at the reception. You looked so much like your mother at the ceremony, I had a hard time swallowing it."

Dylan blinked, not expecting such a human response. In the back of her mind she began to fit pieces together. Her Uncle didn't hate *her*. He hated her mother for something entirely different. She only resembled what he hated, so it was easy to project it on her. Dylan suddenly wanted to ask a million questions while the door to his past seemed wide open.

"Will you… tell me about her?" Dylan's voice tiptoed.

"If you tell me why Effingo left." Damen's eyes narrowed. "He had been on track for Zirk's throne. He was a good friend of mine, actually; and then one day he just… disappeared. I found his pendant and robe left on my desk with a short note of his resignation. He had gone completely off the grid until, well, you seemed to reappear."

"Oh…" Dylan was shocked to hear words other than disgust spoken about Tristian from someone in Elon, and a King at that. She had gotten so used to his tarnished reputation that she actually began to believe Tristian was just another soulless liar.

She looked at her Uncle and tried to recall if Tristian had ever mentioned anything about Elon other than her sabotaged *Binding* day. "I—he mentioned something about hating it here," Dylan shook her head as her embarrassment ebbed at not knowing Tristian better. "Sorry, he didn't tell me much about his life here."

Something behind his eyes shut, and she knew the brief moment of nostalgia was gone.

"That's a real shame." He began to turn away but rethought his decision at the last second. "Your mother is not what she seems, Temperance. She likes to paint bright pictures to mask a dark world. I would stay far, far away from her if I were you." He glanced at the Portal. "You should go. It will be good for you to see." He placed a piece of paper in her hand and left. His long robe swirled around his ankles as he disappeared.

She wondered what he was trying to tell her, and why he chose to tell her that. Was he only trying to scare her away from the Elementas? Did he think she was lying, planning to go through the Portal to see them?

He must think she held the key to their location. Except... if he did, why wasn't he trying to fish it out of her? Unless he already held the key.

Dylan unfolded the piece of paper and found the coordinates for the mission. She looked at it and where King Damen had stood, understanding how much trust he was conveying. What was stopping her from going anywhere she wanted?

It was a test she was determined to pass.

After pulling on a hood and securing a few weapons, she stood in front of the Portal and thought of the long sequence of numbers, letting them run through her mind. She jumped.

Unlike last time, Dylan was able to keep control inside the tornado. She crossed her arms and locked her legs,

feeling her stomach fling up into her throat. She kept her
eyes firmly shut, repeating the numbers over and over again
until she felt her feet slam and stumble onto ice.

She smiled, feeling pretty great that she had managed it
by herself, until she caught sight of the desolate grounds.

Ice and wind propelled against her suit that was designed
to protect her from the cold. But there was a different kind of
chill that began to seep out of her pores, bonding her feet to
the ice as she stared up at the sharp, black rocks surrounding
the old worn castle.

Memories of terror, pain, and heartache punched her
chest as she fell to her knees. *"You should go. It will be good
for you to see."* She hadn't understood until this moment.
King Damen hadn't been talking about seeing her parents,
but Zadar—Silas' castle. He wanted her to go through *this*
box of pain. Except, she couldn't do it.

Not yet.

She wasn't ready.

Three years wasn't long enough to be able to revisit what
happened here. No matter how confident she felt lately, this
place punctured her nerves like a thousand needles, crippling
every inch of her body and crushing her like a tin can.

Physical pain began to form in her shins and she knew
she needed to find the others to be able to leave before she
froze out here. As far as she knew, Soren held the only key
to create a Portal that connected solely to the Glass Tower;
and he was *inside*.

Standing, Dylan told herself to shove it all back inside, to
just turn it off and move. One foot in front of the other.
Nothing else mattered. All she had to do was find her crew.

Silas, Lucia, the worms—none of it was here anymore.
The castle had been abandoned, she hoped.

The door creaked loudly as Dylan stepped inside the
marble throne room. Despite being out of the harsh weather,
she felt colder, lonelier, and defenseless. She wrapped her
arms around her stomach and looked around. Everything was

the same. Same elaborate cathedral ceilings, marble pillars, blood-red carpet runner; same dark and twisting throne.

Her breath plumed and she pushed herself to step toward the same path she had taken day after day, week after week. She stopped at the mouth of the dark hallway.

Dylan's fingers shook as she reached for her hood. She yanked it over her head and the night vision kicked in. At the sight of an empty passageway, she released her held breath. A part of her had almost expected to come face to face with something in the shadows.

She stepped into the blackness now lit with an eerie, neon-green glow from her hood as text flitted across the screen.

LOCATION: ZADAR
LOCAL TIME: 08:05
TEMPERATURE: -25 F
HUMIDITY: 0%
VITALS: NORMAL, ELEVATED HEART BEAT

Her vitals almost made her laugh. She didn't expect her heartbeat not to be "ELEVATED" here.

She passed a row of unlit sconces and traditional oil paintings caked with dust. After awhile it felt like the hallways stretched on past what she remembered. Dylan looked behind herself at the long stretch, feeling disoriented and lost. She hated standing openly in the dark. Yes, she had her night vision, but it only kept reminding her of the blackness surrounding her.

Her heart began to beat faster when she realized she was standing outside her old room. She froze as her gut screamed to run away and find her crew mates as fast as she could, while her curiosity burned hot. Had the room been touched? Was it still filled with blood and destruction? What about the wedding dress that haunted her dreams? Did Tristian's body still lay there with a dagger penetrating his bones? ...because he had to be bones, right?

The door was ajar unlike the others, and it took her

several moments to muster enough strength to push it the rest of the way open.

Dylan's hand came up to the polished wood and shoved.

Her mouth popped open. She didn't think it could be worse yet, somehow, seeing the remade room sprang tears to her eyes.

No blood.

No white dress.

No Tristian.

Leave him here to rot...

"*No-no-no,*" she slurred, rushing inside and spinning around in the room as it blurred together. Where did they dump him? Why would someone do this? She felt as if she had gone crazy. Surely it all had happened? Was she even in the right room?

Dylan sniffed a couple times and pulled back her hood. The skylight above slipped a soft, bluish glow over the furnishings and she sat on the bed wafting the familiar vanilla scent. The smell triggered her mind with a series of memories. She thought about her dreams on the beach, laughing with Peppi, and even Silas reading to her... kissing her.

Dylan ran her fingers along the soft bedspread, feeling the memories rip through her, one by one, breaking her down until she was weeping and wanting nothing more than to hide from it all under the covers.

She abruptly got off the bed and backed away until she hit her spine against the bathroom door, unable to catch her breath. She didn't understand her longing for those moments. This room hurt her heart so much yet, as she stared at the open door, she found it hard to leave. Tears slipped down her cheeks accompanied by a silent ache. Aching for the girl she was, for how young and trusting she had been. Silas had taken that away from her. He had carved out her soul, leaving her as nothing more than a damaged shell of a person.

How could she go back to Elon? She already felt like a fraud every time she stood next to Soren with their fake relationship with her fake uniform and her fake smiles. Everything about her life was becoming a lie. What if she just... stayed? What if she just disappeared? Would anyone honestly miss her?

A noise startled her, interrupting her thoughts. Dylan immediately unsheathed her *Daleon* and peered out into the vacant hallway. It felt like the past all over again. Fear of who lurked around the corner. Did the servants still live here? The worms?

Dylan snapped her fingers and lit the sconce closest to her with her flames and like magic, they all lit.

She stole down the corridor, trying hard to shake the feeling of being captive again, of treading on Silas' personal space all alone. She easily came to the end of the hall. The stairs that lead to the *gym* in front of her... Another far away sound came from her left. She quickly followed the noise, grateful it didn't seem to be coming from the pool. The real Silas still visited her there from time to time and she wasn't entirely sure she'd survive actually seeing it.

Dylan passed the dark dining room. The elaborate chandeliers sparkled and the table was still set carefully for three with fine linens, china and crystal all layered in dust as if the it had been arranged for dinner just before everyone vanished.

Dylan stopped next to the library, ignoring her instincts to continue on. Her fingers traced the delicate carvings of dark fairytales etched into the wooden trim around the door before peering inside. Her breath caught from the beauty. The ornate columns, the stained glass skylight, the whimsical balconies. the antique rolling casters... the *books*.

My God the books.

So many priceless novels just sitting there collecting dust in the dark of a desolate world never to be inhabited. Dylan itched to go inside and take as many books as she could carry or at least look for the first edition Charlotte Bronte she had spotted during her time here. Maybe she could speak with King Damen about bringing them all to Elon and creating a true library worth visiting. A library everyone was welcome to use. Maybe then all of this pain might actually be able to become something beautiful.

Dylan pulled herself away from the library when another sound creaked down the hall. She had never been this deep inside the castle alone, and a part of her wondered if maybe this was where Lucia and Silas slept.

Dylan lit another series of sconces, noticing how the walls were starting to transform into something less ornate, more aged and gothic—like the castle's original setting. Was this the North Wing Silas had tried to steer her away from? Why wasn't it redone like the rest of the castle?

Dylan forced herself to take the first couple steps forward. The golden sconces turned into raging torches. She felt déjà vu claw at her insides and it didn't take her long to place why. She had been here once before in a dream with the demon doctor.

With that in mind, she remembered she was supposed to be searching for her crew and very possibly a rogue demon. Her muscles stiffened at the thought of Silas or the mystery demon being here. Would her Uncle send her here knowing that?

No. She shook her head as if to reaffirm the thought to herself. He may harbor some ill feelings for her but he didn't want her to die or be taken again. No, he wouldn't want to lose Elon's weapon.

A laugh came from the other side of a set of steel doors. Dylan picked up her pace, recognizing Astrid's voice. The others had to be just up ahead. Dylan pushed through the doors and slammed to a halt.

It was like she had fallen inside her nightmare. Six glass tubes, each large enough to fit a person, filled the middle of the room surrounded by equipment. Ian and Astrid were making jokes while taking pictures of the wires, examining tables and medical tools off to the side while Augusto silently kept watch.

The tiny hairs on the nape of her neck rose as she focused on the tubes. Isabel and Aria weren't here, like her nightmare, but these were filled with people—actual bodies submerged inside greenish water.

Soren stood in front of Peppi, the frail girl with chestnut hair and a black servant's dress. She seemed to be screaming. It didn't take a genius to recognize the girl had been shoved inside alive. But the most disturbing part was she looked *changed*. Her limbs appeared twisted and more muscular. Her teeth elongated with fangs and her fingers curled into claws. She looked like she was becoming a werewolf… perhaps, the demon doctor had been tampering with her, after all.

The doors behind Dylan flapped closed and the Shadow Horde all turned to look at her, mostly shocked she had come or maybe because they hadn't noticed.

"I thought you were being cruel," Dylan suddenly said, unable to take her eyes off of Peppi—her friend who sacrificed her soul so that Dylan may live. Tears began to fill Dylan's eyes as she imagined the hell Peppi went through just before she died. Dylan blinked hard, forcing the emotion away.

"No," Soren said. "Making you come here would have been cruel."

"Is he here?" She surprisingly didn't need to specify that she was talking about Silas. Soren knew like always.

"No."

"*Why?*" Except she wasn't asking why he wasn't here, she was asking why all of the servants appeared to have been changed then murdered.

"We don't know. We got a tip on some demon activity here, hoping it was the Plantos." He sighed and pointed to Peppi. "You took her *Essence*, right?"

"Yes," Dylan said, barely above a whisper, remembering that day again like a slap in the face.

Make me numb to this life, Dylan... Dylan could only hope she had.

"That's what I thought."

"What?" she asked, snapping out of her thoughts from the past.

"This wasn't for sustenance."

"What does that mean?"

Soren ran a hand over the scars on his skull. They looked frighteningly congruent to Peppi's claws. He dropped his hand and looked at Dylan.

"I'm beginning to think your birth was merely a coincidence and your parents had nothing to do with the War."

He was thinking about the Day of Mourning and the Scarred's attempted kidnapping with the two werewolves. But why would her parents run if they were innocent? Why would they hide? Everything was becoming a jumbled mess in her head. What if her parents were only badly mistaken for the enemy when it was really the Plantos the entire time?

"That would mean everything everyone has believed…"

"Was a lie," Soren finished for her just as all of their watches started beeping.

Dylan looked down at her wrist, still unsure of what all the TAC watch did or how to use it. She pressed her finger to the flashing icon and an aerial view of the castle showed several flashing red dots closing in on five black dots.

That couldn't be good.

She looked up and noticed everyone arming themselves and Soren creating a Portal. Next thing she knew, Soren was yanking her toward the blue window.

"You need to go home. This is about to get messy."

"*What?*" Before they could get very far, Dylan pulled her arm free of his grasp. "*No*. I can help."

"You are not even supposed to be here," Soren growled.

"Are you serious?" She yanked out her dagger, determined to fight whatever was coming for them; even Soren if he tried pushing her toward that Portal again.

"King Damen sent me here." Dylan ripped down the zipper of her jacket just enough to be able to expose her shoulder. "I'm a part of this crew."

"Barely!" he yelled in her face, trying to grip her arm again. "Just because you have a tattoo doesn't make you ready."

"You need to start treating me like an equal. I'm sick of needing to prove myself. I'm tired of everyone walking on eggshells around me! Let me help. I'm good. You *know* I'm good at fighting, Soren!"

The beeps started getting louder on their watches and she knew they only had seconds before they faced a small army.

"This isn't the time for one of your tantrums."

A burst of fire erupted in her palm when Soren tried to grab her again. He recoiled and cursed as she expected him to.

"I'm staying," she snapped. "Anyone else have an issue with it?" She looked around the room at the others who were trying to conceal their smiles.

Astrid shook her head. "By all means, Pyro. We could use some fire balls."

"*Gigantic* fire balls," Ian corrected.

Dylan smiled wolfishly before looking down at her watch, knowing the red dots were coming from the hall she had just walked through. She faced the double doors, her right hand armed with her *Daleon* and her left scorching with a ball of flames.

Screw Soren and his doubt. She needed this. *God*, she needed to kill some Scarred soldiers for everything Silas had done to her. Silas was the reason she was who she was now; and she wanted him to watch his army die just like he made her watch Tristian die. How fitting that it would happen here of all places.

The feeling of Augusto's heavy hand landing on her right shoulder momentarily froze her. It was already so rare that he interacted with her at all that his touch was paralyzing. He nodded and released her before crouching down in a one handed stance against the floor, posing to launch himself at their guests.

Dylan looked around Augusto, where Ian and Astrid stood. Ian weaponless, his hands already commencing a small wind storm and Astrid grinning at her shiny katana sword that had been sheathed on her back.

Soren finally stepped up to Dylan's left. She looked at him and he at her as an understanding settled between them. He would accept her position here whether he wanted to or not.

"Fight with your mind, never your heart."

Dylan took a deep breath and settled her gaze on the double doors when all of their watches fell silent.

Dylan frowned, about to look down at her TAC, when Ian surged up into the air as dozens of odd soldiers burst through the doors. A cloud of wind flew out of his fingertips throwing the creatures back. He held them off, creating a temporary wall and giving the Horde a direct view of their features.

The creatures stood on two legs like men but their backs were hunched, thick with muscles and covered with fur. Their faces were deformed by snarling fangs and long, wet snouts. And their eyes... Dylan felt her breath hitch when she noticed their demon eyes.

How was it possible? What *were* they? In all of her demon studies not once had she come across a werewolf-demon creature. Not even after the attack by Nadia when she dove into any and all books on werewolves. This sort of mutation just didn't exist.

The ground buckled and Dylan jumped back losing the grip on her fire ball as Augusto sent an earthquake across the room. Every single glass tube behind them burst as oily water and bodies hit the floor.

Creatures began escaping the wind wall but Astrid and Soren were already there to take them down. They ripped through creatures left and right. Astrid's Katana blade appeared through a creature's abdomen, then disappeared before she tore through another creature in a grinning twirl.

Liquid touched Dylan's fingers. She looked down as the burning scent of gasoline hit her nose. She quickly stood and jumped out of the way of the fingers of fuel slipping between the cracks in the stone floor and heading to the brawl. Why would the bodies be submerged in gasoline?

"Temperance!" Ian barked from above.

Dylan flipped around just in time to sink her blade into a creature's heart. In its last efforts, the creature swiped at her and Dylan struggled to hold on to her *Daelon* while simultaneously evading the creature's claws. It swiped at her again and again until Dylan finally let go of her weapon to grab both of its arms, burning fur and flesh with her flames until it dropped.

Her heart was hammering against her rib cage as she stared at the lifeless wolf-thing at her feet.

This is your purpose. Dylan told herself. *This is what you were made for.*

"There are too many of them!" Astrid screamed, stumbling back as three encircled around her.

Dylan ripped her *Daleon* out of the dead creature and lunged forward to help Astrid. Dylan grabbed one of the creatures by the hair and pulled it off her friend. Astrid then gutted one before throwing up her hand and shooting a bolt of ice into the other's heart.

If it wasn't for the snarling and snapping creature trying to claw her to death, Dylan would have gawked at Astrid's frozen powers. Could all Terras do that?

Dylan ducked the creature's claws then rammed her blade into its chest over and over and over again until it stopped and collapsed to the floor. She then quickly helped Astrid up with bloody fingers.

"We have to get out of here," Dylan panted, trying to ignore the splatters of bitter blood against her lips. For every creature they killed five more took its place. Staying would be suicide.

"There!" Astrid gasped, pointing to a staircase toward the back of the room. It led to a second floor balcony with a couple of alcoves that could be exits or dead ends. There was no time to deliberate. They rushed to the steps, grabbing Soren and Augusto on the way.

"What's going on?" Soren hissed, slitting the throat of a creature.

"We need to go!" Dylan yelled over her shoulder.

They got to the top and looked over at Ian still holding a majority of them back.

"Ian, are you okay?" Astrid called out.

A few creatures escaped, but Soren and Augusto were slaying them before they could take more than a few steps on the stairs.

Ian nodded, his gazed focused heavily on the creatures. "Yeah, but I don't know how much longer I can keep this up. What's going on?"

"It's a trap," Dylan said breathlessly. "The tubes were filled with gasoline. My flames would have burned the castle down."

"That makes sense. I thought you were panicking when you didn't incinerate the creatures," Astrid volunteered.

Dylan nodded, choosing to leave out the part when she did panic. If it hadn't been for Ian's warning, Dylan would have been in shreds by now.

Soren suddenly took hold of Dylan's wrist as he pressed a series of numbers into her TAC watch. "Stay with Ian and Augusto. I've sent an emergency message from your TAC. Someone will respond. I'm just not sure how long it will take. Astrid and I will try and find an exit."

"Why not just create a Portal?" Dylan asked.

"I exhausted the key when I tried to send you back."

"*What*?" Dylan snapped. "And that seemed like a good idea to you?!"

"Getting you out of here would have been worth it."

Dylan glared up at him. She didn't understand how he, their commander, could put them all at risk just because he couldn't stand the thought of letting her fight beside him.

"Just go," she snapped, turning away from him.

Soren and Astrid disappeared in separate alcoves in a flash. Dylan blinked uneasy thoughts away and turned back to Ian and Augusto still fighting. Ian looked exhausted. His complexion was paler than she had ever seen. She honestly didn't think he would last more than ten minutes more before passing out. She needed to help lessen the load.

Dylan leaned over the balcony and unsheathed a handful of sleek throwing knives that always reminded her of flat knitting needles. She was suddenly thankful for all of the tedious lessons with Soren, even if he was an absolute ass. He had never let her finish a throwing session without making ten kill hits in a row. Dylan opened her palm and counted ten knives. Hopefully it had helped.

Dylan lifted her arm and took a deep breath, feeling the light steel in her fingers. The weight of death was in her hands. She let out the air in her lungs and flicked her wrist, just missing the first creature's skull.

She gritted her teeth and aimed again, nailing the next creature. It dropped and Dylan continued until nine were down and she was out of knives.

It should have helped but more creatures filled the gaps she created. There had to be a room or a doorway they were coming from. She glanced at her watch seeing the cluster of red dots only in the hallway coming through some sort of... door? If she could get around them somehow, maybe then she could nip the army in the bud. Dylan pressed her fingers to the screen and expanded the map until she was looking at an x-ray of the room they were in. She could see where the halls behind them snaked around the castle to closets, storage rooms, and a passageway that ran parallel to the hall with the red dots.

She snapped her head up. Her eyes zeroed in on the secret passage off to the side. If she hadn't been looking for it, she would have missed it. It was the same texture as the walls. The only part that gave it away was the slight indent around jam.

She rushed to it, killing a couple of creatures on the way with her *Daleon*. She brought her hand to the door and pressed, popping it open. The room inside was so dark she couldn't make out the interior. It could have been the gates to Hell for all she knew, but Dylan had to check it out. She yanked her hood on, letting the night vision take over. She smiled. There were servant passages all throughout the castle and it appeared as if she had found one.

Dylan looked behind herself once. Ian was still holding the wind wall in place as Augusto tore through the creatures one by one. Neither one of them noticed her departure. They would be fine for the time being.

She settled her sights back on the dark corridor as an inkling of fear settled in her gut. She shoved the feeling away and made sure her hood was on tight. There was no time to be cautious; so, without a second thought, she sprinted down the dark hall until she came to her first door. She lifted her TAC watch again and checked to make sure she was coming out a good distance away from the red dots.

As quietly as she could, she opened the door and froze. Her suspicions had been right about the creatures somehow coming through a door. There was a glowing Portal near the entrance to the room Ian and Augusto were in. Creatures stepped through the ethereal door in single file, just waiting for their opportunity to escape the wind wall and attack. Keeping the Portal open was a Scarred soldier with a red band tied around his upper arm. If she could get to him, maybe she could close the Portal and kill as many creatures as possible.

Dylan felt adrenaline pump through her veins, speeding her heart rate.

This was it.

Now.

She tightened her grip on the *Daleon* and emerged from the servant's passage with as much stealth as possible. It helped that Ian's wind sounded like they were inside a tornado.

She was almost to the Scarred soldier when one of the creatures near the Portal noticed her with its heightened senses.

Its head snapped back, locking its beady eyes on her.

Dylan's step faltered when she should have lunged. A mistake Soren would have punished her for if this had been a lesson. Even though it was barely a delay, it was long enough to lose her chance at the Scarred soldier.

The soldier looked over at her and smiled, expectantly. "I was beginning to wonder when one of OP's trash would find their way out here." The soldier stopped the creature that had noticed Dylan from passing him.

"Drop your weapon."

"Sure," Dylan shrugged, flipping her Daleon in her hand before effortlessly ripping her arm forward. The dagger slammed into the creature's neck and it stumbled back before dropping.

Damn, she thought. She had been aiming for the soldier not the creature. She was really off her game today.

"There," Dylan yelled, lifting her hands out to the sides as flames licked up from her fingertips. "Should I drop these as well?"

The Scarred soldier looked wary for a moment before smiling coyly and darting his hand out. A bright green vine jutted out from his palm and snapped around her wrist. He yanked Dylan forward with a start and she had no choice but to release the flames in order to break her fall.

"What the—" she gasped as she quickly tried to untie the tightening plant. She was not expecting *that*.

When it wouldn't come off, Dylan wrapped her leg around the vine, hoping to stomp it off.

Another vine suddenly shot out and wrapped around her neck as he stalked forward. He looked down at her before lifting her up to eye level by the vine. Dylan continued to struggle, looking for any opening between the plant and her neck, but there was nothing. She knew if she got a finger in, the vine would probably break it. It felt like she was slowly being strangled by an anaconda.

Numbers and warnings began flashing across the screen of her hood.

"LOW OXYGEN. INCREASED HEART RATE. EXCESSIVE BODILY STRAIN. WARNING LOW BLOOD PRESSURE. LOSS OF CONSCIOUSNESS IN 30...29...28..."

The soldier suddenly ripped off her hood, silencing all of the data. She squinted at the light, feeling less trapped without her hood but more aware of the bulging in her eyes and cheeks, and the desperate need to breathe.

Dylan looked into the soldier's golden eyes as recognition hit him hard. He released his hold only slightly to allow her to breathe and she fell to her feet. Dylan coughed and gasped in lungfuls of air.

"Well, looks like today is my lucky day."

"Or mine," Dylan coughed just before grabbing hold of the vine at her neck and conjuring her flames.

The plant blazed instantly like two long ropes of pyre. The soldier cowered backward and released his hold on the flaming plant. Dylan hastily unwrapped herself and held both flaming vines in each hand before flicking her wrists out like whips. She smiled. This was better than throwing knives. Perhaps the OP wouldn't be against making something like this for her.

"Shut the Portal and I'll let you go." Dylan flicked out

306

one of the vines until it latched itself around the soldier's ankles. She yanked and he fell embarrassingly easy. "Now."

The soldier began to writhe against the pain of his searing flesh. "Okay! Okay!" he screamed as he crawled to the Portal with jerking movements. He removed something from the Portal's opening and the window shut instantly. "Now, let me go."

Dylan stared at him wishing she could just let him go. Unfortunately, that would only keep one more enemy on the other side.

Something in her expression must have given away her thoughts because before she could answer him the soldier was yelling to the creatures behind him.

"Lycans!" the soldier shouted. "Attention!"

Dylan tensed when every single werewolf-demon creature behind him turned and stared at her with hungry eyes and snapping jaws.

On the plus side, at least Ian could rest.

"Shit."

Dylan took in a deep breath and flicked out the other flaming vine, wrapping it around the dead creature's foot. She yanked him towards her just before the vines turned into ash.

She wrenched out her *Daleon* from its neck and looked up before she turned around and ran.

"Capture her!" the soldier screamed. "Do not kill her!"

Dylan dashed down the hall, never fast enough to lose them, but fast enough to keep them from catching up to her. She glanced back only once to see Augusto stalk toward the Scarred Soldier with his knife drawn.

She was near the art room where she had first spoken to Silas when she flipped around and brought both of her hands together. She pushed her *Unda* and summoned her flames. She strained against the pressure until she could see and feel nothing but fire and then she let it all go.

Dylan released a fireball only Ian could appreciate and

307

watched proudly as it exploded on the pack of snarling creatures like a grenade.

Screams curdled her eardrums as the heady smells of burned hair and charred flesh roiled her stomach. Dylan slapped her hands over her ears in an attempt to silence their pain but the agony wouldn't stop. It was like their cries were stuck inside her head, playing over and over again on repeat.

Seconds flew by like minutes before she could manage to pry open her eyes and remove her hands from her ears. The creatures were all dead on the flaming floor but their screams remained like a scar in her mind.

Dylan stumbled away. Her ears ringing. Her pulse thundering. She found herself outside her old room again where she fell against the wall with the cries reverberating inside her skull.

This wasn't her purpose.

She couldn't do this.

She had killed so many.

It had been so easy to shut her mind off and just do what Soren had been drilling inside her heart for years. But it was like their cries had broken through her armor and pierced her bones.

Dylan forced herself to function and paged Soren using her TAC watch. She had killed everyone. Now they could leave. Now they didn't have to worry about the wall of creatures closing in on them. Now she could rest.

Dylan felt herself slowly sliding against the wall until she was sitting on the floor next to her old room.

Her mind throbbed and her body was weak.

She shifted her head up and rested her eyes on the impeccably dressed blonde leaning against the wall across from her. His arms were crossed and his blood-orange eyes locked on her in amusement.

"You killed a lot of my soldiers, Tempy," he tsked.

Dylan drew in her legs and gripped her *Daleon* harder. Her knuckles were white as stone.

"Silas," she managed, using the wall to help herself stand. Chills of fear ran rampant, spiking through her veins like a river of ice.

Once she was on her feet, Dylan bolted away from him.

Silas expected this. He easily pushed off the wall and followed her through the maze of his castle. It was her dream all over again. Dashing through the halls while Silas' laugh stalked her.

"You can't run from me forever, Tempy!" Silas' voice came from in front of her and she flung herself around and sprinted down another hallway.

She panted. Each corridor smudging into a blur of red and gold as she searched for the front door. She was searching for her crew so that they could get the hell out of here. This mission had been nothing more than an ambush and they all fell for it. Even her Uncle had fallen victim to Silas' sick game to capture Temperance. Now she was right where her kidnapper wanted her.

Dylan turned another corner and almost vomited when she saw Silas grinning wildly from down the hall. She tripped over herself and slammed into the corner of the wall. She winced and Silas was next to her before she could even gasp. He reached for her but Dylan was already swinging her *Daleon* like a crazed woman brought to the edge of sanity.

Silas may have gotten the chance he wanted when she showed up here, but that was only because she never truly believed he'd show his face and risk everything to take her. Now, she wouldn't dare risk losing the opportunity to finish him. To show him exactly who he was dealing with. She had changed and he was in for a rude awakening.

Silas ducked out of the way of her maddening swings and Dylan threw out her other arm, slamming a fire ball straight into his chest. Silas grunted and stumbled backward a step from the force. Dylan smiled. It may have been a small fire ball, but it showed his vulnerability to her power. Silas was going die a slow painful death inside her flames.

This was for Peppi. For every day wasted inside this abominable castle. For the loss of her life—the death of Dylan Prescott.

Dylan lifted her palm reveling in the rush of her *Unda,* the sparkling heat that pulsed and ignited from her bones and shot through her veins like an arrow. She whipped her arm across in an arc as the flames sprang out from her fingertips like a whip from Hell.

A rush of water seemed to come out of nowhere as if someone had broken the line of a fire hydrant, knocking her flat of her back and dousing her raging whip of flame. She sputtered and coughed up water as she struggled on the floor. She barely moved before Silas snatched her hair and forced her, face-first against the wall, pinning her knife-laden hand above her head.

He gripped her wrist and squeezed until her fingers seized and her *Daleon* crashed to the carpeted floor. Silas hastily grabbed the knife and brought it up to her neck. Dylan stilled at the sharp prick against her skin.

"I've missed my feisty girl," Silas crooned softly as he used the knife to push her sodden hair out of the way and expose the back of her neck. "Have you missed me?" he asked, bending to kiss her nape.

"Screw you," Dylan spit out, already conjuring her flames. The burning in her blood. The roar of the satisfaction as she imagined him toasted and then burned to a crisp. She didn't need a knife because *she* was the weapon. She was his Angel of Death. And today he was going to die and rot in his own castle.

Except… something wasn't right. She pushed herself further, feeling the heat burst from her skin and immediately cool. She gave it a solid three tries before she began to panic.

Silas laughed wickedly. "Haven't you ever wondered why you couldn't die by your flames but you could in the water?"

What? she thought, still trying and failing, still in denial that Silas might be able to control this, too.

"You can only be immune to one," he continued. "You might be strong, my love, but you're not invincible."

Dylan realized with a start that it was because she was wet. Silas was keeping her from igniting with his own powers. She didn't even know he could create water. The only element she had been able to create was fire... fire and that flower. She was merely a manipulator of water; and air was still practically nonexistent.

Silas dragged his nose down the side of her neck as her earlier terror blossomed and seeped deep into her bones. She wanted to stop him. She wanted to prove to herself everything she had felt for him before was fake. But, there was a certain comfort within the terror. It was like she was back in her room. His prisoner, again. Would it be so bad to just give up and let him have what he wanted?

"Surrender to me, Tempy. Stay with me." He pulled her head to the side easily and kissed her throat. One of his hands slid down from where he held her wrist. Dylan stayed strangely still. Her fingernails dug into the wall while her mind was rapt on his movements—anxious to see what he would do next. Silas began to rove around her body, feeling and pressing. She felt her breath hitch as the ember she had kept hidden from the worlds and even from herself flickered to life underneath his touch.

Why didn't she want to go with him?

She didn't fit in Elon. She didn't fit into the Horde. And the screams after she killed. My God the *screams*.

She could just follow him and disappear. Hadn't that been what she was after for her entire life? Escape? Freedom? Why was she driving herself crazy by fighting this? Maybe if she just let go he would set her loose.

Silas continued, running his hands down each leg. It took her a moment to realize he wasn't feeling her up but checking for more weapons.

More weapons.

311

More weapons because she had tried to kill him. Because she *wanted* to kill him. Because he was only manipulating her right now. She didn't want him. She hated him! What the hell was she doing just standing here and not fighting back?

His hand slipped up between her breasts, lingering, always lingering and taking his sweet time, feeling confident that he had her.

"I've been watching you since the moment you walked into this castle. I saw you dive onto your bed. I saw you miss me." Silas groaned. "You're going to come back to me."

Dylan glared at the wall and turned around in his arms before he could finish feeling her up. She had grabbed one last weapon as an afterthought before she had jumped into the Portal. It was tiny, but deadly.

Her backup.

She hadn't ever used one before but she didn't think it would be that hard to figure out. All she had to do was pull the trigger.

Dylan looked up into his eyes, conjuring old feelings of innocence and awe.

"What would I be to you?" she asked as her fingers edged behind herself—millimeter by millimeter—so slowly, she hoped he wouldn't even notice her reaching. "Do you still want to marry me? Or was that only a ploy?"

She searched his debilitating eyes as she spoke, trying to shove the feeling of disgust out of her mind. When she was done speaking there was something in his gaze that flickered. Confidence and greed. He believed her.

Stupid boy.

Silas' lips quirked. "I want you by my side, forever. Just like before."

Dylan suddenly grabbed him by the lapel and yanked him close to her lips. It was a bold move and she almost expected him to push her away, maybe even yell or hit her. But, he didn't. He pressed his hands on either side of her head like he was afraid to touch her now that they were about to kiss.

312

Dylan felt the coolness of steel and an emptiness settle inside her as she held the gun no larger than the palm of her hand. She looked at his mouth. "I won't go with you," she said, gently.

He tried to jerk back but she held him against her with every last bit of her strength.

"*Tempy*," he warned.

Dylan took a deep breath, savoring the fact his last word was going to be her name.

She opened her eyes and looked deeply into his, "Goodbye, Silas." She pressed the gun against his heart and he jerked violently. His eyes were wide with anger, terror, pain, then disbelief… he looked down at his chest where the blood began to stain his shirt; bleeding through the fabric and growing, saturating every fiber it touched.

Dylan stared at the gun she hadn't fired then at the blood slipping out of his lips. Perhaps, she had fired and blocked it out? Was that even a thing? Was shooting like that?

Silas looked back up at her with what she could only describe as acceptance before he collapsed, revealing Soren behind him.

Her comrade held a bloodied knife and a scowl.

Dylan met his glare with equal measure and cut him off before he could start.

"*How could you?*" she hissed and dropped down to the floor where Silas was gasping and reaching for her.

She let Silas grab her jacket in desperation as the light quickly drained out of his eyes. Dylan bent down to his bloodied chest and tried to feel for a pulse or listen for a heartbeat, for a breath, for anything that might tell her he was still alive.

Moments ticked by and she slowly sat up, shaking with angry tears streaming down her cheeks. She wiped at her face, knowing it had nothing to do with losing Silas and everything to do with the fact she had lost her chance to make him suffer. Soren had taken her revenge before she even had a chance!

"How could you take this away from me?" she growled at her commander as if that was all he was. No. That *was* all he was. After today he was nothing to her.

She pressed the gun against Silas' temple and clenched the trigger, but it was useless to shoot him. He was dead or almost. Shooting him would only be merciful at this point. She ripped the gun away from Silas' head and looked back up at Soren. "Are you happy, now?"

"Immensely."

"*Immensely*?!" she hissed. "You knew how important *this* kill was for me. You promised me!"

Soren's eyes finally flicked to the gun in her hands as her plan registered in his thick skull.

"Everything has been a competition to you. You wanted this kill, just like you didn't want me to fight. Just like you want me locked up back in my damn room." She sniffed. "Admit it, you would be satisfied if the Kings' *Bound* me again. At least then you wouldn't have to waste so much energy trying to keep me grounded. *God*, you almost killed us all by wasting the damn Portal key on me!"

All emotion had slipped out of his face and that somehow made her even angrier.

"Everyone is waiting by the Portal," Soren said as he sheathed his bloody blade. "So, if you're done, it is time to go."

Dylan ground her molars and looked down at Silas who was now a pale version of a warped Gerion. She sucked in a sharp breath and recoiled. She had almost forgotten who he really was. She wouldn't ever forget now. No, death had a funny way of conjuring the truth out of even the most skillful liars.

Dylan got up and found her *Daleon* in Gerion's back pocket. She sheathed her remaining weapons and followed Soren to the front door of the castle.

"Ugh! You both must be the slowest creatures alive," Astrid yelled, perched precariously on the arm of Silas' throne. "What the hell were you doing?" She swung her leg off the side and jumped down. "Don't tell me you were making out in this screwed up place."

Dylan shoved past Soren, and snapped, "It's none of your Goddamn business."

Astrid balked with wide eyes. "Fine. *Whatever*." Astrid scowled at Soren. "Ready?"

Soren mumbled an expletive under his breath and began creating the Portal with a series of codes from his TAC.

As Dylan waited for the Portal to be generated, she kept her hands tightly clasped and her eyes trained on the crimson carpet runner that had been her pathway from her room to the front door for the months she spent here.

Dylan couldn't wait to get out of here and back to Elon where she would safely be several worlds away from everything that was Silas. She wanted to feel relieved everyone was dead, that her monster was finally unable to terrorize her any more, as she should... but she could still hear the screams as she burned the creatures alive. She could still feel Silas holding onto her jacket during his last moments. A shiver struck her nerves and she suddenly itched to get out of these bloody clothes. But it was more than just the blood that made her feel anxious and suffocated. It was the uniform. After today, she never wanted to wear it again.

"All right," Soren said.

Dylan perked up and stepped over to the Portal hanging midair like a mystical cloud. She couldn't wait to take a long shower and put several doors between her and everyone else.

Dylan was already thinking about her destination when their watches started beeping again. Dylan slowly tilted her head down and looked at the ominous watch that only ever seemed to bear bad news.

Not again.

Dylan looked back at the others who looked just as

315

surprised and equally worn out.

"*Go,*" Soren snapped at Dylan, prompting her to focus back on the Portal. She nodded furiously in agreement. They all had to get out of here. Now.

Dylan quickly imagined Elon and the Portal, the room with the weapons, the only way to enter into the Glass Tower. Then she dove into safety.

CHAPTER 17

"His thorns never were my pain to bear."
Sarah Jave

SEVERAL hours sluiced by like trying to wade through sludge. Her coffee had long since turned cold as she pressed her fingers tightly against each other in the deserted cafeteria late at night, waiting for her crew mates to return home. She had stupidly jumped through the Portal, expecting the others to be right behind her. She should have known Soren would do this. He didn't want her in Zadar, but more than that, it was painfully obvious he didn't want her fighting as a member of the Shadow Horde.

After she realized what he had done, Dylan rushed to King Damen's office and begged for the coordinates again. He hadn't been pleased by Soren's continual exclusion of her, but he wasn't happy about her temper, either. He had told her to get cleaned up and accept this command, that he must have good reason for sending her back. Dylan had bit her tongue and gone to her room to scream, shower, and change. When she still couldn't sit still, she found herself seated in the farthest corner of the cafeteria cradling a cup of coffee.

I should leave, she told herself for the twentieth time. *Screw waiting for them.*

Dylan picked up her coffee and took an icy sip, knowing damn well she wouldn't be going anywhere until she knew

317

they were all right, that Ian hadn't passed out or Astrid hadn't overestimated her abilities.

She dropped her head into her hands, her fingers digging into her scalp. Why did she care so much if they made it? Of course they would. Soren had been doing this job for almost half a century and Augusto even longer. They were the best of the best. Besides, she was supposed to be pissed off that none of them came back for her after Soren's dirty trick; and she was. So why did her chest feel like it was about to collapse if they didn't show soon?

It had been too long. Maybe she should tell King Damen so they could send reinforcements. What if they were stranded without a Portal key or dead because the castle blew! Dylan suddenly stood just as Astrid's winded voice broke through the stagnant air, interrupting Dylan's dire thoughts. She held her breath when she heard Ian's hesitant reply to Augusto's deep timbre.

Dylan watched them round the corner, filing in. Their faces serious and somber.

Augusto.

Astrid.

Ian.

She felt her breath release as Soren rounded the corner, limping with a wince.

Oh God. Was he hurt? Did something happen? Her eyes quickly assessed everyone. Despite being a little pale, they all appeared okay.

Dylan suddenly wanted to run to Soren, to hug him and ask him if he needed something before she screamed and kicked him in the balls; but she stayed suspended somewhere between launching herself at him and being glued to the floor by her pride. His recent actions had made it pretty clear she wasn't welcome as a friend or foe.

Besides, she had a difficult time dealing with someone who repaid her warmth with insults.

As if sensing her presence, Soren's shadowed eyes lifted

to hers. It was a look she knew too well. A look that swallowed her whole and imprisoned her. He was just as pissed as she was, and for the life of her, she couldn't imagine why.

Soren said something to Ian then headed toward her. Dylan's heart pumped harder the closer he got. She rubbed a hand over her chest and tried to still the unexplainable growing sensation threatening to burst inside her chest.

"Hey."

"You're hurt." Her voice unfortunately hitched as she glanced at his side, ripped and stained by blood. She tried to stay unemotional but it was hard to act unaffected by his wound when there was that much blood.

"It's nothing." He looked mentally exhausted as if he had been fighting his own inner demons this entire time instead of a throng of creatures. "Astrid patched me up. I'm fine."

"What happened?"

"Nadia Burke showed up with another dozen Lycans."

"Are they all dead?" She didn't expect them not to be.

Soren nodded once.

"Good," Dylan whispered. Now all that was left was Lucia if she didn't drown herself in a case of wine first. Or if Soren didn't beat Dylan to the punch, which was just as likely, considering.

Soren's eyes bored into Dylan as an impossible silence stepped between them. "I'm not going to lie. I assumed this would go a lot differently."

Dylan shook her head. "You need to start treating me like I'm a part of this."

He laughed at that, but it sounded pained.

Dylan crinkled her nose. Would he ever take her seriously?

"I am a part of this crew, am I not?"

"*Dylan*," he said under his breath and only for her to hear. Her name felt wrong on his tongue. It made him sound like he knew her; as if they were something more than what they were. "We've been doing this for decades. Yeah, you're sworn in and you've killed, but I can't have you in a situation like that. You're just..." He looked off to the side.

"Just what?" she prompted with an edge.

"Nothing," he sighed, like the conversation bored him. She knew he only stopped before he dug himself into a deeper hole. "Look, it's late. I'm exhausted. Let's just not do this now."

"I won't ever forget what you did back there." Dylan stood her ground. "The least you can do is tell me the damn reason."

"Fine," he admitted, "You're inexperienced, and I can't fight *and* make sure you don't die while playing G.I. Jane."

"*Inexperienced*? That's bullshit."

"Why do you think you were accepted in the Horde?"

Because I'm an Elementa that can create fire. Because they want to control me, she thought both but didn't say either.

"Did you really think they just decided to promote you after a couple of lessons because you earned it? If you do, you're an even bigger idiot than I thought." Soren met Dylan's scowl with one of his own. "You are just a strategy. A fucking pawn to shove in our enemies' faces. You're not ready to fight a battle like the one we had today. You're too irrational. *Too damn reckless,*" he snapped and Dylan bristled. "But, don't worry. I'm sure you'll learn how to control yourself in a few decades."

Dylan's jaw had dropped somewhere in the middle of his confession. She refused to believe him. She couldn't. She had been throwing herself into training; trying so hard to be good enough. She expected someone, anyone else to say those words but not him. He knew how hard she worked. How much she had needed it to heal. Perhaps that had been the very reason why he hadn't said anything before.

"Screw you," she said, hating how everything he said made sense. "You'll let me fight next time. I'm good and

320

you know it," but even she couldn't put confidence behind her words.

"I won't sponsor this fucked up death wish of yours," he said dismissively. "So, you might as well let it go."

She couldn't even open her mouth to rebuke because she was so mad, wondering why she was fighting him when in reality she wanted nothing do with the Horde. She wanted nothing to do with him.

He smirked at her silence. "You'll do what I say. I am in charge, and if I want to send you back, you go. No questions asked. Understood?" His tone was firm. It brooked no argument or misunderstanding, but it didn't stop anger from simmering beneath her skin and erupting.

He turned away and headed back to the others who tried to act like they weren't listening. Dylan noticed her feverish skin with a start. She was covered in a fine sheen of sweat. A tell-tale sign of her impeding combustion. If Soren had provoked her much longer she knew the fire in her blood would have taken over the conversation for her.

She *was* out of control. And just like that, a deep sea of despair dragged her under its crushing waves, cooling her flames.

Dylan strode past the Shadow Horde, wanting nothing more than to complain petulantly to King Damen and tell him how much of a dick Soren was being. But that wasn't realistic. Her Uncle didn't care about her bruised ego; he wanted soldiers and soldiers stayed in line.

Once Dylan made it through the double doors and out of sight, her chest seized up and she gasped for air as she fell against the wall. It was always going to be like this. Two steps forward, five steps back. She thought about her uniform thrown haphazardly on her desk chair and it all suddenly felt like one big joke.

Dylan took a deep breath, forcing herself to ball her emotions and shoved it into one of her mental boxes. Control. She needed control. She could not break down.

She was about to retreat back to her dorm yet again, when she heard Astrid bark hasty words at Soren. Dylan edged around the corner of the door and halted when she could clearly hear them while staying out of sight.

"She's right. She should have stayed."

"Yeah," Ian added, "You should have seen how she tackled those Lycans from behind. We could have used her when Nadia attacked."

"Maybe then you wouldn't have been clawed," Astrid continued.

"I didn't see either of you voicing this opinion when I sent her away."

"Would it have mattered?" Astrid accused. "Soren, I'm not stupid. That fight would have lasted half as long with her there. She's good. You know she's good, *you* trained her."

"And what the hell was that about the OP only wanting her here for show?" Ian asked. "Why are you lying to her?"

"I wasn't lying. She would have been a liability," Soren said.

"I mean, come on," Ian said, "I know you care about her, but this… this is different… it's like you're holding her back."

"What is going on here?" Astrid asked. "Is it still your vendetta against her family? For killing Ella?"

"This has nothing to do with Ella!" Soren snapped.

Dylan could hear the passion and hate in his voice. Whatever happened to this girl, she knew then that Soren blamed her and the Elementas. It suddenly made sense why Soren was always so conflicted about her.

"Then what is it!" Astrid yelled back. "Unless…" she trailed off with uncertainty woven into her voice.

"I want you to think really long about what you're about to say, and then I want you to think about it even damn longer because it's about me."

The door Dylan was leaning against squeaked when she leaned on it a bit too much. Her eyes shot wide and she

322

flipped around and dashed down the corridor. She was almost to her dorm when Soren caught her arm.

"Dylan—"

"No!" she screamed, wrenching her arm away only to have it grabbed again. "Goddammit, Soren, leave me alone. You've made it painfully clear what you think of me."

"I'm not—"

"Oh?" she snarled. "Admit it, I make you sick every time you have to look at me. Probably the only time you couldn't mask your disgust was when you woke up after the Scarred attack. At least then you weren't a damn liar! I trusted you! You're no better than Silas, except you only want me for your own selfish reasons. Well, I'm done!" She shoved against him, but he only tightened his grip and backed her against the wall until she was completely and embarrassingly submitted. "I fucking quit!" she cried out as a last resort.

Dylan tried pulling away from him a bit harder before pushing him harshly. Dammit, he was strong. Had he ever used his real strength on her?

"No. You don't get to quit." His voice lowered an octave. "I forbid it."

"You *forbid* it?!" she laughed, humorlessly. "I heard you. You hate me. You hate me for whatever my parents did. It's why you don't want me fighting. It's why you killed Silas when you knew what it meant to me. Why the hell would you want someone like me fighting next to you?"

He turned his head to the side briefly before focusing back on her with a defeated sigh. "I couldn't stand," he grit his teeth, "how much it pissed me off that you were willing to go back to Gerion for me."

"*What?*"

"When I saw you at my bedside asleep. I was relieved we were okay but I was also pissed off that you had given yourself up just to save my life. I was pissed off because, for the second time in my life, I had lost control of everything around me. I was fighting with my heart because I couldn't stand the way those demons had laid their hands on you. And that is why I tried to send you home today."

"What?" she repeated with less vigor.

"Don't you see, Dylan? I can't trust myself fighting next to you."

"Well, isn't that convenient." Dylan made an irritated noise as he let go of one of her hands.

Soren looked at her like she had gone completely mad. "You're so damn stubborn and difficult." His hand hovered over her neck almost as if he wanted to choke her. "And fucking uncontrollable!"

She ignored his remarks and shook out her hand full of pins and needles from how tight he had held it. She still couldn't believe him. This possessive excuse was only masking his true hatred.

"*Dylan*," his voice had dropped, dripping with husk as he pleaded with her to listen with the simple proclamation of her name.

She hesitantly looked up and into his eyes.

"The thought of anyone else touching you makes me go crazy; and that is why I killed Gerion. Not because I hate you. And not because I want to hold you back."

She was already shaking her head. He was lying; he had to be. He was only trying to humiliate her or hurt her. "You hate me. My family killed the people you loved—"

"They are *not* your family," Soren chided, cutting her off. "You are nothing like the Elementas. Out of everyone in Elon, I would be the one to know, don't you think?"

Dylan could only shake her head, speechless. He wasn't there as she incinerated those creatures. He didn't see her smile at Silas just before she pulled out the gun she hoped would kill him. She was worse than the Elementas because... because she had liked it all. She had wanted it to stop because she couldn't face that dark part of herself taking over. She was afraid it would somehow show on her face and alter the part of her she thought was still human.

"Stop telling yourself otherwise. *I know you*. I've seen everything... remember?"

When she refused to open her eyes, he suddenly growled, slamming his fist against the door in desperation. "Look at me."

She did and glared at him. "What the hell do you want from me?"

He leaned down until she could feel his breath slipping across her face. Her heart began to beat so strong she knew he had to be able to see it shaking her entire body. He wanted to kiss her. She could see it in the way he stared at her lips with a molten mixture of curiosity and desire. He had the same determined set to his jaw right after she'd wrecked his bike.

She felt ill from the conflicting feelings strangling each other within her. Half of her wanted to pull him closer; the other half wanted to knee him in the balls for everything he had said in the cafeteria; for everything he had done in Zadar. For everything he had done since they met.

"Don't," she warned.

"Don't what?"

She stared at him unable to deny how terrified she was. She knew none of this was the answer, but somewhere deep down, she begged to be touched, caressed, loved until she couldn't think a second longer. If she could admit it to herself, she'd know she was just alone and needy. She didn't really want to get tangled in another relationship. It had just been so long since someone loved her. Since someone held her without motive.

"Don't kiss you?" He brought his fingers down the side of her face without actually touching her, just tracing the angles with his sapphire eyes. "Why? What are you so afraid of?"

Everything. You. What will happen to us when we cross this line. That I won't be able to give you what you want. That I'll somehow try my hardest and still fail. That you'll

325

only take and take until I'm washed up and broken beyond repair. And then you'll die like the others. You'll die and leave me alone to pick up the pieces.

Always alone.

Her entire body tensed up as he lowered his mouth just above hers.

"Tell me you don't want this and I'll back off. Tell me you haven't thought about me kissing you." He moved away from her mouth, and her breath caught when his lips gently touched below her chin on the soft skin of her throat, "Licking you." Her knees quivered when he suddenly dragged his tongue slowly down the sweep of her throat. His free hand slipped down her side, hungrily running his fingers along the curve of her hip.

She swallowed forcefully and her chest heaved against his.

He shifted next to her ear. "Tell me what you want, Dylan," he demanded, softly, moving her chin with a single finger until their eyes met.

The way his expression darkened, she knew she didn't have to say a word. He knew exactly what she wanted.

"You," she breathed.

His lips found hers and she gasped, shocked so much by the ferocity she couldn't respond, couldn't do anything other than kiss him back. And holy hell was it a kiss. His tongue sliced into her mouth deep and relentless, coiling with her tongue.

She breathed his breath and he feasted on hers. They had a certain synergy that pulsed between them. A brutal hunger that swept her up completely until the world around them vanished into thin air. He was like raw ice, jagged, intense—almost painful if she held on too long, but she couldn't let go. No matter how much it hurt to face that she was moving on, she wouldn't let herself let go of him.

Soren deepened their kiss, pressing and locking their hands high above her head until it was obvious who was in control.

He ground his hips harder against her, and in that instant, she imagined him having no qualms about taking her right there in the hall.

"*Really*?" Astrid called out from down the hall. "There is a freaking room right behind you."

Soren pulled away, panting as if he'd felt every single feeling that had been coursing through her, and more.

Despite being spotted, Dylan had a hard time opening her eyes, too lost within the earthquake Soren had caused to her mind, body, and heart.

When she did open her eyes to see not only Astrid but Ian, too, she cringed.

Oh, dear God, Dylan cried inside, wishing she could dissolve into the wall. Now she probably looked ridiculous after denying their relationship countless times over the past few years.

Soren appeared unaffected by this, like everything else, as he looked over at their friends, and told them to kiss his ass in Latin.

Good, she thought.

She was glad he wasn't turning on her at the last second. But, that didn't mean she was going to stick around so that he could remember he hated her. Using her free hand, Dylan inched her fingers toward the door knob beside her hip while Soren dealt with his friends. Dylan wasn't even sure why she was kissing Soren. He was supposed to be her commander, and maybe even her temperamental–somewhat friend on a good day. Kissing him would only muck things up, especially since now all she wanted to do was kiss him more.

"I'm good, but thanks for the offer," Ian winked at Soren with a mock saccharine smile before grabbing Astrid by the shoulders and physically turning her around so that they could leave the way they came. "C'mon, babe, now you know they made up, let's go grab a drink at Traverna."

Just as Dylan's fingertips touched the metal door knob,

Soren covered her hand, stopping her. She felt the air in her lungs deflate in a sudden rush. She should have known running from Soren was pointless.

"Better be a big drink to make up for that 'babe' comment," Astrid responded to Ian.

"You got it, *babe,*" Ian laughed, as they finally disappeared around the corner.

In the silence, Dylan could feel the weight of Soren's stare pinning her down. He was waiting for her to make a move; whether to run or stay, it was all on her.

"You're going to need to learn how to control yourself when we fight," she whispered, "because I won't just sit back like I didn't earn my title."

"I knew from the moment I laid my eyes on you 'sitting back' wasn't a trait you harbored."

"Soren."

"Yeah?"

Dylan looked up into his eyes framed by silky, onyx locks. "I want you to kiss me again."

His lips curved in a devilish smirk before taking her mouth once more. He released his hold on her hands to hike her up on his hips. Dylan fisted his hair between her fingers, and before she could help it, madness overtook her sensibility. She reached backward for the door handle and shoved it open with a bang against the wall. Soren rushed into her black bedroom and kicked the door shut, letting the darkness envelope them.

Dylan slid down to the floor already pushing his jacket off. She fingered the edges of his shirt and her heart stuttered when he broke their kiss to rip it off. She stumbled backward into the darkness, barely lit by the glow of the red moon.

Soren stalked toward her like a shadow hunting in the night—a demon after his next meal. Dylan stopped when her thighs hit the edge of the bed. With nowhere to go, she stood still, her heart racing.

Soren towered over her as his hands pushed the jacket off

her shoulders and gripped her tank, lifting it high overhead. With her arms still above her head, he coasted his fingers from her wrists, down, down, down, teasing her along the edges of her body. He hooked his fingers inside the waistband of her pants and bent down, slowly dragging them off of her and to the ground.

Dylan stepped out of her leggings and fought the urge to shield herself. She suddenly felt naked but more than bare—the scars mapped out across her body throbbed like flashing neon signs in the dark. No guy had ever seen her scars, let alone felt along them with desire. In her dreams with Tristian she had simply removed them, changing herself to be what she wanted him to see. She wasn't proud of it, but at the time they were only her dreams. Except this was real. There was no changing herself in front of Soren. He would see what she so desperately tried to keep hidden from the world.

Dylan could barely breathe as Soren kissed across the self-inflicted scars on her thighs and stomach. He stood and one of his hands slipped across her forehead, gently pushing away the veil of pale hair she was hiding behind, before resting his fingertips just below her collar bone.

"Sit."

He pushed her down to the bed and she had no option but to fall. She took in a lungful of air, feeling the wind knocked back inside her chest with the simple command as her hands landed on his hips for stability.

Dylan suddenly realized how much she had thought about touching him since the first moment she saw him in the gym, wielding those swords, his hot skin glistening with sweat. She had wanted to feel his muscles taut underneath her fingers so much it had hurt to admit, and the pain had continued until today. It had only been subdued by practice.

Yet, as she sat here, knowing she had free rein of his body, her need flooded back full force—urging her to feel along his tight grooves and trace along the spirals of raised ink marking his chest. With her eyes adjusted to the dark, she was able to appreciate the angles of his body and the scars that marred him in a totally different way.

She pressed her fingers along his stomach, along the intricate tribal design of two suns etched into his muscle. She met the gauzy fabric of a bandage and his stomach tensed.

She flicked her eyes up to his. "Are you sure you don't need to see the Medic?"

"It's fine," he hissed.

She nodded, understanding. Soren kept his scars, too. Hesitantly, she leaned forward, placing a slow, gentle kiss over the wound.

He sank his fingers into her hair and gripped her just on the verge of being painful.

"I need to see you."

She shook her head as her hands found the buckle of his leathers, finding her movements to be frighteningly automatic.

"Keep the light off." She blushed immediately at how bad that sounded. She knew it was selfish, but it was the only way she could go through this without her brain getting in the way.

His hands stopped her from undoing the buckle.

"Please," she whispered. She wasn't sure what all she was begging for because the word felt laden with more than just a plea for the dark.

After a moment, he released her and she tore off his weapons belt, chucking it to the floor.

Dylan couldn't help but wait for Soren to change his mind about her. For the questions, the hesitations, the excuses just before he left. But, no, he only tilted her head back and kissed her harder and more —his kiss ripping the air straight out of her lungs.

He tore his lips off of her, and growled, "Get on the bed and turn around."

Dylan hesitated before slowly flipping around and crawling onto the bed. She felt him behind her as his hands landed on her hips, pulling them back against his leather pants with a noticeable hardness. His hands gently pulled her hair back into a ponytail before wrapping it around one fist.

"Breathe, my pet," Soren hissed, as one of his hands slid roughly down her spine, shoving her rear down until her legs were spread wide. She panted feeling light headed and drunk. She really hoped he didn't plan on having sex with her this way. The pain... could she handle the pain? She should tell him.

Her mouth opened just as his palm came down across her ass in a stinging bite; snapping her out of the strange haze since the moment he kissed her.

"*Ah*!" Dylan whipped her head to one side. "What the hell?!"

His gaze was nothing but serious, staring down at her with pupils dilated black, flaring in possessive need.

"Don't act as if this isn't want you want."

"*What*?" Dylan snapped. *What the hell was he talking about?*

"Beg me," he demanded, rubbing where he spanked her, easing the pain.

"What?" Dylan asked again, feeling infinitely confused.

"Beg me to punish you. Beg me, Dylan."

Her stomach dropped and fear filled her insides which strangely made her want him more. She didn't understand this side of herself. How could being afraid spurn this kind of desire? She trembled as she forced herself to process this request.

Beg him to hurt me?

His fingers slid down. She gasped at how good it felt. The pain. The pleasure. She wasn't unfamiliar with pain; but, this new sensation of weaving pleasure deeply into it opened her mind up and shut down what she thought was right.

His fingers left her and she tensed just before his hand came down swiftly against her rear again. She swore.

331

"*Well*?" he bit out. "Do I need to remind you of every smart comment, of every dismissed command?"

"Go to hell," she hissed through the burning seared onto her skin.

"Give me what I want and I won't have to punish you more than you want, my pet."

More than she *wanted*? This was demeaning. Shameful. Disgusting. Yeah, sure she used to hurt herself in the past, but that was something completely different. Sex was supposed to be passionate, intense and hot, not painful. Spanking was for freaks in pornos or underground clubs. She didn't want this!

"You're nothing but a sick—" his hand came sharply against her rear and she fell face down into the mattress.

"If you hate this so much, why haven't you stopped me?" he demanded, releasing his hold on her hair.

"You haven't given me a chance!" Dylan fumed, turning her head to the side on the bed. Not caring in the slightest that she was practically spread eagle as her ass throbbed.

"You're hands are free, yet you keep them pinned to the sheets."

Dylan stilled before pushing back up and staring at her hands that hadn't moved since he started. She had been too focused on the pain and the desire… she hadn't even thought about stopping him.

"I've seen the scars and the memories," Soren husked, kissing random spots along her spine. "I know you crave pain with no outlet but the gym. It's why you push yourself until you're bleeding or starving. Let me be your outlet, pet. *Beg me.*"

That wasn't true! …was it?

Dylan frowned down at the rumpled sheets, knowing in that moment he was right. She not only wanted this, she needed this. She needed to release the pressure that had built beneath her skin. She needed the tightness constricting her heart since the moment she left Los Angeles unraveled.

332

She needed Soren to free her.

She had only been too afraid to admit it. Just because she had put cutting behind herself didn't mean she had put the destructive need to rest.

She swallowed, throwing down her walls and bracing herself to take a risk. *God*, she really hoped she wouldn't regret this.

"Make me feel," she whispered, squeezing her eyes shut. "Please, Soren."

His palm came down even harder; and this time she cried out his name. Her voice became raw and stripped of everything but emotion.

She barely had a moment to breathe before he was flipping her over onto her back and kissing her. Capturing her lips beneath his need. He lowered his mouth to her neck, tasting her ardently down the column of her throat. "I knew you were like this," he rasped, "Shit, you're so beautiful."

Dylan's breath caught as he continued sucking and kissing down the center of her sternum. Soren sank his teeth into the soft skin of her hip and she jerked at the sharp bite just as he began stroking his tongue over the ache. She pressed her thighs together as she watched him, entranced by the way he sucked on her flushed skin. There wasn't anything special about that part of her body but his mouth managed to make everything thrilling.

Dylan abandoned the sheets and knotted her fingers in his hair, pulling him back up to her lips and succumbing to every dangerous, dark thing she craved. Their tongues met, wet and wanting. Beneath him, she felt pieced back together and scattered all at once. She was so completely lost. She felt free.

Soren rocked against her, kissing her, rubbing her, breathing in her skin until he was all she could think about. Her breathing got faster and all she could do was smell him all over her, inside of her.

"I feel you everywhere," she said breathlessly.

"Ah, shit, *Dylan*..." Soren let out agonizing moan before ripping himself off of her.

He abruptly stood and Dylan sat up, confused.

"Where are you—"

Her voice was cut off by a cry when he grabbed her ankles and yanked her to the edge of the bed. He pushed her legs apart before covering her with his mouth.

"*Soren*!" she choked, trying to snap her legs shut. But, he only groaned against her as he worshiped her with his tongue. Her back arched as tight as a bow. Her muscles tensed. All of the sensations running through her body concentrated to that one spot he stroked.

When it all became too much she bucked, needing him to stop, needing him closer. His arms were wrapped around her thighs. His fingertips bruising her skin as he held her down. Her head swam and her toes curled. In one blinding moment, she cried out as the universe exploded.

Dylan threw her head back and writhed against him as her intensity burned and pulsed through her and into him until she was left panting, drowning in pleasure. Too intoxicated, too shattered to do anything more than moan his name softly.

◇◇◇

"I can't believe the plan worked!" Aria beamed, sitting up in bed. One hand holding a glass of champagne while the other held the tablet connecting her to the worlds.

Asher clinked his glass with hers before finishing his half glass of Dom. He felt genuinely light as if a harsh weight had finally slipped off his shoulders. A weight that had been bearing down on him since he came back from Zadar.

When he initially left to find and kill Gerion he hadn't expected this moment to come. He expected to die or fail. That was until his amazing mate proposed the idea about leading the Horde and Nadia to Zadar to kill each other. They just hadn't expected Silas to show. According to the

Elon News, the demon and werewolf leader were dead along with over a hundred demon-bred lycans. He knew Nadia wasn't the only werewolf leader in cahoots with the Plantos, but her death was vital if they ever wanted to return to Los Angeles.

Asher leaned over and took the tablet out of Aria's hands as she chugged the last bit of her champagne.

"Now we can relax," he grinned, already fantasizing about being back in the city and choosing their new home together.

Aria jerked back when he tried to kiss her. "What do you mean relax?" she said as Asher's smile slipped. "Now we rescue Dylan."

Asher sighed and sat back. "I thought we agreed that plan wasn't going to work." He grabbed the neck of the bottle of Dom Perignon and took a gulp, forgoing a glass. It was a good thing he loved his mate because he was pretty sure she was trying to kill him without realizing it. "Besides, you saw her. She looked happy."

After they had snuck into The Gates to watch Dylan's *Signing* into the Shadow Horde, he had sat down with his mate and his friends, whom all agreed to let it go.

"I won't believe it. I know her," she said vehemently. "There was nothing genuine about her that day. She looked uncomfortable... as if she was being forced up there against her will."

Asher had no idea what she was talking about. Dylan looked proud that day standing next to her new mate and accepting the rank.

"How the hell could you not see that!"

"Look, I don't know what to tell you," Asher said. "I spoke with her and she seemed fine. A little angrier than I remember, but fine."

Aria suddenly fished the tablet out of the covers and found the article about Dylan and Soren after the ceremony. "You're telling me *this* looks fine to you?" Aria shoved the

335

tablet in his face and added, "She looks freaked out."

Asher took the tablet and stared at the photo he'd unfortunately seen too many times to count, just to humor her. Dylan did look caught off guard if you looked really close, but the image was a bit grainy and could be morphing their faces from the truth. He looked up at his mate and she groaned.

"I don't know what you want me to say." He offered the tablet back to her. "We promised to let it go. This isn't our fight. Not anymore."

Her face crumpled and it killed him to see her hope crushed like that. But, it had to be done. They had been immensely lucky to have pulled off the plan in Zadar. It would be suicide to press their luck further.

Asher tossed the tablet onto the bed again and grabbed his beautiful mate and held her as she cried over her friend for what he hoped would be the last time.

CHAPTER 18

"She was an angel craving chaos
and he was a demon seeking peace."
Forever the Sickest Kids

ALMOST nose to nose, Dylan stared at Soren while he slept. Her eyes tracked along the subtle imperfections that only seemed to make him that much better looking. There was a bone in the middle of his nose slightly askew, a tiny freckle on the base of his espresso lashes, and a crease just between his thick brows—probably from his ever present scowling. He had already grown a full shadow of stubble along his jaw. The same stubble that had grazed against her belly the night before.

I need you to beg me, Dylan...

She felt along the inside of her mouth. The taste of him was still on her tongue. It was a strange thing to be next to him, naked and aching in all of the right ways. They had practically done it all, but that one tiny thing. He hadn't even asked as if he knew without asking. As if he knew how important that step was to her.

I know you...

She hadn't slept much after Soren passed out; mostly from her mind racing at warp speeds. It was so easy to lose herself in the dark but now, in the bright light of morning, all she felt was fear. And not the steamy fear that had pulled hidden desires out from hiding but real fear of what came

337

next. What if he didn't want her anymore? What if last night had been the start of something she wasn't ready for?

Soren stirred a bit and mumbled, "Didn't anyone ever tell you it wasn't polite to stare?" His eyes opened. The startling contrast of his eyes like indigo marbles against the backdrop of tanned skin was enough for her breath to get lodged inside her lungs again. *I can't do this.*

The urge to flee crawled along her skin like ants.

"I'm not from here, remember?" she joked, but her eyes lacked any enthusiasm. She swallowed, visibly.

"This doesn't change anything between us if you don't want it to," he groaned, closing his eyes and stretching his tight muscles. "If that is what you are so worried about."

"I know." Dylan quickly rolled out of bed and tried, as discreetly as she could, to grab her scattered clothes without revealing too much. It was stupid to try and hide from him after everything they had done, but being with him in the morning was so much different, so much harder, than hiding behind the night.

She felt his stare burning into her until she closed the bathroom door.

She finally let out a sigh and threw her bundle of clothes into the sink. She looked at herself in the mirror and ground her teeth at the map of scars across her body. Each one told a story. Stories she never wanted to forget, but some were too personal for anyone to see, even Soren. They were ugly stories; ugly memories of solace through self-harm. With them exposed, all of her ugliness would be revealed. And who would want someone so ugly?

"Dylan?" Soren said, his voice muffled by the door.

"Yeah," she mumbled, unable to let go of the sink.

A little bump sounded at the door and she briefly squeezed her eyes shut. She could just imagine his stance—arms braced on either side of the door frame, forehead resting on the door. It unnerved her how well she knew his mannerisms without knowing a thing about his past.

Beg me, Dylan.

God, the night before had been amazing. She just didn't know how to proceed from here. He had somehow managed to alter everything she thought she knew about her herself in a single night.

Dylan let out a frustrated groan. This was just too confusing.

"Open the door." His voice was so deep and terrifying, even through the door, that she felt on the verge of tears.

Taking a deep breath, she quickly pulled a towel around her midsection and unlocked the door. He was standing just as she had imagined, shirtless and unbuttoned leathers. His face showed a mixture of caution and suspicion.

"If nothing has changed," she blurted out before she could help it. "Then why does it feel like, like I lost— like I *can't*—" She shook her head unable to say what she wanted. How could she tell him she didn't recognize herself anymore? She had changed so much since finding out she was demon. Who the hell was she?

Soren snatched ahold of her towel and yanked her into his chest. It smelled faintly of soap and spicy cigarettes. It was so unlike him to just hold her that she awkwardly tensed up.

"You regret it."

Dylan only shook her head no. That was the hardest part. She didn't regret a single moment with him, ever. That was what made her feel the most shameful. She should hate him for everything he had put her through since they met, but she didn't. She couldn't.

"We shouldn't do that again," her voice was smothered against his arm, "until I can figure out what I... want."

Soren pulled her head back by the tips of her hair. He gazed down at her.

"Do whatever you want. No one's stopping you, least of all me."

Dylan nodded and tried detangling herself from his hold, so she could get dressed when he took hold of her locks and yanked her back to his mouth.

She sucked in a breath, not expecting her entire body to weaken so fast.

He looked into her hooded eyes and grinned at her reaction. "Mind if I shower here?"

Dylan grabbed a blueberry muffin and coffee, her mind focused solely on Soren, last night and their morning together. It had taken all of two seconds for her to turn the light off and follow him into the shower. He didn't question her about the light or about anything, really, except for maybe where the shampoo was, making them both laugh.

After they were dressed, he explained that he had paperwork to do. Apparently, Gerion's death wasn't official until the Kings stamped their approval, even with a rotting body in the Elon morgue as evidence.

Soren told her he would catch up with her after morning practice—which was probably for the best. Dylan needed some time to herself to filter through the amazing madness of the last twenty-four hours. Silas was dead and she had almost slept with Soren.

Dylan stepped away from the espresso machine and slowed her stride when she noticed how hushed the cafeteria was. How everyone's eyes seemed to be glancing in her direction. Her ears flamed with embarrassment. It felt like high school all over again. As if any moment a stuck-up blonde would tap her on the shoulder and *accidentally* pour red fruit juice down the front of her white pants.

Dylan squeezed her eyes shut and told herself to calm down. She wasn't back home, she wasn't wearing white pants, and most importantly, to them she was dangerous. It would be a stupid thing to mess with her.

Her eyes opened and no one seemed to be staring at her anymore.

She was seriously losing it.

"Temperance!"

Dylan jumped, almost dropping her breakfast.

"Looks like it's just the two of us this morning," Astrid said, holding a tray effortlessly in one hand and hooking an arm through Dylan's with the other, steering her toward their usual table.

"It is?" Dylan asked, wanting to scowl at Astrid's naturally lithe movements.

The girls sat and Astrid immediately dove into a stack of pancakes, taking a bite that was way too big for her mouth. She quickly chewed and swallowed. "Augusto and Ian are still sleeping last night off and if I know Soren at all, he's doing paperwork on the mission from yesterday... amiright?" she asked, stuffing her mouth again.

"Yeah," Dylan murmured, waiting for the questions about her and Soren. Questions Dylan couldn't answer even in her own mind.

"Do you want to go shopping?"

Dylan halted mid-chew of her muffin. "Shopping?"

"New clothes... shoes..." Astrid looked down at Dylan's shirt for a moment, "leggings, whatever... yeah, shopping. Want to go with me?"

Dylan shrugged and swallowed her bite before washing it down with her latte. "Sure. I don't have any money but I can keep you company."

Astrid slammed down her fork. "What the hell do you mean you don't have any money?" She held out her hand impatiently. "Come on, give me your TAC."

Dylan obliged, watching curiously as Astrid clicked through the screens. A few moments passed by before an incredulous smile hit Astrid's lips.

"Mission bonuses are the best part of our job," Astrid said, handing Dylan her watch with the screen brightly displaying Temperance Elementa's bank account with a recent, hefty deposit of a million *peira*.

"What's a million *peira*."

"A *ton* of money," Astrid smirked.

Dylan just looked at her, waiting for her to continue.

"Ohhhh, a million *peira* is good." Astrid nodded, eagerly, tearing another enormous bite of pancakes from the stack. "You can probably buy your own bike *and* a closet full of clothes." She shoved the food into her mouth, chewed and swallowed. "Or a house if you're into that."

Dylan stilled. "A house?"

"You don't seem to be grasping the fact," Astrid stared at her seriously, "you killed one of our biggest enemies of the century. The OP won't forget that. Hell, the worlds won't forget that. Haven't you noticed everyone talking about you?" She waved her fork around the cafeteria.

Dylan frowned at her. Perhaps she wasn't losing it after all. "But, I—" Dylan stopped speaking, wondering if this was Soren's way of making it up to her—telling the worlds she had been the one to kill Gerion. Except the fame and glory didn't matter to her. She cared about the kill and Soren had still taken it from her. A million *peira* wouldn't change that. "When do you want to go?" Dylan said instead.

Astrid polished off her pancakes and spoke through a full mouth, "Now."

The girls walked out the front door of the Glass Tower and headed for town on foot. They passed a few scattered merchant carts selling oils, fabric, and spices along the main road.

There was a woman dressed in a blush pink dress covered in vines. She sold herbs grown from the "palms of her hands," or so she advertised.

The woman spotted Dylan before they could pass and offered her a bright green flower like the one Dylan had made in the damned domain with Soren.

Dylan stared at it, feeling unsettled. It reminded her of the Scarred soldier in Zadar. The flaming vines. She shook her head at the woman. "No, thank you."

Astrid grabbed Dylan's hand and pulled her away from

the merchants.

"She was certainly *organic*, now wasn't she?" Astrid snickered under her breath. "Terras can be so weird. I promise we're not all tree-hugging lunatics."

"I didn't think you were," Dylan said, as they wove through countless narrow alleyways, deciding not to remind Astrid that Dylan, too, was technically a Terra. "I'm sure she's just selling what she's good at. You can't blame her for that."

Astrid shrugged and let go of Dylan when they reached the mouth of the alleyway.

Dylan gawked left and right at the wide cobblestone street lined by exclusive glass-front shops and outdoor restaurants. A floral aroma of wisteria, honeysuckle, and jasmine filled the air, quickly followed by savory scents of fresh baked bread and juicy tomatoes. It suddenly felt like she had entered another world full of bright color and warm air. It felt like spring on Rodeo Drive.

"Where are we?" Dylan wondered, already rolling up the sleeves to her jacket as they turned left.

"Welcome to Nova," Astrid sighed, dreamily.

Dylan ended up removing her jacket and tying it around her waist as she struggled to follow Astrid underneath the ivory awnings. "Is this another world?" Was it possible to jump worlds that easily without a Portal?

"No, we're still in Elon. We've just entered a bubble; hence, the weather change."

"Crazy," Dylan murmured, eyeing a brunette walking across the street in a white eyelet sundress and chatting on her cell with two lizard-like creatures nervously shadowing her—their arms full of shopping bags.

"Nova is the *it* place to go for, well, everything," Astrid said over her shoulder as she hurried into a small boutique. "And *this* is the best place for clothes."

"Ah! Ms. Crystellos," exclaimed a woman with ashy hair in a skin-tight purple dress and winged, red frame glasses.

343

"Welcome back." The girls kissed each other's cheeks in greeting. "What can I do for you?"

"Tori, this is my friend."

Dylan smiled.

"She needs clothes... sexy clothes," Astrid held back a giggle, "no leggings."

Dylan sighed. She hadn't realized today was "Make Over Temperance Day.

"Oh, yes," Tori grinned, practically showing dollar signs in her eyes. "Please, follow me Ms. Elementa."

Dylan only shook her head at the not so subtle way Tori gave away her knowledge of who Dylan really was. Not that her face wasn't recognizable.

"Is there a specific event, ladies?" Tori asked, as she snapped her fingers to a couple of her employees to come running. She was already fingering through racks of dresses, shirts, jeans, and even lingerie.

Dylan couldn't help wondering what Soren would think of her in this stuff. He had only ever seen her tanks and leggings except for that one time she went out for her birthday. Although, Soren hadn't looked twice at that sexy dress. Perhaps, clothes weren't his thing in comparison to rope and a blindfold.

"No event, but there could be. Can't hurt to be prepared," Astrid shrugged looking through a rack of graphic tees and pulled out one that said '**book dragon**' in bold lettering.

"Is there a library in Elon?" Dylan asked Astrid once Tori was out of sight. "You know, a better one than the one in the Glass Tower."

Astrid checked the tag on the shirt. "There's the citadels in Nollah or book stores, but no, no public libraries that I've seen."

"Sucks," Dylan mumbled, thinking about all of the books in Zadar again. Maybe that was what she could do with her money... build a library. Dylan eyed a simple, grey, tee-shirt dress and the tag of one thousand *peira.* She cringed. That was, if she didn't spend it all here.

"Seriously," Astrid agreed. It took Dylan a moment to remember she was talking about the libraries.

"Ladies," Tori called from the back of the shop. "Ready for the viewing?"

Viewing? Dylan thought as she followed Astrid into a small room with a short runway in front of two plush, leather chairs and a bottle of champagne chilling on the table set between.

"Wait, I'm not trying them on?"

"Hell, no," Astrid said, taking a flute from the glass table and making herself comfortable in one of the chairs. "That takes way too much time that we don't have. Besides, no one does that in Nova."

Dylan grabbed a glass of champagne and took a sip as the first girl walked the runway in a fitted emerald dress and gold pumps.

"This is the Lois," Tori said from the side. "A softly tailored shift that works for the office as well as evenings, it comes in silk crepe de chine, with a deep V-neck and a matching fabric belt that secures with a twenty-four karat D-ring. It drops to a length that's both flattering and chic."

Dylan cocked an eyebrow at the deep neckline. In what office would that be considered appropriate?

The next five outfits were more of the same in different colors and neck styles. All way out of Dylan's league.

"I'm not feeling it," Dylan whispered to Astrid who had already claimed three of the six dresses for herself.

"What do you mean? These are *hot*. Maybe we should go out tonight and show them off."

"Well, stay, um, view. I'm going to walk around and see if I can find something else more my style."

"Sure," Astrid waved her off, "I'll page you when I'm done here and we can meet up for coffee."

Dylan quickly got up and left, feeling much better as she strolled down the street and window shopped alone. She perused a couple clothing stores and purchased a few basic items. Skinny jeans, tee shirts in colors other than black, and a ruched tank dress in teal blue with a slinky tulip-hem. It was the sexiest dress she had come across that was more *her* than whatever Tori was selling.

Dylan browsed an antique book store before coming across a metal-work vendor. She went inside and stepped up to the case filled with glittering chains, rings, knives, and bracelets. Dylan pressed her fingers to the glass and asked the clerk if she could see one of the items. He brought it out with white gloved hands on a felt burgundy tray.

"This is one of our newer editions. Traded in just a couple months ago."

Dylan carefully picked up the silver ink tip pen and twisted it until she could clearly see the three red stones on the cap.

"Who traded this in?"

"I'm sorry. This person requested to remain anonymous."

Dylan could feel her heart pummeling against her rib cage as she stared at the pen her human father had gifted her.

The morning of her eighteenth birthday, Isabel had given Dylan a letter from her parents; one they had written on her first birthday, detailing all of their hopes and dreams for her. It had broken her, but in a way, healed her. They had wanted her to live and to be more than she was allowing herself to be. That was also when she had been gifted her father's pen and cherished it until Tristian took it to gain her attention. Yet, someone had taken it from her room in Los Angeles and traded it *here* of all places.

"I want to buy this. Please tell me about the demon that sold this to you. No names, fine, but tell me about his eyes."

The clerk looked confused as Dylan's hands shook as she gripped the pen. She knew exactly what she was praying for in that moment.

Green.

She wanted him to say they were the greenest eyes he had

ever seen. That it was like the tender shade of budding leaves in spring.

Was it so bad to want this to be Tristian's way of trying to tell her something? Was this why Cassandra couldn't find him through the chain? Was he already alive? Was this some way of reaching out to her without looking for her?

"Um, yellow… gold," the clerk finally said.

And just like that, the brittle hope left over from Tristian's death shattered. She felt so foolish for hoping the impossible but it was a habit. A tendency she would give up on because it could only rip her apart the more she held out faith he'd return to her in the future.

Dylan's hands didn't shake as she paid the three thousand *peira* and refused packaging, slipping it into her pocket. She didn't know why it was here or how that person that sold it got ahold of it in the first place.

A coil of dread hooked into her stomach as she hurried to the alleyway that led back to the Glass Tower. Her thoughts stuck on Peppi's disfigured body in that tank. Aria had been the last person in contact with the pen after Tristian had set it on her doorstep. Was she okay? Was Isabel?

In no time Dylan was outside King Damen's office where a soldier from the interim army stood in her way.

"I need to speak with my Uncle," Dylan panted.

"He's in a meeting right now," the girl replied squarely. "You will have to wait."

"Please," Dylan begged. "Please, just ask."

The soldier pursed her lips and nodded. "Wait here."

Dylan fell against the wall still gripping her shopping bags tightly as the soldier disappeared inside Damen's office. She came out almost immediately.

"You have two minutes."

"That's all I need. Thank you," Dylan said, pushing open the heavy door to the office that smelled of sandalwood and lemon cleaner.

Her Uncle's office was neat, but not obsessively so. The

347

walls were a soft champagne color, and the many
bookshelves and cabinets were a shiny mahogany with
twisted iron handles. He had an understated desk in the
center covered by stacks of paper and books, a computer
somehow poised in the mix of it all. Two leather chairs were
set in front of the desk with Soren in one working on his own
stack of papers.

Soren abruptly stood, startled by Dylan's visit.

Dylan bowed to her King. "My Master. I'm so sorry for
the intrusion but I need to speak with you in private."

King Damen looked at her over his frames.

"Is something wrong?" Soren asked, already putting on
the mask of her protector without knowing a single detail.

"I don't know," she admitted before deciding to ask her
Uncle for what she needed in front of Soren. What he
thought about her worries didn't really matter, anyway. She
turned back to King Damen who was waiting patiently. "I
need to check on my human family."

He raised his eyebrows and Dylan hurried to finish why
she needed to see them. "I was at Nova today and I came
across an item I had in the human world. There is no way it
made it here without someone having access to my things.
The only three people who did are either human or dead. The
salesman told me it was sold recently. What if Gerion got to
them. What if they are trapped somewhere and now that
Gerion is dead…"

Soren was next to her, taking her bags and urging her to
sit. She did, but her legs wouldn't stop bouncing from
anxiety.

King Damen leaned back in his chair and crossed his
arms. "Let's say this is the case. Then why sell this item
here. How would he know you would see it? I will have
them checked up on but I want you to relax. This is most
likely nothing to be worried about."

"There are scavenger demons in every world that like to
take forgotten demon things," Soren added, gently. "Just

because you found it here doesn't mean something bad has happened to your family."

"I will feel better when I know they are safe. And it's not a demon thing. It's just an ordinary pen."

"May I see this pen?" her Uncle asked.

Dylan took an unsteady breath and reached into her pocket, removing the silver pen. She set it on the desk.

King Damen stared at it for a moment before picking it up and examining the stones.

"This is from your human parents, the Prescotts?"

"Yes." Dylan swallowed. "Why?"

"This *is* demon made." He turned it over. "These are Elementa family stones."

"But… I," Dylan stopped speaking, remembering her ring. Isabel had found both items in the boxes. Dylan had always just assumed the pen was her father's. "But how?"

"I wouldn't know," her Uncle said, setting down the pen and pushing it toward her. "Only you could answer that. You and maybe the creature that sold it." King Damen leaned back in his leather chair again. "I will send a soldier to question the merchant and to check on your family, and then have them report back to you. Is that all?"

"Y-yes," she stuttered. "Thank you."

Dylan picked up the pen and carefully set it back into her pocket. After she wrote down Isabel and Aria's names and addresses, she grabbed her bags and Soren walked her back to her room.

Dylan stepped inside her room and tossed her bags on the partially made bed.

"Do some shopping?" Soren asked from the door as Dylan pulled out the folded clothes she had bought.

"Well, I am a million *peira* richer from supposedly killing Gerion," Dylan said, putting the clothes away in her dresser and shutting the drawer a bit harder than necessary.

"I couldn't accept the money for stealing your kill. It was the least I could do to make it right."

Dylan turned around to look at him. "Oh, so that wasn't what last night was?" She crossed her arms and rested against the dresser.

His eyes zeroed in on her, deadly and flat; and she knew she had struck a nerve.

"Was that what it was for you?"

Dylan chewed on her bottom lip, suddenly wishing she could shove her words back into her mouth. Wishing he wasn't blocking the doorway so she could escape the conversation.

"I don't know what it was for me." She looked away. "I'm still trying to figure that part out."

Soren pushed off her door and stalked toward her. "Do you need me to remind you?" he husked.

Dylan shivered as she hesitantly found his eyes again. Of course she wanted him; but, it felt like surrendering if she admitted it.

When he got near, his fingers traced along the back of her hand hanging at her side and her heart jump-started at the simple touch. How was it that the slightest physical contact from him sent lightening through her nerves?

"I don't think I could love again," Dylan whispered, throwing her heart out onto the table for Soren to see. "I don't even know if I want to be in a relationship." After seeing the pen in the shop, and how hard she had hoped for it to be Tristian who had sold it, she knew she still wasn't ready for another love. That Soren couldn't have her heart because it still belonged to someone else.

"This isn't about love," he stated flatly. "This has never been about love."

"Then what..." Dylan trailed off as he leaned in closer to her until all she could sense was him. Intense warmth radiated off his skin. The smoky pepper of his scent encircled the air around her. The invisible pressure of his gaze upon her, throwing all of her nerves on high alert.

"I want to taste you, again. That's all I want."

"Oh…"

A loud knock slammed against the door and she jumped.

"What the hell!" Astrid's voice screeched through the door.

Dylan slouched against the dresser with a forced sigh. Yet, neither of them moved toward the door. Soren cradled her jaw in his palm, tilting it up gently until their eyes met.

"We build each other up. We are each other's strength. That is all we are." He glanced down at her lips. "Strength."

Another succession of bangs rattled the door. "Oh, *come on*! You just ditched me!"

Soren ripped open the door. "*What*?"

"Great," Astrid barked back, "Did I interrupt another impromptu fuck?"

Dylan blushed. She had completely forgotten about Astrid once she saw the pen. And now… now she was alone with Soren again and about to kiss him; despite knowing full well she shouldn't.

Before he could reply, Dylan slipped out underneath his arm.

"I'm sorry," she said to Astrid, "I had a personal emergency. Soren was just making sure I was all right."

"Whatever. I'll see you around." Astrid said before pivoting on her heel and storming off.

Dylan turned towards the gym and started walking away from both of her comrades.

"Wait." Soren dashed to catch up with her. "Why are you running? Why are you always running?"

"Because I can't do this."

"Do what?" Soren growled and snatched her arm to stop her. "Do *what*, Dylan?"

"This! Us!" She groaned and tried to remove his hand from her arm. "*Soren*," she warned.

He released her and she immediately continued on to the gym. He followed her there in silence, which was more infuriating than him forcing answers out of her. She just

351

wanted to be left alone.

No friends. No missions. No expectations. No discoveries.

Nothing.

If Soren hadn't been following her, she knew she probably would have done something stupid like head to Traverna and get drunk. She would just have to make do with a pack of throwing knives and a target to forget about everything.

Dylan had already thrown several plated knives before she felt Soren's hand come around hers as he corrected her form.

"Ian told me you kicked ass during your suicide mission in Zadar."

Dylan wanted to roll her eyes. Soren didn't know what he was talking about. Jumping to the front lines to help her friends was not suicide. She had hoped to win. Those times she had tried to die there had never been any hope.

"It wasn't so much a suicide mission as a mass murder." She tried to hide a smile threatening to break through and flung the next knife, hitting the bullseye.

"Watch out," Soren plucked the next knife from her fingers, flipped it, aimed, and threw. He somehow succeeded to wedge it right next to her bullseye. "Someone might think you actually like this job."

A bit too much, she thought. *But, only you would understand that.*

"Maybe," she admitted, throwing another and meeting Soren's perfect throw in the center.

"I need you to be honest with me," Soren said, as Dylan fingered the remaining knives. "Do you really think Gerion sold that pen before he died to gain your attention?" He faced her. "Do you know how many of those pens were made? Probably hundreds. The odds that it was *your* pen are slim."

She remained silent, staring at the slivers of light running across the blades from the bright windows above.

"What's going on with you?"

She shook her head. How could she even begin to put it into words? How could he understand that she was mourning a man, a demon, that had kidnapped then terrorized her for years? But more than that, she was mourning herself. She didn't recognize the girl that laughed in the faces of her prey and begged her lover to punish her.

"Dylan…"

She suddenly turned and looked him in the eye. He didn't flinch as she expected him to. It was one of the many attributes she admired about him. Courage. He was always the one you could count on to take on an enemy. He stood up to her ridiculous mood swings and never backed away when it seemed like everyone else did.

He was here. He was always here even when she thought he wasn't. He was the true hero of her story. Not Temperance. Not the girl who was more sick and twisted on the inside than she would ever willingly show.

"He's finally gone, and yet I can't seem to stop wondering what I'm supposed to do now. Why am I throwing knives? Why am I still training?" When Soren just stared at her as if she was a puzzle he couldn't figure out, she went back to examining the knives in her grasp. "I should be relieved that he's dead. I am. I just…"

Why do I feel so lost?

It felt like she was reading a story and the book suddenly ended with "the villain died and the girl lived." The villain died… then what? How did the girl live? How did she cope? Did she get therapy for PTSD? Or was she truly happy? Then why couldn't Dylan be happy? It felt like the emotion had been robbed from her, leaving only anger and devastation. What the hell was she supposed to do now?

"I should have let you kill him."

"I don't think there would have been anymore closure if I had."

Dylan lifted her arm and let a knife fly to the target.

"Why didn't you have sex with me last night?" she asked, unable to keep it inside a second longer. Didn't he find her attractive? Was her 'submissive' not enough for him? It seemed like he enjoyed himself just as much as she had... but then again, "seemed like" wasn't the same as had.

Soren didn't even pause at her sudden off subject question. "You're a virgin."

The words slammed into her and she felt her face instantly burn. Dylan knew she shouldn't feel ashamed about the fact, but it felt like a weakness he was stating, not a part of her anatomy.

"So?" she said with a nervous laugh, gripping the knives until she felt the sudden slice of pain she was looking for.

"*So?*" he repeated, scolding her, softly.

Soren stepped closer and wrapped his intensely warm fingers around her wrist before firmly removing the blades from her shaking hand.

His voice lowered an octave, "You can't even handle letting me see you with the light on. Is that seriously how you want me to have you?"

Dylan kept her lips tightly sealed. She didn't really know how she wanted something she had never had.

"You know I'm not your prince charming. It won't feel good. It'll hurt. And after, you can't expect me to love you."

She inhaled sharply. "Maybe I don't want your love. Have you ever thought of that?" she said before stalking toward the target.

She ripped out the knives, one by one, before posing to throw again.

CHAPTER 19

"But I love you, said the knife to the wound."
Anonymous

DYLAN *stood in the middle of a wild and overgrown field. Her boots crushed fallen twigs from the towering oaks and the faint smell of flowers and dried leaves put her startlingly back at the cabin Tristian showed her in a dream.*

She felt his presence as she always did, but instead of gentle touches or the whisper of promises, she saw him so clearly as if they were actually there.

Tristian looked up from the Elon Newspaper he was reading as he sat on the porch steps. Dylan felt frozen and ensnared in the crosshairs of his stare. A strange sensation of guilt gripped her as if she was caught intruding on private property.

Why was she here? And why weren't they running to each other?

His voice entered her mind and her skin prickled.

"I need you to stop looking for me."

"What do you mean?" she asked aloud. What was he talking about?

"Then you were not the one trying to conjure me?"

What... "Oh," Her words died off, remembering the conversation with Cassandra. "... Yes."

He pinched his features in frustration. "Don't bring me

back Dylan. You won't like what you see."

"I can't—" she stopped herself, not even knowing if that statement was true. She still needed to talk to Cassandra about their deal. Maybe she was still trying to reach him and he denied her?

She took a step toward him and stopped when it became obvious she wasn't welcome. "Do you not want to be with me?"

"I'm nothing but a dream." He motioned to everything around him. "How can you be with a dream?"

Tristian snapped his fingers and suddenly the beautiful cabin and enchanting forest were gone, replaced by a frame of singed, exposed timbers. She flicked her eyes every which way, absorbing the blackened field that smelled of sulfur and ash. Heat and tendrils of smoke wafted up from the ground as if a fire had recently swept through, destroying everything.

A gasp burst from her lips as she assessed the damage. It's only a dream, *she hastily reminded herself.*

"It doesn't have to be a dream," she implored. "If you just accept the magic."

"Stay away from that shit, Dylan." He glared. "It's not worth it. The price to pay is too high."

"Nothing will ever be too high. Please. Please, let me make this right. Even if we can't be together. Just accept it, for me, please."

"I'm at peace with the life I lived. Let that be enough for you."

She felt dizzy and spellbound by such a final statement. He didn't want her help. He was content in death while she struggled to go on without him.

Dylan suddenly started for him in determined strides, black twigs snapping beneath her boots. Her soul ached for its mate. Ached to catch fire from his touch. Ached to burn from his intensity. She needed him, even if it was only a dream. Even if none of this was real.

She barely made it across the field when he looked away.

Dylan blinked as the morning light of her bedroom in Elon washed away any remnants of her dream. Everything around her spoke of happiness, even the body sprawled next to her, but she felt anything but warmth. A tear was still caught on her cheek, frozen over the chill of a broken heart.

She couldn't believe it. Tristian's ghost had just broken up with her.

She looked over at the demon who seemed just as hesitant about her as she felt about him. He was staring at her. His eyes as hard as stone. She bit her lip and looked away. The traitorous tear finally slid down her cheek. Soren caught it with his thumb and eyed it like a foreign object for a moment before flicking it away.

The fact that he didn't even want her tear told her he was pissed. And she had a feeling as to why.

"Nightmare?" he asked, as something edged in his voice.

"Would you believe me," she swallowed, "if I said it was worse?"

She didn't even realize Soren had slipped into her bed in the middle of the night. He had been at his family home for the entire day and she only assumed he decided to stay the night. It wasn't like she needed him any more now that Silas was dead.

Soren sighed and stretched before threading his fingers behind his head. "I can't help with heartbreak, Dylan."

"He…" Dylan tentatively shifted her head to look at him. She wanted to confide in him even though she couldn't tell him the entire truth. "He wants me to let go."

"Sound advice from the dead."

She scoffed, "right," as she rolled out of bed and headed straight into her bathroom. It was always so black and white with Soren.

"He has nothing to offer you anymore," his voice broke through the crack in the door.

Dylan paused as she brushed her teeth. Was that how he

saw love? Was that why he didn't want her to love him if it were even possible? What happened if the person who gave you all of themselves had nothing new to offer? Did he just end it?

"His memory is only holding you back," Soren added in the doorway.

She spat her toothpaste out and turned to look at him. His chest was deliciously bare and she forced herself not to deviate from his steely eyes.

"Holding me back from what exactly?"

"From moving on and being happy with me."

Soren walked closer to her, causing her to crane her neck back just to meet his eye. Her body responded to the closeness. Ever since the night they came back from Zadar, she had found that she wanted him more and more each day, which caused her to push more and more distance between them. Was it even possible to fall for two men?

No. She loved Tristian and lusted after Soren. Not that either relationship mattered.

"I can't just fall out of love. It takes time."

He did his own version of an eye roll then reached around her and stole her toothbrush.

"You are so infuriating," she groaned, snatching an extra toothbrush from under the sink for him. The one he was *supposed* to be using.

"Meh?" he mumbled with a mouthful of her minty foam. "Look in eh mirror." He spat then made eye contact with her reflection. "I'm not the one in love with a ghost. That," he pointed the brush at her, "is infuriating."

"Why?" she flipped around and stole her toothbrush back before chucking it across the bathroom and crossing her arms over her chest. It was a childish move, but an effective one. "How in the worlds would that even affect you?"

Soren stepped closer to her with a snarl. "It's fucking annoying when you don't see reason; when you lead with your heart and let it make your decisions. It's infuriating because it's going to get you killed. Love will ruin you. Why is that so hard to see?"

Her scowl softened a bit, albeit not completely. She knew he was only projecting his own issues onto her and trying to intimidate her with his weird protective nature. He just didn't want her to die for a reason he thought of as foolish.

"Well, I'm sorry if my heart gets you in the dog house with the OP." She curled her lip. "Wouldn't want your precious title tarnished."

"Oh, for fuck's sake... Look, I'll put it simply for you. I'm a jealous demon. I don't share. Not even dreams. Got it?"

Dylan managed a meek nod before Soren cupped the back of her head and kissed her, harshly. His teeth closed down on her bottom lip and she hissed, digging her nails into his shoulders. He laughed at the pain and hiked her up onto the vanity, slamming her back against the mirror with a loud crack.

"Seven years bad luck," she gasped as he licked her neck.

"Who cares," he groaned. "We'll be in it together."

And for the first time that morning, she found herself smiling.

God, they were lunatics.

Before hitting the gym that morning, Dylan made her way into the cafeteria and grabbed the first plate set in front of her in the breakfast line. Eggs and toast. Not that it mattered. It would probably taste just as awful as everything else up there.

Dylan scowled at the espresso machine while she waited for her coffee to brew. Her patience was wearing thin. After that awful dream, and Soren demanding some sort of monogamous non-relationship, she only wanted to hit or break something until her fists bled.

Ugh, maybe I should see someone about all of this pent up anger.

A couple a chimes sounded, silencing the room. Dylan turned around and came face to face with Queen Vashti's haughty smirk.

Dylan stopped herself from kneeling when it became apparent that it was only a very lifelike hologram of the red-headed goddess. She was standing near her in a stunning silver dress with diamonds cascading down her body like Elon's tears.

"Hello, Elon," she sang, standing with perfect posture and fingers steepled near her sternum. "I apologize for the intrusion on your busy day but we, the Omnipotence, would like to keep the populous informed through this sudden shift in our economic standing.

"As you all know, we were recently ambushed by the Plantos and several of their allies during a mission in Zadar. Even though we won, a great deal has come to our attention, causing the werewolf alliance that Elon has been working on for the past ten years to be unfortunately severed. Any and all were-refugees that have taken residence here have one week to gather their belongings and leave.

On an even more unfortunate note: The Vat of Souls is wearing thin due to several attacks materializing without our knowledge. We are still investigating how they are pulling this off and will keep you all informed as we learn more. Nevertheless, we are ordering a mandatory collection amongst all general citizens. Please, proceed to the Rose Hall for your list of contracts. Thank you."

The hologram thinned into a single shaft of light before disappearing altogether.

Ever since Nadia Burke was pronounced dead along with her ally, Gerion Planto, Dylan wondered about the Queen's secret meeting with the werewolf leader. It made sense if they had been working on the alliance but, after hearing about a leak in the Vat most likely brokered by a traitor, Dylan wondered if perhaps that traitor was the Queen herself.

Dylan mentally shook off the thoughts that could kill her if voiced aloud and grabbed her tray of eggs and toast from the buffet line. She stepped up to the Horde's usual table, not surprised that Soren wasn't there. With as much time as they spent together, it seemed like he was equally absent.

She plopped down as the others were discussing the Queen's message.

"I wonder if I can take a break to help collect even though we're not the general public," Astrid said.

"Nah, the OP needs us here," Ian said, taking a bite of buttered toast, "especially if someone has been tapping into the Vat without anyone noticing."

Dylan finished unwrapping her silverware and began stabbing the rubbery clumps of protein. *Yum, eggs.*

"Where's Soren?" Astrid suddenly asked.

"Probably checking on his mother," Dylan mumbled. She lifted the fork to her mouth and paused, noticing everyone silently picking at their entrées.

"What?" She glanced at each demon before slapping down her fork and asking again, "What?"

Astrid opened her mouth, looking almost hesitant to say anything.

"My God, *what*?" Dylan prompted, again.

"Soren's mother is dead," Astrid blurted.

Dylan's eyebrows pulled down. "But I... How? *Today*?"

"Years ago," Astrid said. "From heartbreak."

"Depression and suicide," Ian corrected.

Astrid scoffed at him. "Depression and suicide *because* of heartbreak, you dunce." Astrid looked back to Dylan still frozen with shock. "It wasn't long after his dad died. But I wouldn't blame her. Your children die after the love of your life kicks it. Too much on a sweetheart like her."

"Children?"

"His brother died while fighting the Elementa War and his sister disappeared when she was only a preteen while on vacation to the Sponlands. Faerie jerks."

361

"Then… why does he go there?"

"We all assumed to just take a break. Check on things. Hell, do laundry. I don't know."

Dylan thought about the woman she saw and felt a ripple of anger simmer in her blood. Why was he allowed to be mad at her for loving someone who was dead when he had his own living, dirty secret frolicking within his family home? No wonder he didn't want her there. It'd ruin his two-timing ass!

Dylan sprang up out of her seat and shook her tray off in the garbage before plunging herself through the exit.

It took her what felt like seconds before she pulled up right in front of his house on her new bike that Soren had helped pick out the day before. There was no need to hide this time. She wanted Soren and whatever bitch he was hiding to see her. She wanted to make an entrance they would never forget.

She marched up to his front door and lifted her fist as the door swung open and Soren's dark mood filled doorway.

"What are you doing here?" he said so coldly Dylan sprouted goosebumps. He tried to shut the door behind him, but Dylan wouldn't have it. She pushed at him only to have him overpower her and backed up against the stucco exterior. Her fists locked embarrassingly above her head.

"Let go of my wrists before I light you on fire!"

"I told you to never come here again," he hissed, ignoring her threat. "I'll ask again. What are you doing here?"

She scowled at him, injecting as much loathing as possible into a single look. "And here I felt bad for *you;* for dreaming of Tristian while he broke up with me, while you," Dylan stabbed a finger awkwardly toward his house, not really sure what she was going to accuse him of. Cheating? Lying? They weren't technically together and he had never answered who the girl was. "She isn't your family, you— you ASS!"

Soren's deep breath released in a single rush as he studied her, contemplating his next move.

"You're right. We aren't related."

Dylan's mouth popped open to scream "no shit!" but Soren quickly continued, "She isn't my lover, either. I wasn't kidding when I said I was a jealous demon. I don't expect my woman to cheat and I wouldn't cheat on you."

Holy shit. …Was she his woman?

"Then who is she, and why doesn't anybody know about her?" Soren loosened his grip and Dylan hastily wiggled out of his hold.

His jaw visibly ticked. "Who all did you ask?"

"No one. I didn't have to ask. It was obvious no one knew."

Tension left his shoulders and it made her even more curious as to why that girl was a secret and who she was.

"Soren, I'm going to need to know who she is if we're going to continue… whatever this is."

He simply stared at her again, and she had to restrain herself from fidgeting.

Soren closed his eyes a moment before looking back at her. He slowly stepped back just enough for her to slip past him.

Dylan moved before he could regret his decision and stopped just inside the small foyer covered by white-washed wainscoting, unsure of where to go. She felt Soren against her back as he shut the door, taking with it the day's light.

Dylan suddenly felt claustrophobic on this side of the door as she waited for her eyes to adjust to the dim lighting. Once she did, she didn't feel much better. The hall was long and narrow with rooms sprouting off to the right or left. She started to walk when she felt Soren's hands on her shoulders as he leaned down and brushed his lips on her neck. The touch sending a shudder down her spine.

"Welcome to my home."

She closed her eyes, wishing they could be effortless like

this moment but they were far from it. Soren thrived on their fights and she needed the fear of his darkness. They were messed up together and yet, she desired everything about him.

Dylan's resolve and curiosity thickened and she left Soren's warmth to head forward. She passed stairs to the second story and a quaint dining room with a walnut farm house table and a short vase holding an explosion of cream Gerbera Daisies. White plantation shutters covered the picture windows completely snuffing out the daylight.

"I have to be careful about the windows," Soren's deep voice said from behind her. "I have nosy neighbors."

Dylan only nodded and continued down the hall, following the glow of firelight flickering around the corner. There was a strange energy radiating from it that heightened her senses. Soren stopped her.

"You must know, this isn't about trusting you," he said. "It's about protecting *her*."

"Who is she?" Dylan asked, looking at him over her shoulder. The flickering firelight made his irises look black as their gazes met.

"I guess it's time for you to see for yourself." He stepped around her and grabbed her hand, tugging her behind him.

The room beyond wasn't anything out of the ordinary. It was a library or office of sorts with large, French windows covered by more plantation shutters, rows of books, an inviting plaid couch and tufted leather chase facing the crackling fire. Dylan's pulse leapt in the presence of flames like it always did, but it was nothing in comparison to the sensation gripping her from the young woman curled up on the chase lounge.

She was wearing a modest baby-blue dress with a boat neckline and three-quarter inch sleeves. *The Alchemist* covered her porcelain face, framed by rebellious red curls.

As they got closer, the girl glanced up at Soren and Dylan watched as her eyes lit up and her fingers quickly set down the novel on the foot of the lounger as if she were bracing herself to be touched by the man she longed for.

"Caterina, this is Temperance. The new soldier I was telling you about." Soren turned to Dylan, "And my mate." Their eyes locked at that and for the first time Dylan didn't immediately deny it in either her mind or out loud. It felt right. It felt frighteningly real.

"Temperance, this is my sister, Cat."

Caterina's pale green eyes flicked to Dylan, and each girl blinked at the other trying to compose her shock.

Sister?

The fact that his sister was alive wasn't even what had Dylan so mystified. It was the fact that this demon wasn't a demon at all… but a human.

What the hell was this?

"I thought…" Dylan glanced over at Soren, wondering why he was keeping his human sister a secret. Or why he even had a human sister. "When did you find her?" Dylan asked Soren. "And why on earth haven't you told anyone?"

"Maybe we could go into the kitchen," Caterina offered, before Soren could reply.

Dylan was startled by the soft cadence of her voice and a strong chill prickled her skin as she picked up on Caterina's *Essence*. She was a human in Elon and she still had her soul. How was this even possible?

"I can put on a pot of tea…" Caterina trailed off as she seemed to suddenly regret speaking, looking like she was caught eavesdropping on a conversation even though she was part of it.

"Come on," Soren sighed, placing his arm around Dylan and guiding her by the small of her back to the hall covered by colorful four-by-four paintings in thick wood frames.

Dylan let Soren guide her down the hallway and through a carpeted living room with a gun-powder grey sectional facing a red-brick fire place and flat screen. Artwork decorated the milk-white walls and French doors leading to the backyard were covered by more shutters.

Overall, the home had become less stifling. Light colors and cozy spaces filled it with the scent of apple spice. It somewhat reminded Dylan of her grandparents' home on her mother's side before they died.

Just past the living room was the farm-like kitchen she remembered from her creeper mission a month prior.

Dylan sat at a worn oak kitchen table and fidgeted restlessly.

"I am not really his sister," Caterina finally said, as she set down a plate of shortbread cookies. Soren yanked out the chair next to Dylan and placed a firm hand on Dylan's jittering legs, forcing herself to still.

Caterina went about the kitchen, filling the kettle, turning it on then preparing the cups and tea bags and small bowl of sugar.

As Dylan watched her, she couldn't help the inkling of a memory that danced on the tip of her mind as if she was having déjà vu.

"But I'm sure you already knew that," Caterina added over her shoulder, blowing a stray curl away from her lips.

Another sudden rush of memories fingered down Dylan's spine from that particular mannerism.

"Do we know each other?" Dylan asked, wondering if it was possible to have met Caterina before.

Caterina turned away from the counter holding a pearlescent porcelain tray filled with three white tea cups on saucers and a matching teapot. She set the tray down and distributed the cups, filling each one carefully.

"Now, that would be impossible wouldn't it?" Caterina hummed, plucking a few Earl Grey tea bags up and dropping them in the cups before finally pulling a chair out and sitting, like a delicate flower, after years of etiquette schooling.

"Because you don't get out often?"

"Or at all," Cat managed with a composed smile. She dunked her tea bag and added a small spoon of brown sugar, ignoring the fact that Soren and Dylan hadn't touched a thing.

Dylan shifted her eyes to her supposed mate and raised a single eyebrow. "At all?"

"I've smuggled and hidden a human in my home for over two decades," Soren said coolly. "Do you really think she could get away with making a simple trip to the market?"

Tea suddenly felt too sober for this conversation. "So, tell me this… why even have a human in your home? Why haven't you taken her back to earth?"

"This is my home," Cat answered with creased brows. "Soren nor I know who my parents are… if they are even alive." She shrugged, lacing her fingers around the tea cup and bringing it to her lips without taking a sip—just feeling the steam.

Dylan felt the déjà vu slam into her again but this time she recognized it for what it really was. Dylan lifted a hand to her mouth as the memory tapping at the recesses of her mind registered. It wasn't of Caterina herself, but of her mother. Dylan's mother—Léa Prescott. The same fiery locks and willowy frame. Caterina even held her hands in a similar fashion as she sipped her tea. It was something Dylan had always done because she had watched her mother sip her coffee that way, every day, until she died.

"You—you're…" Dylan stumbled over her words, dazed by the possibly that Caterina could be the real Dylan alive and stuck here in a demon world. Soren covered Dylan's hand on the table and squeezed it to let her know her suspicions were accurate.

"Soren saved me when I was set to die here," Caterina said. "His family raised me as one of their own. And when other kids started to ask me questions about my powers, about why I seemed so different, we faked my disappearance. But as you can see, I never actually left."

"You're alive." Dylan's vision blurred. Her mind swirled around thoughts of a grieving Isabel. The beautiful, selfless

Prescotts that had lost their true daughter within the stirrings of a dirty plot. All of those years wasted loving a demon when they could have been cultivating memories with Caterina. They had gotten into a car wreck on the way to Dylan's ballet recital. What if Caterina disliked dancing... would her parents still be alive today?

Dylan shoved her chair back sharply and stood on wobbling knees. "I need to go."

"Hey," Soren said, standing up as well, his voice cutting across her haze like a sharp knife.

Dylan felt her throat constricting and she swallowed hard, suddenly hyperaware of the leaking faucet and the sound of her own breathing. Dylan forced herself to look at Caterina––at the girl that was a perfect mesh of her biological parents; and then Dylan just... snapped. Dylan grabbed Caterina by the shoulders and the girl shrieked, dropping her tea cup.

"You can't just *stay!*" Dylan suddenly cried out, shaking the girl as the spilled tea spread and covered the table. "You have to go back! Why are you doing this to them?! You-you selfish *bitch*!"

Soren was suddenly in Dylan's face, shoving her back until she hit the kitchen wall, shaking a few frames of the grinning Verbeck family off their hooks.

"Arghh," Dylan growled at the pain, at the regret and the guilt. How could they not give a shit? What the hell was *wrong* with them?

"You need to get a grip on yourself because if you ever lay a hand on her again, I can't be held accountable for what I might do to you."

Dylan looked hard into Soren's eyes not expecting any less of a response. If anyone laid a hand on Aria or Isabel out of spite, Dylan knew she'd chop it off.

"Soren, you don't understand. She *has* to go home. She can't..." Dylan trailed off, a sob trying to scramble her voice.

"*No*. You don't understand. She has long since given up

on that dream. Don't you dare give her false hope."

"How is it false when there is a real family waiting for her? My grandmother probably thinks I'm dead or sold to some Arabian gun lord!" She looked into his dark eyes, hoping to relay how important this was… but it was obvious that he thought what he was doing was equally important. "Why not just *try?*" she implored.

"*Dammit!*" Soren slammed his fist into the wall, rattling the pictures again. "You don't understand how hard it will be for her to adjust. She can't just take your place."

"This isn't a life. She's trapped here. She can't even go outside! Don't you want her to live, to love, to have a real family?"

"Of course, I want those things."

They both looked over at Caterina standing nervously by the table in disarray as she tried to and failed to clean the tea off her dress. She gave up and crossed her arms tightly around herself like she was urging herself to stay put. "But Soren's also right, I can't leave. To try and assimilate now?" She shook her head with a resigned smile that appeared forced. "I have chosen to stay after many years of considering it. I have Soren." Her eyes found Dylan's and dared her within the stare. "He's all I need."

Soren released Dylan and walked up to Caterina murmuring to her in Latin too low for Dylan to hear, and Cat spoke back curtly. Dylan glanced between them before rushing out of the kitchen and down the hall towards the front door.

She couldn't be around them a second longer. Caterina, in her ridiculous way, obviously loved him, and Soren was a blind, stupid boy. He was the reason she didn't want to go, and Dylan didn't blame her. If he was the only man to grace her presence for almost two decades, of course she loved him!

Dylan ripped open the front door and started down the hand laid stone path that cut through the grass and connected

369

to the sidewalk.

"Wait."

She stopped in the middle of his yard and spun around.

"She's only staying because of you." Dylan ran up to him, bringing her hands up and shoved him right in the chest. He stumbled a bit, caught off guard. "And you don't care. How can you say you saved her when you keep her here like a caged animal?"

We're all just pets to you, she thought bitterly.

Dylan scowled at him. "Why are you keeping her here, really? Tell me the truth."

"You heard her! She doesn't want to go. There's not much more to it. I'm only doing what I promised my mother. I'm looking after her. I'm keeping her safe. My debt has been paid. If she doesn't like it, she's free to go. No one is stopping her."

Soren stepped closer and Dylan matched his moves backward.

"That's all, Dylan. Anything else is your damn imagination."

She gasped in disgust. "You think I'm *jealous*?"

"Aren't you?"

Soren suddenly reached out and pulled her against him by her jacket as if he'd been holding in the dire need to touch her.

Dylan's heart stumbled into overdrive. She didn't even think when his lips met hers. She just kissed him back, her palms splayed against his chest in that hopeless position of wanting more and wanting to flee before she fell hard.

Their tongues met, biting and tasting. It was the kind of kiss that left its victim breathless and spinning. A kiss that was like free falling through storming skies. She felt herself crumble and her fingers tangled in his jacket, yanking him deeper, succumbing to the desire screaming inside. She had nothing to lose. No one to feel guilty over.

His hands ran down her body, claiming, angry, and

370

desperate as they slipped underneath her clothes and gripped her curves, unable to decide whether to rip her apart or devour her whole. And she almost wanted him to, right here; right out in the open…

"*Soren*," she gasped against his lips, breaking the connection.

She fought hard for a breath, setting her forehead against his chest. His arms wrapped around her back and fisted her jacket, begging her to understand.

She couldn't.

But, she would keep his secret because it wasn't hers to tell. Because this promise to his mother meant something to Soren. She could only pray Caterina might see reason sometime soon.

"I have to go," she said, again.

When she finally opened her eyes to find Soren's jaw clenched tightly, she pulled away. She was running like always. He knew she was running… Yet, how far could she really go?

"Dylan—"

"I won't say anything, to anyone." She offered a small reassuring smile, but underneath it all, she only felt the hot rush of sorrow for keeping Isabel's happiness out of reach. "I'll see you back at the… back at *home*."

She pushed her hands into her pockets and hurried to her bike before she did something foolish like tell him to hold her.

Starting the engine, she looked back at Soren on instinct and caught sight of Caterina watching raptly through the window instead. Dylan blinked away the feeling of her conscience trying to tie her down and took off.

CHAPTER 20

"He's more myself than I am.
Whatever our souls are made of,
his and mine are the same."
Emily Bronte

DYLAN sped through the city streets until she found herself outside of Traverna again. There was one last item on her checklist before she could accept this new chapter in her life. She needed to heed Tristian's request and call off the resurrection; even if it pained her to do so.

He didn't want to come back, so what could she do? Force him? *You won't like what you see.* What did he even mean by that? Would he come back as something different or would he just come back royally pissed off?

Dylan forced her mind to quiet as she entered the vine-covered door and found a seat at the bar near a few regulars already wavering and stinking of liquor. Cassandra's mate was attending the bar, wearing a grey hoodie and black beanie.

Dylan waited patiently as he finished pouring a few drinks. When one of those drinks came sliding in her direction, she shot her hand out and stopped it before it could fall to the floor.

"Vodka, water with lime, right?"

"Right, thanks," Dylan said, staring vacantly into the glass.

Cassandra's mate leaned on the oak slab across from

Dylan, sipping on a tumbler with dark brown liquid. His green eyes assessed her for a moment.

"No problem. Want to unload?"

Dylan looked up. "Excuse me?"

"Just looks like you have a lot on your mind." He shrugged. "Most of my regulars come here for therapy. Their own kind of therapy," he added when Dylan looked befuddled.

"I do have a lot on my mind, but no... not looking to burden anyone with it." Dylan took a long sip of her drink, wincing at the burn from the vodka. It was definitely more Vodka than water. "I need to find Cassandra, though."

"She's out of town... collecting."

Dylan nodded, "Right. The mandatory collection."

The vestiges of a smirk crossed his lips as he stared at her unflinchingly. His candidness made her nervous.

"Have you had time to look at that book Cassy gave you?"

Dylan reached inside her pocket and pulled it out. Ever since Cassandra had given it to her, Dylan kept it on her body at all times. She had looked through it several times, hoping for some kind of revelation, or at the very least, some peace of mind from the poetry. So far it was just a book with pretty words. Her parents' location wasn't stashed inside and the affirmations didn't soothe the anger, guilt, or pain.

Dylan fingered the worn edges of the tiny, leather-bound booklet.

"Yes. You can have it back if you want." She pushed it toward him upside down on the polished oak bar top.

"Cassy gave it to you." He pushed it back. "Keep it."

Dylan sighed and picked up the book, flipping it over and back again. "Poetry's not really my thing."

She studied the back engraved with a map of the human and demon galaxies. Dylan traced her fingers around Earth's solar system surrounded by several demon worlds—a few she recognized, like Zadar and Baal with Elon on the furthest side.

"This looks different from the maps I've seen." It was a strange way to lay out the worlds. After all of her studies with Anna, this drawing looked backwards and mixed up.

"Yeah," he said, draining the remaining contents of his glass in one swallow. "This is an old map." He brought his finger to the booklet and traced along a thin line surrounding the human solar system. "This is the balance that keeps our worlds separate from the humans."

She remembered Anna talking out it but never explaining it. "Balance?"

"It's like a void." He cleared his throat. "If any human tried to cross it... they'd just," he motioned with his hands and mouthed the word 'poof.' "Like The Bones. No one really knows what goes on in there."

"Hmm," was all Dylan could think of to say.

She brought her glass back up to her lips and took a larger sip, almost finishing the glass.

"Want me to tell Cassy anything?" he said as he reached below the bar and poured straight Vodka into her glass.

Dylan stared at the clear liquor and swallowed thickly as old memories gained purchase. She forced herself to push them back under lock and key—a reflex, usually quick and effortlessly done after so many years. But, it was harder now, which she could only attest to meeting Caterina.

"Yeah," Dylan blinked it all away, "Tell her to stop doing what I asked for. The deal's off."

He frowned at her but nodded nevertheless. "You got it. Another?"

That night Dylan couldn't sleep. With the news of Catarina and the awful "break up" with Tristian, she was afraid of what she might dream. Afraid of what her anxious mind might conjure. The last thing she needed was an opening for Silas' ghost to say hello, if that was even possible. Knowing her luck, it would be. Hell, if Tristian could enter her dreams in death, then why couldn't Silas?

So, she stared at the crow perched outside her window, too drained to pace, thinking about the train wreck that had been the rest of her day.

Dylan had gotten a bit drunk at Traverna and shamefully had to walk her bike back. Soren had been waiting for her on the steps with his condescending scowl set in place like a parent waiting up after curfew. She had parked her bike and tried to evade him and his questions as she hurried back to her room to sleep. But, he just followed her.

"Where were you?"

"What happened to your bike?"

"Why do you smell like liquor?"

"Are you seriously drunk? It's fucking nine in the morning!"

She had flipped around when he wouldn't take a hint that she wanted to be left alone and ignited her entire body in flames, making him stumble backward more out of shock than fear. She wasn't proud of it but she just couldn't stand his hovering and she snapped.

"Just stop." Dylan raised a palm out in front of her in a truce before he could try and invade her space again. "I'm okay, I promise. I just need time to myself."

He didn't even respond. He just disappeared in a flash of black and steel.

Dylan stumbled to her room, expecting answers, expecting the holes in her punctured armor to patch up from the acceptance that she couldn't do a damn thing to change anything. Tristian didn't want her or her help. Caterina would prefer to never feel the sun's warmth on her skin again if it meant she could still have Soren. Silas was dead. Her relationship with Soren was nothing but a confusing, hot mess. And here she was on her bed, trying to still her head from spinning. Just like when she was a teen trying to escape her life.

Dylan rolled to the side when she thought she might

vomit. She groaned when she could only heave acidic air.

God, she hated puking, but more than that, she hated this feeling of being completely powerless. This chill of loneliness she couldn't fight. At least the alcohol was doing its job by keeping her mind preoccupied with a different kind of suffering.

Dylan's door suddenly opened and she groaned again at the sight of Soren in the doorway.

"Can you not take a hint?" she trembled, clutching the sides of her head.

She felt the bed dip before she could make herself open her eyes.

"I want to be alone," her voice hitched, as his fingers delicately slipped under her clammy head and pulled her into his lap where he stroked her hair. Tears surfaced in her eyes and spilled down her cheeks.

She didn't understand why he was still here, trying to soothe her with his obedient silence. Not after what she did to Cat, not while she mourned another man.

Soren was a good demon and she was ruining him. Tearing him down as she held on to his jacket through hiccupping sobs.

She was still staring at the crow that night when Soren's fingers came over to her chin and shifted her head to him. They stared at each other silently for a moment before he spoke, "Feeling better?"

His eyes were as hard as ever as he looked at her. She often wondered what he saw in her or if her eyes remotely showed the shattered walls of her rambling thoughts. It didn't make sense why he'd choose her as a mate. Didn't he want someone more stable and more mature? Then again, was she *really* his mate? Perhaps the introduction to Catarina had only been a part of their front and Dylan was reading too deeply into it.

She shook her head not wanting to lie to him.

"I'm having a hard time finding my place," she mumbled.

"What do you mean? Your place is on the Horde and by my side."

Dylan shifted her eyes back and forth between his, looking for the lie, for the contempt. But there was only Soren's unwavering gaze staring back at her.

She turned on her side towards him and rested her head on her hands. "What about what you said about the OP only using me to stick it to our enemies."

A malicious glint showed itself in his features—a look Dylan had come to known as his particular passion. Seeing the darkness was like a breath of fresh air after everything she'd gone through all day.

"*Our* enemies?"

Dylan laughed and playfully hit him in the chest. Soren acted wounded through his throaty laugh.

"Shut up. Of course, they're *our* enemies."

He brought his hand to her jaw, running a thumb over her lips. "You're so beautiful when you smile."

"Stop changing the subject," she chided, while secretly adoring him in this moment. He seemed different, more at ease. Not hiding behind his scowl.

He sighed, removing his hand from her mouth. "Prove to them you deserve your title and no one will ever question where you belong."

He pushed his hand into her hair and leaned over to kiss her. She always felt caught off guard when he kissed her. Her single gasp against his lips was becoming a ritual. It didn't matter how much of a warning he gave. When his lips touched hers, it always startled her as if he'd shot a bolt of *Unda* through their kiss.

What started out as innocent quickly escalated as he moved his hard body on top of her. He tugged on her bottom lip, sinking his teeth into it, stroking it—working her mouth until it felt swollen and tender. His painful kisses lit up her body and broke through her walls. His touch was like a sledge hammer to her darkness, breaking free everything she craved and forcing her true self to the surface.

Yes, she wanted this… she wanted him.

He tore off her tank top and she moaned at the feeling of his bare chest against hers. He grabbed at her body and she gripped his long hair, pulling him deeper into her mouth. One of her hands slipped along the ridges of his scarred scalp and he growled, capturing her hands and pressing them above her head. He slammed his hips into her and she cried out. Desire spreading through her like fire.

She remembered when she had asked him why he hadn't slept with her. He had told her it would hurt and he wouldn't love her. She knew before then sex with Soren would be painful and not just physically. She had a feeling he knew how to take her broken pieces and cut her until she knew nothing and wanted nothing but his sinful torture.

A hard shudder took hold of him and he growled, circling his hips in a way to show her what he was like. He suddenly sat back and kicked off his pants and she did the same— hastily slipping her leggings and panties down her legs. His hard eyes stared at her after he grabbed a condom out of his discarded pants' pocket. It was like he was asking *and* telling her they were going to do this. She nodded, feeling her body hum with fear and desire.

His lips hooked into a devilish grin as he slowly crawled on top of her like an animal stalking its prey. An odd feeling came over her and she tried to shake it off… but it was there, closing its fingers around her neck and tearing open all of her mental boxes. His eyes flicked to hers and she felt frighteningly defenseless beneath him. The way he stared knowingly into her, it was too raw… too invasive.

She suddenly felt *everything.* Every. Godammed. Thing. She wasn't even sure if he realized he was reaching her mind until it was too late.

"*Soren,*" gasped.

Her fight or flight reflexes kicked in, too late, as a flash of memories crashed down around her. Memories she hadn't ever seen before. Feelings she didn't recognize. It didn't take her very long to realize they were Soren's memories, not hers.

Soren was standing inside the Kings' Chambers as King Zirk, Queen Vashti, Lord Tristian Effingo, and a Necromancer prepared to Bind the Elementa baby to the Omnipotence.

Queen Vashti suddenly gasped, connecting her long fingers to the tiny forehead of the infant. Her touch setting off a heart-wrenching wail.

"Human," she growled, before pointing those very fingers at the Elementa Carrier who had brought in the baby. "Seize her!"

The Carrier dashed for the door and Soren lunged; but, he wasn't fast enough. The Carrier spun around him and slit the throat of the woman soldier to his right. She staggered and dropped. Her chocolate hair turning black in a pool of her own blood. Soren hesitated for a split second at his fallen mate but it was a moment too long and the Carrier stabbed him straight into the throat with a pointed pick attached to her wrist. He fell to his knees as blood spurted out of him.

The Carrier darted across the room and grabbed the Necromancer, using him as a shield against King Zirk and Lord Effingo.

Blood was everywhere. It saturated Soren's uniform and expanded around the love of his life that lay unmoving in front of him. The feeling of devastation blasted into him when he couldn't help her. Then a sudden blinding rage for the Elementa Carrier giggling with every life she took. Soren applied pressure to the nearly fatal wound on his neck and forced himself to leave his mate. He snuck up on the Carrier and slit her throat, when all he wanted to do was lay next to Ella and will the life back into her body; even if it took his own life to do it.

Tristian was screaming now; barking orders for Soren to

kill the screaming infant.

Dylan could barely recognize Tristian. He looked so cruel. There seemed to be a grey aura settled around him, crackling like a storm cloud, making his beautiful eyes appear smoky and vile.

When Soren couldn't make himself murder the baby, he took it to the only person he trusted to look the other way for him: his mother. She was lovely with inky hair and porcelain skin.

Soren was shaking, bloodied, and silent in his family home as the news of the war hit the local broadcasts. He peered outside as demons ran through the streets slaying anyone that supported the Omnipotence. Soren quickly ushered his mother into the cellar with the baby as a window in the kitchen shattered.

She placed a delicate hand on his fingers. Her china blue eyes peered up at him, relaying all of the love and warmth in the worlds for her son. She reassured him that he did the right thing; that everything would be okay.

"Come back alive. It is all I ask," she said before disappearing into the darkness of the cellar.

His father was now dying next to him in the street as the smell of blood and burning homes filled the air. "Run," his father gasped on the pavement as Soren tried to stop the bleeding gushing out of the demon's stomach. "It's not worth it."

Soren looked down the road at the creature that had torn a gaping hole in his father's side. A wolf creature trained its wide lupine eyes on him as it ripped through another screaming soldier. It snarled with a mouth full of dark blood.

It was so much bigger than Silas's creations. It made Dylan wonder why this thing hadn't been documented. Why weren't they more prepared for another one? Why hadn't they known about this before the battle in Zadar?

Rage filled and hardened Soren's heart. They were taking everything from him. His mate, his loyalty to the OP, his family. He didn't need to be an Oracle to know his mother wouldn't survive his father's death. She was weak. They were all so damn weak.

He roared a battle cry as he charged for the creature head on as his father's last breath echoed within his mind. Soren freed a long sword off his back and flipped it in the air, tearing it across the creature's broad, furry chest in a flash. It howled and batted him away like an annoying gnat. Soren jumped up amid the pain but the creature was faster than any demon he'd ever fought. It easily overpowered him and stole his weapon, flinging it to the side.

It didn't use weapons.

It used teeth and claws.

It snatched Soren's head. Nails digging inside his neck and skull. Dylan could feel him accepting the inevitable, allowing death to consume him. His fight, his rage, depleted as his mouth filled with choking blood. There was nothing he could do.

He barely felt it when the monster was ripped off of him and burned to a crisp by none other than King Damen.

It was like everything he hadn't been able to say about that day, flooded into Dylan the only way he knew how.

Dylan gasped for air when she came back.

The devastation, the terror, it was like she had actually been there in his place, feeling every wound and every thought. The true Soren he hadn't shared with anyone until now.

Tears rolled down her cheeks and he dipped down and kissed her cheeks, licking up her tears.

Dylan sobbed as he held her, murmuring how sorry he was for hurting her over and over again. That he just wanted her to see.

Dylan wanted to scream. To hide in the corner and cry for him. How could she handle his burden on top of hers? It had been so cruel to force his pain into her mind and make her relive his darkest scars.

381

But wasn't this what he did daily?

Every time he took her scars, he added them to his own. Building, reliving, tearing him open and stitching himself back together. No wonder he was so solid; why he needed the fight; needed the blood and pain to keep himself above water. They were alike in so many ways. He needed to feel what was real just like her. He needed what was present when he had nothing but devastation from himself and others in his past.

Everything about him was fitting together like pieces of a puzzle and she was taken aback by the picture. She knew any sane person *would* be fleeing but she was enraptured by his trust. He was giving her what she had always wanted and she wouldn't run now. If he could bear her suffering, then she would bear his, as well.

"I know *you*," she said, choosing to use the words he told her the first time they kissed. Because she finally did. She finally understood why he was the way he was.

Soren was suddenly there, kissing her fiercely. Dylan wrapped her arms around his shoulders and neck. His hips shifted up and she registered his hardness just before he pressed deeply into her.

Dylan bit her lip and dug her nails into his arms at the initial slice of pain that was almost too much. But, she would never tell him to stop, she realized. To stop would be like telling herself to stop breathing.

Soren peppered kisses along her brow and cheek, soothing the creases she forced along her face.

"Dylan," he husked, slowing but not stopping. Her thighs tensed around his hips, almost as if she were afraid he might leave her even now. "Look at me."

She took a shaky breath, only realizing then she was squeezing her eyes shut. She blinked a couple of times and compelled her eyes to focus on him.

"I need to know you're with me," he said, pressing into her again. Dylan cried out softly with the wonderful burning.

"I'm here," she said breathless; and before he could speak anymore, she pulled him back to her lips and kissed him.

Anchoring herself to him.

Losing herself in him.

Finding herself with him.

Showing him there wasn't anywhere else she would rather be.

He brought her leg in the crook of his elbow and rocked against her in a slow, delicious rhythm until the pain receded. Until it started to feel more than good but amazing.

Her eyes closed, just feeling. Feeling his heart within her. Feeling the violent passion that shone so bright it burned.

His lips slipped across her jaw as her head tilted back, allowing him access to her neck. His teeth grazed her, nipping at her flesh.

She moaned, loving the small bites of pain as the quivering in her belly grew.

She clawed her fingers into his hair as he moved faster, harder, spurred on by her breathless pleas, until she was bracing her palms against the headboard behind her. His movements became rigid as they lost sense of the world around them. Their passion peaked in the most beautiful ecstasy.

Her orgasm came quick and hard as he ground his hips into hers. Soren groaned in response to her gasping cry as if he couldn't get enough. As if he never wanted to stop. As if he wanted to infuse himself inside her blood until his name was the only word she seemed capable of sounding.

Soren suddenly whipped his head back and howled so deep and raw it vibrated her very being. A sound she desperately wanted to hear again and again and again.

Soren's head collapsed onto her damp shoulder as they both collected their breaths. When he finally lifted his head, his eyes were hooded and sated as if he'd just fed. Dylan's body trembled as he rolled off of her and pulled her tightly against his chest.

Dylan laid her head across Soren's bare sternum, listening to the drum of his heart, as he drew lazy circles along her spine with his fingertips. Her eyes were fixated back on the crow still perched outside her window but her mind was a thousand miles away. Too busy sifting through the day.

She could still feel the adoration Soren had for that brunette—a carefree, young love that didn't match with the person he was today. She guessed that was what he was trying to convey. He had been a different person until the morning of Dylan's birth. He had to watch his love die, then his father and brother, only to barely make it himself.

Dylan shifted, switching ears so she could look at Soren. His eyes flicked to her from their stare at the ceiling.

"Who was she?"

His fingers stilled on her back and she worried he might act like he didn't know what she was talking about; or perhaps he hadn't meant to share those memories with her?

"Ella Bryant," Soren answered to her relief, his voice gruff.

Dylan searched for lingering feelings or any despair within his expression, something to match the devastation pouring out of him in the memory, but there was none. He said his ex-mate's name with as much emotion as a doorknob.

"She was in the Shadow Horde?"

Soren closed his eyes and loosed a breath. Not in exasperation but as if he was preparing himself to speak without letting her memory unravel him. "She was training to be." He opened his eyes and looked at Dylan again. "But, she didn't have it like you and I do. She was too trusting and too kind. She was one of the few that actually believed your parents wanted a child out of love." He shook his head. "I blamed you, your family, hell, I even blamed Cat for the longest time for their deaths." Dylan nodded, understanding.

384

"When in reality it was my fault, as you saw."

Dylan listened, afraid to speak, afraid to move, when all she wanted to do was reach over and smooth the frown lines deepening the space on his forehead, and tell him blaming Dylan and her parents was okay; because how on earth could it possibly be his fault?

"She shouldn't have been there that day," he said, answering her inner question. "King Damen ordered me and Augusto to accompany King Zirk. I knew how much she wanted to be there." Finally, regret reached his face. "I snuck her in."

This time, Dylan reached over and smoothed her fingers along his brow, his cheeks. She leaned down and gently kissed him once. "I'm sorry."

He slipped his hand around her nape and pulled her back down to his lips, briefly. "Don't pity me," he said in rush against her mouth.

He flipped her over and Dylan yelped.

"I wasn't," she breathed. "I'm being empathetic."

"That's right," he murmured. "You have lost a great deal, as well." He pressed a hand down her hip, eliciting a shiver that produced goosebumps down her legs.

"That creature... it was different from Gerion's. Bigger. Or was that just your perception?"

"No, that one was a monster. I've never seen anything like it since."

She thought about the long sword he'd been using on the monster. The one she knew he practiced with alone, in the middle of the night. The one she could not only see the emotion tearing out of him but feel it, too.

A buzzing started on her nightstand and her head flicked to the side, to her TAC watch. Soren's started buzzing as well and she felt her pulse speed up.

A mission.

Soren shot up, alert and ready as he yanked on his clothes. She moved to the edge of her bed and pulled on her pants and jacket before sitting back down to lace up her boots with shaking fingers. She felt sore and gritty, wishing she had time for a shower.

Dylan eased up, pulling her hair into a messy ponytail and glanced at the blood spots on her white sheets. The sight struck her like a ton of bricks.

She had just had sex with *Soren*.

Soren stepped over to her. "Don't worry," he said with a frown as his thumb tipped her bottom lip. "We're going to talk more when we get back."

Dylan nodded, feeling light years away and present all at the same time.

He pressed his lips to hers and a hand came up and around her, possessively gripping her neck. He tilted their heads as a bloom of heat unfolded within her. But, he broke away before they ended up back in her bed.

"Now, let's go before the fucker gets away." Soren grinned at her and dashed out of the room.

Dylan shook her head ruefully at his thirst for blood and ran with him to the Iron Portal.

Dylan's feet slammed to the flat roof of a building and she stumbled on the asphalt before planting herself defiantly. She smiled to no one in particular, wanting to happy dance at her control just as Soren appeared next to her in a crouch. Ian and Augusto were tracking the demon while Astrid stood on the edge overlooking the five-story drop and scouting their surroundings.

Dylan lifted her wrist to assess her TAC watch and stopped when she noticed the moon's reflection on the dark screen. She whipped her hood back and looked up, taking in the hazy hint of tiny, white dots like shimmering diamonds across the velvety-blue sky.

Stars, she thought, feeling entranced and overcome by something that she had once taken for granted.

Soren's hand slipped into hers and she knew he

understood exactly how much this moment meant to her.

"There!" Astrid called, pointing to a shadow zipping between two adjacent buildings.

Wind slapped against Dylan, and it took her a moment to register that Ian was using it to jump down to the street.

"*Cheater*," Soren murmured, with excitement laced in his eyes. He let go of her and rushed to the edge where they all scrambled to get down.

Dylan was last getting to the fire escape, but instead of waiting, she spotted an awning that ended on top of an adjacent building's lower balcony. She ran to it, hoping Aria's many spy movie marathons might actually pay off.

Dylan kicked her feet over the edge, remembering James Bond doing a similar move in his latest movie. With a sharp inhale, she shoved herself off. She slid quickly and caught the lip at the bottom, letting herself safely drop to the balcony.

She climbed down another fire escape and jumped down to the alleyway. She heard boots skittering behind her and she darted after the sound, sending all of her nerves and panic to the back of her mind. After the last mission, she wanted nothing more than to prove to the Kings she could be a part of his crew; that perhaps she wasn't as fragile as they assumed.

She tore through the maze of warehouses until she came to a dead end. She stopped and looked up and around, wondering if she had taken a wrong turn or if the demon had scaled the building... when she hit the building's brick facade face first. She cried out and held her gloved hands to the sharp pain over her right eye.

The rogue demon then quickly yanked her backward by her jacket and threw her down, taking advantage of the surprise. He grabbed her Daleon when she reached for it and held it against her throat. Dylan held her hands up in surrender and stopped trying to fight him off.

The demon wore a recently torn, white dress shirt and

jeans. His hair was a mane of tousled caramel strands. He looked her over and started deliriously laughing.

Dylan recognized that laugh immediately. She had used it herself after her first collection in Silas' castle.

"What is this?" he struggled to say through his stark laughter. "I take a soul and I get a beautiful woman?"

If it wasn't for the magic blade at her throat, she probably would have laughed, too, at that ridiculous statement. He was obviously a new demon and she wondered if he had any idea beforehand. Did he even know what the Shadow Horde was?

Her mouth curved into what she hoped was a seductive smile. It felt crooked. "Of course," she said a little too high pitched. "Didn't you know?"

He took his eyes off of her face long enough to appreciate her tight leather uniform, giving her the opportunity to roll out from under him and unsheathe the double-edged dagger. She jumped up and blocked his unpracticed swing hard enough to knock it from his grasp then shoved him against the wall.

His eyes turned sinister in the shadows. He may have been a new demon but it was obvious there wasn't a single good trait in his makeup.

The rogue demon thrashed out and before she could pin him back to wall and call for back up, a shape came hurtling passed her. It gripped the demon in its teeth, slamming him to the ground and knocking him out.

The shape in the dark snarled at the unconscious demon and then turned its growl on her. Dylan gasped and stumbled backward onto her rear. It was a huge wolf with a thick, silvery mane and salivating, sharp teeth. Its fur was the same shade of silver as the werewolf from the barn she and Soren had almost died in.

Nadia's wolf.

It stalked toward her, slowly, backing her up until she hit the alley's dead end. It was definitely the same wolf. She could never forget those eyes.

"Get back!" she screamed, whipping out her Haladie knife.

The beast stopped and it happened so quickly she wasn't entirely sure what had happened until she was staring at a completely naked man, half of his face still covered by shadows.

"Dylan... Are you okay?*"* asked a strangely familiar voice.

Her eyes narrowed in suspicion until he stepped out of the darkness.

Her mouth parted in awe.

"*Garret?*" she gasped belatedly. "You—you're a *werewolf?*"

His kind eyes smiled just as she remembered. "Yeah—"

"You're naked," she blurted out.

He laughed and shook his head, abashed.

A thousand questions flooded her mind as he helped her stand. "How did you know it was me? What are you doing here? Is this something new? Did someone do this to you?"

He laughed even harder at her interrogation. "I, uh... I found my friend unconscious down the street," he hooked a thumb to the side, "and I followed the rogue demon's trail where I saw you. I can't believe it's you." He reached out to touch her and then seemed to think better of it. Probably remembering he was still very much naked. Dylan felt heat rise in her cheeks as she tried to keep her eyes averted.

"You were after him?"

"Yeah, I usually try to stay out of demon business." He hesitated. "Well, since Nadia died. Thank you for that by the way."

Her eyebrows lifted. He seemed genuinely grateful.

She looked away unable to accept his thanks. It got silent between them for a moment as she recalled the night in the barn. Garrett never stopped Nadia from trying to take her. He just stood by, concealed by his fur, and let it all happen.

She remembered how he warned her with his bark just before he escaped into the Portal like a coward, leaving her and Soren there to die.

The rogue demon on the ground jerked and Dylan cursed. She quickly took out her *Binding* wire and tied his wrist to a steel pipe protruding from the building. The demon grabbed her ankle with his other hand and she sucked in a breath before stomping on his hand until he let go. When she turned back around to face her old friend, his face was grim.

She bristled, hating the way he patronized her with a single look. She was just doing what had to be done. *It isn't like I have a choice*, she mentally added in defense. Maybe if she told herself that enough, it would start to feel true.

"For the longest time I had wondered what happened to you after the Tristian and Asher found you. I never heard any updates other than knowing you were in Elon."

"What do you mean, Tristian and *Asher*?"

"We worked together to find you. They went on to Zadar while I took your friend Aria home."

Dylan gawked. "Aria knows?" she whispered.

"Well… yeah. Didn't you tell her?"

Dylan couldn't believe it. She didn't know how they all got connected but it made sense that her best friend and her boyfriend would go looking for her. She just didn't know how Asher or Garret fit into the picture.

Her TAC watch began speaking her name and asking her location. She peered down at the black screen when she realized she never turned the GPS feature on. She brought her wrist up and struggled to press the right button before relaying her location that then flashed on the top of the small screen.

Dylan looked back up at Garrett. "They're going to be here soon…"

He gave a curt nod. "Welcome back, Dylan."

She opened her mouth, but he was already a wolf again and sprinting down the alleyway.

Her eyes followed him it finally hit her.

She didn't need to pull on her hood to know she was back in Los Angeles.

CHAPTER 21

*"Silence, I discover, is something
you can actually hear."*
Haruki Murakami

DYLAN stood off to the side on a street teeming with clubbers and tourists mingling, laughing, and walking into restaurants and venues. Warm air, muffled jazz music, and an earthy smell wafting from the newly wet streets invaded her senses, pulling at her heart—a wistful longing hitting hard with each recognizable landmark.

Part of her still couldn't believe she was back in her home city. She knew it was bound to happen at some point; she just hadn't prepared herself for it to be this soon.

Once Garrett had left, the rest of the group came and congratulated her on subduing the demon first. Ian quickly took the one soul the rogue demon possessed illegally. It made her wonder exactly how many creatures lived among humans like her and this demon—unbeknown to what they were.

After Dylan took the demon's life in a quick pierce to his heart, Soren patched up Dylan's busted eyebrow with firm, yet gentle, fingers. He didn't say much to her, just clipped commands—*come, tilt, better?* She could feel him analyzing her and trying to understand the distant look on her face— whether it was from him or the demon dead on the ground. He didn't know she had run into an old friend or that they had brought her back home.

A group of girls in mini dresses walked by, glancing at their leather clad group arguing on the sidewalk whether to stay or head back to Elon. Astrid and Ian wanted to celebrate, like always, and Soren seemed eager to return.

Augusto stood silently like Dylan. His hooded, wide-set eyes scanning their surroundings and taking in the nightlife.

"I know of a place," Dylan said after awhile.

Everyone silenced and Dylan looked at Soren only briefly, his icy eyes making her squirm under their scrutiny.

"She *knows* a place." Astrid stuck her tongue out at Soren as if to say *three against two, suck it*. "Is it far from here?" she asked Dylan.

Dylan shrugged and turned around to figure out how exactly to get to the underworld club under *Spin.*

"How do you know a place?" Soren asked, his expression bordering on incredulous.

"This is where I used to live."

Soren surprisingly relaxed at this and asked her if the club was the only place she wanted to visit.

Dylan whipped her head up, taken aback by his offer. "No."

His lips held the hint of a smile as if he expected that answer. "Where is the club?"

After they sent the group to *Spin* in a cab, he laced his fingers with hers and led her down the street. He was silent for a good while as if he were taking in the lights and sounds. It oddly felt like a date, the way he stood close or smiled fleetingly at her after stopping to watch a street artist finish up a couple of amazing spray paint pieces. She wasn't sure what they were planning to do or if he really was going to take her wherever she wanted to go; so she started pointing out famous hotels and relayed useless information about the Chinese Theater or the Walk of Fame.

"You've never been to LA?" she asked. It seemed unlikely considering how large the city was.

"We come here a lot."

"Oh," she smiled apologetically. "You probably know all of this stuff, then."

"Actually… no. It's pretty rare that we stay in a rogue location longer than necessary."

Dylan nodded. She could see that. Soren didn't seem like the type of guy to go clubbing or party until the sun rose. Which was kind of good thing, because neither was she.

Minutes ticked by as they walked, talking about some of the favorite places he'd been. Then Dylan admitted she hadn't been anywhere outside of Los Angeles other than the Amazon with him and Zadar.

They spotted a couple of demons laughing next to yellow Yamaha motorcycle. Soren quickly started up a conversation, placing a glint of worry in both of their eyes. It was obvious they were trying to remember if they had done anything against the Law. Dylan wasn't all that surprised when they handed Soren the keys to the bike when he asked for them. She watched them scurry off.

When Dylan turned back to Soren he was already straddling the beast and starting the engine, revving it in two short bursts. "Come on, my beautiful pet."

He grasped her hand and she fell forward against his chest.

"What did you do?" she asked, a breath away from his lips. The air around them felt heavily charged and it took so much for her not to lean into that last inch to his lips.

"Nothing," he said it in a way that she knew she wasn't the only one feeling the heat. "Just a couple demons wanting nothing more than to stay away from the eye of the Law."

"That's not nice," she said, in mock seriousness as a breeze tossed a couple of rebellious strands of hair across her face.

"I never said I was nice." He glanced down at her lips and back to her eyes. "Now, where is it you want to go?"

She tilted her head, finally giving in, and kissed him.

"Feel like meeting my real family?" She looked up at him through her lashes.

"Get on," he husked.

She grinned and slipped on behind him. Soren waited for her to wrap her arms tightly around his waist before taking off.

Hectic energy and busy streets quickly bled into stunning homes with posh gates—but no matter how quiet and settled the area became as they got closer and closer to her grandmother's house in Brentwood, Dylan couldn't stop shifting restlessly behind Soren. It was like her body couldn't be contained, too keyed up and on the verge of bursting with anticipation.

Since the moment she was taken, she yearned for Isabel's guidance and strength; not that she felt entitled to it. She suddenly wanted to shake herself. Isabel loved her whether she was truly her granddaughter or not. As someone who wanted everything for the other, Dylan knew she needed to tell her about Catarina, then the both of them could persuade Soren to lay down his resistance and give her up. Both women deserved to be with family, more so with Dylan unable to return home.

Dylan breathed in the exotic smoke and leather of Soren's scent as she rested her head against his back. It brought lust, fear, and solace into her heart, tangling with her struggling emotions until he was all she would let herself think about. Soren had become her safe house and she loved that about him. He knew the right buttons to push and when to hold back. More importantly, he saw *her* above everyone's expectation of an Elementa. Soren cared for her and she was starting to really care for him in return.

They navigated the neighborhood streets, stopping in front of the old, vine covered, Tuscan villa on the dead-end road of Leven Lane.

Not waiting for Soren, Dylan jumped off the bike and briskly walked over the grass and cobblestone and up the horseshoe drive until she was standing in front of a heavy, wooden door with iron detailing.

Her nerves fired, flipping her belly as she clenched and unclenched her hands, remembering the only other time she felt this nervous standing in this very spot: the day a social worker had held her hand and knocked. Isabel had answered with all smiles and kisses, moving past her own immense pain of loss. Dylan needed those kisses and hugs now more than ever.

Soren brought his fist up and gave a good solid knock for her. Voices murmured indistinguishably from the other side of the door. It unlocked and a man Dylan didn't know peeked out.

"Can I help you?"

Dylan just stared, dumbfounded. Where was Isabel?

The man looked at Soren and raised a bushy eyebrow. Soren placed his hand on her lower back and sent a steady stream of confidence into her with his powers.

The touch jolted her and she spoke, "Is there an Isabel Prescott here?"

"Who? Oh, oh," the man wedged the door open a bit more, making room for his large belly. "She's the owner, right?" Dylan slowly nodded, still in some sort of daze. "I'm not really sure what happened to her. A lady down the street rented us this place about a week ago."

"Oh…"

"You family or something?" he added.

"Down the street?" Dylan asked, ignoring his question.

"Huh, oh yeah," he pointed behind them. "She lives in that one story with the gnomes. That's where I drop my rent, at least—"

He continued, but Dylan didn't stick around to hear it. Her sights were on the quaint cottage with two gnomes and a wooden swing on the porch. Dylan was there in a matter of moments, knocking, not wanting to waste any more time entertaining the awful thoughts swimming around her brain.

Isabel had to be okay. She had to be on the other side of this door. Was it possible Dylan was too late? Had she died? She wasn't that old, but Dylan had seen what grief could do to a person.

She was shaking and trying not to cry when she felt Soren's calming presence behind her. He brought his hands down her arms and kissed her neck, whispering notes of reassurance. She wanted to hug him. He was being everything she needed, and more.

Even though she knew she wouldn't love him, he was as close to it as she would allow herself. He'd seen all her cracks, all her flaws and scars, and instead of cowering away he showed her his. He may never take the place of her soul but Soren wasn't afraid of the black void that remained. He knew her and that was enough.

"*Dylan?*"

Dylan opened her eyes and Soren moved away from her neck to look up, as well.

Dylan gaped at Aria's presence. Aria slammed herself into Dylan with an *oof,* hugging her hard. Dylan didn't even have to think, her arms immediately came up and around her best friend just as the tears came rushing down her face.

Aria suddenly forced Dylan back, looking her up and down, unbelievably.

"It's you?" She laughed once through her tears. "It's really you?"

Dylan nodded, unsure whether a sob or laugh would come bursting out if she tried to speak.

Aria continued to looked her over as if she couldn't believe it. "Look at you." She smoothed her hands down her arms and around her bruised face as tears shined on her cheeks. "Dylan, you look so…" Dylan felt herself locking up. A thousand adjectives ran through her mind, beating herself up one by one. *Sad, broken, evil.*

She definitely wasn't prepared for her friend to say, "You're so *hot.*"

Dylan's eyes widened in shock and then she laughed, so happy her friend hadn't changed... well, except for her natural hair color.

"What is this?" Aria frowned, motioning to Dylan's wound, already going full-fledged mother bear on her.

"It's nothing," Dylan brushed off.

Soren shifted and Aria's eyes flicked to him as if noticing him for the first time and not liking what she found.

"Oh!" Dylan motioned to him, "This is Soren... my, uh, boyfriend."

"Soren," Aria said, all humor gone, and held out her hand politely. "Aria, the *best* friend."

After they exchanged forced pleasantries, Aria practically yanked Dylan inside and started a pot of coffee. She continued to gush to Dylan from the kitchen about everything Dylan missed, friends or celebrities who married, the latest gossip, how she was finally finishing her degree after taking some time off. Topics she knew which soothed Dylan because they were superficial and light.

Dylan sat on a beautiful tweed sofa and listened as Soren looked around guardedly, as if he expected an enemy to appear at any moment. Dylan rolled her eyes at him but couldn't stop herself from taking in the space, as well.

In front of the tweed sofa was the same antique coffee table from their apartment in college, adjacent to a vibrant, yellow, leather chaise and stack of unopened moving boxes. Coral, light blue, and ivory frames decorated the light grey walls. It all fit her friend to the T. Her home was quirky and eclectic, just like the girl who lived in it.

Aria reappeared, still all smiles, holding two purple mugs of coffee. She leaned down in front of Dylan and handed her a cup. "Milk, no sugar and..." she shifted around to Soren, handing him the other. "I wasn't sure what you take," Aria said, hiding a grin, "but assumed you'd want straight up black." Dylan snorted into her coffee as Soren thanked her with his usual frown and took a cautious sip.

Aria walked over to Dylan and sat, her flirty, red, wiggle dress accentuating her shoulder tattoo.

"Now, fill me in on everything."

Dylan's smile slipped and she placed the coffee on the table as she struggled to tell her friend that she had been taken and forced to become a monster who hunts others for money; it wasn't an option not to tell her anymore. Keeping it all from Aria and Isabel had been the first mistake after she initially found out.

"You know I'm a demon?" she said, waiting for her friend to laugh or call the mental hospital. Despite what Garrett had said, she still didn't truly believe her friend knew.

"Yes, I know."

Dylan exhaled in relief. "How did you find out?"

"Tristian came to me after Erez took you."

Dylan glanced at Soren and she suddenly didn't want him there anymore; and by the looks of it, neither did Aria.

"Wait, does Isabel know?"

"No," Aria shook her head, briskly. "She wouldn't have been able to handle it. She barely survived your disappearance."

The way Aria spoke about her made her heart drop. "Oh God, is she…"

"Oh, no!" Aria smiled, sadly, "She just moved to Hawaii. She's doing good. She has a *boyfriend*." Aria winked and it made Dylan giggle under her breath. "I could tell she was just too sad staying in that big house by herself. She needed to move on."

Dylan swallowed forcefully past the lump trying to clog her throat. "*Thank God.*"

"Yeah, I manage her assets here and the tenant," she looked in the direction of Dylan's old home as if she could see it. "It's the least I can do." When Aria looked back at her, Dylan noticed how tired her friend looked. Her big smiles and energetic attitude had masked it well at first.

Dylan grabbed Aria's hand and squeezed. "I'm sorry."

Aria sighed. "Don't be. It's not your fault."

Dylan disagreed with her statement but she didn't want to start a pointless argument. "It still looks like it took a toll on you, so I'm still sorry."

Aria laughed and flipped her sleek hair back. "Is that your nice way of saying I look tired? *Thanks.*" Aria shoved her friend mockingly in the shoulder.

"It's because she's pregnant."

The girls startled at Soren's comment.

Dylan looked at where Aria's hand instinctively covered her stomach.

"With who?" Dylan blurted out, not even asking how Soren knew because there were still a lot of demon things she didn't understand.

Aria glared at Soren, but he looked indifferent as usual.

"Do I know him?" Dylan prodded further.

Aria sagged against the couch and whispered, "Yes."

"Is it *Matt*?" Dylan asked, thinking about her last boyfriend.

"No…" she trailed off and that was the moment the front door opened and shut. They all looked over to the foyer as Asher walked in to the living room in a pair of dark jeans and a leather jacket; a black Shoei helmet under his arm and a handful of mail gripped in a hand.

He stopped short at the sight of the Shadow Horde being entertained by his girlfriend.

Dylan looked at Aria and then back at Asher as Aria quickly got up and hurried to Asher's side. "Dylan, you remember Asher? He's my boyfriend."

Dylan glowered at Asher, not liking one bit that a demon was screwing and impregnating her friend. And not just any demon, but a demon who had manipulated her for information.

Asher kissed Aria's hair sweetly and murmured, "You should have called me. What have you been talking about?"

His eyes flicked over at Soren and the two demons nodded at each other, coolly. It suddenly hit Dylan that by bringing Soren, it had been like bring the OP into their living room.

Aria looked into Asher's eyes and the passionate love they obviously shared for each other warmed Dylan a bit. "Just about the baby."

Asher suddenly lit up, "And how's my girl?" he tossed his helmet and the mail to the floor and bent down to kiss her flat stomach.

"It's a girl?" Dylan asked, still a little wary.

"He insists," Aria said, pulling him up with a smile when he started nibbling at her stomach. "But I'm only seven weeks. We won't know for sure for a little while."

"Have you told your parents?"

Aria sighed with a look Dylan remembered well, and walked back over to the couch and sat. Aria's parents were a bit controlling, to say the least.

"They want us to get married... traditionally."

Dylan didn't see the problem. "What's wrong with that?" If they loved each other with a little one on the way... what was the big deal?

"It's what I keep saying," Asher grumbled, on his way to the kitchen.

Aria looked uncomfortable. "I just don't see why you have to get married if you're pregnant. It's not like my family is suddenly going to think I'm less of a black sheep."

"Has he asked you?" Dylan whispered.

"About a thousand times, Dylan," Asher called from the fridge.

If possible, Aria looked even more tired as she eyed a tattooed ring on her left hand. "I don't know how you do it."

"Do what?"

"Always get me to start talking about myself."

"Ah, a deflection within the deflection," Dylan smiled. "I guess old habits die hard."

"True *that*," Aria said, knowingly.

Dylan looked over at Soren still standing as a big reminder they probably needed to go soon. At least his expression was a bit less reserved.

"You have to go, don't you?" Aria said.

Dylan nodded and Soren piped in, "I'm sure she'll be back. We get called to Los Angeles a lot."

Aria smiled, "Good."

"My darling non-wife, where's the bottle opener?" Aria frowned along with Dylan. Couldn't Asher just use his strength?

"Hold on a moment." Aria jumped up and walked into the kitchen for whatever chat he obviously wanted to have with her in private.

Dylan stood and ambled over to Soren. The closer she got, the fierier his eyes became.

"Thanks for this."

He brought his hand to the side of her face and toyed with a loose lock of hair that escaped from her pony tail. "I will do anything to see you light up like that."

Dylan smiled. "Let me go say goodbye and we can get out of here."

"Sure, I'll meet you at the bike."

She turned around and picked up the coffee cups off the wooden table and made her way into the kitchen, a ghost of a smile on her lips. It felt like things were strangely working out in her world. She was closing doors and opening new ones. She had surpassed an ugly time in her life and she finally felt a surge of power to take on who she was. Her past had scarred her forever, and some things might never leave her, but she was stronger now and would overcome whatever she needed in order to live.

Her thoughts were on Soren and his words and the next time she would see Aria and Asher. Whether her friends would finally be married with a determined toddler running them in circles. She was caught off guard when she realized they were whisper-arguing near the stainless steel sink.

402

"I don't want them here ever again," Asher snapped. "Next time don't answer the damn door!"

"You don't get to dictate this about my life," Aria hissed. "She's my best friend, Shadow Horde or not, I would give her a damn kidney; and I know she'd do the same."

"She's a fucking demon, now. Don't be so naive to think she's the same person she was when she left."

"Wow," Dylan drawled, catching their attention. "And here I was warming up to you, *Asher*."

"Can't exactly blame me, can you," he stated, "not after threatening my life in Elon. Why would I want you around the love of my life and our baby?"

"Wait... *threatening your life?*" Aria asked Asher in disbelief.

Dylan lifted her hands still gripping the mugs in one hand as if to say, *you got me there.* "I can understand why you don't like me; but, Soren's never done a thing to you. He's been nothing but respectful." She thought about how he'd been the one to diffuse the situation at her Signing ceremony and kept politely silent while in their home.

"*Respectful?*" he laughed, with an ugly edge that rubbed Dylan the wrong way. "How about next time you come, try not to bring the trash in with you?"

"*Asher*," Aria admonished. "He's her boyfriend." She raised her eyebrows at him and Asher visibly thawed.

A cell phone chirped on the charger behind Asher and he grabbed it. Aria quickly reached for the device but Asher held it away from her. His expression disbelieving.

"You said you'd let this go," he handed his girlfriend the device forcefully.

Aria slowly took it, glancing down at the screen for a moment. She didn't say anything.

Dylan frowned. "Let what go?"

They both looked at her in a way that suggested maybe there was something more than they were keeping from her.

"Let what go?" she asked again, more clipped.

A tiny part of her began to beat, so far away it was nothing more than a light tapping. The longer they took to answer the heavier the beat became until the noise slammed and shook her body. It was stupid to want to hear his name, even if it was in the past tense, even if it was some messed up dedication Aria or Asher felt towards a corpse. She just needed to hear it. They knew him like she did. Only they would understand how she could love who he was.

She began rubbing her hand over her chest absentmindedly, the wound of his death reopening and constricting her heart.

"You still love him," Aria said, with wonder coloring her voice.

"I will always love him," Dylan whispered through the ache. "What Soren and I have is… different." The tone Dylan used to describe their relationship was so *clinical* that it made her wince. She took a deep breath as Aria turned to Asher and he shook his head vehemently at her.

"*Goddammit*, just tell me," Dylan gasped. "You hate Soren because he's with me and Tristian isn't? Well, I've spent years mourning him. I'm…" she lowered her voice with a wary glance over her shoulder. Soren knew she still loved Tristian but he didn't need her shouting it within earshot. "I'm still not over him, and I honestly don't think I'll ever be, but I have to at least *try* because Tristian isn't ever coming back. *God*," she groaned. "Please, just be happy for me, because I'm trying to do the same for you both."

"He's not dead," Aria blurted out and Asher cringed, leaning back against the countertop and resting his head on the cabinets in irritation.

Dylan dropped the mugs in her hand and they shattered on the floor.

All the blood drained from her face and she suddenly felt sick. The pounding inside her body grew again as she shifted her eyes from Aria to Asher and back again, unsure if she had heard her friend right. They didn't say anything, but by the looks on their faces, she knew she hadn't just hallucinated.

"Dylan?" Soren said from the kitchen's threshold.

Dylan flipped around and wordlessly conveyed how sorry she was. In return she watched as something shut irrevocably within him before hardening like the cold steel he was.

Dylan paled from the obvious pain she had caused. She knew then they wouldn't ever be the same.

Dylan hated how whoever she loved ended up hurt. Whether it was death or heartache, her soulless being sucked the life out of anyone willing to share their life with her. With those tumbling thoughts, she gave into the blaring craving to *run*.

She slipped past Soren and bolted out the door and down the street to the bike. Dylan peeled out, distancing herself from the street she grew up on and successfully fleeing from Soren. Not that he'd run after her. She knew better. If he wanted to stop her she wouldn't have made it out the front door.

The night was a blur of tears as she tore down the wet streets to Sunset Blvd. Before she knew it, she was stumbling on to the grassy patch of the beach in Santa Monica—grieving Tristian all over again with hiccupping sobs and angry screams.

She couldn't believe he was alive. Why would he let her go on thinking he had died? He had even told her as much in their dreams. What was the point? To screw with her head? To see how bleak life was without him to light up her soul?

Tasting the ocean salt on her lips, Dylan absorbed the feeling of the cool air and damp, warm sand. Waves crashed against the shore. The moon was merely a thin cutout of light amongst a sea of millions of stars.

All Dylan could think about was how she needed her mother, Léa. She needed to touch her parents' souls and be held by their memory.

Her eyes squeezed shut as she forced herself to feel for

them. They had to be here. She couldn't think otherwise. A large knot of cotton felt stuck in her throat as she tried to bring herself to speak. It felt as if she had lost the right. Lost it after discovering the real Dylan. Catarina was their daughter, not her.

Temperance's parents were terrorists according to the Omnipotence. Evil, despicable beings yet, she held a need to go to them and it planted deeper and deeper inside her gut each and every day. Was Tristian with them now? Was he living with the Elementas and missing her despite his plea for her to let him go?

The energy of another creature sliced through the crisp night air. Dylan flipped her head towards the dark shadow to her right. Her pulse leapt. The situation was all too familiar. As it moved closer, she laughed at her pathetic hope when she recognized Aria closing the distance between them. She wore Asher's leather jacket and her arms were wrapped tightly around her midsection to fight off the night's chill.

Dylan had forgotten Aria knew about this place.

Her friend sat on the grass. The silence between them was suffocating.

"Where's Soren?"

"Asher drove him to your crew," Aria said. "I think he said the club, *Spin*."

Dylan nodded, wondering how Soren was taking the news; if he was planning a manhunt.

"After you were taken initially," Aria started suddenly, "Tristian… he didn't waste a single moment in his search to find you. There were road blocks and failures but he found you. He did everything he could to get you back. He loved— loves you."

Dylan instinctively ducked her head against her knees and tried not to cry. How was it just as equally painful to hear that? But he didn't love her. If he loved her, he wouldn't have lied to her about this.

"You have to understand," Aria continued, "even after he

406

woke up after his coma from Zadar, he couldn't stop looking for ways to rescue you from Elon. The obsession *consumed* him."

Dylan tried to imagine it but she couldn't. He could have sent word. He could have said *something* in their dreams to renew her hope.

"God, Dylan. He figured out a plan, a really good plan."

"Then why didn't he execute it?" Dylan snapped. "I dreamed with him almost every single day for *years*. He never said a damn thing."

"I didn't know you talked—He never said anything to me." She sighed. "He was there the day of your Signing into the Shadow Horde. We were all there. Asher snuck us in to see you."

"You were the woman that waved?" Aria nodded, and Dylan felt suddenly sick. Tristian was there. He was right there as she held Soren's hand and let the worlds think she'd fallen in love with her commander. An angry tear slipped down her cheek. "Why did he change his mind?"

Aria cast her eyes away to flick an ant off her dress. "It had only been a rumor up until then, but when we saw you with Soren, it was kind of a reality check. He wanted to step back. He made us promise to let it go after we led Nadia and the Shadow Horde to Zadar."

Something inside Dylan cracked. "You guys were the demon activity we registered there?"

"Yeah," Aria offered a weak smile. "Asher had managed to slip some false information to Lord Struo during your ceremony." She sighed. "We just wanted to at least weaken Gerion's army. You know, so that he wouldn't be able to take over Elon any time soon. We never imagined Gerion would show up or that you'd kill him."

Dylan thought about how Silas clung to her during his last moments, then focused back on her friend. "Is Tristian... still working on a plan?" She couldn't contain the wistfulness that coated her words.

Aria's face fell with a slight shake of her head. Dylan thought about the countless articles on her relationship with Soren and the way Tristian seemed to be reading the Elon paper during their last dream together.

"Not being with you ruined him," Aria said to the sand and then suddenly looked at her when an idea surfaced. "Go to him. It isn't too late. You both obviously love each other––"

"I can't," Dylan whispered cutting her off. "Our love... it isn't real." She closed her eyes. How could she explain that if Tristian truly did love her, he wouldn't have told her to move on? He wouldn't have lied to her and made her believe he was dead. He wouldn't have made her mourn him. Dylan shuddered as cruel thoughts hooked into her heart and twisted. No, their love wasn't real. It was only a dream, just like he said.

"Oh, Dylan," Aria sighed. "Of course it is real. I think for a while Tristian still held hope underneath all that stubbornness that you both would end up together."

"I fought for us," Dylan swallowed, "even when I knew it was ridiculous. I held on to him so tightly until only..." *Until only hours ago.*

"I know," Aria said, boldly clasping Dylan's hand. Dylan accepted the comfort, feeling drained and overtly confused.

Dylan groaned in frustration and gazed out at the black ocean. A bird cawed in the distance and she musingly thought of her crow looking out for her. At least now she knew it was just an animal and not her reincarnated lover.

Something tiny and sharp cracked in her chest.

"I have to go." Dylan got up and dusted off her uniform. As much as it pained her, she needed to go back to Elon with her crew like nothing happened. "I'm sorry about the mugs."

Aria just waved her off. "It's fine. I've broken my fair share, as well."

The girls hugged goodbye before Dylan quickly ran back to the bike.

CHAPTER 22

"Darling, even though your eyes may be wide open,
you still cannot see."
J. L.

IT seemed like the perfect night as Dylan zipped down PCH on the borrowed motorcycle and turned on to Sunset Boulevard. The city was clear and clean from the recent rain, and the air was comfortable against her skin. For all intents and purposes, it should have been the perfect night; and it was to everyone, but her.

Dylan was merely minutes from the underworld club when she found herself slowing down in front of Tristian's apartment building. She wasn't sure what she was even doing as she parked her bike illegally in front and walked inside the polished reception area. Her eyes squinted slightly at the stark contrast between the dark streets and the bright, reflective space.

She marched to the mirrored doors of the elevators just as a woman called out to her.

"May I help you?"

Dylan looked at her with a frown and remembered, belatedly, to smile.

"Um…" Her thoughts dried on her tongue. *God*, what was she doing? How did she know if he still lived here, or even wanted to see her?

"May I get the occupant's name?"

"Tristian Eff—Stewart." Dylan cleared her throat. "Tristian Stewart."

"Mister Stewart." The woman smiled and clicked several keys on her computer before looking up. "His specific residence has a key or 'call only' request." The woman tilted her head.

"Um—" Dylan said again.

The woman's compassionate smile stayed in place as she picked up the black phone. "Your name?"

"Dylan Prescott—Oh no. Wait."

The woman stopped, the receiver still pressed against her ear and her fingers hovering over the dial pad.

Dylan shook her head. She couldn't do it. She needed to leave. This wasn't her life anymore.

"Miss?"

"Don't worry about it," she exhaled, "I think I'm in the wrong apartment, sorry."

The woman nodded a bit and slowly set the receiver down.

"Miss?" Dylan turned her head to the receptionist just before pressing her palms to the glass doors. "You said Dylan Prescott?"

"Yes," Dylan whispered with a frown.

"Oh, he has you here on the pre-approved list." The woman smiled sweetly. "You may go up, if you wish to."

Dylan's eyes widened, and she slowly looked over at the bank of elevators that seemed so ominous. Her legs apparently decided they weren't going to work.

"Miss?"

"Right," Dylan cleared her throat and urged herself to move, even if it was rather slowly. "Thanks."

Trembling, she made her way into an elevator. An attendant clicked floor thirty-three and left her alone. She watched the floors pass with the long Art Deco needle and by the time she reached his level, she had bitten a nail until it bled.

The sets of two doors opened and she stepped into the small, marble foyer that evoked so many painful feelings. Knocking on his door would be like intentionally busting open one of her mental boxes. Yet, if she chose not to knock... she could go on as she had, letting Tristian be a part of her past just as he wanted.

Would she be able to live with the regret?

She pulled back, knowing she needed to let this one be. It didn't matter how much she hated him for doing this. She was afraid at how much seeing him would alter her life.

Panicked thoughts swirled through her mind and she flipped back around, just a few seconds too late. The elevator had closed and was already racing back down to the lobby. She stabbed two fingers quickly against the down button willing the car to speedily reverse its path.

The elevator dinged and, with one last hard look at his door, she turned just in time for the car doors to slide open.

"No, stop."

Dylan froze. Even her heart felt shocked and unable to beat. Angry tears collected inside her eyes, refusing to fall. The elevator dinged again and shut its doors, showing her distorted reflection and a hint of the person behind her. Yet, she still couldn't turn around.

"*Dee.*" The sound of his pained voice sent a soundless gasp into her lungs and two tears racing down her cheeks.

Another moment passed before she found the strength to turn, to face a large shattered piece from her past.

Her eyes moved off of the floor and slowly slid up his body. He was barefoot, his jeans pooling around his ankles. She continued to travel up and over his firm stomach and chest covered by a black T-shirt. His jaw was dusted with the perfect layer of stubble and his hair was styled in the same purposeful mess. He looked exactly the same while she felt different in a million ways.

It took her a full moment to realize he actually stood in front of her. She had so desperately wanted him to be alive for so long that it felt like a fantasy. Only it was real and she felt debilitating fear... fear, and so much anger.

Anger for mourning him so intensely. The entire time she hurt, he *knew.* He knew and he did nothing but plunge the pain deeper with each dream.

Her tears were flowing in raging drops when she finally spoke. "Was this your fucked up way of breaking up with me?" She licked a tear dangling precariously on her upper lip. "You know, there were a million better ways..." but she wouldn't even finish her sentence because her tears were flowing too heavily.

"No."

Her eyes flicked up to meet his red-rimmed green eyes. It looked like he was hurting just as much but she couldn't accept the possibility.

Dylan suddenly marched up to him, needing him to feel *her* hurt. She needed him to feel the pain she endured, the agony she faced grieving him. Her face twisted and she met her palms against his chest and shoved. He stumbled back.

She needed for him to feel the nights she screamed in his absence, the guilt that plagued her. She shoved him again for making her lean on someone else. Shoved him again because he wasn't just hurting her, his presence hurt everyone in her new life, too—everyone who felt like they could trust her. How could they trust her now?

She cried, pounding her fists against his tense chest because she knew she could never give herself fully to anyone in the future if he was alive. Her palms landed with less and less vigor as her cries increased, until she was sobbing and gripping his shirt for strength.

Tristian had allowed her to take her emotion out on him until it was obvious she had lost the war to her heart. His hands slowly came around hers, his eyes full of ache.

Feeling the shock of his warm grip snapped her out of the hysteria. She pushed him away and pointed an accusing finger. She didn't want his pity. He was the reason for her

412

agony. The reason she was even in Elon. If she hadn't met him, she would still be living blissfully unaware.

"You. *You* don't get to touch me," she croaked, her features contorting from the feel of her heart ripping open. Stitch by stitch, the seam burst. "Because of you I died inside!" she screamed. "Why do you get to be okay? Why did you have to do that to *me?*"

"*Dylan.*"

"NO!"

He moved so fast, she barely had time to react. His body loomed over her crumbling one. He grabbed her leather jacket, pulling her weeping face a whisper from his.

"Dylan," he groaned, "Let me explain, *please.*"

She shook her head, shying away from him.

"Please, *please* come inside. Let me tell you why."

Dylan felt a strange sensation bubble up her throat. It was the wrong reaction, at the worst time, and it made her feel crazy. *He* made her crazy.

She laughed.

Her mind had snapped back to the first night she was in his apartment. How he begged her to just listen to him and *explain.* She had been so terrified of him... just as she was now, but for completely different reasons.

Tristian frowned at her reaction and it only made her laugh harder until it morphed into a bizarre mixture of sobs and giggles.

"You know how crazy that sounds?" she finally asked, her voice still tight with tears.

He seemed to think about it for a moment before offering a small, sad smile. "Please," he begged as his smile dissolved along with her hysteria.

They looked at each other for a moment before she nodded warily. He stepped to the side to allow her in and she slowly moved past him, really hoping she wasn't making terrible mistake.

Dylan stood off to the side and next to the hallway that

413

led to his bedroom and library while he closed the familiar red door.

He stepped in front of her and she noticed his muscles were tensed as he forced his fists not to clench. It made her wonder what emotion was rippling through him. Anger at their friends for telling on him? Her unannounced arrival? Whatever it was, maybe this was only a giant inconvenience.

Let me explain. *Why? So I won't turn you in?* She hardened at the thought.

"Coffee?"

She looked up into his haunted eyes and he set his jaw. Something was off with him. It wasn't anger she was seeing, but fatigue. Tristian looked… empty. The cocky attitude she remembered was absent, but not from lack of Essence. He looked drained of *life*.

"Okay," she whispered in a rush. She didn't think she could force herself to consume anything right now. Still, it was a distraction for them both.

He nodded and proceeded to the kitchen that opened up like a fan to a large, modern, living and dining room. Floor to ceiling windows acted as a panoramic view of the glittering Los Angeles skyline.

Unlike last time, the apartment appeared as if it hadn't been cleaned in a while. Discarded clothes were tossed around the room and abandoned glasses and containers of take-out littered most surfaces.

Dylan sat a bit awkwardly on the leather barstool at the kitchen island as he pulled out two mugs and prepared the French press. She watched as he sniffed the milk before tossing it in the trash. He then reached into a cabinet for the sugar and paused, retracted his hand and closed the door.

He finally sat next to her, two black coffees in clear mugs placed in front of them. She set her fingertips on the lip and twisted the mug in slow circles, unable to look at him.

"Make me understand." She swallowed forcefully, still twisting the mug. "Make me understand why you did what you did." She peered over at him, noticing how he was staring at her hand. She quickly stopped the compulsive action.

"I didn't do it on purpose... not a first." He took a deep breath. "I was so close to death. I remember everything: the pain, how you held me... all of it until you told me you loved me and everything went black."

She twisted the mug once more, remembering each detail and more.

"I don't know how much Aria or Asher told you," Tristian continued, "but when I become depleted, my powers continue to work and I black out. I barely breathe, my heart barely beats. I am like a corpse. I wasn't all that surprised when I woke back here, pronounced dead to the worlds. I was just thankful they didn't insist on burning me in the Valley of Ashes." He curled one side of his mouth slightly, but his making light of the situation darkened quickly at Dylan's frown. "I immediately began doing research on you." He looked down at the table again. "I had so many plans for rescuing you—then, with the passing of time, came reason. I knew that if I interfered more than I had, I would only do more harm than good. You were becoming someone else there and I, I didn't think you would want the life I could give you anymore."

Dylan felt a scream trying to take form in her throat. *That* was his awful excuse? Why didn't he just tell her the truth— he was jealous of Soren and he thought she had moved on!

Dylan thought about everything she endured since she left Zadar.

"Are you *shitting* me?" Dylan shouted. "With every dream we had together you just assumed I didn't want you anymore?" She suddenly stood and backed away from him. "I shouldn't have come here." She pivoted around, but stopped when he blocked her path.

"Step aside," she demanded, panting furiously. She couldn't listen to any more of his lies. Too much time away had painted a damn good picture.

"No."

"Step. ASIDE," she seethed, feeling her flames sizzling inside her veins.

"I need to finish—"

"YOU BROKE ME!" she screamed in his face. *How could he possibly explain that?*

He flinched as if the words had an effect on him, but she knew better.

Tears blurred her vision as she fought for her own sanity.

"I can make you move. I'm a part of the Horde. I can—" her words broke up. She brought a trembling hand her lips.

"I wanted to go to you every single day."

For a split second her body swayed toward his. She squared her shoulders, grounding herself, even though staying away from him felt like trying to pull apart two magnets.

"Who cares," she whispered. "You didn't and that's all that matters."

She turned away from him again, and grabbed the sides of her head in tortured vexation. Why was he doing this to her? Why was he telling her this *now*? Didn't he know how much it had hurt to accept that he was gone? Now she had to embrace the fact he was alive?

"I tried so damn hard," Tristian hissed. Dylan glared up at him. "but I was wrong. At least you thought I was dead. Think how I felt!" He took one of her hands and brought her wrist to his mouth so quickly she was stunned. He inhaled, closing his eyes in ecstasy, as if her body was his Essence— the only thing that could truly keep him alive. She knew she needed to take her hand back but his touch was electric, shocking her heart into terrifying speed.

"Think how I felt," he groaned against her tender flesh, "having to watch you constantly, knowing I could never have you. That I could never smell your fucking scent or taste the succulence of your skin." He ripped her arm away from his mouth and leaned in close to her. "Then I had to see you with him." His anger was so palpable, she jerked. "I had to watch as he *touched* you, *supported* you in the ways I wanted to. You're supposed to be *mine*," he growled, even though something in his voice sounded uncertain. "I only have myself to blame. I pushed you into his willing arms because I wanted you to be safe. And you're not safe with me."

"Don't you see? I'm *still* yours whether it's safe or not." Her eyes spilled surprise at her spontaneous words.

Without another thought, his lips crashed onto hers, silencing her gasping cry by the touch of his beautiful mouth. She crumbled in his arms as if the contact of his lips had yanked the floor right out from under her.

His lips were mesmerizing and greedy. It was too easy to forget their issues when he consumed her like this. She basked in the familiarity of his taste, unable to place a finger on what he reminded her of… but then it was there.

Home.

He was *home*.

He growled and kissed her harder as if he had to; as if he'd go crazy if he didn't and had almost waited too long. He drove his tongue into her mouth and their teeth clashed hungrily. He spun and lifted her onto the kitchen island. His hands shifted from her waist and up the smooth skin of her hips that peeked out from under her jacket. The simple act had her gasping for a breath that had been stolen from her three years ago.

Drunk butterflies flipped in her belly as he shoved her jacket off her shoulders.

"I love your body," he husked against her lips as his hands slipped beneath her shirt, grabbing at her and pulling her closer. His lips ran across her cheek and down her throat. "I don't think I'll ever get enough of you."

He licked and sucked viciously. His wet tongue sent a drumbeat of animalistic need racing straight through her.

417

"Ah, *Dee*," he groaned, kissing her again. "I love you. Shit, I love you so much it hurts." His hands blindingly pawed at her leather pants, trying to undo the hem quickly, not realizing she could just slip them off. "Don't ever leave me."

She stopped him and grabbed the sides of his face, wanting nothing more than to kiss the pain away. To heal him the way he healed her.

"Never," she said looking into his beautiful eyes. "I can't." What she felt for him in that moment, seeing his passion and the relief in his eyes of finally having her, was so incredible it was heady.

Too fast, she thought. She was falling too deep, too fast back into what they were.

"Tristian—"

She suddenly felt claustrophobic, the leather suffocating her.

"Get them off," she moaned, falling back on the island.

Tristian grunted in frustration before digging into a drawer to his left and grabbing a pair of kitchen shears. She felt the cold metal against her belly and then he was cutting them off.

Her heart knocked against her chest. The feeling of his hands sliding along her bare thighs, disfigured by scars, as he yanked her pants the rest of the way off had her going crazy. His fingers hesitated over the tiny cuts along her inner thighs and then the larger one from her attempted suicide, but she ignored it. She felt needy and hot... and sore.

Dylan gasped as the cloud cleared from her mind and she pressed her hands to her scars, covering them.

"Hey," Tristian said hesitantly, motionless and still staring at her legs. "What is this?"

"Get off," she demanded, frantic for space. It was then she became aware of the hot well of tears shimmering her eyes. She couldn't do this. She had *just* slept with someone else.

418

Soren.

Beautiful, steady Soren. The way he looked at her just before she left him at Aria's house began burning across her vision.

Tristian slowly moved off of her as something dark and deadly flickered in his eyes. The moment she was free, she jumped off the island and stood a couple of feet away from him. She wound her arms tightly around her rib cage.

She hated herself in this moment.

"Did they do this to you?" Tristian visibly swallowed. "Did *Gerion* do this to you?"

"No one did this to me, Tristian," Dylan whispered, unable to look him in the eye. "This is me." This had always been her. Not just the scars, but this way she managed to hurt everyone she loved. She was a walking curse. A force that conflicted agony on anyone that got close to her. She finally had something good with Soren and just look at what she did to him. Look at what she was doing, now, to Tristian. She had always been so focused on what life was doing to her when every terrible thing had been because of her decisions. She was single handedly ruining the people in her life. Not only had she hurt her best friend and boyfriend but here she was tearing a gash into Tristian, as well.

Little by little, Dylan was able to force herself back into the moment. She needed to pull herself together and accept the consequences of her actions; and to do that, she needed to see Soren and tell him the truth.

A second had barely passed before Tristian was yanking her to him, unexpectedly, clashing their naked chests together. As if he knew Dylan's immediate instinct was to shove, he planted his ground with a firm grip.

"I have to go," she gasped.

She continued to struggle against him but if she were being honest with herself, she'd stop because her heart wasn't in it. She wanted to be next to him even if it ended up crushing her further. There was something about his scent and enraptured heat that slipped her into a vivid high so intense it paralyzed her. She closed her eyes. Every inch of her skin was still alive, her temperature soaring.

Her eyes fluttered open when she realized they were both silent. She didn't move a muscle. The moment was too delicate. She just wanted to listen to his breathing, to his heart beat steadily against her ear. *He's alive.*

"I just thought it would get better over time," he rasped.

She could feel the vibrations of his deep voice against her ear. She turned her head to look up at him.

"Yet, here you are. I can't believe I ever thought that would work," he added, pushing a couple of errant locks behind her ear.

"You died," she whispered. "You died in my arms." She felt wary as he held her even tighter, afraid to let her go. "You gave me my life and then yanked it away from me. I didn't know who I was anymore."

"You're Dylan, *my Dee.* You'll always be mine, just as I will always be yours."

She could almost see that person he wanted her to be, that person she was before Silas entered her life. It was so easy being this close to him. It was so easy to fall back into what they were. But, that person she once was remained distorted and senseless. It was like trying to feel through frosted glass with no way of reaching herself; no matter how hard she beat and threw her body against the image. She had changed whether she wanted to or not.

"I'm so sorry. I shouldn't have come here. I shouldn't have let you kiss me."

Tristian set his jaw. "Why?" he asked, but the cold, resigned look he resorted to told her he already knew why.

"It was—"

"A mistake?" he finished for her. They stared into each other's eyes for a full moment until it felt so laden with the past she had to look away.

"I'm not the same person you love, not anymore." He let

go of her and that that single act hurt more than any physical wound she had ever endured. "Maybe you were right all along. Maybe we just need more time."

"Let me get this straight…" He laughed, but the pain in his eyes was insurmountable. "You came here just to yank me around before you went back to him? No, you aren't the same person I once loved."

His words continued to hit her hard. *Loved, not love.*

"You're everything to me, Tristian," her voice was small. "But… Dee died… with you."

"You are the last person I ever wanted to hurt."

She nodded, knowing there was nothing they could do to take back what had already happened. She had always thought seeing him would suck her back into who she was. She never dreamed it would only hurt to simply look at him and not kiss him.

Dylan hesitantly brought her hand up to the curve of his jaw, hoping to relay her emotion when words escaped her. She expected him to draw away, but he didn't. His hand covered hers, moving it over his lips and kissing the heel of her palm. Her fingers grazed his stubbly cheek and his eyes slipped shut as suffering washed over him.

She never felt more connected to anyone in her life, and she didn't understand it. How she could feel this way about a person she had actually spent so little time with? But maybe she wasn't supposed to understand it—Maybe, just maybe, she was supposed to accept it, just *feel.* The way her heart beat in his presence rocked her. If she thought she was alive with Soren… *Soren.*

She stepped away, needing to leave before she convinced herself she could stay with him forever. She pulled on her tank and looked down to pick up her pants, remembering he had completely ripped through the material in the heat of the moment.

"Wait here." Tristian dashed away and was back so quickly she hardly had moment to question what he was doing until he held out his palms.

He was holding her old jeans.

Her fingers ghosted over the faded denim. The rips, tears, and faint stains somehow reminiscent of that bittersweet night. The night that she met Datu. The night she used her powers for the first time. The night that she fell in love with Tristian.

The night that had changed... *everything*.

She let out a long whoosh of air, looked up at him.

"Why do you still have these?"

Tristian just turned away from her to grab his keys, not wanting to answer her. Dylan took a deep breath and pulled on the jeans that fit like a worn glove.

He grabbed her hand as they made their way to the door. Their steps were painfully loud and slow against the beat in her chest. He stopped just short of the door and she turned to look at him.

He looked as if he was about to say something. Perhaps, beg her to stay? Her heart sped up as she imagined him locking them in and kissing her again as she threw everything away.

This love... it isn't real.

She suddenly reached out and opened the door before a single word could fall from his lips.

Dylan stood in front of Tristian's apartment building. Her eyes locked on the borrowed bike as she yanked the zipper of her jacket up to her chin. She was desperately clawing at straws, trying to push herself to straddle the beast and leave.

"Dee," Tristian husked.

She flipped around, letting herself be engulfed in his embrace. He dug his hands into her hair, pulling her against him in a hug so wistful it twisted and contorted her heart in painful agony, breaking it all over again.

How could she do this?

"Give me another chance," he said against her hair. "I

can't fix what I did, but I can dedicate my entire life to trying."

She looked up at him through renewed tears. It was everything she ached to hear since the moment Aria told her he was alive. If only it could be that easy. Even if she said yes and went back home... how would that even work? He was supposed to be dead, a dead *rogue* demon. If he suddenly came back to life, the OP would have him executed.

"How can you say that?" she said, glaring into his eyes. "When would we ever get to be together? In my dreams? In secret?" she panted. "Coming out would be suicide!"

His chest huffed and he seemed to be holding back something deep. But she didn't want him to hold back. She wanted him to show her he cared. Show her this was just as much torture for him.

"I don't give a damn if you think you aren't the same person. You, Dee, are still in front of me. I've never felt this with anyone else... I have never *felt* this emotion."

Dylan ran terse fingers through her hair, realizing she had lost her hair band somewhere in his apartment. She dropped her hand.

"I *want* us to work... but, God, Tristian, I want a lot of things and it doesn't mean I can have them." She took a deep breath and rubbed the pain in her chest that felt like she'd swallowed razor blades. The right thing shouldn't hurt this much.

"I love you," he hissed, pressing his forehead against hers. "Don't ever think otherwise."

She could only nod against him. She tilted her chin up and kissed him, despite knowing it was wrong.

Tristian suddenly grit his teeth and shoved himself away from their embrace, stealing her heart, and leaving her once again cold and dead inside. He seemed to stumble from the earthquake of his own heart shattering. His hands lifted to cover his face and he crouched, roaring into his palms.

Dylan jumped and quickly backed away until her hands blindly found the bike.

She hopped onto the leather seat and kick-started the engine. She whipped her head back in his direction and searched his eyes.

He stepped toward her once then stopped himself. She squeezed her eyes shut, still feeling the whisper of his beautiful kisses against her lips.

"Goodbye, Tristian," she said, her voice splintering.

Before he could protest, respond or simply see her break, she revved the bike's engine and gained momentum, peeling out onto the dark road.

"I will always love you, Tristian," she whispered into the wind, crumbling anything human left inside her.

Kicking the shifter and pulling the throttle, Dylan told herself to drive, to get as far away from him as possible. The distance would remind her that Tristian and everything that had happened this night was nothing but a fantasy, a dream that needed to be contained and forgotten to protect him. To protect them.

She'd barely made it five minutes down the road when her resolve began to falter and fail. Doing the right thing suddenly felt like arms wrapping around her and crushing her lungs. She gasped, wondering if she could even survive this new pain.

The ache built up in her body and the tight hold around her chest contracted in severe spasms. Her vision glazed over with gathering tears and she felt the bike wobble as she swiftly pulled it to the side of the road. She tumbled off. Grunts and gasping sobs spilled from her trembling lips. Her palm pressed to the open wound in her heart as she fell into the grass, unable to catch air. She felt her worlds crashing in on her and her newly glued together soul crushed once again just as it had been when he died.

She knew she needed to get up and make her way back to Elon, her home. Just the thought of returning to Soren scared her. She couldn't fathom kissing someone else. How would she move on as if this night never happened?

Dylan hated herself for wanting to turn around and fly back into Tristian's arms. Soren was finally opening up to her and all she gave him in return was a hardy slap in the face. He had been with her every single step of the way following Tristian's death. A man that was loyal to a fault. Yet, it took her less than a week to betray his one request of their relationship.

God, she wanted to scream!

Cars with cones of light zipped past her as she moved to the curb and placed her head in her hands. She felt a dizzying rush grip her when she realized she smelled like him. The same damn smell that she loved so much. That simple sniff spun so many memories through her. She couldn't believe she had forgotten how wonderful it was in as little as three years. What would she forget in a hundred? Two hundred?

She threw her head back and looked up at the sky catching a glimpse of diamonds through the hazy sky, feeling helpless against who she was.

The wind sifted through her tangled hair and it gave her sense of self, as if the breeze was a supportive touch reminding her she could survive this, even if she were on her own. She knew she couldn't continue to be so thoughtless, *so selfish.* She wouldn't tear Tristian, Soren, or even herself down. This was her life. She was a part of the Law because she chose it, and she needed to own up to her decisions.

There would be no more running.

Dylan felt like she understood now why Tristian let her believe he was dead. Before she signed her commitment to the Omnipotence, she would have tried to escape and search for him. She would have never let go, never *tried* to live, to trust, to understand her powers.

Wiping her tears tersely with the back of her hand, she stood and sniffed, gaining control of her emotions and throwing her established, emotionless, exterior back up. She could do this, she had her crew, she had her Uncle, all of whom had become her family; she had her life... How many more reasons did she need to keep moving?

Stepping through the same velvet curtain that only three years ago started her on this very trek, she scanned the cavernous space of the underworld club of *Spin* looking for her team, for her *mate*. She had selfishly left him back at Aria's after discovering Tristan was alive. She never told him where she was going. For all he knew she had run straight to Tristian, which in a way, she had; and now she felt guilty. A familiar stabbing feeling radiated throughout her chest, but this time it was with worry that she had lost her best friend.

Her eyes searched the packed club. Nephilim, faeries, vampires, warlocks, and sirens littered the dance floor jumping and rolling their hips to the upbeat song. All the alcoves were occupied with sinful activities. Dripping blood, bottomless liquids, and blissful drugs. It almost made her smirk at the thought of her former naive self wandering down here so guilelessly.

All the way at the end, Dylan spotted him with his fist gripping a short glass filled with a honey brown liquid wallowing around ice chips. It was the first time she had ever seen him drink on a mission and it threw her stomach into knots. Soren never wanted to be anything other than at the top of his game one hundred percent of the time. Even in sleep he was ready to slay the enemy.

Dylan swallowed her nerves and made her way across the club to her boyfriend.

Soren sat with a grim look staring straight forward at the dance floor. But she could tell he wasn't looking at the sexy creatures undulating their curves to the beat, or at anything in particular. His was grinding his jaw and one of his legs bounced in agitation.

426

As he took a long sip of his drink, Dylan closed the curtain and sat next to him. He never once looked in her direction.

"He's alive?" he asked, his voice like wet gravel.

She didn't say anything.

"You met with him," he asked more as a statement than a question.

She still didn't say anything as her pulse thundered in her ears. He finally looked at her then at her body before letting out a deep throaty growl. He suddenly slammed his drink on the half-moon wooded table, ice splashing out of the glass. She jumped.

"What were you thinking?" he glared at her. "Did you think I wouldn't find out? Or that I wouldn't give a shit?" His voice came out strained before it hardened. "You fucked him didn't you? You let that bastard in your pants after ten seconds of seeing him!"

Dylan just sat there too stunned to deny his accusation; because she might as well have slept with Tristian. She had wanted to. She had loved another man for an hour without ever considering what it might do to Soren.

He abruptly stood and began pacing the tiny space. "What the hell am I even doing?" he asked aloud. He stopped and looked at her. "You know what? It doesn't matter what I think, because he's in violation of the Collector's Code, and you not bringing him in makes you in violation, too." He paced a bit then stopped. "For fuck's sake, *say something*!"

Dylan opened her mouth before she could make herself form words. "I found out he was alive." Renewed tears pricked the backs of her eyes and shame formed a large lump in her throat, making it hard for her to look at him. "I went to a place I used to go to think before I knew what I was. It wasn't to see anyone; it was only to be alone… but I had forgotten Aria knew about that place, too."

She looked down at her tensed hands, clasped tightly

427

together. Soren had sat back down, but she knew better than to think he was relaxing by her words.

"She talked to me," Dylan continued, "and told me everything that had happened in the last few years. I still couldn't handle it. I left… I was planning on leaving and never looking back when I found myself…" she closed her eyes for a moment, summoning the courage to be honest. "I found myself outside of his apartment. I didn't even know if he still lived there." Dylan swallowed. "I won't lie to you about any of it, but he is only my past." She moved her gaze to his tensed profile. "I know you won't bring me in, because even if you deny it a million times over… you care for me." She held up a gentle hand to his cheek and he jerked away as if she were engulfed in flames.

His rejection hurt, but she earned it.

She looked at him, painfully. It had been so hard to leave Tristian for her life in Elon; and Soren was a part of that life… couldn't he see that?

Soren suddenly stood and looked at her, his hands balled into fists at his sides and his teeth clenched around his words, "Then you tell me the truth. You kissed him?"

Reluctantly staring into eyes hard as stone, she nodded her head ever so slightly before looking down.

His eyes flicked down to her jeans that weren't part of her uniform. "He touched you."

Her face crumpled, unable to answer him. She knew that had to have been the biggest insult. It felt as if she had slapped him, the sting radiating in her heart instead of her palm. She had promised to be faithful, to not even dream of her old love.

He growled. "You *fucked* him."

"Soren, I—"

"No," he snapped, silencing her. "I don't want to ever know what happened tonight." Her eyes flew to his in disbelief. She was so stunned she couldn't speak.

His eyes kept running up and down her body as if he was

428

trying to understand or remember her. He stopped at her chest before flicking up to her gaze in an eruption of anger. "Actually, I'll forget it if you take off that fucking chain."

She gasped, clutching the only semblance of Tristian she seemed allowed to keep... until then.

He grunted and lunged, snatching the thick necklace and ripping it off of her.

"No!" Dylan squealed, reaching out for it.

He whipped around holding it in front of her face. She reared back.

"You think I didn't know? You think no one knew this was *his*?"

She panted, eyes wide. No one had ever said a thing about it.

"This metal work, it's demon made. Did you know that? Did you know that Tristian's mother carved this particular type of jewelry? This is a man's chain, a direct correlation with her exquisite weaponry. Once you marched into this world everyone with fucking eyes knew this was Effingo's!"

She trembled in her seat.

"And don't fucking forget, the same *weaponry* was used on Ella." He spat the word "weaponry" like a bad taste on his tongue.

Dylan whimpered as a few traitorous tears slipped down her cheeks. She had no right to cry, not when it was because of something she did that instigated their fight.

"Take your time. I don't care when you leave," he ground out before marching out of the alcove, jerking the curtain around him and letting it fall back into place.

Dylan sat there for a moment, alone, grasping her naked neck. It felt as if a limb had been torn away. An empty, bare feeling added to the insurmountable pain already in her heart. The pain was growing and swallowing her.

Letting her head fall into her hands, she groaned. She never wanted to lie to Soren, but the look on his face, the way he reacted to her touch. If she ever saw Tristan again and he found out about it, she knew he wouldn't think twice before giving her up and never speaking to her again. Hell, even the look in his eye told her he might strangle her if she even dreamed about him.

She needed to remember the good that was in Elon. Soren had slowly made his way into her heart. Tristan may *be* her heart, yet Soren was the tape that wrapped the broken pieces back in place, holding it together.

Her strength.

Without him she would have been nothing but a bleeding, fractured shell. He was the reason she had even embraced this life and because of that he deserved so much better than her. He deserved someone loyal and fierce. Even if Tristian had remained dead, she wasn't being faithful to him. She still pined over a ghost and, probably in some small way, would always do so. She needed to end things with Soren before she hurt him again.

Several minutes passed before Dylan could summon the energy to stand. She downed the rest of Soren's drink, giving herself enough courage to wipe the tears off her face, push herself up, and return home.

Parting the curtain, she immediately spied Astrid grinding against Ian in a sultry roll and he gripped her like only a lover would.

Dylan looked around for Soren and spotted Augusto instead. He was apparently chaperoning Ian and Astrid with his arms crossed tightly across his broad chest.

"Hey, have you seen Soren?"

Augusto flicked his cool gaze to her momentarily. "He went back home."

"What?" she panicked, then groaned.

"You need me to send you back?" he asked in a clipped tone. "He left the new Portal key."

"Yes," she whispered. Soren drinking and leaving duties to his subordinates wasn't like him at all.

"Something going on between you two?"

She stilled, surprised every time Augusto spoke without prompt, but even more so by the fact that he was asking about her love life.

"No... yes. I mean... nothing you should worry yourself with." Augusto was the last person in the worlds she wanted to confide in.

"All right."

"Um..."

"Yeah?"

"Why won't you just go dance with her?"

He looked at Dylan, contemplating her question. Opening his mouth, he shut it again with a crease to his brow. He looked the most thoughtful she had ever seen him.

"I see the way she looks at you, you know," Dylan continued. "What do you have to lose?"

Augusto didn't say anything as he gazed back over in their friends' direction while Astrid laughed at something Ian said.

"It's not too late—" Just as Dylan said it, though, Ian lifted Astrid's chin and kissed her, an unusual tender look blanketing his face.

Augusto clenched his jaw and without saying anything, stepped around writhing creatures and exited the club. Dylan sighed and followed him. Followed him back to Elon, to her mate, to a painful future only half alive.

CHAPTER 23

*"Heavy. From keeping everyone I've ever loved
anchored to my heart."*

sm

DYLAN stared down at her palm cradling a vibrant leaf. It was autumn in Elon. Instead of things turning brown and dying, the leaves blossomed like flowers turning stunning shades of pinks and oranges as the ever-present cool air seemed to grow warmer.

All around her was intense color that should have been beautiful, like the leaf she held. It was hot pink scattered with ribbons of green and white, but the hues were muted as if a film covered her eyes. Life was suddenly congruent with her white-walled room. Color, love, happiness all absent within her new prison: The Shadow Horde.

Once she got back in Elon, everything that happened in Los Angeles felt like a dream bordering on a nightmare. Tristian was alive… completely, physically and emotionally *alive*. She touched him, kissed him, and cried with him. The world that was only starting to turn again, spun out of control until it broke off its axis and toppled into ruin at her feet. Something inside her felt unfixable.

But she was stronger now.

She wouldn't break down like Soren expected her to. She would try to forget. What happened in Los Angeles was closure. Something that no one got from a dead loved one—

432

but she had. She pleaded with a higher power for years to give her one last conversation, one last touch, a real kiss… and she had gotten it. So, why didn't she feel better?

Immediately, once she had gotten home, she had gone looking for Soren. She checked everywhere, even his home. Catarina had looked surprised and told her she hadn't seen him. There was a curious tone to her voice that Dylan hated, knowing the woman hoped their relationship was on the teetering brink of collapse.

The next day flew by without any word on Soren, either, so Dylan decided to ask her Uncle.

"The King is in a meeting," the female solder said, blocking Dylan from entering through the door that was slightly ajar. "But it should be over soon. You may wait here."

Dylan nodded and slouched against the wall. Her mind scanned the places Soren could be, knowing he couldn't be too far. Maybe he was at the Valley of Ashes? Or Traverna?

"Is this about your last mission?" King Damen said, his voice filtering through the open door. Dylan looked away and tried to force herself to stop listening.

"It's about all of our missions," Soren replied, causing Dylan to straighten. "Well, all of our mission's that she has been on."

"Oh?"

Dylan could almost imagine her Uncle looking over his glasses at him, and setting aside whatever he worked on.

"She's out of control."

"I'm going to need examples, Commander Verbeck," King Damen said, the tone of his voice was a mixture of caution and interest.

"She disappeared for several hours during our last mission, she completely broke down in the Amazon, and she was absolutely out of control in Zadar. She disregarded her orders—"

"Did she come back?" King Damen sounded bored and

shuffled some papers. "Did she subdue a contract?"

"Yes—"

"I will have a chat with her about her place on the team again and how crucial your orders are as commander. Anything else?"

"I don't trust her."

"What are you proposing I do? Kick her off the Horde? You can only imagine what kind of impact that would have on her loyalty. Not to mention, what will the populous think?"

"No…" Soren hesitated, "Perhaps, just keep her at a disadvantage?"

"You do realize the seriousness of what you're suggesting?"

"*Yes*. But I feel like it's only a matter of time before she runs. She needs to be *Bound*."

At Soren's answer Dylan tensed up in shock. *How could he?* She couldn't believe Soren would stoop so low as to wanting to control her again. What was she to him… his toy?

No, his pet, her inner-self sneered. A pet that had stepped out of line and needed to be disciplined.

"Well, I trust her loyalty, even if you don't," King Damen said, surprising her. "I will not *Bind* her again. She's too useful to have her at such a disadvantage. But…I will not force you to date her publicly. Her reputation is excellent and her future holds great promise on the Shadow Horde. Nice work."

"*My Master*—"

"That will be all, soldier."

What? Her mouth dropped open. His mission was to *date* her? Why on earth… That was when it snapped into place.

Her loyalty.

King Damen wanted someone on the inside of her heart, to know her deepest secrets. It was the only way he felt like he could trust her.

Her mind quickly ran through each and every conversation, touch, and kiss, and with what she knew now, everything Soren did made sense and then some. He hadn't changed. She hadn't unlocked a new man. He had simply driven his psychotic game farther in the name of his old flame. The fun would be in taking her virginity, dumping her, and then debasing her until she tried to kill herself again.

Dylan bristled when she noticed the other soldier seemed to be in just as much disgusted shock. She too, had overheard Soren.

Dylan heard their farewells and she quickly ducked into a neighboring room just as Soren exited. She watched from the little window at the side of the door as he earned a glare from the female soldier before stopping short in front of the door Dylan hid behind. His eyes were hard, unlike anything she'd ever seen, and it boggled her mind that she had ever thought she knew him at all. He squinted slightly before he seemed to shake off whatever bothered him and continued down the hall.

No, she didn't know him at all.

She hated that she had left Tristian for him and Elon. Her relationship with Soren turned out to be a sham, and after her missions and how they all treated her, she was beginning to wonder if her spot on the Horde was also just to keep her *contained*.

Dylan slipped out from hiding and looked over at the soldier when she called Dylan's name to go in. Dylan nodded and walked into her Uncle's office.

King Damen sat behind a large wooden desk just like the last time she had been here. He looked over his glasses at her.

"You know it's not polite to eavesdrop."

Dylan didn't even try to deny it. She just sighed and plopped down into one of the leather arm chairs.

"Well, I couldn't help it... not when it's about me."

"And what do you think of his request?"

435

"To be frank," she cleared her throat, "I'm pissed off." She crossed her arms and huffed. "I wish you wouldn't have made him date me."

She bit her lip at her words, forgetting for a moment that he was a King and not her friend. She suddenly remembered she hadn't bowed or used the customary greeting.

"Oh!" she abruptly stood, startling him, and bowed, "*My Master.*"

King Damen chuckled and took of his glasses to look at her. "Enough. Sit."

She swallowed and sat.

"I didn't make Soren do anything other than shadow you."

"But I heard—"

"At first." King Damen cut her off. "He was the one to bring up the rumor concerning the two of you while you were incapacitated on your birthday. He wanted to stop mentoring you because of your attachment." She thought of the way she threw herself at him on the bike that night in front of Traverna. "I told him no, that your attachment would pay off with your loyalty. Whatever more he chose to do with you after that was his idea."

She frowned, even more confused than before. "Do you know if it all was a lie?" she hated how small her voice sounded, how needful it was.

"You'll have to ask him that."

The following afternoon Dylan was doing just that. Despite all of her anger, she still had too many questions that needed answering. A part of her needed their relationship to be a lie to justify what she had done with Tristian.

King Damen had been right, though. To everyone around them they were the perfect, dangerous couple. The population loved her with him and it was a smart move even if it hurt her. They expected her to love someone rogue, but she had proven them wrong. She had sworn into the Shadow Horde and began dating her law-abiding commander—a soldier the worlds seemed to love more than the Kings.

One of the attributes she admired the most about him was his brutal honesty. It hadn't ever stopped him from tearing her apart before so why keep *this* from her? Why kiss her passionately and talk to her like she was the only one who knew him on the inside? Was he really that fucked up to go that far for his own sadistic form of fun? Even if he didn't want to admit it, part of her thought he genuinely cared for her.

The center of the leaf she held in front of Soren's house glowed, catching her eye as if a light had been pressed against the other side. A snake of smoke drifted up just before the leaf caught fire. Dylan watched it burn into a pile of ash on her palm before letting the cool wind carry it away. She rubbed the singe off her palm with the side of her new uniform and stared back at the simple home that had experienced too much death and an abundance of love.

Dylan stepped forward to Soren's front door until her fist met solid wood. She knocked twice. She heard the peephole cover unlatch then latch back from inside. The door opened a crack and she took the invitation to step inside. Catarina stood off to the side, wary with her sudden, and second, unannounced arrival.

"I'm sorry about attacking you the other day," Dylan blurted out. "I wasn't thinking clearly."

Caterina sighed and shut the door behind them. "It's okay. I mean, it wasn't but I can understand why."

Dylan nodded before digging into her pocket and pulling out a piece of paper from her empty notebook. She held it out to the other girl.

"I know my—*your* grandmother would love to meet you," Dylan said, as Caterina took the note with her grandmother's contact information on it. She had wanted to leave this alone like Soren asked of her, but she just couldn't ignore that Cat was in danger living in a demon world when there was a human family ready to love her safely.

"I don't understand why you want to get rid of me so bad," she said. "Is it because of Soren?"

Dylan frowned. It was painfully clear that Catarina loved him, but could that honestly be the only reason deterring her from an actual life?

Dylan shook her head. "No... look, I grew up literally in your shoes. Our mother and father *died.* All I had left was my grandmother. I was all she had, too, and I was taken away. I *can't* go back. So honestly? I'm pissed off you would just throw that away for an empty house and a demon who might never love you the way you wish he might."

Dylan tersely wiped away a few tears. She had cried so much in the past few days, she wondered how she wasn't all dried up and blown away by the wind like the ashes from that leaf.

"She's getting older," Dylan continued as Cat stared at the paper, "I know age means nothing to you here, but to a human... she may only have fifteen years left. She deserves to know you. *You* deserve to know her." Dylan took a step toward her as Catarina's eyes were swelling with impending tears. "She's so wonderful. If I could go back—If I could continue my life near her, I would in a heartbeat—"

"Would you now?" Soren's voice boomed from the stairway.

Dylan turned her head in his direction, surprised he was coming out of hiding. She had expected to comb through the house then hit the Valley of Ashes.

He stood in a shadow like the demons of her nightmares—a deadly, dark figure with only glowing eyes taking shape.

"Of course, I miss my grandmother," Dylan said with a slight edge to her voice, "I won't deny it today or a hundred years from now."

He narrowed his eyes and shifted, angling his body against a wall and letting a bay of firelight from the library swath over him. "What are you doing here?"

438

"Looking for you," she answered, honestly.

"Come here," he said, his voice was deep like syrup over jagged rocks.

She was intrigued. She wondered how far he would go, if he would continue the charade after Los Angeles. Or if he'd finally just tell her the truth.

Dylan walked over to him, challenging him with her stare. She was still so confused about what King Damen had said. She wanted to believe Soren wouldn't do that to her after everything they had been through or everything they had done… it was too passionate for it all to have been a lie… but that didn't stop it from being one.

Once she was in reaching distance, he grabbed her and crushed his mouth on hers, pushing her against the wall. She sucked in a breath, not expecting him to kiss her again so soon after the mission. The feel of his lips was familiar and grounding, and of all things Soren wasn't—it felt safe. His hips moved against hers and she couldn't keep herself from glancing to the spot where Catarina was standing. The girl was gone. Soren's hand slipped underneath her jacket.

"I can't stop thinking about you," he whispered, pressing their bodies further against the wall. "How it felt to be inside you."

She shifted her face away and tried not to grimace.

Deceit.

Games.

Soren was a psychopath and she couldn't let herself forget she was frolicking in the lion's den.

Dylan looked back into his eyes and knew she still needed him to tell her that it had all been a ruse for her loyalty.

"We need to talk."

He looked at her a long moment and she wondered if he could tell where her mind was. If he could tell she knew. He finally nodded curtly and led her upstairs to his childhood bedroom.

As soon as she stepped through the door, her eyes flitted across the sparse space. She expected a teenager's room, like her room at Isabel's. Well, like her room *had been* at Isabel's. Posters, pictures, anything to show what his life was like then… but his room was devoid of anything personal. There was a wooden bed with a white comforter tucked tightly against the far wall and a wooden dresser on the opposite wall near a round window, a row of first edition novels collecting dust.

Dylan moved to the only picture that hung on the wall. She recognized Soren and his mom. Soren was in uniform. He looked young and even more breathtaking—the hard, unyielding exterior and vibrant scars absent. On his other side were two men who looked like his brother and father, also in uniform. And on the far right was Ella, the stunning brunette from the vision. It must have been Soren's Signing day into the Shadow Horde because he looked so incredibly *happy*.

Rough fingers wrapped around her wrist, yanking her away from the photo.

"I don't want to talk," he said, gripping the back of her head and kissing her so hard she hissed. He pulled her with him to his bed and he sat, but her arm was taut between them, keeping him at a safe distance.

Something about him felt desperate and she wondered again if he knew she had overheard.

"Too bad…" she smiled coyly hoping for levity, "because you're not getting any of this," she motioned to her body, "until we do."

He boosted an eyebrow at her challenge and she was suddenly on her back with Soren straddling her. "You think you can resist my charms?"

"We need to talk about the other night," she said, seriously.

He moved off of her with an unreadable expression and stood. "Fine. Talk."

She nodded and figured she start with Tristian.

"We can't just act like nothing happened, as much as I want to." She sat up, pulling her knees up to her chest. "Since we've been back, you've been... absent. I hurt you, and I need to tell you how sorry I am." Soren just stood silently facing her. His jaw ticked from her words. "I mean, put yourself in my shoes. What if you suddenly found out Ella was alive?" His entire body tensed like a bow ready to shoot an arrow into her heart.

"Well, I wouldn't have fucked her, that's for sure," he spit out.

Dylan narrowed her eyes at him, realizing he still believed she had sex with Tristian not even a couple of hours after they had slept together.

"But you would be mad, angry that she lied to you. Confused as to why. But you still love her... right? So wouldn't you want to see her?"

"It's not the same thing. Besides... love fades with time... and reason."

She tried not to let that statement sink in like he wanted and went back to the subject.

"So maybe Tristian hadn't been dead as long but it is the same thing."

"No, it's not," he argued. "She wasn't rogue or conspiring with enemies!"

"Who you knew wasn't the same man he is with me!"

"Was!" Soren snapped.

Dylan suddenly stopped herself from defending Tristian. There was no use in doing so. "I just need you to think from my perspective, that's all. I acted on impulse. My emotions were shot. *I wasn't thinking,*" she urged. "But I am now. It was a mistake. I'm sorry. I should have stayed far away."

He rubbed his mouth a bit, mulling over her words.

"Why were your leathers off?"

Dylan swallowed against a huge rock of bile in her throat. *Lie,* she told herself. *Just lie.* "He tore them off me," she

441

whispered.

"He tore—" Soren couldn't even finish his sentence. He began pacing. He stopped and turned to her. "Did you fuck him? Answer me and I'll tell you where my damn head is at!"

She moved to the edge of the bed. Her words continued to remain calm, a complete contradiction to the screaming inside her mind. "I didn't have sex with him."

"Then what?" He marched up to her and pushed her back on the bed harshly, she gasped. He gripped her hips, pushing his legs between hers. His strong hands moved down her torso roughly. She didn't expect any less.

"Did he touch you here?" He growled close to her lips as his hands suddenly fisted her rear.

She cursed and shoved him off of her. Soren fell onto the floor and she quickly darted to the door.

Pausing, she turned back around to face him, trying to rid the plaguing thoughts of Silas forcing himself on her.

"I will not let you do this to yourself."

Soren shook his head from side to side repeatedly. "I'm going out of my damn mind." His eyes moved up to hers, and she was surprised to see pain in them. "After all the doubts, after everything you've seen and heard about him, you still spread your legs for him." He chuckled maddeningly. "Oh sorry, but you *didn't have sex with him!*"

She ground her teeth at his condescension. She knew he was thinking about the first night they were together.

"What was I to you?" he scowled. "Tell me, Dylan. Did you think of me at all while you ran to him, while he touched you? Was I even a damn dot on your radar?"

"Of course you were. But I was… blinded by him."

"Well, I'm blinded by you."

She frowned at his words.

"What?" she asked. He couldn't…

Lies, she suddenly remembered. He was only continuing the scheme. Her shock turned into a stone-faced glare.

442

He looked down at the floor as if looking for answers within the aged grain. "I still remember the way you first looked at me, how you always look at me, like my sole purpose in this life is to protect you. For the longest time, I didn't want to see it. You were an Elementa! Why would you need me? I wanted to hate you... and I did... I hated you so much until I..." He glanced up at her angered expression.

"Stop it. Stop it right now. I know, okay?" She looked at him disapprovingly. "You don't have to continue with the game. We played, I lost. Just stop it!"

"Dylan—"

"Stop pegging me for a fool. I know you went to Damen and tried to have me *Bound* again," her voice rose, "I know you tried to have me kicked off the Horde!"

He stared at her, disbelieving at first. "I thought I sensed you there... but it seems like you're everywhere these days and I thought I was only further losing my mind."

"Great. I'm glad we cleared that up," Dylan said, dryly. "I should go... No, wait," she stopped herself from leaving. "Just tell me what was the point of taking my virginity? Was it all just a matter of score to you?"

Soren looked confused but she didn't buy into it.

"The Kings told you to date me for my loyalty, fine. But, you didn't need to take it that far! No one told you to screw me!"

"Dylan, I wanted to... Do you regret giving it to me?"

"Of course I do!" she screamed, even though it felt like the biggest lie of her existence.

Soren flinched.

"I regret falling victim to your games and giving you something that was important to me."

"My *games*?" Soren glared at her. "I may have tried to *Bind* you again and yes, I admit, I started dating you publicly because I thought it was a good strategic move. But, I never lied to you. I hung out with you because I wanted to. I slept in your bed every night because I wanted to. I kissed you because I wanted to. I made love to you, because I fucking love you!"

Dylan silently gasped.

"You don't even believe in love," Dylan forcefully swallowed. "It's a weakness, remember?"

"I've been staying away from you because *you've* become my weakness."

"Goddammit, Soren!" Dylan snapped and she turned for the door.

He jumped up and hurried over to her, blocking her path.

Dylan stilled. It was all a lie. He had taken advantage of the situation. He didn't love her. He couldn't ever love her.

"You don't love me," she said, weakly, stating the fact and hoping it would be true.

He stood before her, his heart raw and bleeding out in front of him. "I do. I fucking hate that I do, because you love someone else. But I do."

She began backing up, but he stopped her, gripping her wrists. "I don't beg for many things, but please, *please* don't give up on what we have just because he's alive. You're right, I am hurting. And that's the problem. I understand jealousy, anger. But this pain? It only comes from the thought of losing you, not kissing you, not sleeping next to you, not having a future with you. That's love… isn't it?"

Dylan stood in front of him their hands clasped. She flipped his and focused on the calloused skin and creased lines laid out like a map of kills along his palms.

She puckered her brow, unable to ignore how honest and pained he sounded. It was like a dagger to her heart. It was easier to think he was only lying because… if he loved her… then what she did with Tristian hurt him badly.

Dylan opened her mouth to gasp but she couldn't make herself take in air. She felt strangled at how terribly she had screwed up. It hurt to think of not having those things with Soren too, but one question clouded her thoughts: Would she have forgotten him so easily while with Tristian if she did love him?

"I—"

"Don't say it. Don't say it just because I said it." He gripped her hands and she looked up and into his stormy blues. "I'm only telling you like it is. I told you not to love me, so I understand if you don't. This is my doing and I will have to live with it despite what you do or don't feel."

She tried not to twist her features. He made it sound like loving her was a disease, something he needed to get over… but wasn't it? Didn't all of the people who loved her end up getting hurt?

"I… don't know what I feel." She pulled her hands out of his grasp. *This is for the best*, she told herself. *Run.* "I'm sorry."

She slipped around him and left his room. Left her mate standing in his room with an accepted look on his face.

Dylan stormed down the old steps and ran into Catarina. They both squeaked in surprise.

"Sorry," Dylan muttered, moving past her.

"Dylan—"

Dylan froze. She hadn't told Catarina to call her by that name. Soren must have told her. She began to wonder just how much Soren had told the human about her. Could she honestly trust his word on anything anymore?

"That's your name," Dylan sighed, still reeling from her conversation with Soren. Before the girl could reply, Dylan spoke again, "You should go to him. He needs someone," *better*, she mentally added.

Catarina frowned but nodded and started up the steps.

CHAPTER 24

*"They whispered all their flaws
And inhaled the storm together."*
Randy Mascorro

DYLAN quickly headed back to her motorcycle and sped to the Glass Tower. She parked and shuffled up the large steps, entering through the main foyer to take a walk through Astrid's plot of green space.

Dylan smiled politely to Lord Struo and glanced at the nearly empty Vat. Her face pinched and she picked up her pace, bee-lining to the door within a dark alcove that she knew led to the Thorn Gardens.

Stepping through the arched door, she gazed at the stunning arrangement of life before her. Bushes of burgundy peonies, crimson hanging amaranthus, and champagne roses surrounded ghostly birch trees covered in tangerine and emerald leaves with tiny white blossoms.

She followed the cascading slabs of glittering stone that led her around the side of the Glass Tower to a grassy lookout with a small, aged gazebo covered in vibrant, green vines.

Dylan moved to the stone railing and stared out at the bustling city. She felt in her pockets for Cassandra's Affirmation booklet. Needing solace, she pulled it out and opened it to a random page.

"May I stand amazed in the presence of the gods.
May the rhythm of my heart stir
music that enslaves darkness.
May my heart witness what my hands create,
the words I utter, the worlds I think.
May my flesh be a sail propelled by
the breath of dream.
May I ride in calm waters toward destiny."
—Awakening Osiris, The Egyptian Book of the Dead

Dylan groaned at the poetry but the answer to the Elementas' location had to be inside. There just wasn't any other reason for the demon to give it to her. Dylan flipped through the pages, peeked inside the binding and finally shook it out vigorously before chucking over the railing. She sat down onto the iron bench in the gazebo and rubbed her hands down her face.

What was she doing? Did she really want to find her family or was this just another desperate plea to run away from her problems?

She honestly didn't know what to think when it came to Soren. What she heard outside of King Damen's office had been one thing and what she had experienced in his home had been another. It felt impossible to pick apart the truth when she was so inclined to believe the former because of her damaged past. Yet, even that felt too *easy*.

Dylan rubbed her temples before bending down to pick up the bookmark and small envelope that had fluttered to the ground, escaping the book's damaging fall. She started to throw it over the edge as well when she found herself examining the woven fabric of the bookmark with worn edges. It appeared to have been handmade and used over many decades. It was a deep blue and across it were numbered solar systems and stars with a noticeably starless horizon around what she guessed was Elon and Zadar. It felt personal and special and even though Cassandra had

447

expected Dylan to keep the book, she just didn't feel right about keeping *this*. She suddenly felt badly for having thrown the book.

She started to place the bookmark inside the envelope that Cassandra had sent the chain back in when she remembered the note.

Dylan had initially ignored it, guessing it was only to bring her the bad news. She pulled it out now and unfolded it.

New friend,
I'm sure your spirits are low now that I have sent back the necklace. As you now guess, I haven't been able to locate the soul you sought attached to it. He is either alive or truly past on. I pray you find solace. Please study the booklet I gave you. There is a spiritual balance that can have a healing effect on the flowing energy between the mind and spirit. Do not take this lightly, because what you choose... you won't ever be able to take back.
C

Dylan frowned harder. She was obviously trying to say something without saying anything. Tristian was alive, she got that much, but a spiritual balance with the book? And what was Dylan supposed to be choosing?

As she pondered the message, Dylan's thumb ran absentmindedly across the bookmark. Her nail caught on a pulled thread and she looked back down at it— realizing the numbers on the planets were out of order just like the back of the book. She ran her thumb over the planets and the flowing void blocking humans from the demon realm; the *Balance* as Cassandra's mate had called it. She wondered again, why it was laid out in this order. But not only that, the numbers on this solar system didn't seem to make any sense. It was almost like they were something completely separate from the picture.

Her eyes widened.

A spiritual balance. A flowing energy. The Balance.

The balance lies where the energy flows…

Coordinates! The numbers were coordinates for a Portal!

Dylan gawked at the bookmark, frozen as she listened to her pulse's galloping; the sound filling up her ears. It was something she had secretly wanted since that moment in Tristian's apartment when he told her she was a demon, and now she had found them!

Holy crap, she knew where they were.

Her mind was already concocting scenarios and plans how to go there whenever she was called for their next mission. She thought about how easy it would be to do it. All she would have to do would be to make sure no one touched her as she entered the Portal. The Horde would arrive at their destination, and only then, they would realize she was missing, just like when Soren tricked her in Zadar; and by then it would be too late.

But… what would happen on the other side? How could she get back if she screwed up? Or what if they weren't there anymore, or she changed her mind? Only the commander held the Portal key and she couldn't ask Soren to take her. Perhaps she could get a key herself?

Dylan sighed, closing the envelope and stuffing it back into her pocket. She shouldn't decide anything drastic now. She was still upset with Soren and herself.

She knew what she needed to do, whether or not she stayed. It hurt her deep inside, but it was the only answer. She needed to start cutting ties and she needed to start with Soren. To tell him it was over. She couldn't decide her fate while worrying about love; real or fake.

Dylan felt the sudden need to clear her mind and sift through all of the nonsense until she felt comfortable with what her options were.

She left the gardens and quickly stepped through the side door and entered the gym. It was the one place she felt whole and balanced.

Dylan marched through the doors under the words **"VINCIT QUI SE VINCIT"** which she knew meant: *He Conquers Who Conquers Himself;* and halted at the sight of Ian and Augusto speaking closely with each other. Augusto touched the side of Ian's cheek softly before leaning over and kissing him.

Ian noticed Dylan first and tensed.

Augusto turned and looked at Dylan as Ian slouched to the side nonchalantly, his flushed cheeks betraying his aloofness.

Dylan just continued to the glass enclosure where she could practice her powers, not wanting to deal with any more personal revelations of any kind from anyone.

Dylan fogged the glass and punched in several codes before an inferno of fire erupted in front of her. She zipped up her jacket to protect her clothes and grabbed a handful of fire. The flames cradled her fingers and she closed her eyes for a moment to take a deep breath and to bask in the numbing feeling.

In that brief moment, she understood how one might become consumed in the fire. All she wanted to do was to spur it larger, to step inside; to disappear until everything dissolved and all of the answers to her problems became clear.

Dylan opened her eyes and flung the fireball at the target so hard it cracked.

Her chest heaved from the amount of emotional burden she had forced into that throw. She scowled at the stupid target—unable to decide if she wanted it to crumble underneath the hit or withstand everything she offered. To live or to die. Wasn't that always the choice?

Dylan snatched another fireball and hurled it against the same target. It splintered down the other side. This time she wanted it to break, because breaking something else was far better than falling to pieces herself.

Dylan glared at the stupid piece of wood that only seemed to remind her of her broken life—one big target filled with cracks and gaping gashes from everyone who had had a try at her, while the iron shell of her armor refused to crumble no matter how hard she sometimes wanted it to.

Her parents' death.

Her high school days.

Silas' greed.

Tristian's death.

Elon's hatred.

Leaving Tristian.

Soren's *love.*

She slammed another fire ball against the target, exposing a large, glowing gash, sputtering sparks as the magical wood fought off the flame and kept it from igniting.

How could Soren claim to love her after what she had done anyway? Shouldn't he hate her? It certainly sounded like he did from what she heard outside of King Damen's office.

Besides, Soren didn't love her. She had felt how much he cared for Ella during those memories and there was no way he felt that for Dylan. He liked her company as a friend, as a friend with benefits. He took what he wanted and in return gave her what she needed, like a master feeds and sustains its pet. That wasn't love!

But what about those other times? Her inner self demanded out of nowhere. Those times it felt like she was all he could see. The way he let her into his life, his mind. The way he kissed her like he needed to… and the passion, holy shit the passion. She could still feel him even now as if his touch had been tattooed onto her skin and deep inside her bones.

Dylan gripped the crucible, trying to convince herself she didn't need him like he needed her; but just the thought of never waking up to his sapphire eyes again, or having to watch him love someone else, tore her up inside. Because it would happen, all of it.

She couldn't do this—no she could. She had only become attached to him because of his constant role in her life. She needed to cut the cord. They would both move on… eventually.

Dylan suddenly dove into the fiery pit and gripped the rest of the violent blaze before she could allow another thought.

In one big, angry snap, she threw it at the targets. The room exploded with heat, throwing her backward.

Moments later, she tried to sit up, but everything seemed to be rolling in slow motion. A sharp ringing filled her ears, and black smoke clogged her lungs. She gagged, gripping the polished edge of the bowl of fire. It felt like she was being strangled by a ghost.

Dylan clawed at her throat as the room tilted and burned. She knew she couldn't die in her own flames, but no one ever said anything about smoke. Several tubes dropped from the ceiling and shot white dust onto the violent conflagration but it almost seemed too strong to be extinguished.

She was still coughing and sputtering through the thick cloud sitting heavily in the air, when a pair of arms wrapped around her and pulled her out of the room.

"Stop, stop. I'm fine," she whispered hoarsely to whoever was behind her. The demon dropped her harshly as the glass doors swooshed shut, cutting off a thin trail of smoke from its origin.

"You told me you wouldn't try ever again," Soren's pain-filled voice struck her. She jerked her head back and looked at him.

"What are you doing here?" she rasped, her throat burning. The words ignited a bout of coughing that she couldn't control. All she could do was hold her chest and huddle against him.

Soren's face contorted and he ignored her question.

"You told me you wouldn't try to kill yourself again!" he

roared an inch for her nose. "Is my love that fucking difficult to bear?"

"I wasn't. I swear… I wasn't."

"Then what the *hell*?!"

She looked back at the room, the glass fixed back to translucent. The walls were charred and all three targets incinerated. The only places untouched were the large bowl that initially held the fire and a smudge of her body's outline on the floor.

"I just…" *needed to think, to clear my head, to forget about you and Tristian and my life…* "I just needed to *breathe*."

He snatched her face and pressed his mouth to hers. All smoke and scorching pain.

"Don't you see?" he growled, like the world was crushing around him. "I'm under water and I need *you* to breathe." He yanked her to his chest and she let him. She closed her eyes as a couple of tears slipped down her ashy cheeks.

"You really love me," she said as more of a statement than a question.

She shifted her head and gazed up into his striking eyes.

"Of course, I do."

Her unsteady hands covered his bunched ones gripping the length of her neck, and gently fused herself with him. She could feel the abyss of his pain.

"I don't deserve you."

"Why don't you let me decide what and who I deserve, okay?"

"I was so selfish…" She cast her eyes down.

Did her wants and needs even matter anymore? Protecting the Kings, her image, her abilities above others came first. Demons depended on her for safety. She had to stop being so egocentric. As painful as it was to bear, her and Tristian wouldn't ever be and neither would her and the Elementas.

Soren brought one of their melded hands up her face,

cupping her cheek, as he leaned in brushing a soft kiss against her lips. He pulled away, wiping at the dark singes on her skin.

"I'll wait until you are past this, if you ever get past this. However long it takes."

He let go of her hand and began ripping at the tight knot on his wrist with his teeth. The action momentarily stole her attention. When he got the leather braid loose, he pulled it from around his wrist.

"What are you doing?" she asked, knowing he never took it off.

"I don't have a family ring," he started.

"Oh, Soren, please don't." He grabbed her wrist so gently she flinched. He acted as if he didn't notice and started tying it on. "I'm asking you, but I don't want an answer today or in fifty years. Not until you're ready to give everything in here." He brought his hand to her chest. "I'll always be waiting. You have my heart. I'll wait for yours."

She felt on the verge of sobbing. Why? Why did he have to make it so difficult? Didn't he know he needed to stay far away from her?

"Soren, I-I…" *I can't love you*, she urged herself to say the words. *I will ruin you. I am ruining you, don't you see?* But she suddenly couldn't do it because the words felt fake. Because she did love him no matter how many times she told herself otherwise; and she was ruining him by pulling away. It was a love completely separate from Tristian. The easy love that she wanted was suddenly sitting right in front of her. A lifetime kind of love.

He kissed her fingers and she let him, choosing to believe him.

"Thank you. I…" Dylan trailed off, her eyes shot wide at the black shadow silently sprinting towards them. Soren turned his head to where she was looking just as the dark figure brought a swift elbow down on the back of his neck, knocking him out cold.

Dylan scooted back to scream, but a leather gloved hand slipped around the back of her neck and with his dagger in his hand so the handle was cold against her jaw. He jerked her toward him and ripped the ski mask off half-way exposing his mouth and before she could take her next breath, his mouth was on hers.

Dylan struggled and kept her mouth firmly shut, not kissing whoever it was. The man pulled back.

"There's no way I'm letting you go, again," the man said, though heavy breaths.

"*Tristian?*"

"I sincerely hope no other demons try to kiss you like that." Tristian grinned. "Of course, it's me. Now, come on. We don't have much time." He stood and pulled the mask back down. "And make it look a little like a struggle."

Dylan froze as her caught breath slipped out of her lungs.

She had resigned herself to never seeing him again, yet, here he was doing exactly what she had dreamed about for years. He was saving her. Except… it was when she didn't want to be saved.

When his beautiful green eyes met hers, she saw a minute of panic. Tristian bent down, took hold of her hands and pulled her up to her feet. Everything around her felt fuzzy and strange as she followed Tristian's lead, as if her mind had shifted into autopilot. She looked back at Soren, instinctively. He was laid out on the tarmac of the indoor track they had run together for years. The place where she had realized she loved him, too.

"Dylan."

She turned back to Tristian as a hollow feeling flooded inside her stomach. As much as she wanted to be with Tristian, she couldn't imagine leaving Soren. No, she couldn't run. Not even for the boy she thought was her soul.

"*Dylan*," he said her name again, this time it sounded painful on his tongue. "I can't ignore what we have anymore…" He cupped her cheeks and the way he stared deeply into her eyes felt like he was trying to break her out of a spell. "Not after last week," he continued. "It was hard enough trying to forget something carved so deep within your being but now… all I do is crave your scent and your voice. I crave the way my hand feels in yours. I crave waking up next to you and feeling you screaming and writhing beneath me. And most of all, I crave your heart." His eyes danced between hers, pleading with his soul and searching for the passion they shared. Yet, oddly she felt blank, still too shocked that he was here. He was finally trying to rescue her. What did they say? Better late than never?

Dylan started to turn her head back to her best friend, her mate, but Tristian stopped her with a single finger on her cheek.

"You said you wanted me to try harder. I am. Give me the chance to show you. Come with me. *Be with me,*" he implored. "I can't promise that it'll be easy but we'll be together and that's enough for me. Please, let it be enough for you."

Elation from his words fluttered her heart as he edged forward, brushing up against her.

"Come on," he whispered, tilting her chin back as she stared deeply into his eyes. "It's time to go home."

CHAPTER 25

"The fire that beats in my chest is nothing like yours.
Your fire is a hungry, all-consuming beast of a flame
That has licked away your smile."
F.D.L.

WITH his eyes closed, Soren felt the painful succession of thuds as someone slapped his cheek. Lifting a heavy limb, he lazily swatted at the pest.

"He's waking up," said a woman's voice... his mind slowly registering who it was.

"Astrid, why are you here?" he grunted, realizing his bed felt unusually hard.

"You mean, 'Why am I passed out on the floor?'"

He opened one eye trying to focus on his surroundings. The training room—Dylan.

He instantly sat up almost colliding with her, "Where's Dylan?"

"Who?"

"I mean Temperance, where's Temperance?" he demanded, rubbing the back of his aching head.

"She's not here. Soren... what happened?" Her eyes were absorbing the scene around him. But he couldn't seem to knock the dark spots away from his vision.

"I was knocked out. I got sucker punched from behind." His eyes cleared a bit and he focused on what had Astrid wide-eyed. He looked around at the broken floor and the bloody handprints that dragged a few feet. He felt his pulse pick up as his eyes followed the blood to the door that led to the dorm rooms.

"Looks like a struggle," Astrid faltered, glancing around at the damage. Augusto was on the phone and Ian looked uncomfortable with his hands stuck in his pockets.

Tension vibrated within Soren's veins as he eyed the handprints, trailing through the heavy slick of blood. He got to a wobbly stand and began mindlessly following the path of red splatters. He shook his head trying to clear the haze curling around the corners of his vision. What if she was bleeding out somewhere with no one to help her?

He shoved open the door leading to the hallway and stumbled out of the gym.

"Soren!" Astrid yelled, but her voice sounded hollow and far, as if she were calling out from the other end of a tunnel.

"Shit, Dylan, *shit*," he panted under his breath.

Dammit, he couldn't lose her. She would be destroyed, *no,* he would be destroyed. Please, let her be here somewhere. His mind swam with denial clouding his rational thought as he busted out the back door that led to the Void of Bones, following the blood. The drops getting less and less frequent.

Harsh air slapped against him and his body involuntarily shivered when he reached the edge of the courtyard. He searched the ground feeling fear gush into his veins. The last drop was on the rock she used to sit on before she knew what this place was.

"Soren!" Astrid shrilled behind him just as he braced himself to jump into the void.

He lunged, but Astrid and Ian were there, holding him back. He roared and struggled against them for a moment until he fell hard to his knees from a strong gust of wind from Ian's powers.

"Let me go!" he snarled. They didn't understand. He needed to go after her. Someone had her. Someone had taken her. Silas was dead, but that didn't mean a damn thing. He still had an entire family looking for her. Hell, *she* still had an entire family looking for her.

The memories of the last few years shot through his mind like a bullet; starting with the shock as he looked into her pained eyes inside Silas' castle covered in Effingo's blood to the moment in her bed when he realized he loved her. He had thought she saw it too. The stunned realization that their hearts were on the line… that was until *he* came back from the dead. Yet, even then, Dylan had come back.

Soren reached out, grabbing Astrid suddenly by the jacket. He pulled her against his chest and forced his *Daleon* against her throat through the gust of wind. "Ian, stop before I fucking slice her jugular."

"Don't!" Astrid screamed to Ian when she felt the wind begin to die. Ian reluctantly pushed his powers back up.

"*Soren*," Astrid sobbed, "You can't go in there."

"She did!" he insisted.

"That doesn't mean a thing and you know that!" Astrid lifted a steady hand to the blade at her throat. She didn't try to remove it, but he knew better than to think she wouldn't shoot a single icicle into his neck if he moved for a kill. "You need to stop reacting and think. We are not the enemy. Let us help you find her."

The curtain of air retreated around them and Astrid swiftly pulled away just before Soren's hands hit the cold rocks—the fight whooshing right out him.

He looked up at Astrid as his shoulders sagged with the aching reality of Dylan's absence. Astrid's face morphed from aggrieved to pained.

"Oh, Soren, we'll find her."

Soren turned away from Astrid's sympathy as he stood uneasily and stared out at the void. A part of him wanted to collapse again, and he almost heeded the desire, when Augusto and Ian appeared at his sides ready to help him back inside. His feet felt heavy as stones and his chest held a familiar constricting emptiness he never thought he'd feel again.

They walked up the steps and his friends pulled him past the gym and away from the scene of the crime.

"No." He pushed them off. "I need to see it again." What if the soldiers assessing the scene missed something? What if she left a clue for only him to find? He owed it to his mate to do everything he could for her.

"Another time," Augusto said, steering him away from the gym, once again. "Let us handle this for now."

"*No*," he growled, shoving them off. Soren released a torrent of fear from his powers and his friends immediately backed up and away from him. He didn't feel good about it; but it had to be done. He couldn't just sit back and wait while everyone else searched for her.

Several soldiers and Medics quickly moved out of Soren's way as he marched back to where he had awakened. He took it in this time with a clearer head. Something didn't feel right, but not in the way he initially thought. Dylan had become so strong under his wing, which told him none of this made any sense. She could easily take on anyone in a matter of seconds. She had taken on rogue demons, Scarred soldiers, and *saved him* from death, twice. Why was the scene in the gym so amateur? They had made more damage just training together... unless she was caught off guard.

No, he told himself. She had seen the intruder before him, and those precious seconds had been more than enough time to act. It had to have been someone she recognized. Someone that gave her pause. He took in the broken floor, the smeared handprints. She was in a hurry. She wasn't thinking clearly because it was so obvious... to him. It couldn't have been any clearer than painting a giant middle finger.

She had fled.

That fucking bitch had fled and taken his heart. He wasn't sure how she had managed to escape through the

Bones, or how long she had been planning it.

A sadistic chuckle bubbled up in his throat and turned into a full-blown laugh. Several demons peered at him curiously while doing their jobs. He didn't give a damn. It had all been a manipulation to get what she wanted. Astrid had been right all along, Dylan... no, *Temperance* had damn well played him.

He wanted to slow clap for the bitch, but he schooled his features instead. He didn't want to enlighten anyone on his theory that all of this had been an afterthought. Something to throw them off so she would have time to escape. Because he wanted to *deal* with it himself. He could think of only one creature that could persuade her to do this.

He growled deep in his throat.

Effingo.

He suddenly turned around and vehemently shoved his way through the side double doors with an icy smirk.

He'd find them and make sure Tristian stayed in the fucking ground. He'd finally do what he should have done the moment he looked into those terrified, manipulating eyes.

Kill Temperance.

Dylan jerked awake. It took her a full moment to orient herself. She was in a strange bed. A strange bedroom. She squinted around the space with steel-grey walls and a large frosted wall of glass, brightening the air with a muted flood of morning light.

She groaned at the throbbing that cut straight through her skull. It felt as if she had drunk the night away, *twice.*

Why did she feel this way?

How did she get here?

Where was here?

She suddenly remembered Tristian and his grand entrance that included knocking out her boyfriend.

"Tristian?" she called out, trying to sit up. Once the sheet moved she realized she was wearing some white, lacy... bralet... thing. She lifted the sheet and looked down at her scarred body and at the matching sheer panties. *What on earth*—A crow squawked to her right and she jumped, yanking the sheet up over her chest.

A bird was perched on the seat of the side chair, cocking its head and looking at her with its familiar green, beady eyes.

"*You*?" she asked. "What are you doing here?" *Am I still in Elon?*

It fluffed out its feathers before morphing into a grinning demon.

Dylan gasped. "How did you—why would you—why didn't—" she shook her head trying to get her mouth to cooperate with her rushing thoughts, but all that came out was, "*Tristian*?"

Tristian smiled hungrily and was on top of her in a matter of seconds, his mouth claiming and beautiful. She felt her entire body flush from his touch. It was startling, spinning her mind in circles and jolting her heart with life. How she convinced herself she could live without him was beyond her. His tongue licked up her neck. Was she dreaming? No, she couldn't be. She could feel him and taste him just like when they were in his apartment.

"Tristian, wait," she moaned, still dizzy and confused. "Where are we?" He slipped off the straps of her bra and began kissing slow, tantalizing kisses in the spaces he exposed. She slipped her eyes shut. "How did we get here? How— you were just a bird." He suddenly bit her breast and grabbed her wrists, yanking them above her head as her thoughts cleared.

Tristian sneaking into the training room and knocking out Soren. Tristian pleading with her to leave with him. She had told him no. She had asked him to leave before Soren woke up or someone else caught him. She promised not to say anything to anyone as long as he left quickly.

So, why was she here? And then she remembered the pain against her side from an electric shock. The blackness after her head hit the ground.

She screamed when she realized she was looking into Soren's lust-filled eyes.

"This one's no good for you either, *my love*?"

Her shock turned into dread. A cold so deep it seemed sunken into her bones. She didn't need to watch the man in front of her change to know who he was.

"Sila—*Gerion*," she corrected in a whisper. "You're supposed to be dead."

He brought a single black nail down the side of her cheek and over her trembling bottom lip—a signature move that never ceased to make her flesh crawl.

Dylan started struggling mercilessly against his grip, but he was so strong. Why was he so strong?

Silas tsked as he pulled one of her arms down and kissed the inside of her wrist—on top of her new *Binding* next to Soren's bracelet and a three-inch-long gash closed by fresh stitches. She wondered how Silas got his hands on an Elon *Binding* before remembering how Lucia had been wearing a fake one the day of their trial. She must have kept the real one for a time such as this.

"The dead don't always stay dead. You of all demons should know this."

Dylan tried to jerk away as his hand began slipping up her thigh, getting too close to her. She released a sob as he touched her.

"Hmm, No, Tempy," he purred, holding her down. "I think you like Silas better."

"*Get off me,*" she hissed, feeling more courage rush into her soul. "GET OFF! GET OFF! GET OFF!" she screamed over and over with everything that she had left.

Anger flashed inside his blood-orange eyes and she felt a part of herself that was still screaming and chained inside

Silas' castle cower.

He backhanded her, whipping her head to the side.

She felt his lips against her ear as he spoke, "I told you, you are mine. Your thoughts are mine. Your dreams are mine. Your powers are mine," he bit her earlobe and she cried out through a sob. "Your body is *mine*."

His hand was descending again just as a fist rapped against the door. Silas whipped his head to the side and growled, "*What*?"

Dylan trembled as the door opened and she looked at the demon who stood in the doorway. She started to cry for help but her voice cut off at the tip of her tongue, knowing the man wouldn't help her. He looked like Silas but his hair was black and his eyes even blacker. The way he stared at her with his head tilted in careful curiosity scared her almost as much as Silas did. It was the demon doctor from her dream, except, instead of a white coat, he wore an expensive, black suit with a blood-red tie similar to what Silas used to wear to their dinners.

"They're here," the doctor said dispassionately, like he expected to find Silas trying to rape some poor girl.

Silas grinned and the doctor closed the door.

"Come on, my future wife," Silas said as he stood. "Time to meet the parents."

Dylan shivered as he yanked her to her feet. Her legs felt like rubber and her arm throbbed where the stitches lay. She tried to force her mind to clear from some sort of sedation she had obviously been given.

Their eyes connected and he grabbed her jaw so hard it felt bruised and liable to break. He placed a firm kiss against her lips and warned, "I don't want to hurt you, but I will if I need to." He released her and she swayed away from his touch.

Silas pulled a tan and navy striped tie around his head and began tying it against his crisp white dress shirt tucked into a pair of navy slacks.

Despite his warning, Dylan used this time to sweep her eyes all over the room for a plan to get out of here, noticing instantly how large it was. The room was almost triple the size of her suite in Zadar. The slate-grey walls were actually a padded fabric wrapped around them and topped by ivory, stone, crown molding. Near a sleek, marble wet bar on the other side of the room was a bolted shut ebony fire place and a seating area with black, tufted, armless leather chairs, surrounding a small granite coffee table with a square stone vase filled with a stunning arrangement of merlot roses. She had no doubt that it was Silas' room and she had a feeling it was going to be hers, as well.

Dylan returned her eyes to Silas as he buttoned the top button of his shirt, wondering who she could be possibly meeting that she hadn't already. Had Lucia remarried? Or was this just another boring dinner with his mother?

"Who are we meeting?" she found the courage to ask, even if it came out meekly.

Silas glanced at her as he cinched his tie tight. "Why the Elementas, my love. Our family."

In an instant, all of the blood slipped out of her face. Silas lips curved at her reaction and she wondered if she looked as dead as she felt inside. How could her parents do this to her? How could they make Silas, her kidnapper, an ally? Didn't they realize who he was to her?

Once Silas was done dressing he looked immaculate and GQ cover-ready, but Dylan knew better. It was all a lie. It didn't matter how beautiful he could make himself be in the moment, she would never forget the cold, dead look in his eyes, the scarred flesh, and gravelly voice that made Gerion so incredibly terrifying. And now he had her right where he wanted her and it made her absolutely sick.

"Come," Silas commanded under his breath.

Dylan took a step, only hoping he didn't insist on personally dressing her in whatever ridiculous outfit he picked out for her.

Silas locked his fingers with hers and started for the door.

Dylan suddenly stopped before he could open it. "I still need clothes," she hastily reminded, planting her feet until he looked her.

Silas' eyes slithered over to her full of loathing. "You *are* wearing clothes," he hissed. "Perhaps, you should be grateful for what I have allowed." His fist tightened, gripping her impossibly tight like he was warning her not to get out of line, again. Like he would make sure she regretted any act of defiance *later*.

"I still have not forgotten your betrayal back in Zadar," he hissed. "Fool me twice…" he grumbled, while ripping open the door where the demon doctor waited against the hall wall adorned with black and white photos of New York, Venice, London, and Singapore. Directly across from the door, and taking up the entire side of the hallway, was a wall of glass; this one transparent and looking out onto a dark forest. Nothing but wet trees and mist for as far as the eye could see.

"You want to take her like that?" the doctor asked with a sneer of disgust, either at the racy lingerie or her mutilated skin.

Dylan didn't need a mirror to know she was as red as the doctor's tie from how little she was wearing. She hunched her shoulders and crossed her free arm over her bare stomach in a sad attempt to cover herself.

With how much confidence she gained in Elon, she was disappointed to have stooped back down to this… weak, withering, pathetic girl all over again.

"Ah, brother, *of course* I do," Soren pulled her close until she was pressed tightly against his side, grinning icily down at her, no doubt pleased by her complacency. "I can't wait to show off my prize to our guests."

The doctor slipped his hands into his pockets and kept his mouth shut.

Silas led the way down the hall to a massive, white

466

marble staircase. It curled around to the main floor which
was encased by more seamless glass and filled with white
leather furniture, daunting granite columns, and rich fur
throws. Beyond the glass was an azure pool just before the
infinite forest of trees. The home couldn't have been further
from the taste of the castle in Zadar, but it still fit their
family in a way. The Plantos were always extravagant.
Always treating themselves like the royalty they desired.

"Welcome to my home!" Silas bellowed to the guests
below, prompting everyone in the living room to glance up
at them.

Dylan's eyes slipped across the space hurriedly. So many
faces blurring together.

Dylan must have stopped walking because Silas yanked
her after him and she stumbled, falling against him again. He
wrapped his arm around her and possessively pressed her
into his side. He smelled like a spicy cologne that burned her
nose.

When they reached the first floor, Dylan peeked up again
at the many faces. This time, she forced herself to focus on
each one. Her eyes roved over Lucia in an elegant black
dress with cap sleeves, to a couple of paint-free Scarred
soldiers with red-commander bands standing with three
werewolves looking uncomfortable in slacks and dress
shirts. In the center stood her parents. Her mother wore a soft
cream sheath dress and her father donned a matching cream
suit with a pop of ice blue at the collar.

No one smiled except for Silas.

Her mother, Constance, went as far as to glower at the
them like she didn't approve of the spectacle Silas was
putting on. Dylan began to wonder why Silas was parading
her around like this in the first place.

"Let me see her," Constance snapped, skipping any
pleasantries. Dylan's heart picked up as hope blossomed
inside of her. Maybe her mom would finally step up and
save her from Silas?

"Of course, my lady," Silas unhooked Dylan from his hold and shoved her forward like an unwanted animal. Dylan stumbled and fell in front of her mother's nude pumps with a grimace.

Constance immediately couched down and grasped Dylan's chin with her cold fingers, her candy apple red nails digging into Dylan's cheeks. She forced Dylan's face from side to side, examining her before grabbing her shoulder and sneering at her tattoos before standing back up.

"It's her. She has the mark of the Pyro on her shoulder just like her father, Damen," she announced to the room.

Dylan glanced down at her shoulder where a red mole was—the one she had caught King Damen staring at on multiple occasions. She immediately flicked her eyes to Atticus in question. As Damen's identical twin, Dylan wasn't surprised that it felt like she was in the presence of a King. Except, instead of a stern, kind man with unkempt hair and wire frames, Atticus was the picture of perfection with a dash of malice. *He* was supposed to be her father, not King Damen. Had her mother misspoke? Did Atticus know he wasn't her father?

Atticus' deadly eyes connected with Dylan's for a brief moment while Constance whispered in his ear. Dylan knew then that he did know. He had always known, because Atticus and Constance were never mates but business partners.

In a way it made sense King Damen never told her or anyone about his true role in Dylan's life; because that would have meant he had had a relationship with a rogue demon. It was already hard enough on him to have a brother that was going against the Law.

Her mother shifted away from Atticus and clasped her hands together near her stomach. "You may have one heir and then I want her back. Her powers will still be at your disposal, of course, but I request she leave with us tonight."

Dylan felt her being still. *What*?

468

"The deal was a marriage alliance," Silas hissed. "I want her and I want *heirs* if you want access to MY army."

Dylan's mouth was hanging wide open unable to shut it with each passing statement as they discussed her like a bargaining chip between their families. Like an inanimate item to be used and discarded.

"Multiple children will keep her out of commission for far too long," her mother snapped right back. "We need her to man the armies. With her abilities we can soon take over Elon."

Dylan slowly pulled her legs underneath her bottom in a squat as her eyes flickered around the room. It was painstakingly obvious which side everyone was on. The Scarred soldiers were with the Elementas while the werewolves were with the Plantos. Except, one thing was even clearer, no one was paying any attention to Dylan.

"Patience, Constance," Silas glared. "Multiple children can only mean more power."

"Decades from now!" her mother screeched, jolting Dylan into action.

Dylan shot up and ran as fast as her legs would take her... which was about as fast as a human with the *Binding*. She turned down a hallway, passed a stainless steel, gourmet kitchen, and darted through two more hallways before realizing no one was coming after her. It was either because there was nowhere to run or she was running into a trap; neither options comforting her.

Dylan decided then that hiding was the best choice. She began trying door after door, her blood boiling and the *Binding* cutting into her skin each time she lurched forward to use her speed.

Her hand grasped another knob and she fell inside with a soundless gasp. She quickly closed the door and locked it with shaking fingers. She stared at the door as her heart galloped inside her chest. How long could she hide here? How long until they tore the mansion apart? She needed to find a cabinet or closet. Her fists clenched and unclenched as she continued to back up.

A low growl grumbled from behind her.

She flipped around only to stumble back and fall on her rear in shock. She slapped a hand over her to mouth to stifle any screams.

There was a giant cage aglow with a low green light, with plant life and boulders and bloody smears. Standing near the corner was a wolf creature like a beefed up Lycan. Just like the creature she had seen in Soren's vision. A thing that had been tearing through demons before it had almost killed Soren.

Their eyes locked and it slowly listed its head. Its hungry, golden eyes took her in, wondering if she was its next snack. Dylan gulped and began to move up on wobbly legs when the door crashed open and snapped against the wall. Splinters of wood from the lock littered the floor as Silas stepped inside, his eyes alight with amusement and suppressed anger.

"Ah, I see you've met one of my spawns," Silas said on the threshold of the door. "I believe you can thank your little friend Peppi for him."

Dylan couldn't stifle the gasp that shot out her mouth. Silas acted like he didn't hear her.

"Alpha Echo, please meet my new *wife* and your stepmother."

If Dylan hadn't still been thrown by the comment about Peppi, she would have gasped again that her mother apparently agreed to Silas' terms.

The wolf, Echo, started pacing his cage like he was distressed by Silas' presence. Distressed or maybe antsy for food.

Dylan lifted her shoulders and forced her legs to solidify, preparing herself for fight or flight just as Soren had taught her. She had prepared for this. She could take him. She could kill him like she wanted. She *had* to kill him for what he did to her and for what he did to all of the servants in Zadar. She owed it to Peppi.

"Tempy, Tempy, *Tempy,*" Silas sang, settling his eyes back on Dylan as he prowled closer. "You ran away from me."

Her gaze flicked back and forth between Echo and Silas, more afraid of the demon with orange eyes than the lab creature with giant claws.

"You embarrassed me in front of my allies. I thought you understood that I own you now."

Silas brought deft fingers to his neck tie and loosened it languidly before slipping it off his neck and carefully rolling up his sleeves.

Dylan stepped back until her spine hit the wall. She didn't like the way he seemed to be taking his time getting to her as if he was savoring the high of knowing he was going to hurt her.

"However shall I punish you, my love?" He grinned like he was remembering a joke. "That is what you like, isn't it?"

"Please," she pleaded, and he laughed. "You don't have to do this. I will do anything. Make me a soldier or-or a servant." Dylan felt herself shrinking against the wall until she was practically in the fetal position. "Just not… this."

He's manipulating you! a small voice in her mind screamed.

She knew this. Silas was already in her brain, claiming every last inch of her, strangling the fight right out of her and turning it against her until she felt as small as she was trying to make herself appear.

Silas crouched down, almost level with her eyes and ran the beds of his nails down her cheek. She recoiled.

"My sweet, Temperance, I have enough soldiers to take down your precious Kings. So, you see? There's only one role you fit into." He leered. "Besides, I traded ten of my best hybrids for you and I *expect* an heir."

"*Please,*" she breathed as a last resort.

She knew just by looking into his eyes that her pleas would go unanswered. He was done being polite and would finally just take what he wanted. She squeezed her eyes shut and tried to numb herself before he started.

How pathetic and weak she was, even after two years of training with Soren—Elon's best swordsman. *Her* best swordsman. He always knew how to push her. How to make sure she fought harder despite her inabilities, despite every possible situation that could affect her. If he could see her now, she didn't think he would love her as much as he claimed.

You aren't even trying! She heard Soren scream inside her head. *Fight harder!* She whimpered, remembering the night Soren saved her from dream Silas. *I changed my mind... Nothing about you is weak.*

Her eyes snapped open just as Silas began to snake his arms around her to pick her up like a doll. Was she really just going to lay down and let this disgusting excuse for a man take her back to his room? Then what? Play house while he used her to fill some creepy hole in his life?

She was not weak.

She was not pathetic.

Not anymore.

Before Dylan could second guess her actions, she launched herself at him, catching Silas off guard. She grabbed whatever she could. Kicked and kneed anywhere her legs touched. She scratched his chest, his jaw, his forearms as he tried to block her. She reached for his eyes and clawed; wanting nothing more than to tear them out. Her movements became a blur in her vision. She fought even though it felt like there was nothing left to fight for.

Despite the *Binding*, she conjured her strength until blood welled and dripped down her arm, staining Silas's dress shirt and smearing across her chest and belly. She connected a successful knee into his groin and he grunted loudly at the impact.

Dylan tried to shove him off of her during his moment of paralyzed pain but Silas snapped out of it too soon. He snatched her writhing limbs within seconds and slammed her down, pinning her to the carpet. His jaw was swelling from a good right hook and beads of blood trickled out of the deep scratches near his blazing eyes.

They were both panting but Dylan didn't cower. She lifted her chin at his pain and spat in his face, reveling in the way he lurched back in disgust.

Silas may be stronger and more powerful than her right now, but Dylan vowed to never break. To never stop fighting no matter how worthless he made her feel. Silas would pay for everything he did to her. For every nightmare and violation.

She didn't know if she could make it out in one piece or even escape, but one thing was for sure, she wouldn't stop trying until one of them was dead.

"You're going to wish you hadn't done that," Silas sneered, just before whipping his head down and knocking her out cold.

"In all the stories my daughter shall hear…
She will learn to rely on her own sword
in every battle, in every struggle, in every war,
because she will learn how to devour
every single monster from their very core."
Nikita Gill

To my readers,

Thank you for reading my book! I love interacting and hearing from you. Your honest thoughts are highly appreciated. Please take some time and review this novel on your preferred retailer's website. Reviews are the best way to help authors spread the word about their books!

To be updated with the latest info, sweeps, and sales, or to simply chat with me:
Instagram: @sm.yairlevyauthor
Twitter: @DNYL_Books
Facebook: https://www.facebook.com/SMYairLevy
Goodreads:https://www.goodreads.com/author/show/8331593.S_M_Yair_Levy

Acknowledgements

My husband, Ori. I am incredibly thankful for your constant support and patience. You never batted an eye at my outlandish ideas, or doubted me in any way. You are my rock and best friend. I love you, my taco flower!

My children: Nathanel, Mila, and Jordan. My love for you runs deep to the bone. I love how you constantly keep me on my toes. Every day with you is a new crazy adventure.

My editor, Carole. Thank you so much for your guidance and honesty. I know this novel wouldn't have become what it is today without your sharp and discerning eye.

My dear friend, Annie. Thank you for always being there as my alpha-reader. Your long nights and helpful insights will never go forgotten.

My cover designer, Noa Yair-Levy. Thank you for your patience and for creating stunning book covers!

And above all, thank you to all my beta testers and readers/reviewers you guys are the best! <3

.

www.ingramcontent.com/pod-product-compliance
Lightning Source LLC
Chambersburg PA
CBHW051532250626
47157CB00001B/17